SILENT SUBVERSION

Secrets Want Out

Hyrum Jones

Silent Subversion I: Secrets Want Out

First edition: January 2016

Second Edition: January 2018

Third Edition: July 2020

ISBN (Print): 978-0-997-21076-7

ISBN (eBook): 978-0-997-21071-2

Interior Artwork: astrosense.net/astrology-fonts

Cover Design: nickcaldwellcreations.com

Anxiety Publishing

Special thanks to Bernard Burchell for his assistance with the NMG concept, and to
Carlene, Jim, Shelly, Diane, Jared, and Carrie for their feedback of the story and my writing.

CONTENTS

PART I

MOMENTUM

After the fire created

You will see

The beast illuminated

ONE

Gerald

January 2009

Gerald first encountered the jumper, as his mother would have called it, after returning from lunch with one of his legal clients. He noticed the black jumping spider crawling across the top of his office doorway. Afraid the spider would jump on his head, he walked slowly into his office, close to the edge of the entry.

He was tempted to squash the spider but decided to take care of the situation if he encountered it again. He had work to do.

He saw the same spider the next day on the ledge of his bookshelf, just a few centimeters from his fingers. After recovering from fright, Gerald decided to capture the creature in a cup, but when he returned with the cup, it had mysteriously disappeared, likely behind the books. While starting to search for it, his law partner called him from the other office, so the spider vanished again from Gerald's mind.

The next day at his desk, he was trying to remember a disturbing dream from the night, when the same jumper made its third appearance. After it hopped into the space between the keyboard and the monitor, Gerald felt no fear and noticed three blood-red spots on the black spider's back, forming a creepy equilateral triangle. While appreciating the beautiful color and symmetry, he wondered why he hadn't noticed during the previous two encounters. He should really try to appreciate things, he reminded himself, especially the little things.

Instead of jumping away, the creature put its two front appendages in the air as some kind of surreal greeting. It stepped to one side then returned to its original position as if studying Gerald from different angles.

During its strange dance, Gerald recognized this same spider from the dream he was trying to remember. No other details of his dream presented themselves, just the spider. Maybe part of the dream had materialized in the real world, he wondered, but he instantly rejected the disturbing thought. Reality and dreams must remain separate. The tiny creature did seem more important now, so Gerald felt grateful to have spared its life.

"Hello again, big fella," Gerald said, leaning forward as close as he dared so he could see its row of alien eyes. "What were you doing in my dream last night?"

No answer.

Several seconds passed in silence as Gerald tried in vain to recall more of the dream and what part the spider had played. After finally looking away, he noticed how dark his office had become, even at noon. Forgetting the spider for a moment, Gerald turned to the window behind him and spent a while watching the exceptionally dark clouds drift across the Seattle sky. He inhaled deeply, appreciating the double-paned glass separating him from the cold rain. He usually ignored the drab, a regular part of the six-month season of cold and wet in the Pacific Northwest.

Sudden awareness of the darker office seemed to restore Gerald to the present. What was he doing? Instead of resolving his clients' legal issues, he was wasting time trying to recall dreams and having ridiculous conversations with spiders. He should get back to work.

While considering energizing the office lights, the phone rang. Without thinking, Gerald picked up the receiver and prepared to repeat his memorized introduction, but he paused after seeing the caller ID.

Taylor Evans, a friend he'd met at the University of Oregon, waited on the other end of the line, a woman of raw beauty and intimidating intelligence. Despite the physical distance between them, his heart rate increased. Male instincts demanded he act his most charming.

"Hello," he said, imagining her pink lips just a few milliseconds away from his own. "Foster and Fowler law office, Gerald Foster speaking."

The spider watched, motionless. Gerald tried not to notice.

"Gerald Foster," the woman said sarcastically as though she had just won a prize. "I contacted a firm partner on the first try?"

She laughed before continuing.

"Just kidding. How's it going? I hope 2K9 is treating you well! This is Taylor, by the way."

"Taylor Evans," he began but was interrupted by a new memory.

Gerald remembered Taylor extending her hand to him through some kind of dark barrier. It was another memory from his elusive dream. Gerald now had two pieces of his dream puzzle, the spider and Taylor. He took a quick breath.

"It's great to hear from you! I'm doing fine. What's new?"

"Our last conversation was a bit too confrontational, so I thought of a way you could make it up to me."

Gerald suppressed a laugh. He noticed her playful tone, but her voice sounded forced, almost rehearsed.

"That's funny," he said, intending genuine amusement. "If I remember right, you were the confrontational one."

"Yeah, I've been known to start the occasional argument, but it's not my fault there are so many ignorant people out there."

"Right," he said sarcastically. He expected to hear a quick retort, but what he got was a pause and then a quiet sigh of frustration.

"During our last conversation," she began, "if you didn't understand what I was talking about, you should have asked more questions."

"Okay, okay," he said, suddenly remembering how their last phone conversation had quickly degraded when he'd failed to respond sufficiently to her tirade about quantum theory. He did not know enough about the subject to even form a question. He sighed, but a little too loudly. He had to get her back on track. "So, how I can make it up to you?"

"Gerald," she said in exasperation. "I have something very important to discuss and I need you in the right state of mind. Should I call back tomorrow morning? Will you be in a better mood after getting a good night's sleep?"

"Night's sleep?" he asked tentatively. Excitement for the conversation with Taylor was quickly transforming into confusion. His mind scrambled for its next response.

"I'll take that as a yes," she said during his pause.

Click

"Taylor?" he asked but was answered with silence. "Hello?"

Cutting the connection without formally ending the conversation should not have surprised Gerald, but the abrupt end made him pause. Even for Taylor, her behavior was very strange. He would need to be extra careful when they talked the next morning. Hopefully, she would be the one in a better mood.

While slowly setting the phone down, he began mentally preparing for her call the next morning. He looked down at the spider.

"Maybe tomorrow," he said. "I'll find out what she wants."

Gerald hoped she needed simple legal advice. After starting his law firm, former acquaintances including Taylor often contacted him with legal questions. Many of his professional associates found the behavior annoying, but Gerald liked helping people, and he often acquired new clients in the process.

After his graduation from law school, Taylor had first contacted Gerald due to a personal tragedy. Her father had just died, and she'd needed to transfer the ownership of his sole proprietorship business, a machine shop, to her mother. After that first correspondence, she would call at random times, sometimes just to say hello or vent like her recent complaints about quantum theory. But whatever the reasons for her correspondence, Gerald felt honored to be a part of her life.

Her current irritability suggested a possible negative aspect of the present situation. He hoped the reason for her phone call was not as severe as her father's death.

The dream involving both the spider and Taylor now seemed like a bad omen. Dreaming about the spider itself was logical. He sees a spider in his office in strange situations and it appears in his dreams—not unexpected. Taylor's appearance, however, was a little disturbing. He could not remember an instance when any of his dreams predicted or predated a real-world situation, such as her phone call.

In his opinion, the subconscious used dreams to resolve or make sense of current psychological issues. The mind used real-world experiences in elaborate rearrangements as coping mechanisms for all of life's traumas, like solving a complicated puzzle. These experiences, dreams, were only internal, completely detached from the world outside of the mind.

Movement in his peripheral vision redirected Gerald's attention. The jumping spider raised its two front appendages again, then turned and scurried away, disappearing behind the monitor. The creature's exit made Gerald forget about his dream and the strange coincidences.

After this third encounter with the spider, Gerald decided to just let it go. Would it ever return? Probably not in the real world, he thought.

An hour later, Gerald made a cup of tea. The hot mug felt good in his hands and contrasted with the cold rain outside. He set the mug down where the spider had watched him. After taking a deep breath, he opened the papers he'd requested from their largest client, and then he started reading.

When Albert, his law partner, opened his office door about ten minutes later, he poked his head into the room and waited quietly. Gerald pretended not to notice and continued reading. The experience of Albert watching him felt nothing like when the spider had watched him. He could ignore Albert.

When Albert failed to go away, Gerald found a good stopping point in his reading and looked up to see the forced smile, the raised eyebrows. From the look in Albert's blue eyes, he seemed prepared for a potentially contentious conversation. For a moment, Gerald felt a little jealous. Albert was tall like Gerald but had blond hair and blue eyes, and ten to fifteen kilograms more muscle. Gerald had a more slender frame with dark brown hair and brown eyes.

"Hey, Gerald," he said. "Do you have a few minutes?"

"Sure," he answered. He felt like the day was going to get even more complicated.

"Okay," Albert began in a more serious tone. "I found this in the mail."

Albert removed a white envelope from his suit pocket and tossed it on the desk. Gerald reoriented the letter so he could read the name of the sender, an organization called, *End the Fed*. He inspected his name more closely on the envelope. Someone had handwritten his name, rather than printing it in a way that resembled handwriting, a tactic to give junk mail a more personalized touch. This letter was not junk mail.

"Thanks for delivering my mail," Gerald said sarcastically, feeling a slight rise in his heartbeat at seeing the *End the Fed* name. The previous year, a leader in that organization, an undercover FBI agent, had tried to entrap Gerald in a sting operation, intended to give the organization a bad name.

Despite his outwardly cool attitude, he almost started to panic. The experience with the spider had most likely weakened his state of mind.

Gerald thought he would never hear from that organization again or from their secret financiers, the FBI. After what had happened, he'd assumed the FBI would not want anything to do with him, preferring to avoid drawing any attention to their failed entrapment attempt. Gerald had intended to follow the same tactic, not talking about the scandal or sharing the information with the media, basically pretending it never happened. He did not want to provoke them any further.

During the trial, when the FBI had charged him with attempted arson on the Seattle Federal Reserve building, Gerald had shown complete faith in his belief that those with the truth would prevail if they acted intelligently. He was innocent and the arson never happened, so he had little concern. Albert had attempted to convince Gerald of the more realistic view: those who go against the system will lose whether armed with the truth or not.

After clearing his name and exposing the FBI in their attempted entrapment, Gerald had decided to forget the whole affair. Whenever he caught himself thinking about the possible alternative outcomes and how close he had come to them, he would begin to feel a sense of panic. Over time, he had attributed at least some of his success to luck and not completely to his brilliance, which was his first dominant opinion.

At the present, Gerald understood Albert's concern more fully and would continue to follow his plan, spend little to no time thinking about the affair. *Stay optimistic,* he told himself while Albert glared at him. *Stay optimistic, and move on!*

"Do you have anything to tell me?" Albert asked finally. He sat in a chair in front of Gerald's desk.

"I haven't read the letter yet, Albert," Gerald said, taking a deep breath before continuing. He needed to relieve his partner's concern about what the letter might mean. "I haven't been in contact with them since, well you know, the last time. Let me read it first."

Gerald opened the envelope and began reading the handwritten letter inside, a note from the organization that had caused him so much trouble. While reading, he could feel Albert watching him. Before Gerald finished, Albert stood from the chair and stepped to the bookcase on the side of the room. Although several meters away, his partner watched Gerald as though searching for signs of deception.

To salvage the situation, at least with his business partner, Gerald would act as though the letter did not deserve any serious consideration. If Gerald did not respond to the letter's request, the story would end there once and for all. The past would remain the past and not intrude again on the present.

While reading the final paragraph, Gerald smiled and shook his head with a silent laugh.

"What's so funny?" Albert asked, squinting even tighter until only his pupils were visible.

"You can read it and see for yourself," Gerald said after setting the letter on the desk. "But you probably won't see the humor."

"So you haven't joined with them again, right?" he asked, stepping away from the bookshelf and glancing briefly at the letter. He stood very close to the desk, almost leaning over it. His light blue eyes shot at Gerald suspiciously. "I don't want you bringing our little business venture into any trouble."

"No, I haven't," Gerald said. "I told you I wouldn't get involved with them again."

Gerald looked up at his partner and recognized the tactic. Albert had intentionally positioned himself so Gerald had to look upward, an attempt to psychologically coerce him into speaking more honestly. Gerald had every intention to reveal the truth. He wanted to relieve Albert's anxiety about the subject.

"What do they want then?" he asked.

"They want me to come back because they really need my help," Gerald said with thick sarcasm. "It's from the new Seattle chapter organizer, but I don't know him. He apologized for what happened with the Federal Reserve thing, and he claims that they are no longer affiliated with Mr. Alvarez."

"What's so funny with that?"

"Because this new guy sounds just like the last undercover FBI agent." Gerald laughed with as much sincerity as he could muster, hoping to sound completely unconcerned. Albert knew him well enough to recognize any hint of deception. "How stupid do they think I am? *Seriously*! I should probably be offended if it wasn't so funny."

Albert looked at him for a few seconds before responding. Gerald stopped chuckling but waited with a smile. His partner's shoulders relaxed slightly.

"That doesn't make me feel much better," he said. "What makes you suspect he's another FBI agent?"

"It's just a feeling I have," Gerald began, "but I doubt the organization is no longer a front for the FBI. I proved that pretty conclusively during the trial. Don't you think? At least I proved their leader was on the FBI payroll."

"That's what scares me," Albert said and then sat down again, shoulders slumped in final defeat. He seemed to lose all sense of his previous suspicion. "It doesn't matter if you're right if you piss off the wrong people, especially the FBI."

"There's nothing to worry about," Gerald said, hiding the lie behind a smile. "And it *does* matter if you're right."

After Albert left the office, Gerald sat quietly at his desk, staring blankly at the computer screen. The timing of the spider, the phone call, and then the letter all seemed related in some strange way. Three peculiar experiences happening so close together was no coincidence.

Gerald took another drink of his tea, thankfully still hot, then stood and stretched. Before leaving his office to visit with a client, he paused with his hand on the door handle. He looked back at his desk at the space in front of the computer screen.

No more spider.

TWO

Gerald

After meeting with his last client of the day, Gerald drove home instead of returning to the office. He wanted to get to sleep early that night to prepare for Taylor's call the next day. He also wanted to avoid another conversation with Albert who might continue his interrogation about the letter.

A welcome rush of warm air washed over him when he opened the front door to his home. He wiped the cold rain from his forehead then locked the deadbolt to the door and put the chain lock in place. Even after enabling his meager security features, he still felt a little insecure. If the FBI wanted to break into his home and plant evidence, he could not imagine a way to stop them.

Before changing from his suit, he tossed the folded letter on his coffee table.

"Nice try, FBI," he said to the letter, breaking the silence. He would put the letter away later, out of sight. "I'm staying as far away from you as possible."

Ten minutes later, he sat at his kitchen table with his laptop open, waiting for his potato to bake. To keep his mind off food, he quickly checked his email and then searched some of his favorite podcasts, looking for something interesting.

For the remainder of the evening, he listened to a new podcast about the Second World War, the story of when Rudolph Hess flew to Scotland. Gerald hoped the podcast contained new information or a different interpretation of the events, but the speakers just repeated the standard story. In his opinion, the official history left too many unanswered questions.

When finally ready for bed, he closed his bedroom door and spent a while feeding and inspecting his fish. He counted four neon tetra and nine cardinal tetra, all healthy and colorful. He returned the fish food to the shelf, turned off the light, and got into bed. While falling asleep, he enjoyed listening to the bubbler in the fish tank and watching the flashes of color under the ultraviolet light. As usual, the experience helped him relax before losing consciousness.

Shortly after midnight, a distinct noise woke Gerald from a deep sleep. He quickly sat up in bed, his heart beating wildly. After rubbing the life back into his eyes, he looked toward the bedroom door and listened carefully, but his heartbeat was the only sound.

He waited only a few seconds for confirmation of his fear. He had heard the click of the deadbolt on his front door and now the unlatching of the chain. Then he heard the other familiar noises, the turn of the doorknob as the front door opened and then closed.

"Oh, my god," he whispered, his mind racing.

In the following silence, Gerald reached a disturbing conclusion. Only a professional burglar could have gained entry so easily. But a professional would have been quieter. The intruder had not shown any attempt at stealth. Except for the chain lock, Gerald could have easily unlocked and opened the door quietly enough to escape audible detection, but only from the inside. That apparent contradiction helped Gerald reach a more favorable conclusion. He had only imagined the noises while in a semi-conscious state. Now that he was awake, he heard only the bubbler in the fish tank.

As the time continued to pass in silence, Gerald felt more at ease. No one could walk across his floor without making the boards creak. If an intruder had entered his home, they had stopped at the front door and just stayed there. Placing blame on his imagination seemed more consistent with the observations.

"You're just hearing things," Gerald said quietly to himself. The crazy events of the previous afternoon had obviously not worn off yet. His mind just needed time to return to baseline. After lying down again and closing his eyes, he concentrated on the fish tank bubbler until his pulse returned to normal.

Despite his relief, Gerald decided to inspect his home to reassure himself of his safety and the absence of intruders. Only then could he sleep peacefully. He lifted the blankets, preparing to swing his legs to the floor, but before he could start moving, he heard a noise more disturbing than his front door opening. He now heard the soft metallic scraping sound of someone turning the doorknob to his room.

With his heart thumping harder than before, Gerald scrambled to think of an appropriate action. His rational self said to jump from the bed and prepare for an attack, but his body decided to obey a more primal instinct, lie still and attempt to avoid notice. Through extremely narrow eyelid slits, Gerald watched as the door slowly opened wide and then inexplicably closed.

His mind instantly rejected what his senses told him, that his door had moved on its own. No one had entered his room. While struggling to comprehend the situation, he noticed another strange sight. The ceiling near the door was shimmering as though an invisible cloud of hot air floated there.

Gerald stared in confusion as the aberration drifted across the room toward him, finally stopping directly above his head. Curiosity soon replaced fear and erased his instinct to jump from the bed and flee. In the next few seconds, the aberration transformed from shimmering air to blinding white light and continued to intensify until he could see nothing but the light above him. During the transformation, he felt like something within the light was watching him.

While his eyes adjusted to the light, the pressure of gravity on his back suddenly transferred to his feet. The resulting disorientation and dizziness nearly stole his consciousness. The strange experience felt as though his whole house had rotated ninety degrees. Instead of lying on his back in his bedroom, Gerald now stood on his feet, facing a hallway of illuminated white marble.

Contrasting with his state of shock, the air in his new environment felt cool and comfortable. While trying to determine what had just happened, Gerald focused on breathing and inspecting his surroundings. The hallway seemed endless, converging to a single point at an infinite distance away. The view soon became a strain on his eyes, so he turned to the ceiling. He tried to touch the stone surface above him, but his fingers just barely missed or seemed to at least. He placed his hand on the wall to his right and felt a warm and smooth stone surface.

The hallway behind him stretched to the other side of infinity. After looking down both directions, he considered his options. Walking in either direction seemed like an effort in futility. No matter what direction he walked, he would always remain in the exact center of an infinite hallway.

While considering the dilemma and unsure of how to proceed, a sudden movement drew his attention to the floor several meters in front of him. He looked down and noticed a black spider with three red spots on its back. Gerald remembered the same creature from his office, but he felt less panicked with the spider so far away from him.

"Hello again," Gerald said, but he instantly regretted speaking. His voice seemed like a blasphemy to the silence, reverberating through the hallway like an earthquake.

After his voice fled away and the hallway returned to a peaceful silence, the spider began hopping toward the wall to his left. The movement looked strange, and Gerald had to peer closely to see the illusion. The spider only appeared to hop. At first, it would begin vibrating and then appear two centimeters away, leaving a motionless spider copy in its previous position.

The trail of static spiders quickly extended up the wall, then across the ceiling and back down the other side, snapshots of the past but each spider copy remaining in the present. When the living creature reached its starting point, the spider trail became a boundary in the hallway, dividing infinity in half. The living spider no longer seemed to exist and became a part of the boundary line, indistinguishable from the rest of its copies.

The next change happened too slowly to immediately notice. The red spots on every spider copy began to glow as tiny hot coals. When Gerald attempted to focus on them, all of the lights seemed to blur together. While staring at the red lights in front of him, the hallway on the other side began to grow dark, and Gerald soon found himself standing before what looked like a wall of dark smoke.

Gerald started to hear footsteps walking toward him from the same direction he was facing. He listened for a long time until he recognized the sound, leather sandals on stone. Unlike the harshness of his voice, the soft and rhythmic sound felt oddly comforting. After a long time of listening, he found himself looking forward to meeting the person making the noise, although he had no way of determining their benevolence or malevolence.

The walker, a slender person, suddenly appeared approaching from the other side of the barrier, their outline barely visible in the darkness. When the distinctly female form stopped at the interface, Gerald's eyes widened in surprise. Although he knew she was a woman, he did not recognize her. She wore a white nightgown, glowing with a light of its own, the fabric falling just above her ankles. When he looked at her face, he saw her nose and mouth clearly, but she had shadows for eyes.

"Present yourself," she said softly with a voice clear as a bell.

Gerald took two steps toward her and stopped with his face close to hers, the dark barrier shimmering between them. While standing so close, he noticed two pinpoints of light shining from the shadows of her eyes. He opened his mouth to speak, but her voice stopped him.

"Who are you?" she asked slowly, as though she already knew his identity and just wanted confirmation.

"Gerald," he said obediently.

"What do you seek?"

"Truth," he answered without thinking.

"We shall see," she said, her lips curving into a smile.

"Can you give it to me?" he asked.

"Only if you dare," she answered and then carefully extended her right hand through the barrier, her palm facing upward. "Take my hand."

Gerald looked down at the pale white skin of her hand and wrist. It contrasted sharply with her darker skin on the other side of the barrier, rippling as though submerged in running water. When their palms connected, her fingers tightened around his, and she began pulling him forward through the barrier. Gerald closed his eyes.

After reaching the other side, he opened his eyes and looked into the face of Taylor Evans, bright green eyes and pale skin. Her long hair cascaded down her cheeks and over her shoulders, dark red against the white gown. Before speaking, she held her index finger in front of her pink lips.

"Follow me."

THREE

Gerald

Gerald woke to the vibration of his phone on the bed. While reaching over to stop the annoying sensation, he looked through the window at the streetlight shining in the darkness outside. Before realizing why the phone was vibrating, he noticed the time, twelve minutes after six, almost an hour before he usually began the day. Then he recognized the name on the phone, Taylor Evans. If he did not answer quickly, he would miss the call.

"Good morning, Taylor," he said while sitting up and pretending he was already awake.

"Good morning, Gerald," she said, just as cheerfully.

Taylor's voice reminded Gerald of his dream, seeing her face through some kind of dark barrier. Then he remembered seeing his door opening and being afraid, but that part did not feel like a dream. The transition between lying in his bed and standing in the infinite hallway must have been when he fell asleep, he concluded. The whole experience was confusing.

"Oh, Gerald, is this too early for you?" she asked sarcastically during his pause. "You did say to call anytime."

"Yes, this is a fine time," he said.

"Don't tell me you sleep this late?"

"It's only 6:13 in the morning," he said, affronted.

"Oh man," she said with an exaggerated tone of pity. "The life of a lawyer is so hard. You should be happy I waited so long to call you. I could have called much earlier."

"Can I call you back in a minute?" he asked, slightly embarrassed to tell her the reason.

"Got to take care of some business, huh?" she said and laughed. "Sure thing, Gerald. How much time do you need? Two minutes or five?"

"Um..." he said, trying to think of how to respond.

"Just kidding," she said while still laughing. "I really don't need to know."

"I'll call you back in..." he started to say but then realized she had disconnected.

He quickly took care of his bathroom needs. After rinsing his mouth, he looked into the mirror, into his dark brown eyes and brown hair falling over his forehead. Very unkempt, he thought. He drew a deep breath and sighed, attempting to forget the strange experience from the night.

"Just a dream, Gerald," he said to the mirror.

Before tapping the call button on his phone, Gerald rubbed his eyes and swept the hair from his forehead.

Taylor answered during the first ring.

"Everything okay now, Gerald?" she asked with mock concern. "Are you ready to have a serious discussion?"

"Yes," he said, feeling more comfortable with an empty bladder. "I've been very curious about why you wanted to talk to me."

"I've decided that you should be the first one I ask for help, but actually, I think you're the only one I know, who I can ask. I want to show you something, but I need to know your current state of mind first."

"My state of mind?"

"I know this is going to sound strange," she said and drew a deep breath before continuing, "but I need to know if you're capable of helping me with something big. How's your life recently? Any new romantic relationships? The law firm going well? Not falling into any more FBI sting operations, I hope!"

"One question at a time, Taylor," he said and laughed nervously. Her reference to the FBI reminded him of the strange noises from the previous night and that their conversation was probably being transcribed and recorded in some database from his phone. "Life's good lately. Business is going well. I'm not seeing anyone, just a few dates now and then."

"Oh man," she said in frustration. "Sorry. This sounds too much like small talk."

Gerald chuckled. "You're definitely not one for small talk. What do you want to show me?"

"First, I want your agreement to work with me on a project. I'm not going to all the trouble of meeting with you if you're not going to help me, and there's no turning back if I show you what I want to show you."

While holding the phone to his ear, Gerald walked into his living room and flipped the light switch, then turned up the dial for the heat. The wet January night had sucked all of the warmth from his home.

"What can you tell me?" he asked but instantly regretted the question. Many of his clients preferred to discuss everything in person, rarely over the phone. If Taylor had dangerous information to share, it might implicate him. Her anarchistic beliefs exponentially increased the odds he would not want an electronic record of what she planned to share.

While waiting for her answer, he glanced at the front door and his eyes grew wide with shock. The chain at the top hung unlatched. He tried convincing himself he had forgotten to secure the chain, but he distinctly remembered putting it in place.

"Life is full of risks, right?" she began hesitantly, her tone losing the usual confidence. "The bigger the risk, the bigger the opportunity. How attached are you to your cozy life? If you agree to help me, there may be no turning back."

After seeing the latch unsecured, Gerald had difficulty focusing on their conversation. He walked to the front door. "No turning back huh," he said while putting the latch back in place.

"We're always talking about improving the state of the world, right? Well, this could be our chance."

"Hmm," he said, feeling extremely tempted just to agree with her request. But saying the words, *sure, I'll do it*, seemed too easy. Then he remembered his dream when Taylor had grasped his hand. Her proposition seemed connected somehow to the events of the night and the previous day, and it scared him. "Then I will have to think about it."

"That's what I wanted to hear," she said, clear relief in her voice. "If you would have said, yes, I would have told you to think about it some more. Just email me after you've thought it through. I gotta go. It's been good talking to you."

"Yes," he said, taking a quick breath. "It's been..."

Gerald closed his mouth after realizing Taylor had cut the connection on him again that morning. He shook his head and smiled. That was Taylor, too busy for social propriety. From then on, he'd try to expect it. To be fair, whenever he thought about the usual method of ending phone conversations, the final goodbye often felt redundant.

While preparing to visit the office for the day, Gerald replayed their conversation in his mind and wondered what she wanted to show him. What did she consider so important and obviously risky? He did not want to get into any trouble either. After what had happened with the FBI, he needed to avoid any possible attention from law enforcement.

He avoided thoughts of the unlocked chain and did not even look at it while leaving his house. Gerald had simply forgotten to connect the latch. His encounters with the spider the previous days had destroyed his routine, putting his mind out of balance.

—✳—

Gerald had an hour to himself at work before his law firm partner arrived. He left the door to his office open, so he would hear when Albert entered the office. He spent some time relaxing in his chair with a hot cup of tea, staring through the window at the office building across the street. He rarely saw anyone in the windows, especially not during the wet months of October through April. For a few minutes, he listened to raindrops striking the window.

Just after nine, Gerald heard the front door to their offices open and then the sound of Albert removing his coat and opening a briefcase on his desk. When he heard the footsteps approaching his office, Gerald's pulse accelerated just a bit. He was prepared to commandeer the conversation, if needed, and quickly divert the topic from the entrapment letter. Albert stepped into Gerald's open door, smiling.

"Good morning, Gerald," he said pleasantly.

"Good morning," Gerald answered, relieved to see his partner with no sign of contention. "Get any sleep, or did the baby keep you up again?"

"I slept alright," Albert said then cleared his throat. "Hey, before I forget, the wife wanted me to ask if you could do lunch with us and her sister again tomorrow. My sister-in-law really liked you, apparently."

"Hmm," Gerald said, thinking of how to decline politely. Their first lunch double date had seemed like two men dating twins. "I don't think I can. I'm having a meeting with Patrick Franklin tomorrow morning, and it's probably going to overlap with lunch."

"If tomorrow doesn't work with your schedule, what would be a good day?"

"Actually," Gerald began, knowing he would have to decline definitively. The look in the man's eyes indicated he would continue pursuing the issue. "I don't want to give her the wrong idea. I'm too busy for a romantic relationship."

"That's a lie if I've ever heard one." Albert's smile quickly transformed into a smirk, and his blond hair fell out of place onto his forehead. He continued his attack while returning his hair to its proper position. "You're not being very consistent. Weren't you telling me last week, excitedly I might add, about meeting a couple of interesting women?"

"Stop trying to cross-examine me," Gerald said, smiling with guilt. He enjoyed watching his aggressive partner in action but usually against other people. "I'm not on trial."

"Now that you're caught," Albert said triumphantly, "tell me why you don't want to do lunch with us. And don't tell me you're not attracted to her. I remember how you looked at her."

"Your sister-in-law is very nice, and yes, attractive just like your wife, but maybe I'm just not ready to be your brother-in-law and partner-in-law."

Gerald had to think fast before Albert convinced him to go on another date with his sister-in-law. The man was correct. Gerald lacked a good excuse.

"I don't like leading women on," Gerald said before Albert could continue. "That would really make your wife angry."

"Fine, Gerald," he replied, sighing heavily. "Take my advice. Find a beautiful woman, have too much to drink, and wake up the next morning wondering what happened. Best decision I ever made."

"You mean the best decision ever made for you."

"Sure, I'll give you that," he said, smiling again. "But it left us with an amazing little gift."

"Yes, I know...sleepless nights."

"Those sleepless nights sure bring it all into focus though."

"I know," Gerald said, tired of his own facetious replies. "I just haven't found the right girl yet, I guess."

After his partner left, Gerald sat in his office thinking about marriage and children, a frequent subject of contemplation since the birth of Albert's son. To outside observers, Gerald appeared ready for a marriage commitment. He had completed his education, owned a house, had a promising career, but the thought of finding the right woman scared him just a little. He did not fear losing freedom. He feared losing future opportunities, including what Taylor wanted to show him.

If Gerald were married, and especially, had children, he would probably need to reject Taylor's offer. Responsible people did not unnecessarily risk the lives of their dependents. Gerald felt bad enough putting their business in jeopardy by embarrassing the FBI, although the experience had felt distinctly satisfying winning the case against them.

Gerald suddenly realized one answer to his many questions. He wanted to help Taylor and see what she had to show him. Then a more dangerous question materialized. What if they found success? Taking Taylor's hand in his dream suddenly seemed like an omen. Then he remembered the spider looking at him. The memory sent chills through his chest.

"Okay, Taylor," he said, logging into his computer and preparing to answer her via email. He needed to act while he still felt good about the decision. "Let's see what you've got."

After sending a brief answer, he had to wait less than a minute before receiving her reply.

Awesome!

Let's meet on your next visit to Portland. We can have dinner or something.

Just email me the time, and I'll choose the place. My schedule is completely open.

Gerald smiled in anticipation of another encounter with his favorite anarchist, a meeting in the real world and not in cyberspace or over the phone. Whatever happened, he needed to prevent involving their law firm in some scandal and attracting the notice of his law partner.

FOUR

Gerald

Gerald arranged the meeting with Taylor for the next Friday. The date coincided with his monthly visit to clients in Portland, Oregon, where Taylor lived. On that particular trip, he planned to visit a non-profit organization, which provided mental health care for troubled children and youth. His firm helped manage the organization's liability insurance, tax issues, and government grant proposals. Both Gerald and Albert had insisted on providing the service without compensation.

Soon after starting their law firm, when they'd had fewer paying clients and more free time, Gerald had kept busy providing free services to those with insufficient resources to pay for them. He quickly learned how the work earned more than just emotional satisfaction. Through their charitable efforts, he and his partner had made many valuable contacts with other individuals and businesses in need of legal assistance. At that time, their firm had a good mix of paying clients and others who, with a bit of support, were more likely to afford their services.

Gerald imagined himself in Taylor's financial situation and the experience made him shudder, but thankful for his own situation. Taylor had graduated from college during the worst economic collapse in their lifetime. Companies were downsizing, not hiring. Even with her exceptional confidence and skills, Taylor faced a bleak job outlook.

He expected their upcoming conversation would include the collapse of the housing market of the previous year. He prepared himself to hear an epic rant about how the big banks had intentionally orchestrated the event. She would then probably attempt to predict what their financial rulers would do in the future. He hoped the discussion would be therapeutic for Taylor, but he feared the topic would probably generate more anger.

During the next few days of waiting, nothing else strange or disturbing occurred. No spiders. No more strange dreams or chilling noises at night. But he did fall asleep several times with the pleasant memory of Taylor pulling him through the barrier.

Before departing to Portland the next Friday morning, Gerald stopped at the office for some legal documents. He parked on the street in front of their building then ran up the two flights of stairs. After placing the papers into his briefcase, he turned for the door but noticed movement on the bookshelf. He stopped mid-stride, feeling a sudden chill and not from the cold January morning.

"Is that you, my little friend?" he asked while inspecting the packed shelves. Only inanimate books appeared in his view.

After first encountering the spider in his office and then in his dream, Gerald had acquired a strong desire to see it again. Since the time of its last appearance, the spider had transformed from a living creature into an imaginary omen. Another encounter in the physical world might return the spider to its proper place in his mind.

He had considered telling Taylor about the spider and the dream but wondered how the information would affect her. She had a more scientific mind and might offer a more plausible explanation, or she might make him feel stupid. Both possibilities might put his mind at ease.

After turning off the light, Gerald stood with his back to the office and paused with his hand on the door handle. He imagined a set of tiny black eyes watching him from the dark room. Without looking back, he shut the office door and then returned to the warmth of his car. In just a few minutes, the raindrops had evaporated from his hair and shoulders, and the soothing music of Mozart helped him forget about the spider.

Gerald enjoyed watching the sun rise slowly above the dark clouds on the horizon. Beginning a long car ride in the dark always reminded him of his childhood when his parents would take them on vacation. During the beginning of the drive, he thought about his first encounter with Taylor at the University of Oregon.

Shortly after meeting her at the anti-war protest he had helped organize, he'd learned of a recent tragedy in her life, the death of her only brother. His death was somehow related to the Iraq war. Although she hadn't given him many details, he'd come to understand the full impact the tragedy had on her. That personal trauma had intensified her pre-existing anger at the government for all of the lies used to invade Iraq, lies enticing her brother into military service under the illusion of patriotism. Gerald did not like to think about how the same thing would have affected him.

A few minutes past 10 AM, Gerald crossed the swollen Columbia River on Interstate Five and entered Portland. While crossing the large river, he wished he could just skip his work that day and visit Taylor. The time between the present and when he'd agreed to work with her had passed too slowly.

He planned to accomplish as much as possible for his client until 5 PM, giving himself an hour before his meeting with Taylor. Surprisingly, he managed to immerse himself in work and lose track of time. After leaving his client for the day, he felt good about what he'd accomplished, so he felt mentally prepared to see what Taylor planned to show him.

—✳—

Her chosen rendezvous point made him smile. Despite his alternate suggestions, Taylor chose to meet at Burgerville, a fast-food restaurant. Gerald usually met with their clients at nice, upscale places where he wore a suit. He remembered going to Burgerville once or twice in his college days, maybe even with Taylor, although he could not remember any specific time. He never felt impressed by fast-food establishments or wanted to revisit them.

After arriving at the specified location, he saw no sign of Taylor, so without waiting, he got in line at the counter where a short teenage girl with acne waited behind the register. When his turn to order arrived, he still needed to decide on what type of hamburger to order. He saw other items on the menu but felt obligated to purchase a burger at Burgerville. Feeling a little panicked, he ordered the first one on the list.

"Will there be anything else?" the girl asked.

"I uh," he began and smiled. "What's good with a hamburger? Fries, I guess."

A woman behind him noticed his hesitation and tapped him on the shoulder. She had two children with her, a young boy and girl. The younger girl clung to her mother's leg while the woman spoke.

"You should try their rosemary shoestring fries," she said with just a hint of impatience. "They're better than the regular fries."

"Thanks for the suggestion," he said after turning to see her and then smiling at the kids. He turned back to the teenager at the counter. "I'll have what she said."

Gerald chose a booth near the back of the dining area where he could watch the entrance. While waiting for his food, the aroma of hamburgers and fries made his mouth salivate. The oil in the air coated the lining of his nose.

He wondered if Taylor would look any different. Would she have a new hairstyle? Painted fingernails? *That would be a sight*, he thought and chuckled. He remembered how Taylor had always kept her fingernails cut short. They had usually looked scratched and even a little dirty underneath. For some strange reason, he remembered her fingernails.

In college, Taylor had failed to fit the mold of the typical twenty-something female student. She had never worn makeup, or at least Gerald had not noticed any. In his opinion, makeup would have detracted from her appearance. Her dark red hair and bright green eyes added enough color to her Irish-white skin to satisfy even the worst critic. Although her physical appearance had impressed Gerald, her confidence and intelligence had intimidated him. She had a quick wit and rarely hid any impatience or her hot temper. He enjoyed being around her, even when he was the target of her displeasure.

When he saw Taylor enter the restaurant, Gerald stood from the table and eagerly approached her. She looked the same as he remembered, dark red hair in a ponytail, bright green eyes, and an arrogant smile warning people to stay away. She wore a forest green jacket, dark blue jeans, brown boots, and seemed a little more fashionable than in her college days when she only wore jeans and a t-shirt.

Her green eyes fixed on him instantly. She smiled wider and raised her right hand as a motionless wave while walking to the counter. As he approached her, Gerald felt as though they had seen each other recently, which reminded him of the dream.

"Taylor," he said, extending his hand. "It's great to finally see you. Sorry for pushing this off for so long."

She glanced at his hand, acting surprised at the formality, and immediately smiled wider. When she grasped his hand, she pretended to meet him for the first time and shook vigorously.

"It's great to see you too, Gerald. Three years just slipped by."

"Is that the same backpack you had at the University of Oregon?" Gerald asked, remembering the simple yellow canvas backpack.

"Yeah. If something works, I keep it."

She turned to the counter as the man in front of her finished his order. While she ordered her food, Gerald glanced around at the other people in the restaurant. He estimated between ten to fifteen people, filling several tables.

"Is that the table you chose in the back?" she asked, looking at his table where an employee was delivering his food. "I suppose that will do, for what I want to show you."

Gerald recognized the same get-down-to-business attitude he remembered in college. They had written enough to each other over the years, that he felt no need for idle chatter to get reacquainted. After she completed her order and they sat together in the booth, Taylor took a deep breath and her smile disappeared. Gerald wondered if her green eyes revealed how she felt—nervous to begin the discussion.

"You aren't in any trouble are you?" he asked, eyes squinting slightly.

"Not yet," she said, her smile returning. She removed the backpack from her shoulder and put it on the ground between her feet. "But it's a definite consequence if I screw up. That's why I need your help, why I called you. Don't worry, I also wanted to see you. It's not just business."

"Thanks for the vote of confidence."

"Did you leave your cell phone in your car?"

"Yes," he said.

Gerald ran his hand through his hair, not knowing what else to say. He suddenly felt impatient for her to explain the reason for their meeting, and then she surprised him by placing her right hand reassuringly on his. The warmth of her fingers caused an unexpected rush of adrenaline, and the sensation reminded him of the dream when she had pulled him through the barrier.

"Before you get all worried, let me explain," she said then removed her hand. "Although I will need to explain some background information before shooting you with the big bullet."

"Well, I'm intrigued." Gerald looked down at his burger as though still deciding to eat it. "Interesting place for a secret meeting. And we can say it all started at Burgerville."

"Yeah, don't make me wait for my food, or tip someone for bringing it."

As if on cue, a female Burgerville employee approached them from behind Taylor, bringing another tray of food. Gerald looked up at the girl and smiled, and Taylor stopped talking. As the girl walked away, Taylor looked carnivorously at her burger and took a bite. She sighed with pleasure and spoke while chewing.

"Before I start," she said, "let me just say that it's really good to see you. I've been surrounded by shitheads for way too long. Even Mom, God bless her, gets on my nerves sometimes. You're just about the only one I can trust, at least from my pathetically small social circle."

"I'm flattered to be in such an elite group," he said sincerely.

She paused as if considering a response, but then she changed her mind and took another bite. Her words had raised his interest, more than his desire to satisfy hunger. But he did feel slightly uncomfortable watching her eat, so he hesitantly took his first bite.

"After I graduated last fall," she continued, "I finally had a chance to work on this idea of mine, one that's been in my head for some time. I was so damn busy jumping through the stupid hoops required in college that I didn't have time to work on it."

While simultaneously talking and eating, Taylor looked annoyed by the additional requirement to breathe.

"Slow down. I'm in no hurry. We've got all night."

"So I finally had some time to work on this project," she continued, showing no sign of hearing him, "but I never took it too seriously because it just seemed so crazy." Taylor paused to inhale. "No wait, it didn't *seem* too crazy. It *was* too crazy. The idea was too complex to understand, even for me."

"So I came to live at home after graduation to use my dad's shop. It was such an insane idea, I never, ever seriously thought it would work, but I couldn't stop thinking about it. My mind must have been working on it when I wasn't aware because I even dreamed about this thing. If it did work, then I'd be rich and famous, or so I thought. As you know, I don't care about fame, but I wouldn't mind the money. Self-ishness makes the world go round, right?"

"It does indeed," he said, smiling and not wanting to interrupt the story.

"So, since I didn't have any obligations, I quit my dead-end job, moved back home, and became kind of a recluse, a freeloader on my mom."

"Does your mother know what you're doing?"

"No," she said. "I couldn't talk to her about it anyway. She wouldn't understand what it was, or the implications, and I wouldn't want her to freak out or do anything rash. For now, it's in her best interest to remain ignorant. That's why I didn't want to meet you at my house."

"Seems reasonable," he said, barely containing his impatience. Even though he enjoyed listening to her talk, he wanted her to reveal the reason for their meeting.

"Well, a few weeks ago, after endless failures, I finally found success. When the reality of it all hit me, I seriously almost passed out." She paused to breathe and shook her head at the memory. "It felt like waking up in bed, looking out the window, and finding yourself in space. I got dizzy and had to lie down, so I wouldn't black out."

She looked at him with half-closed eyes, and he feared she would decide against sharing her secrets.

"Go ahead, Taylor," he said. "You can trust me."

She looked around again to assure herself that no one else was listening, then she lowered her voice even further. "A few days after I discovered that it worked, I thought I had it all figured out, but now I don't know what to think. There are so many implications, so many little worries that are filling my head. I don't know if they're real or imagined. Is the government watching me? Do they know about it?"

"The government?" Gerald asked, but she interrupted him in a whisper.

"Am I just dreaming all this?" she asked while leaning forward. "What if I'm going crazy?"

Her whisper made Gerald start to feel even more paranoid, so he quickly checked for anyone else in the restaurant looking at them. When he turned back to Taylor, the look on her face seemed to plead for emotional relief, for assurance of her sanity. He leaned forward and put his hand on her forearm. At his touch, she closed her eyes. For a moment, he thought he saw tears glistening in the corners of her beautiful green eyes.

"Believe me, Taylor," he said. "I've seen you far crazier than this."

Gerald laughed, feeling instant relief when he saw her lips curve into a smile. She wiped her eyes and then attempted to look offended.

"Hey, you haven't seen true crazy yet!"

Despite his relief, Gerald was also shocked. He could not recall a time when she had appeared so disturbed.

"You're not crazy, Taylor," he said, feeling sorry for scheduling their meeting so long after their phone conversation. "You should have asked me to come earlier. I would have driven down in an instant. Sorry, you had to wait so long."

When she continued, no trace of emotional distress remained.

"I just need someone to see it, someone to help me plan. I know it's a stupid worry, but I'm afraid it won't work for you, that I just imagined it all. That would mean that I *have* lost my mind."

Taylor drew a deep breath and then pushed her canvas backpack to him under the table with her foot.

"I can't believe I brought it here," she began. "I feel like I have a billion dollars in this bag and I'm about to be robbed. Here, put the bag on the seat."

Before reaching down to pluck her bag from the ground, Gerald hesitated. He felt as though some dangerous creature waited inside, ready to bite. After securing the bag on the seat between him and the wall, he opened the main compartment.

"So this can help change the world for the better?" he asked while looking into its dark interior.

"I believe so, yes."
"Okay, what do I do?"

FIVE

Freddy

Freddy Carlson waited before answering the phone, especially when he saw the caller ID. Most likely, his sister or mother waited on the other end and he had a difficult time deciding which family member induced more anxiety. Considering the late hour, his sister Wanda wanted to ask him for something. His mother usually went to bed early, and she rarely called anyway.

Freddy hated answering phone calls in general, but his employer, Mr. Smith, had already gone to his room upstairs to read a book to help put himself to sleep. In his old age, Mr. Smith had trouble sleeping, so some nights he would sit up there for hours, reading or typing on his computer, but mostly reading.

If Mr. Smith heard the phone ringing, he would have gotten out of bed, and Freddy wanted to avoid that. His sister had purposefully put him in an awkward position. She knew he would not answer her call at any other time.

"Yes, hello," Freddy said after quickly lifting the receiver. While waiting for a response, he checked behind him just in case Mr. Smith was silently watching. He saw only the dark hallway.

"Hey, Freddy," the voice said after a long sigh.

"Who is this?" he asked before she could finish. "Wands?"

Freddy listened to another annoyed sigh.

"Who else would it be, Freddy? You know Mom's gone to bed, and no one cares enough about old Bill to call him."

"Say the word then," he replied in annoyance.

Only his sister or mother could give the correct code word to identify themselves. If they gave the wrong one, he would know another human was trying to deceive him. Usually, his boss answered the phone, and like every other normal person, the old man would know the identification of the owner from their voice.

Freddy had a rare and unfortunate problem. Voices made no emotional connection with him, not even the voices of close friends and family. To recall the identity of a voice, normal humans use their emotional connection to the voice. But Freddy's mind somehow lacked the capacity to form that connection. Without the option of connecting the familiar voice to a familiar person, he chose to confirm identification by another method, a code word.

People in his life had used this particular disability to ridicule him, but he had a long list of other peculiarities they had also used against him. He suffered from social anxiety and had difficulty understanding other humans. Long ago, he had quit wanting to be normal. Freddy now just wanted to be left alone. After becoming an assistant to the old man, only his sister still pestered him.

Freddy waited impatiently for his sister to say the code word.

"Spider, spider, spider," she said in frustration, and he imagined smelling the alcohol on her breath.

The high volume of her shout made him drop the phone with a loud thud. His whole body tensed while listening for any indication that Mr. Smith had also heard the sound. But only silence answered. Although her anger made him cringe, Freddy felt better after hearing their secret code word. He did not want to deal with an angry Wanda, so he changed to a softer tone.

"What is it that you want, Wands?"

"I want to show you something," she said, her tone softening and becoming almost friendly.

"The time is late, and Mr. Smith is in his room. I do not want to disturb him. Can we do this tomorrow?"

"Don't worry. I'll be quiet," she said, and Freddy could hear her raspy breathing between responses. "I want to show you something I bought today. Just let me come over. I'm coming through your neighborhood anyway."

"Well," he said in his final attempt to dissuade her. "You know that Mr. Smith does not want any visitors after he goes to bed."

His boss specifically did not want Wanda to visit unless he could chaperone. When she visited, Mr. Smith became Freddy's emotional advocate.

If his sister spoke the truth and did have something to show him, did Freddy want to see it? Probably not. He could not remember his sister ever giving him a gift unless as a cruel joke. But she had not tried anything like that for several years. Since he began working for Mr. Smith, she had pretended to like him. But no matter how much she tried to act friendly, her vindictive and selfish personality usually rose to the surface.

When Freddy was eighteen years old, Mr. Smith rescued him from the Oregon foster care system and from his parasitic mother and sister. Now at twenty-two years old, he lived with Mr. Smith doing errands and keeping the estate in order. He did almost everything for Mr. Smith, except answering the phones, unless it was after the old man had gone to his bedroom for the night.

"Freddy, just let me in when I get there. It'll just be for a minute. Old Bill won't know I was there."

She cut the connection.

Before setting down the receiver, he held the phone for a few seconds and sighed, wondering how many times he had to play the game with her. Freddy had some consolation. After moving to his present residence, he encountered his sister much less frequently.

Her five-year-old son kept his sister busier lately too. Freddy usually felt more comfortable around children than people his age, but not preschoolers destined to be tyrants. In just a few more years, the child's transformation into his mother would be complete. Freddy tried his best to hide his displeasure at seeing the boy whenever they came into contact. After the boy's last visit, Mr. Smith had forbidden him from entering the house again, and he had told Wanda personally.

Freddy walked into the room at the main entrance of the mansion, the drawing room. He opened the curtains and peeked outside but saw only the street light past the driveway gate. From that location, he would be unable to hear Mr. Smith's movement, so he went to the central staircase and walked silently upstairs. He walked through the hallways until he saw the closed door to Mr. Smith's room. After listening for a few seconds, Freddy heard no movement or sound.

He returned to the drawing room and stood at the closed curtains, watching for light at the main gate. After a few seconds, his diminishing patience forced him to move, so he walked to the grand piano at the other end of the room. He spent the next ten minutes walking from the piano to the window and back again. He counted twenty-one trips before he noticed the light from his sister's car through the curtains.

SIX

Freddy

After his sister stopped at the front gate, Freddy held his finger over the gate entry control, waiting until he felt more mentally prepared to press it. He counted to five then pushed the button. Even though his sister had given him the code word over the phone and the car looked like hers, Freddy would feel better once he saw her face, the only way he could positively identify her.

Wanda parked in front of the main entrance, knocked on the front door, then waited. He looked through the peephole and sighed after recognizing her face. Freddy took another deep breath before inactivating the security system he had installed and then slowly opened the door.

"Hi, Brother dear," his sister said before stepping past him and entering the house.

After he glanced behind her and failed to see her son there, he breathed a large sigh of relief. He closed the door and immediately noticed her hair, which had grown a couple of centimeters since he'd last seen her.

The short section of blond hair near the roots contrasted sharply with the rest of her dyed brown hair and red highlights. Her hair also seemed covered in about three days' worth of hairspray. Like Freddy, she had natural blond hair, nearly white. But she was always fighting nature and wanting something different. In his younger years, she would ridicule him for allowing his nearly white hair to get all bushy.

"What," she said and rolled her eyes. "No hi, or anything?"

"Shh," he said in warning, pressing his index finger to his lips.

"Oh pfah," she said and began walking away. "Old Bill can't hear half of what we say when you're standing right next to him."

He wanted to scold her for speaking disrespectfully about his boss, but he also wanted to prevent agitation. Before following her from the room, he took a deep breath and tried to keep the irritation from his voice.

"What do you want to show me?"

Wanda ignored him and walked through the hallways toward the kitchen as she would through her own home. Freddy disliked how she knew her way around the house so well. He followed her as an obedient child, afraid of being spanked by an angry and loud response.

"I just gotta get a drink first. You're gonna love what I got for ya."

She opened the refrigerator and instantly looked disappointed, probably due to the lack of beer. After rummaging through the contents for a moment, she smiled in triumph and removed pink grapefruit juice. She drank directly from the container.

"I know what you're thinking, Freddy," she said and swallowed. "I'm here to ask for some shit, but I'm not. I just couldn't wait for an old-Bill-approved time to give this thing to you."

Although her statement sounded rehearsed, she seemed genuinely excited. After breaking eye contact with him, his sister placed her purse on the counter by the refrigerator and rummaged loudly through its contents. She finally retrieved her intended object and displayed it in the palm of her hand. Freddy blinked a couple of times before he could focus on the thing.

Wanda held a flat, rectangular crystal with rounded corners, slightly larger than a credit card, and thick, maybe five millimeters, he guessed. While leaning down for a closer view, he felt uneasy being so close to his sister, but a strong attraction seemed to pull him toward the object.

After looking more closely, he noticed a finely grooved crystal surface, which refracted the light from the kitchen ceiling. No matter what angle of his view, the surface threw a beautiful rainbow into his eyes. He admired the light spectrum for a moment until noticing the object encased inside the crystal, hidden at first by the refracted light. His lips stretched into a wide smile when he recognized the spider inside, a creature that both frightened and fascinated him.

The crystal encased a giant spider with outstretched legs, not a real spider, but one composed of what looked like different kinds of stone, and only two-dimensional so that when he looked at the object from the side, the spider nearly disappeared. Several rows of ruby-red eyes lined its light gray head, and the body looked like granite with silver metal streaked across it. Different colored stripes of polished metal encircled its beautiful black legs like a candy cane.

When he attempted to peer closer at the eyes of the spider, his vision blurred and he had to look away. Freddy blinked several times to restore his sight.

"It is amazing," Freddy said while gently taking the crystal from her hand. He turned the rectangular object over and noticed that the spider looked identical from either side. He carefully tossed it up and down in one hand to judge the weight, enjoying the sensation. "It is very dense."

"I know I shouldn't indulge your spider fetish," she said with a genuine smile, "but this had your name on it."

"It does?" he asked and began inspecting the surface for his name.

Wanda sighed then frowned in irritation.

"Just a figure of speech, Freddy," she said. "I bought it for you. Do you want it or not?"

The question struck warning bells in his mind. He closed his hand over the crystal, afraid she would take it back. If he accepted the gift, he would owe her a favor, a big favor. Wanda never gave gifts without strings attached. She would expect something in return, either right then or in the future.

He moved his hand outside of her reach then looked at the spider again. The beautiful object seized his attention and he had difficulty looking away. When he did manage to return his attention to Wanda, she had a strange look in her eyes, some pleasure he had never seen before.

"Yes, I do want it," he said before she could speak. "Thanks, Wands."

Freddy realized something that quickly relieved his anxiety. No matter what his sister did or gave him, he owed her nothing. Even by giving him the crystal and its encased spider, Wanda would still be in his debt. He failed to recall any time in his life when she had given him anything other than grief.

"You're welcome," she said, her dark red lips stretching into a genuine smile.

"Where did you purchase it?" he asked, feigning indifference. He planned on visiting wherever she had purchased the crystal, to see what else they sold.

"A friend of mine had it," she said. "And when I saw it, I had to get it for you, so I bought it from her. You don't know the best part."

"What best part?"

She put her index finger on the center of the crystal, covering part of the spider. "That rock, the head."

"Yes."

"She says it's a piece of an asteroid."

He stared at the head of the spider but remained silent.

"Yep, that little piece of rock was flying through space," she spoke with excitement, "for thousands of years probably."

Freddy resisted the urge to laugh at her ridiculous estimation of its possible age. He wanted to correct her and say billions or trillions of years.

"How did she know that?"

Even if wrong about the asteroid part, he still wanted the crystal. If the head did come from an asteroid, he would desire the object even more, but the true identification of the rock did not seem as important as its creator. He already owned a piece of an asteroid, and even that seemed unimportant. Everything on the Earth had also been flying through space for a long time.

He held the crystal up closer to his eyes and examined it again. He had never owned anything as beautiful, and he could not recall ever wanting something more. How had her friend acquired the crystal object? He could not imagine any of his sister's associates having something of similar quality. The closer he stared at the shiny rainbow surface, the more exquisite it looked.

Typically, some factory in China or Southeast Asia made cheap and interesting baubles like the one in his hand. They looked attractive from afar, but upon closer inspection, their absence of quality or value became painfully apparent. Freddy quickly recognized the high quality of the crystal from his sister. After inspecting the object from several angles, looking for any sign of make or model, he saw no inscription. He planned to use his analytical instruments later for a more detailed inspection.

"The girl I got it from was certain about it being an asteroid," Wanda said, offended. "She would not lie to me."

"Do you know where she got it?" he asked casually, trying to conceal the intensity of his curiosity. He felt something strange about the affair as though the trinket came from a secret government laboratory instead of a cheap labor factory in Asia.

"She wouldn't say, but what does it matter? Can't you just be happy for once and not follow up with a million questions?"

From the tone of her voice and the look in her eyes, Freddy knew he had to stop the interrogation. If he persisted, she might demand that he return it.

"Sorry, Wands. This is great. How can I repay you? Do you want to take some food back home to Charlie?"

Without waiting for an answer, Freddy retrieved a plastic bag from a drawer and began filling it with food from the refrigerator. Whenever she visited, he reluctantly gave her food to take home, but this time he felt glad to return the favor. He filled the bag quickly, so maybe she would leave quickly.

"Thanks, Bro." Her tone of anger was gone. "Bill won't notice?"

"Probably not. I will just go to the store tomorrow or tonight and restock."

"You got a sweet set-up here, brother. Don't ruin it."

After walking her to the front door, he failed to stop himself from asking another question.

"Who is this friend you got it from?"

Wanda opened the door and turned around with the two bags of food swinging in her hand.

"She's not really a friend, more of an acquaintance. I met her yesterday when she was moving out of the apartment down the hall. We got to talking, and I noticed the crystal in a box of her shit. She seemed glad to be rid of the thing. But, she's all moved out. I'll probably never see her again."

She turned and walked away, so Freddy quietly shut the door.

"Now I will never know where she got it," he said to himself.

Freddy walked to the window, lifted the curtain, and watched as his sister carried the bags of food to her car and drove away. During the entire scene, he felt the weight of the crystal in his closed fist. After letting the curtain fall back into place, the soft sound of an elderly voice paralyzed him.

For the next three seconds, he listened to the raspy breathing of his boss standing somewhere behind him. He squeezed his hand tightly over the crystal, not wanting Mr. Smith to see what he held.

"When are you gonna stand up to your sister?" his boss asked. Bill Smith leaned against the piano, holding a polished black cane in his withered hand. "You wouldn't have to see her if you followed the rule of letting me answer the phone."

"I do not know why I picked it up," he said slowly, looking outside again through the thin curtain. His sister was pulling onto the street. "I thought it might be an emergency."

"Everything's an emergency with your sister."

While turning from the curtains, Freddy slid the crystal discreetly into his pocket. In the dim light, the old man had not noticed. If Mr. Smith had seen the object, he would have asked Freddy to show it. For some mysterious reason, Freddy did not want to show his boss yet. Maybe he just needed time to investigate further.

"If you knew she was here, why did you not stop her?" Freddy asked and instantly regretted speaking. The words felt impertinent.

"Talking to your sister requires too much energy," the old man said. "And it's late. I just didn't feel like going through the trouble, since she was here already. She's gone, I guess. That's all that matters."

"How long were you standing there?"

"Long enough to guess that the kitchen has probably lost some more inventory again."

Freddy looked down, ashamed.

"I am sorry," he said. "Next time, I will let you answer the phone. I did not want to wake you."

"I know, and thank you, and don't worry about giving your sister food. I don't mind since it's yours too. I'm going to bed now, again. Goodnight." Mr. Smith turned and began walking from the room then stopped and faced Freddy again. "By the way, did your sister have anything important to tell you?"

"She just wanted some groceries," Freddy said and paused. "As usual."

Mr. Smith looked at him critically, and Freddy wondered if anything ever escaped his notice. Before the old man could say anything else though, he began coughing.

After the coughing subsided, he said, "Goodnight, Freddy." Then he turned and disappeared into the dark hallway.

SEVEN

Gerald

"**P**ut your hand in the main compartment," Taylor said with a casual glance around the dining room in the Burgerville restaurant. "Don't take anything out of the bag. Just put your hand on the box. You'll find a switch on the side."

When Gerald felt the cool metal box, his heart rate began to rise. The box had a grainy surface.

"Okay, I feel the switch."

"Before you flip the switch," she began, "make sure to put some downward pressure on the box."

"It's not going to hurt me is it?" he asked, followed by a nervous laugh. To any observer in the restaurant, Taylor probably appeared calm. The pulsating vein in her neck indicated otherwise.

"Putting pressure on it?" she asked.

"Yes."

"Okay, flip the switch."

He pulled the switch with his index finger and heard a small click.

After failing to notice any unusual activity from the box, Gerald felt the beginning of panic. It was not due to the box but from his fear of her reaction. He braced himself for a shriek from a furious female and imagined her hands reaching across the table to strangle him. Instead, Taylor just looked confused, narrow eyes staring at him almost accusingly. After a few horrible seconds, her eyes grew wide.

"Oh, my God," she said, placing her hand over her heart and laughing. "I know what the problem is."

"That's good," Gerald said in relief. "I thought you were going to kill me."

"I almost forgot," she said, ignoring him. "Here, stick this next to the switch, then flip it. My precautions worked a little too well."

She handed him a shiny piece of square metal, two centimeters long. "This was just a precaution in case someone stole my backpack and found this thing. They wouldn't think it's anything special because it won't work without the magnet activating an internal switch."

Taylor took a deep breath and smiled again.

When Gerald placed the magnet next to the switch, it snapped to the metal with a loud click. He flipped the switch again and the box began to hum with a high-frequency vibration more intense than the notification from his iPhone.

When the metal box began to push up against his hand, he jolted in shock and then fought an unexpected instinct to remove his hand from the backpack. He looked up and met Taylor's eyes, the vibrating box feeling steady and powerful under his hand. Taylor held her breath. For the next few seconds of silence, he felt paralyzed.

"So?" she asked, breaking the silence like the crack of a whip.

"It's pushing against my hand," he began hesitantly. "What do I do now?"

He felt a little stupid and almost wanted to laugh, but the fiery look in Taylor's green eyes prevented him from showing any amusement. Apparently, he'd failed to see the importance of the force against his hand.

"I'm kind of disappointed that you don't get it yet," she said and wiped the moisture from her eyes. "Lift up your hand a little bit."

Gerald lifted his hand, and the box followed as though it wanted to escape the backpack. The small metal box suddenly felt more alive under his hand. Gerald flipped the switch and the box fell back down to the bottom of the bag. Chills coursed from his chest to his neck, but he wasn't sure why. The box did not feel natural.

"What the hell is this?" he asked with surprising impatience. "Sorry, you just need to tell me."

Gerald pushed the bag away and removed his hand. He usually tried his best to act composed and speak in perfect English, so he felt stupid for revealing his emotions. As he looked into her eyes, they seemed to be silently laughing at him.

"So what do we do now, right?" she asked.

"Just give me a second here," he said. He was unprepared to respond and needed time to decode the experience. "I just need to get my head wrapped around this. You invented anti-gravity?"

"Shh," she said, and her eyes opened wide in warning.

"I guess you *might* call it anti-gravity," she said, lowering her voice. "Just like you might call throwing a rock in the air, anti-gravity. A more accurate and cleaner description is *Net Momentum Generation*. I shortened it to NMG, simple and sweet. I'm a sucker for acronyms."

"NMG huh," he said and nodded in approval, feeling like a puppy trying to please her. "At the moment, I don't know what to say. It's a lot to take in. No offense intended, but part of me doesn't believe it. I mean, why hasn't anyone else figured out how to do this? Or have they? People have been trying to do something like this for thousands of years."

"Yes they have, Gerald," she said, a tone of disappointment replacing her amusement. "I've considered two possibilities. Either someone has invented it before, but the military or someone else has covered it up, or I'm just the super genius of them all."

"Don't worry, I give you full credit for being a genius, but you're not the only one, right?"

"Hey!" she said, smiling and nodding slightly. "You have to admit though, there's no one else like me."

"True," he said and relaxed a bit. "I'm just glad it hasn't damaged your humility."

"I just feel so much better after showing you, telling someone I can trust." She threw an entire fry into her mouth and then continued while chewing. "Seriously though, I doubt anyone has invented this yet. Anyone educated in science would have instantly dismissed the idea—my initial moment of inspiration. All of my education claimed it would not work, so I would have dismissed it too, but I couldn't get the idea out of my head."

"Well, I'm honored you decided to share this moment with me. How exactly is this going to improve the state of the world?" Gerald felt slightly afraid of her response. He prepared to hear an accusation, how he had failed to see the obvious answer.

"Because the shitheads at the top like the world the way it is," she began. "They don't want anything to change, except what they can control. That's why they divert all the public money to junk science like hot fusion, projects that will never produce anything. They fear a scientific revolution the most. That will make people less dependent on their system."

"Ah yes," Gerald said, finally understanding. They had discussed this topic many times in the past. "Not every human problem has a technological or scientific solution, but you may be correct in this instance."

"Good answer."

"Okay," he said, "I think I'm ready for your scientific explanation, but give it to me gently. Remember, I'm not a science geek like you."

Her eyes narrowed in feigned outrage.

"Gerald," she said slowly. "I'll try to explain so that even a lawyer can understand. To put it bluntly, I had to break the law, one of the most fundamental laws of engineering, what they drill into you from day one. I broke the sacred conservation of momentum law."

"I'll pretend that I didn't hear that," he said and laughed, "being a lawyer and all."

"They won't like what I did," she said, smiling at his joke.

"You mean other scientists?" he asked. "The institutional ones in charge?"

Gerald began to feel less intimidated and more like a child about to hear an exciting bedtime story.

"Yeah, those ones," she said with a sneer. "The gods of science that everyone seems to worship."

Her reference to the *gods of science* produced a colossal statue in his mind, a college professor wearing glasses, a robe, and a book held to his chest.

"You broke a law, huh? And the first person you told was a lawyer?"

"If I explained in detail how it works," she said, ignoring him, "you probably wouldn't understand, so I'll try to explain in the most basic way I can. This is related to the conservation of momentum, which depends on forces being equal and opposite. That's what is seen macroscopically, net momentum averages to zero. But on an atomic level, I wondered if there was a small time delay that could break the balance, if only slightly. But a little can add up to a lot, and I designed a way to extract net momentum from semi-isolated systems."

"The main problem with fundamental physics," she continued, "or to be more precise, those who study fundamental physics, is the absolute reliance on assumptions and the mistake of failing to reassess them. For instance, the electric forces between subatomic particles..."

A short time after she had begun her explanation, Gerald lost focus and only pretended to listen. While she wasted her time attempting to help him understand, Gerald considered the implications, which were his true interest. He knew the military would have a great desire to acquire her invention and they would likely stop at nothing to get it. Then he understood her frightening dilemma.

EIGHT

Gerald

"So, where do you go from here, right?" he asked, hoping she would stop explaining the scientific details.

"Yes," she answered. "Your initial thoughts?"

Gerald glanced briefly at the backpack sitting on the bench next to him and wondered how to respond. He spoke slowly, not wanting to frighten Taylor any more than necessary.

"My gut instinct tells me that the military would want it, cover it up even. An invention like this would revolutionize war, especially if we were the only military to have it."

"When you say *we*, do you mean the United States Military?" she asked with derision. "Or do you mean, *we*, as in you and me?"

Gerald shook his head in irritation, remembering her feelings about the military and her brother. He was also slightly embarrassed for speaking like a collectivist. He needed to speak more carefully and more precisely.

"I know we can't be blamed for what the U.S. military does," he said. "We just need to prevent them from taking you to a secret military base for the rest of your life. I don't think you want that, but those are just my initial thoughts. You've had a lot more time to think about this than I have. What have you come up with?"

The anxious look in her eyes caused him to feel an intense empathy and desire to help her. So far, he had failed to offer any comfort. He could imagine her excitement when she finally got her NMG device to work and then her realization of all the frightening opposition. Not only would the US military want the NMG, but so would all the others. Being locked away in a military base would probably be the least distressing outcome but would fail to promote what they both wanted, more freedom in their lives. Although he had no solution and needed more time to think, she needed to discuss the situation with him.

"Those were my first thoughts too," she agreed. "I've been trying to think of ways to avoid it, maybe start my own company, flood the market with the device before they can cover it up."

"Hmm, yes," he began. "It's a very delicate situation. You would need to give very little time for your opponents to begin countermeasures. Corporate sharks can smell open market share from far away and they will come to eat it up, and that's only if intelligence doesn't put a blanket over it first. A Nobel Prize might be the best possible outcome from that strategy, a good chunk of money and fame. But that wouldn't be enough would it?"

She smiled deviously.

No, he thought, *a big chunk of money and fame would not satisfy her*. Taylor wanted every last drop of juice from this fruit. No one else could profit from her efforts.

"Nobel prizes are only given to promote political agendas," she said with an angry sneer. "There's also the problem of filing for a patent and all that mess. I'm not sure how easy a patent would be, but doesn't that take forever? That's not going to work anyway. Something this big cannot be kept a secret, especially after passing through the hands of a hundred patent clerks."

"But don't forget–" Gerald began, but she continued.

"That seems like a dead end. One of the corporate sharks, as you call them, will make something similar, ship the production overseas for half the cost, and probably claim I stole the tech from them. We might be able to make it work and make a quality American-made novelty for a niche market but... blah, blah, blah. All that just seems so boring compared to what this is."

Taylor paused to drink her soda.

"God I hate those arrogant snakes," she continued. "They sit in their fiftieth-story boardrooms and steal the sweat and labor of the scientists and engineers, those who do all the real work. They give us a hundred thousand dollars while they take a hundred million."

Gerald prepared to speak again but decided instead just to enjoy her rant. Taylor needed to continue the process of converting her anxiety into righteous indignation. The mind sometimes acted as the stomach and just needed to vomit.

"Thanks for your hard work, we'll take it from here," she said mockingly. "Businessmen, bastards!"

Taylor drew a deep breath and exhaled. The following silence seemed like the eye of a hurricane, peaceful but tumultuous in every direction.

"You're right about the patent," Gerald said with a scoff. He wanted to remain positive but could not prevent her anger from infecting him. "We could not maintain control long enough to fully capitalize on it. The legal team from a company like Lockheed Martin would tie you up in court with fake patent infringement lawsuits, and the government would make the case impossible to defend by classifying it as a national security matter. The public will never hear anything about it."

He suddenly understood another implication of Taylor's underlying assumption, a more dangerous possibility that erased his sarcastic smile and made him gulp. He wondered how Taylor had managed to sleep peacefully at night.

"So you're saying the military won't even want something like this to be invented?" he asked. "Something this big would alter the game for everyone on the planet. It would cause too much uncertainty. Western military dominance might be in jeopardy."

"Western military dominance," she said with a fresh sarcasm. "You don't want to start that argument again, do you? I proved pretty convincingly that all military conflict is managed, at least between all the big players. West against East is just another movie to distract the masses."

She opened her eyes wide, challenging him to argue with her.

"It would be nice," he said with a smile, happy to see some excitement in her eyes, "if we could at least agree to disagree on that subject."

"That's what I thought," she said and sneered, but then her tone changed to resignation. "No matter what we try though, the government will squash us. I don't understand this human world of yours. That's why I brought the problem to you. If anyone can find a way, it's Gerald Foster."

"Thanks for the confidence," he said with a fresh smile. "I will help you come up with a plan, but first let me continue to think out loud. The powers-that-be have unlimited resources to fight whoever threatens their system. They could just follow the simplest and cheapest action, threaten to hurt your mother, so you won't dare to try anything."

He paused to let her respond but then changed his mind.

"Or they'll just poison us and anyone else who knows about it. That's cheaper and easier than paying us for our silence."

"I know, I know," she said with a tone of acceptance and not surprise. When she made eye contact, he saw hope. "I did the hard part, and now I'll just let you figure out the rest."

Her confidence made him feel a little better.

"Here, you probably want your baby back," he said and pushed the backpack under the table to her. "I'm glad you decided to make me a part of this. Despite everything I just said, I do think we can overcome all obstacles."

He stood and started gathering up the remnants of his meal.

"Come on. Let's talk more in my car."

"Sure," she said and placed the backpack in her lap.

Gerald held the exit door open for her and took a deep breath in anticipation of entering the cold, wet night. He ran to his black Ford Taurus ahead of her. While waiting for him to open the passenger door, she drank her soda, smiling pleasantly and acting immune to the cold rain hitting her exposed head.

"Thanks," she said after he opened the door for her.

After entering the vehicle and igniting the engine, Gerald started the heater and placed his wet hands in the cold airflow. He estimated just a couple of minutes for the air to warm up.

"Privacy and a higher temperature might help us think more clearly."

"Sure," she said and rubbed her hands in the cold air, acting as though she faced a raging bonfire.

Gerald turned to watch the raindrops slide down the windshield, the last part of their long journey to reunite with the Earth. The water streams distorted the street lights from outside, and the view reminded him of the dream with Taylor when the barrier had separated them. While staring at the colorful light display on the windshield, the remainder of his dream replayed in his mind.

—✳—

"Follow me," Taylor said when Gerald opened his eyes on the other side of the dark barrier.

Gerald found himself in a dimly lit hallway with dark brick walls. The hallway felt extremely old, perhaps thousands of years, but the bricks still fit together neatly and looked impregnable. While he tried to comprehend his situation, Taylor released his hand and began walking away from him.

He took a step forward to follow her but noticed a light to his right. He paused and turned to see a closed wooden door with a small narrow window at his eye level. In the bright room, he noticed a man lying on a steel cot in the corner, a man who looked disturbingly too much like himself. He wore a white hospital gown and faced the wall in stillness, possibly asleep.

Gerald turned to find Taylor waiting several meters in front of him. She waved her hand in the air for him to continue moving.

"We can do nothing for him now," she said. "Come."

Without waiting, she resumed walking down the hallway. The movement of her body under the gown seemed to have a power of its own and pulled Gerald forward. The sight of her figure quickly replaced the troubling view of the man in the bright room. Gerald passed several more doors, but they had only dark windows.

Taylor led him to the end of the hallway, to a large iron door set in the brick wall with an illuminated keypad on the right. She held her hand two centimeters away from the panel, palm blocking the light. The panel illuminated bright orange through her fingers and then Gerald heard a click of the door locking mechanism.

After passing through the door, they began ascending stone steps and entered a thick fog. Gerald noticed a bright glow toward the top of the stairs, but the outline of Taylor's body through her gown consumed his attention. While following just a few steps behind her, he almost wished for the stairs to continue forever.

At the top of the stairs, they emerged from the fog and then stopped. They were standing between two large stone pillars at the edge of an immense room with polished granite floors. Crystal chandeliers with hundreds of flickering lights hung from the ceiling high above and kept the large space illuminated. Gerald imagined great dances held there with beautiful people wearing expensive costumes. At the opposite end of the room, a wide staircase ascended from the floor with a giant statue on the landing. The stairs in front of the statue seemed like a great place to give a speech.

The statue reminded Gerald of some ancient public figure and seemed to look straight at him. The man had a prominent nose, strong chin, and deep-set eyes. A crown of gold sat on the statue's head, shining with reflected chandelier light. The crown was a pentagon with polished black tips, sharp enough to pierce skin. The room reminded him of a cathedral, but instead of Jesus as the central attraction, the statue of the man dominated the room.

While staring at the statue, Gerald heard voices above him. He looked upward to a walkway surrounding the large room where a pair of teenagers stood talking and leaning against an ornate wooden guardrail. They seemed like typical teenagers but were dressed in custom-fit clothing and looked well-groomed. From the confident look in their eyes, Gerald thought they appeared mature for their age, not trying to impress each other as he remembered acting as a teenager.

Gerald also heard music from the second level, not a recording of music but the sound of a piano. Taylor began walking again, so Gerald turned from watching the teenagers and followed her across the room toward the wide staircase. He noticed geometric patterns carved into the stone floor and wondered if a view from above would reveal some overall design, but the sway of Taylor's hips quickly stole his curiosity away from the man-made pattern.

After passing the statue, Taylor followed the next staircase on the right, which led toward the teenagers. The couple had remained in their previous positions, leaning over the railing and looking down at the floor while talking. Neither of the teenagers turned or made any indication of noticing the woman in the white nightgown leading a barefoot man in his sleeping attire toward them. Gerald initially thought they were tourists in a historical palace, but they looked more like residents, or maybe one resident entertaining a visiting friend. Gerald felt incredibly awkward, but they never paused in their conversation to look at him.

"Where are we?" Gerald asked after they had passed the teenagers and then continued toward the piano music.

"The location is insignificant," she answered. "Time to meet the Dayr Aban."

Her answer seemed like some arcane reference to a well-known story.

The new hallway terminated at an open set of double doors where Gerald heard the muffled sound of several people talking. Taylor led him into the square room, each side ten meters in length. She walked to the center of the room and then stopped to watch the occupants, Gerald standing at her right. Ten people congregated at the sides of the room, some standing and some sitting in elegant chairs. Everyone was holding glasses of colored liquid and conversing together pleasantly. Seeing their semi-formal dress made Gerald feel extremely self-conscious again in his pajamas.

Only one person turned to face Gerald and Taylor, a man sitting by himself in a high-backed chair, behind what looked like an altar on the opposite side of the room. An elegant silk cloth covered the altar, a soft turquoise with a slightly iridescent reflection of the chandelier light.

Unlike all of the other occupants, the man wore a long white silk shirt embroidered with gold and silver thread. A band of woven beige fabric encircled his head, holding black hair neatly away from his face. The dark hair contrasted sharply with his pale skin and hung just above his jawline. His face looked familiar, but Gerald feared to make eye contact and kept his gaze on the altar. In his peripheral vision, Gerald watched the man peer at them closely for a moment, then he looked away as though unimpressed.

When the man no longer faced their direction, Gerald looked up and noticed a large mural hanging on the wall behind him, showing two young girls kneeling on some steps before a throne. The girls were pretending to worship another young girl on the throne while several adults watched in amusement from the side. Each child wore a long white dress, which spread out over a large part of the ground and stairs. At first, Gerald assumed the mural depicted a scene of ancient Greece or Rome, but the fashion looked wrong for some reason, maybe from a more ancient civilization like Sumer or Mesopotamia.

The awkward feeling of social impropriety began to subside as Gerald examined the mural. After nearly a minute, he noticed the side wall on the right of the altar. Two marble columns stood on either side of an opening to another room where the piano music and sound of loud laughter originated. Gerald could not identify the music but thought it sounded like a classical version of some popular rock song. The musician was talented but played as though slightly intoxicated. Gerald suddenly remembered the two teenagers in the hallway. They were probably bored by their parents' social gatherings.

When Taylor gently touched his shoulder, Gerald turned from the entryway to the other room and found her pointing to the altar. And then before Gerald could consciously reject the implied command, he began walking obediently to the altar.

The man behind the altar turned to Gerald, his eyes opening wide in surprise, the first person who seemed to notice Gerald. He stood from his throne.

In his peripheral vision, Gerald noticed several of the people in the room suddenly stop their conversations and turn to stare at the man. But no one else in the room looked at Gerald or Taylor. When Gerald reached the altar, he stopped and knelt with his hands resting on the soft cloth covering the stone surface.

After kneeling, Gerald looked up into the man's eyes and realized why he had seemed so familiar. The man had the face of the statue on the stairs, the one wearing the gold, pentagonal crown.

"Why are you here?" the man asked casually with a deep and resonating voice. "You are not on the guest list."

Gerald broke eye contact and turned to Taylor for guidance, and then discovered everyone in the room looking at the man with concern. No one was looking at Gerald. All of the private conversations had stopped and the music from the other room became more distinct. Taylor smiled as though amused by his discomfort then nodded toward the man, an indication for Gerald to answer him.

"I go where I please," Gerald said, surprising himself at his words. He felt like an actor with no knowledge of his lines. "Don't worry. I will not interrupt your party."

"Then be my guest," the man said, "but give me the honor of your hand."

The man bowed just enough for his dark hair to fall forward and touch the edges of his cheeks. Then he slowly extended his right hand across the altar, vertical and palm facing left. When his fingers reached halfway, they appeared to pass through an invisible barrier. Blue sparks of static electricity crackled at his fingertips and then around his knuckles. The man continued to push his hand forward, the ring of blue electric sparks wrapping around his palm and then stopping at his wrist. Before grasping the beautifully shaped hand, Gerald noticed gold rings on his middle three fingers, each one with engraved spirals.

When their hands connected, Gerald felt an incredibly painful jolt of electricity. The man strengthened his grip and the pain intensified, but Gerald retained eye contact and acted as though he felt nothing. The sound of crackling electricity filled the room. As he stared into the man's dark eyes, he noticed black, swirling clouds around the pupils.

A few seconds later, Taylor appeared next to the altar. She looked down at their hands and then placed the tip of her finger on the middle knuckle of the man's index finger and the electric pain suddenly stopped. The man quickly released Gerald's hand and looked at his own hand in surprise. He turned to where Taylor stood, but his gaze seemed to focus behind her. He began looking around in confusion, anger in his narrowed eyes. Taylor smiled and quietly laughed.

"You cannot remain concealed from us," the man said calmly after returning his attention to Gerald. His look of anger had vanished, replaced by satisfaction at the pain he had inflicted. He shook his hand slightly to dissipate some of his pain.

"We'll see," Gerald said while standing.

Gerald glanced at his hand, relieved to find no sign of physical damage. The man sat back down on his throne and turned away from Gerald, looking perturbed and making no further eye contact with him.

Gerald looked at Taylor in confusion. He wanted to ask her about what happened, but the people on the side of the room caught his attention first. In one of the groups, three men stood with two women and conversed as if oblivious to the scene at the altar. The two dark-haired women wore simple party dresses falling just above their knees. One looked maybe sixty years old, and the younger woman looked like her daughter. The men also dressed casually, wearing sport coats of expensive material, each a different shade of gray.

After examining the two women, he focused on the men and his eyes opened wide in surprise. He recognized two of the men almost instantly but required a moment to accept their identity. Vladimir Putin, Prime Minister of the Russian Federation, stood with the American actor, Robin Williams.

After recovering from his shock, Gerald attempted to understand their speech. They spoke in a language he did not recognize, but it was not Russian or English as he had expected to hear. Robin Williams suddenly raised both of his fists and shook them in mock anger. He said something, that Gerald did not understand, and then let his hands drop to his sides and the small group laughed heartily.

Gerald felt strange being so close to such celebrities, as though a hidden audience was watching them from a dark theater. When he turned to see Taylor, she was smiling at him.

"I want to show you something else," she said, then turned and began walking away from him, toward the entrance to the room.

Before following Taylor from the room, Gerald quickly examined the other group of people but did not recognize anyone. He glanced at the altar again and noticed the man staring at him. His gaze felt like a living thing. Despite the disturbing sensation, Gerald smiled politely and then quickly exited the room.

He caught up to Taylor in the hallway and followed her the way they had come. But instead of returning to the large ballroom, she turned down a new hallway. Gerald followed her past several closed doors and then past one open door, a dark room where a small boy was playing video games on a large flat-screen television. A servant girl sat beside the lad, light from the television flickering across her young face. After glancing into the room, Gerald noticed the man from the altar enter the hallway behind him, walking casually. Gerald pretended not to notice him, and then after leaving the open door and turning another corner, the man did not reappear.

After walking through the halls for a while, Gerald felt utterly lost. They eventually reached a short set of stairs leading to a circular room with flickering candles on the walls. A small wooden desk sat under the nearest window with bookshelves on either side and two divans against the opposite wall.

When Taylor shut the door behind him, the windows drew his attention first and he felt a strong desire to see the natural world again. Taylor sat in one of the divans and watched him as he approached the window above the desk.

"Are we in a tower?" he asked, leaning toward the window.

Before looking outside, he noticed the candles on either side of the window. Instead of actual flames, their flickering light came from LEDs sitting atop smooth white wood.

"Yes, the tallest one," she answered, her voice breaking the spell of the flickering light.

His first glimpse into the night revealed what looked like a large compound surrounded by a tall brick wall. He saw three small cottages below and a large garden illuminated by small light posts. Beyond the wall, Gerald could see only the tops of trees. After inspecting the scene for a moment, he heard a noise from the hallway outside the doors and remembered the man following them. He recognized the soft but distinct sound of footsteps approaching the small room. The man was almost at the door.

While concentrating on the sound, he turned to face Taylor and noticed an opening in the wall at her right, revealing more stairs winding upward. Gerald felt a sudden panic and nearly sprinted to the other set of stairs. He turned and expected to see Taylor preparing to follow him, but she remained in the chair, calmly watching the door.

"Where do these stairs lead?" Gerald asked, just as the door knob began turning.

"Go see for yourself," Taylor said.

The door opened and the man with black hair appeared. He looked around the room without seeming to notice Taylor. Gerald felt momentarily paralyzed.

"The stairs lead nowhere," the man said as though Gerald had asked him the question.

Taylor watched the man at the door for a moment, the corners of her mouth curved in amusement. Then she turned to Gerald.

"You better hurry, Gerald," she said and her smile disappeared. "He can't follow you all the way up, but don't let him catch you."

When the man closed the door behind him, a new wave of panic gave Gerald a jolt of energy. He turned and began running up the stairs, which circled a large stone column. On his ascent, he orbited the column many times before entering another room, smaller than the one below and with the stone column visible in the center. This room had two chairs on either side of the column, each next to a window. Gerald paused and looked outside, breathing heavily. From his higher position, he could see the thick forest beyond the outer wall, nothing but trees in every direction.

After the pounding of his heart slowed enough for his ears to work properly, Gerald heard footsteps ascending the stairs. The clapping of soft leather on stone steps indicated a slow and steady pace. The experience suddenly felt like a dream. No matter how fast he ran, his pursuer would continue to gain on him.

He took a single, deep breath before exiting the room and running up the stairs again. On his ascent up the tower, there were no more rooms, but he passed more candles on window sills, each view showing the ground much farther away than the last. After running for what felt like forever, Gerald stopped when he could no longer see light from the stairs above him.

The man's head and shoulders appeared on the stairs below, and Gerald felt paralyzed again. The darkness up the stairs suddenly seemed just as menacing as the man with the black hair below him. He wished Taylor was there to help him.

"I won't follow you into the dark," the man said, taking a final step closer and stopping within arm's reach of Gerald's legs. "No life exists outside the light."

The man began slowly extending his right hand forward, palm facing left. As the hand moved, Gerald heard the crackling of sparks again and saw the ring of blue electric discharge slide up the man's fingers, then his wrist and arm.

Gerald stared at the hand in terror, knowing its touch meant extreme pain or possible death. He tried to take a step backward, but he tripped and fell onto the stairs. The hand kept moving slowly forward.

Gerald scrambled to his feet, then ran up the stairs and into the darkness. As he ran, the crackling electrical discharge faded into the distance. He orbited the central column several times and then an eerie silence made him pause, so he stopped to catch his breath. Gerald saw only a faint light from below but no sound. The man from the alter had stopped following him.

He began climbing again and held onto the central column for guidance, ascending until all the light had vanished. He passed no more windows or any other sources of light and had no choice but to keep moving upward. Going back down was not an option.

The stone column eventually became a smooth metal pole and Gerald began thinking of the man from the altar as a shark under the water, unable to harm him as long as he stayed out of the light. At that point, he no longer felt afraid of the dark. It provided security. He felt only the comfort of isolation and a curiosity of what lay ahead.

When Gerald could no longer feel the central pole, he kept ascending with his hands on the outer wall to support himself. After a few more minutes of climbing, he ascended one final step and found himself on a platform in a cool breeze. While standing motionless, he looked upward and saw only darkness. He extended both hands into the air above his head and felt nothing. Then he looked down and could see the faint outline of the platform under his feet, surrounded by light from Earth far below.

He stepped carefully to the edge of the platform and looked down. He could see the swirling clouds over Earth and the lights beneath them. The sight was beautiful and full of life. But when he looked up to the black sky again, he felt a chill. The universe suddenly seemed empty. Earth existed but nothing else, no stars, Sun, or Moon.

After several minutes of staring into the black universe, a light burst into existence, a single star in the center of the sky. As he focused on the light, he could see all the colors of the rainbow swirling together. He had never seen anything so beautiful.

"Gerald," Taylor said, shaking his arm. "Earth to Gerald."

Gerald turned from watching the raindrops on the window and looked into Taylor's green eyes. In that moment, her eyes connected the dream world to the physical universe and he saw the same amusement she had shown in the dream. Although he felt stupid for the long pause, the peaceful memory at the top of the tower left him hopeful and excited. Following Taylor in the dream had kept him safe, and he had ultimately escaped the dangerous man by going up.

"I have an idea," he said slowly. "How much can the NMG lift?"

NINE

Gerald

"The NMG can lift nearly any weight you want. If I gave it more power, this little box could lift you." Taylor tapped her fingers on the top of her knee as though counting. "For this design, not this prototype of course, I don't think it would do such a good job for more than a few tons, but I could make a configuration to lift much more. It would blow your mind to see the energy balance equation! Although I didn't find an exact solution, I more or less minimized–"

"So could you fly a 747 with this thing?" Gerald asked, needing to put her words in terms he could understand. A few tons seemed like a lot, but that amount made no connection to anything in reality. He held his breath and prepared to interrupt her again if she continued to explain on a technical level.

She looked annoyed at the interruption, but her lips quickly curved into a smile.

"Absolutely, I mean not this little prototype, but we could design one to do that job. You do understand that flight will depend less on aerodynamics than usual? We would have to consider it though."

Her tone intimated doubt in his mental capacity, but her lack of faith did not affect him. His memory of the dream dominated his thoughts, and his ascent of the tower seemed like a message from his subconscious. Gerald had no idea where the inspiration led or ultimately originated, but it offered a way forward. And they needed direction.

"Okay, here's what I'm thinking," he said, attempting to curb his enthusiasm. "We'll need to build a contingency plan."

Gerald paused for breath and searched her eyes for her reaction. She looked doubtful and a little confused, exactly what he had hoped. He wanted to build some tension before explaining the remainder of his plan, the part inspired by his dream. He hoped the tactic would prevent premature rejection.

"Build a contingency plan?" she asked. "What the hell are you talking about?"

"We make an escape plan, a vehicle capable of flight, capable of escaping the atmosphere. Weren't you telling me that they have very limited ability at high altitude, because of aerodynamics right?"

"Yes, kind of," she said, but not with the tone of excitement he wanted to hear. "If we managed to get high enough, they wouldn't be able to catch us, but preparing an escape plan is not a plan. You need a *plan* to have an *escape plan*."

"Give me some credit, Taylor," he said, hiding his frustration behind a smile. "You were right. They won't want the public to learn about it. So that's what we do, build something to show the public. And if they come after us, we can just fly away in our spaceship."

Taylor looked up at him, her wide eyes reflecting the light from outside. The intensity of her life force felt almost palpable. Gerald gulped.

"Hmm," she said, her eyes narrowing in contemplation. She took a drink of her soda and stared at the backpack resting in her lap. "I thought of space travel but not as a means of escape. We wouldn't have the resources to live in space."

"I don't mean we live in space, but if we can escape up there, and let people know. There's no way they can hide that. Every astronomer could see it for themselves."

"We can make a banner and drag it behind us," Taylor said, laughing and dramatically waving her hand in the air. "Suck it! Assholes!"

"Besides," he said, pausing to chuckle politely at her comic outburst. "It'll give us time to think of how to do it best, or come up with an alternative."

"It's definitely fun to think about," she said with a serious tone again. "But I cannot make a spacecraft all by myself, and I doubt you have the money to pay for the materials. An escape plan would be nice though."

"We'll need to bring someone else on board then."

"I don't know, Gerald," she said, pausing to consider the suggestion. "I can't trust anyone else with this."

From the tone of her voice, Gerald knew the plan had taken root in her mind. He also liked being the only one she trusted.

"Okay," he said, speaking in more of a business tone. "The right person needs to, A, gain your trust, B, have the necessary skills, and C, possibly help with the financing. Are those your requirements?"

"Have fun with that," she said with a sneer.

"I already have a couple candidates in mind," he said, breathing a sigh of relief and ignoring her lack of faith. "Start thinking about what you need, and let me acquire the resources."

"You can't expect the universe just to provide the way," she said. "I know you always seem to think there's some positive force out there to help us, but I wouldn't count on it. We might have to devise another plan."

"We'll make this work," he said and then extended his hand to her. "Let me have the bag. I want to try it again. I'm not afraid anymore."

Taylor hesitated almost imperceptibly before returning her precious backpack to his possession. After he placed the bag in his lap, he opened the main compartment all the way so that he could see the mysterious box. He expected to see a shiny metal surface, but instead, he saw a dull black surface.

"A black box," he said with a quick smile. "Seems fitting."

"Hmm," she said with pleasant surprise. "Didn't think you'd appreciate that."

He touched the cold metal surface, activated the device, and suddenly felt like a child opening a present on Christmas. His broad smile expanded even further when the box came to life and pushed up against his hand. Before deactivating the object, he let the black box lift completely off of his lap for a few seconds.

"Wow!"

Taylor smiled with pride but then frowned.

"I hate to burst your bubble, Gerald," she said with disappointment. "But after thinking about it, I think *your* plan's got too many holes."

He wished Taylor had the capacity to sugarcoat potentially disappointing news. He thought they had both agreed with the plan. Sure, a spaceship seemed like an impossible and impractical task, but after seeing her invention, the impossible seemed possible. Only a spacecraft could escape the grasp of the government.

"What's the matter?"

"Don't get me wrong, I like where you're going with this whole escape option, but I think you might be fantasizing again. You do have the tendency to avoid considering major obstacles."

Despite his disappointment, his lawyer instincts never left him speechless. He would tackle her concerns one at a time.

"What specific obstacles are you talking about?"

"Oh, I think the most glaring one is money," she said. "It'll cost more than you've probably considered. Then there's the problem of the facilities we'll need."

"You're thinking about it too closely," he said, feeling frustrated again. "You've got to look at the big–"

"Oh don't get all worked up, Gerald," she said, holding her hand in the air. "I still think your idea is worth pursuing. We have to start somewhere. The plan to show the world might not work, but I can't argue with *build a spaceship*. We do need to find help though. Success will require more than just one engineer."

Gerald sighed in relief then returned his attention to possible candidates. One name quickly rose to the top of his list, causing him to feel his smile stretch to his ears.

"I might know the perfect person," he said. "I helped him with his business start-up a few years ago, just after he moved here from Mexico. You'd like him."

TEN

Freddy

Freddy stood at the window and listened to Mr. Smith walking up the stairs. When the sound of the old man's movement faded to nothing, Freddy continued counting how many steps the old man would need to reach his room. After feeling satisfied that Mr. Smith had reached his room safely, Freddy closed his eyes and cursed himself for doing what his sister had wanted. At least her visit had resulted in the amazing gift stored safely in his pocket, the crystal with the spider.

He did not care much for his sister anymore, then wondered if he would ever have any positive feelings for his mother. They had contributed only misery to his life. Now that he lived completely away from their control, he had only to act politely when they interacted with him. All encounters with them reminded Freddy of his childhood. Those memories felt like flies at a picnic. They never went away, and he could only try his best to swat them away from his life.

When Freddy was four years old, his father had abandoned them, and Freddy had never heard from him again. For all he knew, his father had died. He'd even forgotten the man's name and face because his mother had disposed of any picture of his father or document mentioning him.

With all of her emotional issues, his mother could only manage one child, the daughter who had no special needs or abnormal mental issues. Freddy had required more effort than she could emotionally provide. He never blamed her for what happened but concluded that people like her should not have children, especially after seeing the kind of adult Wanda had become.

His mother blamed Freddy for her husband's abandonment, and she never let either child forget it. Due to her constant reminders, his sister Wanda had also learned to resent him. As a young child, Freddy had believed them and that belief had obliterated any hope for positive self-esteem or confidence.

His mother taught him only one lesson about life, the reason for his predicament. Having no man in the house had caused all of their problems and all because of Freddy. As an adult, Freddy still accepted the same conclusion but with one consolation. The poor mental state of his parents had been the major contributor to their irresponsible decisions.

Without his family's influence, young Freddy had developed another belief about life, an idea that often occupied his imagination. Malevolent gods, he believed, designed specific situations for each person and at least one of those gods enjoyed watching Freddy suffer. Although that theory provided a reason for his situation and strangely helped him cope, the idea seemed more likely with every passing year. One day, he hoped to meet this malevolent god and return the favor.

State officials had ultimately convinced his mother to let them take Freddy from her. Other families were much more capable of fulfilling her son's special needs, and for an extra thousand dollars a month from the state of Oregon, they would eagerly accommodate those needs.

His first foster family, the Coopers, had two children, one boy two years younger than Freddy and one boy a few years older. When he joined the family, the other boys quickly learned to divert their father's anger at him. Not only could Freddy absorb the punishment they would have received, but they also enjoyed watching their father's abuse of others.

They also learned to use their influence to control Freddy. If he displeased them, they would invent some story to get their father angry or they would misbehave somehow and then blame the stupid foster kid. Freddy quickly learned to do what they said and stay out of their way as much as possible.

During his second day there, the oldest boy got peanut butter on his father's video game controller and then blamed Freddy. Before Freddy could even deny the accusation, Mr. Cooper took him to the kitchen table, in front of the boys, and hit his knuckles so hard with a ruler that they bled. Paralyzed with terror and tears streaming down his cheeks, Freddy just stared at the man.

Mrs. Cooper frightened Freddy even more than her husband frightened him. Her light brown eyes reminded him of a reptile and seemed devoid of empathy, and maybe even life. Her cold gaze made him shiver.

As she explained his chores, he attempted to concentrate on what she was saying by closing his eyes and humming softly, something he often did with people. Since Mrs. Cooper thought he was not listening to her, she called her husband to deal with him and the man used the only method he understood, inflicting pain. He squeezed Freddy's upper arm so hard that he stopped humming and opened his eyes. Mrs. Cooper rarely punished her children, but she usually watched her husband do it, her eyes devoid of emotion.

Whenever Freddy felt stress or if situations caused him any form of anxiety, he would attempt to remove himself from the world, but with the Coopers, he quickly learned to delay his instincts until he could be alone. He often went to bed early and spent many hours in the fetal position, humming silently. Retreating into his mind was his only refuge.

During most of his younger years in foster care, Freddy made no friends and learned to avoid other children his age. He would occasionally visit his mother and sister, and for the first time in his life, they treated him better than anyone else. But despite their improved treatment, they ignored his complaints of abuse in his foster homes.

Those visits with his family taught Freddy the futility of crying when it was time to leave. He learned to accept his fate without outward emotion.

Overall, Freddy spent his childhood with five foster families. He preferred to forget about the first four, but in his fifth and final foster home, he experienced a small reprieve from emotional distress. His final foster parents were an older couple who had grown children with families of their own, and they wanted the least interaction with Freddy as possible. Raising their own family had exhausted all of their patience for any child other than their grandchildren.

They used the foster care compensation money to help pay for their retirement and left Freddy to care for himself. But despite the neglect, he liked living there the best. He preferred solitude.

—✳—

The blissful neglect of his final foster parents helped Freddy cope with the next phase of his life—friends and heartbreak. Shortly after moving in with them in Portland, Oregon, he met two older kids from the neighborhood who quickly became his first real friends, Sadi Jacobsen and her younger brother Brian.

Freddy and Brian attended high school together. They met at the beginning of the school year at a park when Freddy was playing by himself on a swing set. Brian was two years older and a senior and asked Freddy to settle a dispute between him and his friends, an argument about some song they were trying to create. Brian played two different chords on his guitar and asked Freddy to decide which one sounded better. He felt too intimidated to make a sincere judgment and just pretended to like one more than the other, the same one Brian seemed to prefer.

Brian played the guitar and sang in a band with some friends and spent a lot of time at home, practicing in their garage. He liked to have Freddy just hang out with them and give feedback about their music. Even Brian's friends liked to have Freddy around and treated him as a younger brother.

When Brian brought Freddy to his home and introduced his sister, Sadi, Freddy just stared into her beautiful blue eyes, speechless.

"Good to meet you, Freddy," she said and then shook his hand, breaking the spell enough for him to reply.

"It is good to meet you too."

Sadi smiled at him and then glanced at her brother, amusement on both of their faces. Although Freddy knew they were silently laughing at his awkward way of speaking, he did not feel like the brunt of a joke. It was a new experience for him.

He fell instantly in love with Sadi and came to view her as the model female. Although he failed to hide his affection, she never showed irritation or awkwardness about it.

The next day at school, her brother gave Freddy his first lesson on social interaction, how long to look at people during conversation. Instead of the usual feeling of embarrassment and shame for his lack of social skills, Brian made Freddy feel confident in himself. He required a few weeks of practice before he could just glance at Sadi during a conversation without staring. With other people in his life, he had preferred to look away. But eye contact with Sadi always seemed to put him in a trance.

Although she never reciprocated his adoration, Sadi always treated him kindly and even seemed to enjoy his company, the first pretty girl to ever give him any positive attention. Freddy never considered the possibility of having a romantic relationship with her and did not need her to love him. He just appreciated her femininity and tried his best not to stare. More than anything, he feared to ruin his good fortune by making her feel uncomfortable.

Her brother Brian wanted only one thing in life, to have fun. He did not care about popularity, although he was popular, or his education. He acted when something interested him, and for some mysterious reason, he found interest in Freddy. Brian was tall, had a strong physical presence, a captivating smile, but an almost tangible confidence drew people to him.

Sadi was definitely the more intelligent of the two, although she lacked the same confidence and seemed drawn to her brother as everyone else. The two siblings also acted differently than the other people in his life and forced Freddy to reassess his conclusions about humanity. Not everyone in the world was cruel, shallow, or self-centered.

"Hey, Freddy," one of Brian's friends said one day. "You're a smart kid. Can you get this piece of shit working again?"

Freddy looked at their damaged mix-board and felt like a surgeon given the task of restoring a mangled accident victim. He took the mix-board home and by the next morning, he had restored it to full functionality. Electronics became his new fascination and he began teaching himself how electronic equipment worked.

That small accomplishment became the second major confidence boost in his life. The first boost was becoming friends with one of the most popular kids in school, Brian. In Freddy's experience, the popular kids had always been the most cruel and often found pleasure in preying on the socially weaker kids.

When Freddy first met them, Sadi had already graduated from high school but still lived at home and worked at a part-time job. She was often present when Freddy visited, usually reading a non-fiction book about science, history, or biography. Freddy always wanted to talk to her and quickly discovered an easy method of approach, asking about her latest book. At first, he just wanted to hear her talk, but he eventually discovered his own love of learning and often borrowed her books after she had finished reading them.

When the other kids in his high school had learned how Freddy spent a lot of time with Brian Jacobsen and his sister, they left him alone, and he could focus more intently on his school work. For the first time in his life, he felt no social fear while walking through the hallways and sitting in his classes, unafraid of what people would do to him.

Then he discovered something else about himself. Not only did he enjoy learning, but he also absorbed information like water into a dry sponge. He would soon begin earning the top grades in all of his classes, and other kids began asking him for help, although he still felt social anxiety talking to them.

Brian and his band friends, and Sadi had all liked to get high, their only activity that made Freddy uncomfortable. They preferred marijuana but experimented occasionally with hallucinogenics like LSD and DMT, or addictive drugs like cocaine and heroin. Brian and his friends claimed that the drugs helped them create better music, and Sadi said she just liked the experience.

Sadi intervened the first time Brian attempted to give Freddy a joint, telling her brother to leave him alone and not pressure him. Freddy had felt afraid to reject the offer and cause offense. Brian always listened to his sister and never again offered drugs to Freddy.

Later in private, Freddy had asked Sadi about her intervention. "Why did you not want me to inhale from the joint?"

"I'm a nobody," she answered with a frown. "So, it's okay for me. You're special, and we shouldn't mess with that."

During his time with the retired couple, his visits home became more frequent, usually on the weekends, but the situation had reversed. His home no longer seemed like an improvement to his situation.

The next horror in his life began when Freddy made the grave mistake of telling his sister about his new friends. He had hoped to impress her, but Wanda quickly found a way to use the information to her advantage and turn Freddy into her slave. If he ever refused to follow her demands, Wanda would threaten to tell Sadi all of his embarrassing secrets, like how he felt about her.

Other than doing her chores, his sister would force Freddy to go shopping with her. The first time the mall security caught him shoplifting became the most embarrassing experience of his life. Because he had no prior record, he escaped punishment by the mall authorities, but not from his mother who yelled at him and confined him to his room for the rest of the weekend. The next time he got caught, they sent him to juvenile detention, and he had no one popular to cushion him from all of the emotionally disturbed inmates there.

Freddy learned an unexpected lesson from his fellow inmates at juvenile detention. He learned the amount of control he had over his own life. Whenever possible, the other kids ignored the rules and did whatever they could get away with. Rules and expectations suddenly became just one set of many possible options and Freddy realized how he had the choice to follow them, something he had never previously considered.

After returning from that horrible experience, Freddy decided never to visit his home again. When his mother or social worker said he had to visit home, he would either refuse or be somewhere else when they came for him. He also swore never to fear Wanda's threats again or trust her with any information about himself. He felt especially stupid after realizing that Wanda had no way of finding Sadi or Brian to tell them anything.

"Where have you been?" Brian asked Freddy at their next encounter, a few weeks later.

Freddy did not want to tell him, and Brian immediately accepted his decision to remain silent. But Sadi was more persistent and eventually got Freddy to admit where he had been and the reason for his detention, although he refused to tell her how Wanda had blackmailed him. That level of embarrassment would have been too intense to bear.

"Give him a break, Sadi," Brian had said, trying to intervene. "If he doesn't want to tell us, he doesn't have to."

"What a bitch!" Sadi said after he'd told her, sincere anger in her eyes. "Want me to mess her up, Freddy? Where do they live?"

Her offer shocked him, and Freddy quickly refused. He imagined a disturbing but pleasant vision of Sadi yelling at his sister and making her feel like a horrible person. Strangely, his imagination of the encounter satiated any desire for revenge, but he would often fantasize about what Sadi might have done. Her anger also surprised him, and he felt afraid for anyone on the receiving end of that anger. Sadi never asked him about it again, and the final trauma inflicted by his family soon became just another fly at his picnic.

After Brian had graduated, he and his band friends moved into an apartment in Portland and Sadi went off to college. Freddy visited Brian two times at his apartment and promised to attend one of his concerts, but he never saw Sadi again. He spent the next two years in high school without the social buffer of a popular friend, but no one bothered him intentionally again.

He often thought of Sadi and her brother and wondered what they were doing. Whenever painful memories haunted him, he would think of them. One memory in particular usually reappeared before all of the others. Sadi had called him one day on the phone, pretending to be his mother, and then had laughed after learning that she had successfully tricked him. She eventually got Freddy to confess his problem with voice recognition and then offered the idea of using a secret code word. She suggested he use the word, *spider*.

"You're quiet and calculating," she had explained. "Like a spider."

ELEVEN

Freddy

When Freddy was a young child, the doctors diagnosed him with autism, and the social worker assigned as his case manager planned on sending him to a home for autistic children after he graduated high school. He dreaded the thought of living with children unable to care for themselves. No one who knew him thought he belonged in a place like that, but he suspected that money from the state helped motivate the people running those special homes to include the most children as possible. As his graduation from high school approached, he worried about getting a place of his own and a job.

Freddy felt sorry for other children with abnormal social and psychological behaviors like his own, but he thought the doctors had incorrectly diagnosed him with autism. Like autistic children, he had required more time to read and speak and had trouble connecting with other people. He specifically remembered having difficulty associating words with the objects and ideas they represented. Unlike children with autism, Freddy could make eye contact with people if required, and he sensed humor sometimes but was too self-conscious to react.

His peculiar symptom of failing to associate voices with identities had made his true diagnosis even more complicated. Ultimately, he had decided not to categorize himself with any official psychological condition. No single word would define him.

Although thoughts about getting a job or going to college filled him with anxiety, he was confident in his ability to achieve success if he tried. He wanted to call Sadi for advice but feared the possible consequences. She might not want him to contact her. If she preferred to keep their relationship in the past, he preferred not to know. He could not bear the thought. He did not trust her brother's opinion about school enough to call him. Brian loved music and his band more than an education.

The hope of a life without abusive or neglectful foster parents, and the fear of being sent to a special home, had given Freddy the necessary motivation to ask someone for help, so he asked his new case manager, a friendly Hungarian woman named Malika. Earlier in his life, he had attempted to seek assistance through his appointed state servants, but they had never improved his situation. Although he knew Malika was overwhelmed by the high number of cases she managed, he had hope for obtaining her assistance.

Freddy contacted Malika several times before he became her priority. Then one day shortly afterward, Malika's sister needed an urgent favor. Her sister worked as a housemaid for an old man named Bill Smith, and she needed someone to help clean the estate before her boss returned from a trip. In the owner's absence, her sister's friends had held a party there and trashed the place. She had turned to her sister for help, and Malika had turned to Freddy. It was the first time in his life he would earn more than a few dollars.

He accepted the offer with excitement and then actually enjoyed the work. Freddy liked the task of restoring the beautiful home to its former condition and was amazed that people lived in such luxury. But to the horror of both Freddy and Malika's sister, Bill Smith returned home before they had finished. He fired Malika's sister and offered her job to Freddy on a temporary basis. Then after only a single day on the job, the old man asked Freddy if he wanted to live there and take care of things for him on a permanent basis. Freddy moved there the next day and never talked or spoke with his foster care parents again.

—✳—

At the beginning of their professional relationship, Bill Smith insisted on being addressed as Bill. But after the first six months of living together, he stopped trying to convince Freddy to call him by his first name. Freddy only felt comfortable addressing his employer as Mr. Smith.

Although Bill Smith always treated Freddy with respect and never intentionally made him anxious, Freddy required a long time to feel comfortable with their working relationship. He often wondered if Mr. Smith genuinely liked him or if he was just acting politely. His doubts eventually dissipated.

Fear of getting fired caused Freddy to delay telling his new boss about his problems. Of course, Mr. Smith could see some of Freddy's peculiarities, just not his inability to recognize voices. The first few times Mr. Smith had called him from somewhere out of sight, Freddy did not immediately answer but instead would come into view before responding. Mr. Smith refrained from saying anything about the incidents until one day when he called the home and Freddy did not answer.

When Mr. Smith finally confronted him about the strange behavior, Freddy confessed all of his problems and expected to get fired. Instead of the expected angry reaction, Mr. Smith called Freddy's case manager for more information. When she failed to answer his questions, Mr. Smith paid for a psychiatrist to come and evaluate Freddy. The psychiatrist subsequently determined that Freddy had some extremely rare psychological traits.

"He seems to have a condition similar to Asperger's syndrome," the doctor said in Freddy's presence, "but I hesitate to put him in the same category. Every case is unique. His most interesting symptoms are related to what is known as phonagnosia, exhibited as an inability to recognize voices that should be familiar. Freddy requires vision to confirm the identity of people, even the ones he already knows. This case is very peculiar."

The psychiatrist also explained how Freddy failed to fit the classic model. In every case the doctor could recall, phonagnosia could be traced to physical trauma to the head, but Freddy had shown no signs of such trauma and had no history of it. The psychiatrist wanted to enroll Freddy in a psychiatric research program. Freddy had found no reason to object, but Mr. Smith had.

"He is who he is, and he's not going to be a lab rat."

TWELVE

Freddy

Later that night, after his sister had left and Mr. Smith had gone to his room, Freddy entered his bedroom in the basement and removed the crystal from his pocket. He looked at the beautiful crystal for a moment then placed the object on the top of his dresser. He had to push the science fiction novels and a textbook out of the way to make room.

Freddy dressed in shorts and a t-shirt, his standard sleeping attire, then walked to the mirror at the head of his bed to inspect himself. Motionless brown eyes stared back at him while he straightened his shirt and shorts. He spent a few seconds on his bushy white hair, trying to make it look more presentable. He slid his left hand through the thick hair then stopped after realizing the futility of the effort. He'd never had the patience for comprehensive grooming. Other activities always seemed more important.

After completing the nightly ritual of inspecting himself, he glanced at the other spider hanging near his door. The realistic black spider hung from the ceiling by a linked silver chain. Freddy would often transform the object into a pendulum and enjoyed watching it swing back and forth. If an intruder ever entered his room, Freddy hoped they would first see the hanging arachnid and then have a heart attack as a penalty for the intrusion, or at least a healthy shock. When Freddy had first warned Mr. Smith of what to expect and showed him, the old man laughed.

"You might have just saved my life," Mr. Smith had said, clapping Freddy on his back. "The shock would have killed me."

After looking at the motionless spider for a few seconds, Freddy decided to remove it. Compared to the new treasure on his dresser, the hanging one seemed pathetic. He slowly untied the inanimate object and put it in his top drawer with all of his other trinkets. While shutting the drawer, he felt as though another chapter of his life had just ended.

Freddy carefully placed the new crystal spider in the palm of his hand, the cool surface flat against his skin. Before inspecting the object more carefully, he glanced at the digital clock on the wall and noticed the time, ten twenty-seven.

He enjoyed watching the light refract off the crystal surface, spilling rainbows onto his shirt and wrist. While sitting on his bed, he noticed the smooth covers ripple under his weight. The sight reminded him of the light waves refracting off the crystal.

While inspecting the numerous red eyes on the spider's head, he realized something strange. The eyes only appeared red but were actually composed of other colors. When Freddy tried looking closer, he experienced an intense sensation similar to vertigo, nearly making him lose consciousness. He tried to focus for only a few seconds before the intensity forced him to look away. After the vertigo subsided, he felt different. Something in his environment had changed.

Freddy looked around the room, searching for evidence to validate his suspicion, and thought the digital clock looked strange. He stared at the time for several seconds before realizing the problem. The clock now showed ten forty-five. Freddy had been staring at the spider for eighteen minutes, but the time could not have been longer than a minute. He failed to remember any thoughts during that time. If anything had happened, his memory of the events had vanished.

"Must be tired," he said to himself.

For the next five minutes, he tried to convince himself of being mistaken but ultimately concluded that something strange had happened while staring into the eyes of the spider. He stepped to the light switch and turned off the lights then crawled on top of his covers, holding the spider in his hand.

"You are a strange little thing," he said to his new lifeless pet.

He carefully set the crystal on his chest and closed his eyes. He usually fell asleep on his back on top of the covers, and then always woke on his side, but never under the sheets. He liked them as smooth as possible. He could not fall asleep under wrinkled covers.

While slowly losing consciousness, he tried to understand the reason for his sister being so considerate. She had never shown such generosity, at least to him. He would have paid a lot of money for the crystal, and she should have known that. He fell asleep attempting to solve the mystery.

THIRTEEN

Freddy

Freddy awoke, as usual, an hour before the sunrise. Light from the street lamps filtered through his windows, allowing him to see the outline of his bed and the other objects in his room. He felt a panic immediately after waking, afraid of discovering that the events of the night were just a dream. But he quickly found the crystal on the bed beside him. He slid his fingers over the grooved surface and felt immediate relief. It was smooth and cool on his skin, and the excitement from its touch wiped the residue of sleep from his eyes.

Freddy had an easy job. His primary responsibility of keeping the estate clean required the least amount of his time. His employer always cleaned up after himself and hardly ever disturbed anything. Freddy had free reign over the entire residence, even Mr. Smith's room. His other responsibilities included cooking, shopping, reading mail, and whatever else Mr. Smith asked of him.

At the start of every day, he made breakfast for them both and then they ate together. Mr. Smith liked to have something different every day and had a list of things he liked. Freddy just had to prepare whatever he wanted from the list, randomizing the decisions as much as possible.

Mr. Smith came from a long line of wealthy and influential people. Freddy accepted that fact without resentment and never investigated where they had first acquired their money. He only cared about one thing, his financial security. As long as he worked for Mr. Smith, money would never be in short supply again. After just a few months of employment, Mr. Smith had given Freddy his own bank account and made an arrangement with the bank for the account to remain at a balance of one hundred thousand dollars. Freddy never became fully accustomed to the idea, and he never felt the temptation to take advantage of all the wealth at his disposal. With money in such endless supply, the fear of destitution slowly faded to nothing.

"I trust you, Freddy," Mr. Smith had said. "This will make it easy for you to take care of things, and you can use it for your own expenses as long as you live with me. I know you won't abuse it."

He never abused the trust given to him. He felt too afraid that he might. The possibility always waited in the back of his mind, a fear that Mr. Smith would find something abnormal in the account and fire him. And whenever he considered something he wanted or needed, he nearly always consulted Mr. Smith. Freddy remembered the first time he had felt a desire to buy something for himself.

"Freddy, why don't you go get that telescope you were telling me about the other day," his boss had suggested. "It is a fine idea to study the sky. Astronomy is a worthy pursuit."

Freddy had agreed and dared not argue with the logic.

His boss even seemed to enjoy indulging Freddy's interests. After more than three years in his employ, Freddy had accumulated three different telescopes, several computers, various other tools, and a well-equipped laboratory with microscopes and many other scientific instruments. If he'd wanted, he could have even bought himself a car, but he already had access to any of the three vehicles at the estate.

So far, college remained Freddy's largest expense. He felt guilty about the drain on his account, but Mr. Smith always insisted they were just part of his wages. To stay in Mr. Smith's employ, Freddy needed to attend a nearby college, so he chose Portland State University.

"An education is more about the effort you put into it," Mr. Smith had explained one day, "and less about where you go. If you work hard, you can get a fine education at just about any university."

Motivated partly by his interest in spiders and what he had already learned in school, Freddy chose to major in biology. He had a great interest in biological organisms like animals, insects, and plants, but he found more interest in the cellular and molecular levels of life. In his free time, he explored the world through his microscopes and telescopes. Those extreme aspects of the world made more sense to him than the one his usual senses detected.

In both of those activities, he hoped to find something that might help him understand the purpose of his existence. Maybe the secrets of life lay hidden somewhere inside living cells, the basic structure of life, or in deep space, detectable only by enhancing normal human senses. Exploration became an obsession.

As a side effect, he found friends on the internet. They existed only in cyberspace and lived all over the world. He felt no strong connection to any of them and considered most of them as too immature. Most people, he discovered, were usually too centered on sex and entertainment. While often disagreeing with their view on social topics and their personal lives, he enjoyed talking to them about science and technology.

He secretly played games online with some of his friends, games like chess, go, and a few role-playing games, but he kept those activities from his employer, fearing the information might lower Mr. Smith's opinion of him. He might think the time was wasted. Now that Freddy had the crystal, he had two secrets to keep from his employer.

Freddy spent a few more minutes in bed, rubbing his fingers over the grooved crystal surface, and then he began getting ready for the day.

He placed the crystal in his clothes drawer under his socks. Although he had no real concern that Mr. Smith would find the crystal, he disliked the thought of leaving the object exposed. Sometimes, Mr. Smith had visitors, and maybe one of them would take a tour of the lower level, his domain. Freddy did not trust some of Mr. Smith's guests.

After having breakfast together, Mr. Smith gave Freddy an update about all of the tasks he needed accomplished that day and then Freddy left for his classes. To Freddy's relief, Mr. Smith neglected to mention anything about Wanda's visit the previous evening.

For the two hours between his morning class and afternoon laboratory class, Freddy studied in the college library. He had two tasks to perform in the library that day, his homework for biochemistry, and then he needed to find some astronomy books for Mr. Smith. Freddy's interest in the subject had inspired Mr. Smith to study astronomy himself. He had recently found particular interest in the motion of the planets and how ancient astronomers had theorized about the structure of the solar system.

Before Freddy had purchased his telescopes and specialized cameras, he used to show his boss images from the Hubble Telescope. The images had impressed the old man, but after seeing Orion's belt through a telescope himself, Mr. Smith had become as hooked as Freddy.

FOURTEEN

Gerald

"Don't worry, Taylor," Gerald said reassuringly. "The man I want to include is not an illegal alien."

He hoped to relieve Taylor's anxiety about his friend from Mexico. His words might have sounded a little racist, so he wanted to correct the impression before she made a sarcastic comment.

"Actually," he said and then paused as the rain began pelting the window again, scattering the lights from the restaurant signs across Taylor's face. "He's more of a political refugee. He used to be the governor of a large Mexican city. You should hear his story. It should be a feature film."

"A political refugee?"

"I'll let him tell the story, but it has something to do with a drug cartel and their candidate who ran against him."

She looked more concerned.

"Is he in any danger? I mean, are people still after him?"

"I don't know, but he doesn't seem to be worried about it. I think you'll like him, personally and professionally."

"What do you mean?" she asked.

"Well, he runs his own machine shop. You like making things. He likes making things. He has a lot of customers from the local Latino population as well as several large manufacturers. He's doing really well, at least the last time I checked on him."

She leaned forward, interested. "So what makes you trust him?"

"He shares our views, and he's very passionate about it. His son and wife were killed by the drug cartels. It's very sad. He hates the war on drugs, or I should say, *the war* to keep drugs extremely profitable. He has direct experience with the real drug war, not the story they tell on the news."

"Oh, my God!" she said, her eyes coming to life. "Poor guy. What's his name?"

"Cesar Sanchez," Gerald said, feeling relieved. "He's an older gentleman and lives in Seattle with a friend, only about thirty minutes away from me."

"Before we tell him anything," she began, and her eyes widened as a challenge. "I need to meet him first. You say we can trust him, but I just need to see for myself. It's my baby, and I call the shots."

He had no intention of arguing with her. On the contrary, he felt honored to be part of her discovery. Even more, her lack of further argument gave him hope for including Cesar in their plans.

"I promise," he said, "that I won't reveal anything to anyone without your prior approval."

Since she wanted to meet with Cesar personally, Gerald said he would arrange the meeting as soon as possible. He had to stay in Portland that night and would call in the morning.

They talked for another hour, mostly about what they would need for a temporary visit into space. At Gerald's request, they took money constraints out of the picture. Taylor never had much money in her life, so she worried more about finances than Gerald. To him, acquiring the money became just another task on his list, another small hill to climb.

As he had explained, they merely needed to recruit the right people, and then they would have plenty of access to money. Keeping her invention a secret while they prepared was the real problem. Even if they only recruited people they could completely trust, they would still carry a major risk. The probability of exposure increased exponentially with more people aware of the secret. A random remark to the wrong person would eventually travel to a dangerous pair of ears.

Without any conscious effort, Gerald started planning. They would need a secure way to communicate with more people in the group. He and Taylor had already considered communication by telephone and regular email as too insecure. Their project needed a secure website and Gerald had a friend who could build one for them, someone who did not need to know the whole story. Gerald planned to ask for Taylor's permission after they met with his friend from Mexico.

When their conversation ended for the evening, she agreed to meet his Mexican friend as soon as possible. Gerald would contact her again in the morning.

After she drove home, Gerald checked into a hotel. For almost two hours that night, he lay on the bed in a futile attempt to sleep. How could he sleep after being part of possibly the most important development of the millennium? Even with his limited and incomplete understanding of the implications, he knew his life would never be the same again. He liked the feeling and would have to keep his partner, Albert, ignorant of the situation.

The more he thought about her invention, the more his excitement grew. He attempted to think realistically, but he kept thinking about space travel as a permanent escape and not as a temporary means. While lying in bed, listening to classical music, his mind grasped the idea like a life preserver and then ignored his rational mind's command to release.

When sleep finally overcame him, he dreamed of leaving Earth and traveling into the cosmos. No more being forced to pay for war, or massacre, or some dictator in the third world. No more force-fed democracy. No more IRS. In space, he would be completely free.

FIFTEEN

Gerald

When Gerald awoke the next morning at six, he called his friend Cesar Sanchez. In his excitement, he had decided not to wait for a more decent time to call, especially on the weekend. Once Cesar had seen what they wanted to show him, Gerald felt confident he would forgive any intrusion on his sleep. To his relief, Cesar answered the phone immediately and spoke without any indication of a rude awakening.

"Good morning, Cesar," Gerald said then quickly continued. "This is Gerald Foster. Sorry to call you so early, but I have something important I want to talk to you about."

"I'm sure you do," the man said and laughed.

"I would like to visit you later this morning with a friend. She needs your help for a complicated project."

"What kind of project?"

"I'd rather discuss it with you in person."

"Then does this friend of yours have a name?"

"Ah yes," Gerald replied, not wanting to provide the information but knowing he had no other choice. "Her name is Taylor Evans. We're in Portland now, so it will be a few hours."

"Of course," the man said politely. "Let's meet at my shop. I look forward to your visit, Mr. Foster."

Gerald drove faster than usual to Taylor's house, irrationally afraid of hearing police sirens and feeling like a bright beacon in the early morning darkness. After arriving in her neighborhood, he followed her request and parked at the curb. She wanted to leave without waking her mother.

"So, our story is that I have a shop project for Cesar," Taylor said as they pulled onto Interstate Five, heading north toward Seattle. "And I want to go over the plans with him."

In case she felt uncomfortable revealing their secret to Cesar, Taylor brought some drawings for another project she had wanted to do one day. Gerald said he would pay for the decoy project if that happened, but he seemed assured Cesar would gain her confidence.

On their drive, they talked again about the idea of traveling into space, more than they talked about her invention. She still seemed excited about the possibility, but Gerald feared she was just humoring him. She had many concerns and knew more than he did about the requirements of traveling in an environment of total vacuum, conditions where the only thing standing between the passenger and death is a leak-tight design and expensive equipment. While listening to her, he also began to have doubts.

He both loved and disliked that aspect of her personality. While his head usually floated in the clouds, she kept her feet on the ground. She needed him though, someone who could proceed without letting major obstacles stop them. Gerald felt little concern for the specifics of a project or the costs. He liked to think of plans as a river, weaving its way around all obstacles or just forming a lake until it found an escape route.

"If we were forced to escape into space—" he began.

"And we survived," Taylor interjected with a smile.

"NASA and the military would probably have a nasty panic attack," he said sarcastically. "We would be viewed as a security risk. Bureaucrats and government officials don't want potentially dangerous people above them, people with a chip on their shoulder."

Requiring permission to leave the planet infuriated him as much as international travel requirements. The copious amount of permits, taxes, and other special permissions required by governments always caused him frustration.

"And how could the IRS collect their precious taxes?" Taylor asked with thicker sarcasm. "Send the IRS auditor in a rocket?"

"True," he said, glad for the interruption.

Even if they had to change their plan, Gerald had faith in their combined talents. *You'll find a way*, his mother had always said. Then he remembered one of her other sayings. *The future is dark, but only before it arrives.*

"Too bad we can't just go live on the moon, or Mars, or find another solar system to live in," Taylor said and sighed. "The cost of that would be beyond our reach, no matter how much of your fluffy optimism you throw at it. Even if we were able to carry enough fuel to visit another solar system, the probability of finding an inhabitable planet in our lifetime is practically zero."

During the next few pauses in their conversation, Gerald thought about the possibility of finding other inhabitable planets, something he had not considered. As they entered Seattle, Gerald turned to Taylor and saw her watching the Space Needle coming into view.

"So, if you believe there are more planets like Earth out there, does that imply you believe in aliens?" Until that moment, Gerald had never seriously considered aliens.

"In my opinion," she said without looking in his direction, "the existence of other inhabitable planets is a certainty. But reaching one? The nearest star is something like five light-years away. The probability of alien existence seems pretty certain to me too, considering how many galaxies exist and how we happen to live on a life-containing planet out of only a handful of other planets in just one solar system."

"Do you think aliens are in contact with anyone on the Earth?" he asked.

She laughed. "Who's the conspiracy theorist now?"

"I'm serious."

"Gerald, aliens aren't going to help us. We have to figure this out on our own."

"I know," he said.

Later, he would investigate if credible evidence existed for aliens. He had always thought of alien conspiracies as either unfounded theories or military disinformation, diversions from sensitive security issues the military wanted away from public discussion.

"Actually," Taylor said after a long pause, and her smile disappeared. "I wasn't going to bring this up, but while working on the NMG, I had another disturbing thought."

"What was it?"

"Although I'm pretty confident in my abilities, I don't feel smart enough to have thought of this on my own." Taylor paused for a quick breath. "I mean, I don't know where I got the inspiration, and I know what you're thinking."

"I doubt that," he said, suppressing a laugh. As of yet, Gerald had no other thoughts.

"You'll say that I'm just being humble," she said. "I know that I'm smart enough to put this together, but not to have the original idea. It's pretty damn complicated. I really feel like I can't take the credit."

"Well," Gerald said, pausing to convert his next thought into words. "Are you saying aliens put the idea in your head?"

"I don't know."

Instead of continuing, Taylor just looked out the window in silence.

Gerald decided to keep his next thoughts private since they would probably just start an argument. Taylor was being modest, for once. Her talented and disciplined mind seemed completely capable of producing the net momentum generation concept. Where did any idea originate, anyway? Questioning the origin of ideas would lead to a never-ending string of unanswerable questions, a rabbit hole. The possibility did not feel as sinister as Taylor had made it seem.

—✳—

As they approached the machine shop, located in one of the industrial districts near the waterfront, Gerald's anxiety transformed into an intense urge to escape the vehicle and use his legs. The GPS unit in his car used an annoying female voice, compounding his anxiety, so he was relieved when she said they had reached their destination.

He remembered the red brick shop, a two-story building across the street from an old diner. An ornate tin sign hung over the main double doors with the name of his business, *Stainless Forest*, stamped into the metal in big letters. They drove around to the back parking lot and parked two spaces away from the only other vehicle, an old Ford truck.

A small crystal bell rang after they walked through the entrance. They stopped at the front counter, the large stainless steel top littered with papers, blueprints, and a scattering of pens and rulers. A moment later, the door behind the counter opened and an older man walked into the room.

SIXTEEN

Gerald

"Hello, Cesar! It's good to see you," Gerald said cheerfully, then took a quick breath. "Como estas?"

Taylor smiled at Gerald's attempt to speak Spanish. Even Gerald knew he sounded horrible, almost as though he had intentionally tried to speak with an exaggerated accent of the Northwest.

Gray strands streaked through Cesar's coarse black hair, making his black eyes appear even darker. He stood slightly taller than Taylor but much shorter than Gerald. Although Cesar had always been kind and hospitable, his eyes reminded Gerald of a mafia king in a gangster movie. His eyes demanded respect from those around him.

"Bien, Bien," Cesar replied, the tone of his natural accent contrasting strongly with Gerald's forced one. Gerald extended his hand in greeting and the old man squeezed firmly. He turned to Taylor. "And you must be Miss Evans."

Gerald watched Taylor carefully as she interacted with Cesar. When Cesar shook Taylor's hand, her whole body quivered slightly from his firm grasp. Gerald felt pleased to see her genuine smile.

"Strong grip for a girl," he said appreciatively. He turned her hand over to see her palm. "Not too soft either."

"Thank you, sir," she said. "I always try to return what's given."

"So, you say you have some job for me," the man said as he turned and motioned for them to follow him. "Come in the back and we'll talk about it. You can show me your drawings."

They went into the back shop area. Unlike the counter in the front, the shop looked clean and uncluttered. Gerald paid little attention to the machines in the shop or their condition, although he had difficulty ignoring the pungent odor of burning metal. The smell reminded him of fireworks.

As they walked past all of the machines, Taylor responded as Gerald had expected—like a cat on a leash in a mouse factory. Her eyes were almost as wide as her smile. As she walked past each machine, she appeared to be fighting a strong urge to stop for an inspection.

After maneuvering their way through the shop, they entered an office in the back. The walls of the room were lined with shelves and covered with books and rolls of blueprints. Gerald thought the office looked cozy and relaxed, a refuge away from home.

A large portrait hung on the wall directly opposite his desk, easily viewable by whoever sat in the chair. The portrait showed Cesar with an elegant lady standing at one side and three children on the other side, twin boys about fourteen years old and an older teenage girl. All of the children had the same blunt nose as their father but without any other resemblance to him except for the dark hair. They all looked more like the woman standing next to him, each child with the same high cheekbones and wide eyes. Gerald could easily see the biological parentage of each child.

He took a moment to appreciate the woman's appearance. She looked more regal than beautiful, as an ancient Greek statue—tough like Cesar but with kind eyes. When Cesar sat down at the desk, Gerald turned away from the portrait and watched as the man opened a large laptop.

"Before we go over what you want of me, I just have a few questions for you," he said, and his smile disappeared.

Gerald felt a twinge of dread. Cesar turned the laptop around and displayed the results of a Google search with, *Taylor Evans Washington State mechanical*, typed in the search field. There were several results.

Taylor glanced at the screen and then turned back to Cesar. "There I am," she said in the mocking tone of someone proud of their popularity. "So, what did you discover?"

She asked her question with calm curiosity, but it reminded Gerald of when he had first met Cesar. He remembered feeling intimidated by the man. Something about Cesar kept those around him at full alert, but Taylor seemed impervious to intimidation.

"Well, the first thing I discovered was that your team won the best alternative fuel car contest in 2007 and you were the team leader." He stumbled over the word, *discovered*, his accent giving special emphasis to it. "The school article said that you showed amazing promise."

Her lips stretched into a casual smile.

"Yeah," she said. "That was fun."

Cesar still did not smile, and Gerald wondered if he was impressed or angry. If angry, then Cesar was a good actor. He had already acted genuinely pleased to meet her. Then Gerald remembered that the man had been a politician.

"After digging a little more, I found that when your father was alive, he used to have his own machine shop, and it's still in operation. Could you not just use that for this project of yours?"

"I could have, but I need something especially complicated," she began, and Gerald worried about her reaction to the mention of her father. "Gerald claimed that you were the perfect man for the job."

Cesar smiled again at the compliment.

"So, do you often consult with Gerald for technical matters?"

Gerald could see where Cesar intended to turn the conversation. He wanted to interject, but the look from Taylor stopped him. In a small way, Gerald was beginning to enjoy the show, and then he wondered how long Taylor would perform her act. At that moment, she looked sincerely amused.

"Gerald and I talk all the time," she said, still smiling, "and we happened to talk about this project of mine."

Cesar turned to Gerald.

"So, what is this project she wants me to do?"

Gerald gulped and his lips spread into an embarrassed smile. While he attempted to remember what Taylor had told him about the project, she laughed.

"Damn Google!" Taylor said, shaking her head slowly. She cast an accusing glance at Gerald. "This was Gerald's idea. Not mine."

"Cesar, let me explain," Gerald began, then paused when Taylor extended her hand in the air to stop him.

"Not yet," Taylor said, glancing at Gerald and then back at Cesar who swiveled the laptop to face him again so that only he could see the screen. He sat back in his chair and waited, eyebrows raised.

"Mr. Sanchez, I apologize for the deception. Usually, I would come out in the open at the very start, but our friend here has his own way of doing things. Maybe it's just how lawyers think. Anyhow, I wanted to get to know you, to determine if I wanted to share something with you. We do have a job for you, but I'm not sure you'd be willing to do it, or if we can trust you, although Gerald insists that we can."

As Cesar sat forward, his demeanor changed from accusatory to sincerely curious. He reminded Gerald of a hungry man preparing to devour a meal.

"Miss Evans," Cesar said. "Do you want to know what I thought when Gerald called me?"

"Sure."

"My good friend, Gerald Foster," he began with a tip of his head to Gerald. "The man who helped me set up my business and new home in this country, a man who has a true understanding of the world, wants to introduce me to a brilliant young engineer who wants me to help her make a machine, one that could most likely be made by herself. Just from the tone of your voice, Gerald, I knew you were hiding something. I've looked forward to this all morning. Frankly, I was disappointed you thought it would be that easy to fool me."

Gerald faced Taylor, more interested in her reply than in defending himself to Cesar. He wondered if most other females her age would have let the intimidation hinder them, but Taylor hesitated only a moment before responding. Her eyes widened as though glad for a challenge.

"So, what do we do now?" she asked. "Our true purpose cannot be shared with just anyone."

"Of course, Miss Evans. This is obviously very important to you, and I don't want to rush you, although you have my curiosity caught on a hook, so to speak." He looked back to his laptop, lost in thought for a moment. Then after closing the computer, he continued. "Let's do this. Come to my house. We'll relax, have lunch, and talk. You can meet my friends and we can go from there."

"Sounds like a great plan," Gerald said before Taylor could refuse.

Both men turned to Taylor. She smiled and agreed.

Gerald had hoped their introduction at the shop would end as well as it did. In reality, he had made only a minimal effort at fooling Cesar. He knew they would eventually reveal their true intentions, so he felt glad for Cesar's keen perception. He had secretly enjoyed watching Taylor get backed into a corner.

SEVENTEEN

Freddy

Freddy walked through the front entrance of his home to find Mr. Smith sitting in the drawing room in a chair by the piano. After Freddy shut the door, the old man looked up from his magazine, the latest issue of Foreign Affairs.

"How was school? Come, sit down."

Freddy sat on the firm surface of the couch opposite his boss, shifting his position until he felt completely comfortable. The action reminded Freddy of when he had replaced all of the soft cushions with something more firm. His boss no longer complained of struggling to stand.

"Class was good," Freddy said while gently placing his backpack on the floor but keeping his stack of books on his lap. "We finished up a laboratory project that we have been working on. My partner was absent, so I had to do everything myself. Very rude. Very rude."

"Are those my books?" Mr. Smith asked.

"Yes. I picked them up at the library this morning."

"Thank you, Freddy."

"You are welcome."

"I wanted to give you some warning about the next few days," Mr. Smith said, looking directly into his eyes and causing Freddy to look away. "We will have a visitor. My son is coming tonight."

"When will he be leaving?" Freddy asked, trying to hide his anxiety by staring at the floor.

"Oh, he'll probably be leaving tomorrow night. I'm just telling you so that you might want to stay out of sight." He shook his head in irritation. "I don't like having to suggest something like that, but just like last time, I don't think he'll be too friendly. I apologize again for his behavior."

During his last visit, Mr. Smith's son had yelled at both of them after discovering that his father paid for Freddy's schooling. He had spent a significant amount of time reminding his father of the vast difference in social status between them and their servants.

"You've allowed yourself to become vulnerable in your old age, Father," his son had said and then turned to Freddy. "This young man is just taking advantage of the situation, and he will continue to do so."

Freddy remembered the incident with shame. The memory had become a stinging reminder of the trauma from his past, and how all of his childhood wounds had never fully healed and could easily start bleeding again. Until that incident, he had thought they were gone forever.

In the absence of traumatic social experiences for so long, he had become entirely unprepared for the contentious encounter. He had stood as though in a trance and listened to the father and son argue over him and other issues. He had never seen Mr. Smith so angry, and he remembered feeling afraid that his time with the old man would soon come to an end. But after his son had departed, all had returned to normal.

Mr. Smith's relationship with his son had stood on unstable ground already, Freddy realized later, and Freddy had merely added fuel to the fire. He remembered Mr. Smith explaining how his son always looked for reasons to argue with him. He had encouraged Freddy not to take the negative sentiments toward him personally. Had

Freddy been absent from the scene, Mr. Smith's son would have argued about something else.

"It's my fault really," Mr. Smith had said, shaking his head in disappointment and sorrow. "He's grown up just like I allowed him to be raised. I cannot blame him for who he is."

Freddy had required almost three days to forget the pain of the encounter and feel normal again. Mr. Smith had claimed that most of the contention originated from a single motivation. His son wanted him to relinquish control of their business by selling his remaining shares. Freddy lacked the background in business to understand the specifics, and to be honest with himself, the details bored him. The situation reminded Freddy of something in a movie or television drama.

"You've lived your life, Father," his son had said. "Now step out of the way and let me live mine."

At six-thirty that night, Freddy's smartphone began vibrating, a notification from the front gate. After opening the link to the gate camera, he immediately recognized the black sedan and its unwelcome visitor. His heart rate increased and Freddy had to breathe deeply to sustain the increased blood flow.

Before running to Mr. Smith's room, he looked through the second-story window at the car waiting there, and for a very brief moment, he considered ignoring the call and going to his room. But that would only give the man more reason to disapprove of Freddy. As he looked outside, a heavy rain sliced through the lights from the street and seemed to dance on the shiny black surface of the sedan. Freddy took another deep breath and then used his smartphone to open the gate without providing a verbal response to the driver.

"Your son is here, Mr. Smith," Freddy said after knocking on the door to his room and receiving the invitation to enter. "I have opened the gate, and he will be at the door in a few minutes."

The old man grunted while rising from his desk. "Better get to your rooms."

Freddy ran to the basement, shut the door at the bottom of the stairs, and held his ear close to the wood. Mr. Smith's son reached the front door before his father arrived, and Freddy heard the doorbell ring. He listened for a few seconds through the stairwell door and then walked to his room after failing to understand the muffled speech.

—✕—

After shutting his bedroom door, Freddy decided to postpone energizing the ceiling lights and just listen for a few seconds. Due to the heavy blinds and curtains covering the windows, his room darkened much earlier than outside. Freddy liked the feel of the dark. The dark provided cover, protection from harm. The only light in the room came from all of the electronic equipment he had accumulated during his time there. The LED lights made his room seem like a science-fiction version of Christmas.

He owned two desktop computers, one primarily for gaming and both for his school work. They sat on his large oak desk, close enough to use simultaneously. He had contemplated getting either the Xbox game system from Microsoft or the PlayStation from Sony, but his classes, job, and other interests like astronomy and cell biology consumed most of his time. He had decided to limit his gaming excursions exclusively to personal computers with sufficient graphics capabilities.

After convincing himself that no one was likely to visit his room, he went to his dresser, the one containing the crystal. He had been wanting to hold it again but did not have the chance until then. When he saw the two-dimensional spider within the glass, he felt the same excitement as the previous night. Holding the crystal in his hand made him whole again.

The surface was cool to the touch, and Freddy tossed the object carefully from one hand to the other, enjoying the sensation of its weight. A slight paranoia slowly began to creep into his thoughts, and he felt like *Frodo* from *The Lord of the Rings* novels when he had held his precious ring. No one else should see his new possession. They might attempt to steal it. He laughed, but it failed to eliminate the concern.

Then for the first time that day, he remembered the suspicious event from the previous evening when he had inspected the eyes of the spider. He wondered how he could have forgotten about the strange incident and then decided to accept a temporary explanation. The memory loss had occurred right before going to sleep. After thinking for another few seconds, Freddy chose to run an experiment to convince himself of its reality or conclude he had just felt tired.

He considered using a microscope but decided to use a camera first. After carefully securing the crystal with small laboratory vices, he positioned one of his digital cameras, so light from the crystal surface would travel into the camera lens rather than his eyes. Then he connected the camera to his computer and felt ready to begin the experiment when the image on the screen appeared.

Before he could examine the head and eyes more closely, Freddy needed to bring the image into focus, but no matter what he tried, he failed to get a sharp image of the spider's eyes. He only managed to get a slight rainbow blur, mostly red.

"Impossible," he said and then moved the camera so that the focus shifted to the spider's abdomen. To his surprise, he experienced no problem focusing on any other part of the spider. "It is all in the same plane, so why can I not get it to focus?"

In frustration, he held a magnifying glass above the crystal on the table. With the light of a lamp, he examined the sliver of rock that his sister claimed had come from space, and then he looked intensely at the eyes again, and then for the third time since acquiring the object, his vision became blurry.

When the computer screen in his peripheral vision suddenly turned black, Freddy jolted in surprise. His room had become dark again, the lamp and LED's as the only light sources. He took a moment to reassess the situation and realized the computer screen had not turned black while he was conscious. The screen had turned off before he had noticed the transition.

"What was that?" he asked quietly, shaking his head and looking at the time. It was ten minutes after seven. He had just lost consciousness again and this time for at least twenty minutes, long enough for his computer screen to fall asleep.

He left the crystal on the desk and sat back in his leather office chair. After concentrating hard on his most recent memory, he failed to remember one moment from the blackout episode, no dream, no image in his mind or impression, nothing. He felt the same, but he wondered if something about him had changed without his awareness. He would need to continue being scientific about the investigation.

"There has to be a test I can do," he said, swiveling around in the chair.

Before devising a more detailed plan, he decided to ask his sister about the crystal's origin, just one more time. His sister had become his only physical link to the crystal with its embedded two-dimensional spider. By calling her, he risked giving her an excuse for another visit, but he would take that risk. His sister had much less influence over him on the phone. With considerable anxiety, he dialed his sister's phone number and waited through three rings.

"Spider." A female voice answered in an uncertain and impatient tone. "What do you want?"

"Hey, Wands," Freddy said as cheerfully as possible. "I wanted to thank you for the crystal."

"What crystal?" she asked impatiently. "What are you talking about?"

"The crystal you gave me?"

"I don't have any crystals, and if I did, I wouldn't give them to you." The tone reminded him of her usual abrasive personality, unlike the previous night when she had acted almost nicely. "You've got everything you could ever dream of, so why would I give you anything? Is this all you called me about? I'm busy."

Another wave of irrational paranoia washed over him. Perhaps one of his sister's friends had answered the phone again, making fun of him and now she knew the secret word. No, Wanda would not do that to him again, not after so many years. He needed to think rationally and trust his judgment. The female had answered his sister's phone and she had the all-too-familiar irritating attitude. And she had used the code word. She had to be his sister.

To avoid causing more anger or frustration, Freddy decided to end the conversation. After the phone call, he would consider its meaning.

"Sorry, Wands," he said, hoping to sound sincerely apologetic. "I must have been thinking of something else."

His sister spared him more anxiety by cutting the connection.

EIGHTEEN

Freddy

Freddy restarted his computer and followed his habit of writing or typing all of his observations and thoughts, so he could see how they looked in the real world. He liked to use the Microsoft program, Notepad, and made a simple numbered list of everything he could recall. Since his mind tended to race faster than his short-term memory could retain, typing his thoughts helped to keep all of the major pieces of the puzzle right in front of him.

"Yes," he said triumphantly while typing the details of a new idea.

If he had any more blackout episodes, he would record them on video. He went to another room in the basement and retrieved his digital camcorder, opening the doors silently so that Mr. Smith and his son upstairs could not hear him. He heard the faint murmur of human voices and tried his best to ignore them.

After returning to his room, Freddy placed the camera on the desk and then tested the connection to the computer. The video showed just as he had expected. He remembered to increase the screensaver time interval to an hour, so it would not interrupt the experiment.

"This is ridiculous," he whispered to himself. "Nothing is going to happen. It is just a trinket, an inanimate object."

At the very bottom of his conscious thoughts, Freddy wished to be mistaken. He feared the implications of being correct. During his next blackout, he wanted the video to show nothing happening. He started the recording at thirty-five minutes after seven.

After positioning the camera so that his face and the crystal were in the frame, he turned to the computer screen to view his profile and thought his nose looked larger than usual. For a brief moment, he felt as though he was looking at a different person, so he took a deep breath to shake the sensation. After exhaling, he started the recording and then looked down at the crystal, several centimeters away from his face. As with his previous experiences, the more he tried to focus, the fuzzier the spider eyes became. So, he tried harder and the effort brought physical pain to his eyes.

Freddy felt something like a blip in his mind, as though the scene had changed slightly. He tore his gaze away from the crystal, rubbed his eyes, and looked at his watch. It showed fifty-nine minutes after seven. He slowly reached over and turned off the camcorder. Then while extending his hand to click on the video player program, time seemed to move slowly. Before pushing play, he spent a moment inspecting the still image of his brown eyes staring down at the spider.

What if he saw something disturbing in the video? Although the possibility seemed highly likely, the feeling of trepidation soon passed, so he decided to stop thinking and push play. Sometimes, thinking hindered progress and he just had to move forward with action. He clicked the triangle play icon and soon discovered how he had spent the last twenty-two minutes.

His last memory involved trying to focus on the spider's eyes. What happened next caused more surprise than fear. In the video, his eyes grew wide as though he saw something incredible. Freddy watched as his eyes stayed open nearly the entire time, blinking slowly only after long intervals. He felt strange watching a close-up of his face staring at the crystal.

For the first thirty seconds or so, the scene remained the same, but from inside the crystal, blue and orange lights began slowly shining on his face. Despite the intensifying blue and then orange, his face remained unnaturally still, expressionless. Chills raced through his body, and paranoia soon took hold of him, afraid that some ghost would shoot out from the computer screen.

Freddy turned his attention from his face on the screen to the source of the light inside the crystal. Instead of shining like a flashlight, several soft orange lights shot into his eyes like thin laser beams while a diffuse blue light spread evenly over the rest of his face. In another situation, he might have considered the light as beautiful, but the entire scene was disturbing.

He paused the video and stared at the still picture. How could he have no memory of the events? The unknown scared him the most. His imagination could create more nightmares than reality could generate. He thought of all the crazy alien abduction stories where the aliens wiped your memory clean after finishing with their horrible experiments. He had always depended on his memory, but now he had to depend on this video.

Where had his sister acquired the crystal and why had she claimed to have no memory of giving it to him? Did she have a similar experience of losing her memory? Had someone instructed her to deliver the spider and then she had pretended to forget? Too many other questions fought for his consideration. In the end, he made only one conclusion. Someone wanted him to have the crystal.

Freddy began playing the video again and sat forward to watch the remainder of the file. For several minutes, the lights flashed over his face while he remained perfectly still. He disliked seeing himself in a trance. He suddenly imagined his head turning to the camera and smiling wide. But to his relief, that never happened.

Then he wondered if watching the lights in the video would cause him to fall into another trance. Fortunately, the video on the computer screen failed to have the same effect as the actual spider eyes and that observation seemed significant for some reason. The rest of the video showed him in the same trance-like state with the lights but without any other movement. At the end of the video, the lights from the crystal just stopped, and his consciousness resumed.

After he finished watching the video, Freddy noticed the darkness of his room again, but now the scene seemed different. He felt as though he had just watched a disturbing horror movie. Freddy had the sudden urge to turn on the lights, to extinguish the eerie mood. But before he could move, another light came to life. The orange and blue lights began shining from the crystal. Without considering the consequences, Freddy turned to the source of the light and all physical objects in his vision disappeared.

—✳—

Freddy opened his eyes and found himself standing in complete darkness, no longer sitting at his computer. Without any light to distract his awareness, he felt complete emptiness and a strange freedom. He soon forgot about the concept of light and noticed a hard, smooth surface under his bare feet at the same temperature as his body so that he sensed only the texture and pressure. He felt no air or anything else and imagined himself standing at the exact center of the universe with the ground extending to infinity in all directions.

His memory seemed intact, however, and provided a welcome orientation to reality, similar to gravity connecting his feet to the floor. He remembered his room and the video, but the day's events seemed as though they had occurred a long time in the past and his entire life had been a dream, and he had finally awakened to reality.

After enjoying the absence of light for a while, Freddy looked around him. As expected, he saw nothing and then wondered if he should be afraid or feel some other emotion. He evaluated his emotional state for several seconds and found himself surprisingly free of all fear and anxiety. Should he be afraid? Fear seemed like the logical response to his predicament.

The process of thinking seemed strange, he realized, as though he had never before used his mind for that purpose. His thoughts suddenly felt like a pack of dogs pulling him on a sled, ready to run wild and take him where he might not want to go. So, he decided to focus on the present and attempt to understand his new reality. He was standing in a room with walls an infinite distance away, waiting patiently for a play or some other kind of performance to begin.

After what felt like several hours of just standing there, the ground slowly became illuminated from above him. At first, he failed to notice the transformation. It happened too slowly. But when the light did enter his awareness, he noticed the ground. He was standing on smooth, black marble.

When he noticed his shadow extending several meters in front of him, he turned around and saw a single star rising in the black sky. The brilliant orange and blue star ascended slowly from the horizon, growing larger on its ascent and intensifying until the radiation would have vaporized his natural eyes. After the object completed its journey to the top of the sky, it had grown to the size of the sun. He could stare directly at the light without pain and enjoyed watching the surface burn with a brilliant electromagnetic fire.

After staring at the beautiful light for several minutes, he turned to survey his surroundings. Maybe with the light, he could see if anything existed in the distance. But as he had previously guessed, the horizon stretched to infinity and only his shadow, the ground, and the single star existed with him.

"Welcome to nowhere," a voice said from all directions at once.

When the female voice entered his mind, Freddy experienced no fear or surprise. The voice reminded him of a distant wind.

Freddy turned away from the orange and blue star and scanned the horizon. He saw no one, and after a moment of searching, he noticed a large cluster of new stars just above the horizon, moving higher in the sky. Unlike the giant star above him, the star cluster remained dimensionless on its ascent, just multicolored points of light. After reaching forty-five degrees in the sky, they stopped and just hovered there. He could not see them distinctly and when he tried to focus on any single point, the lights became a blurry rainbow haze.

The star cluster suddenly expanded and formed a familiar shape. It had two blue eyes, a pale nose, red lips, a giant nebula of a woman's face against the black sky. The eyes were oval with vertical pupils like those of a cat. The colorful face floated above him an infinite distance away and then transformed slowly into the faces of different people from his life, those he liked and those he did not. He recognized every individual. In every face, the eyes remained fixed on him.

"Hello," Freddy said after a while, but he instantly regretted speaking. Sound felt like an intruder in the silent world and sent shock waves through his mind. He had to wait a long moment for the reverberations to stop. When he spoke again, he whispered. "What are you? Where am I?"

At the sound of his voice, the lights transformed into his own face, and then as though mocking him, the mouth silently repeated his words.

"What are you? Where am I?"

When the face had finished the parody, he heard a female voice behind him, a whisper.

"Freddy."

Although quiet, the sound felt like an explosion in his mind. Before Freddy could turn around and search for the woman who had spoken, he noticed a single white star suddenly shoot away from the face in the sky. The star flew over Freddy and out of sight. He saw no one after turning, but he did see the star hovering just above the horizon, a shining point of light in the distance. Then Freddy heard footsteps from the direction of the light.

While staring at the horizon and listening to the footsteps, he noticed a small black dot appear below the star. Almost similar to watching a mirage, the tiny black dot stretched vertically and slowly expanded into the form of a woman walking toward him. After she arrived within several hundred meters, Freddy could distinguish her dark hair and clothing, simple blue jeans beneath a loose white blouse.

He felt only curiosity at first, but time seemed to stop when he recognized her. Sadi Jacobsen was walking toward him, the only woman he had ever loved, the woman who occupied so many of his dreams and fantasies. She moved gracefully and eventually stopped in front of him. Her dark hair swayed as though moved by an invisible current he could not feel. Only when she stopped did Freddy become aware of his beating heart. Its intense pounding prevented him from saying anything. He could only watch.

The woman smiled and appeared to be studying him.

"Who are you?" he asked after several deep breaths.

"That's a funny way to greet someone you know so well, Spider." She tilted her head slightly. "I know you remember me."

NINETEEN

Freddy

"You are not Sadi Jacobsen," he said. "You look like Sadi, but I know you are not her."

"Isn't it customary," she began politely, "to assume that the body you're addressing contains the same creature as your previous encounter?"

Freddy required a moment to comprehend her question. At first, Freddy thought the question was pointless, the answer too obvious. But other answers suddenly felt dangerous, a threat to his understanding of the world. After ignoring the temptation to contemplate other implications, he decided to keep interrogating her. She was trying to evade his question about her identity.

"You are not Sadi," he said.

The woman did not respond. While looking deeply into his eyes, she tilted her head almost imperceptibly. After finally breaking eye contact, she walked slowly around him and finally looked up at the cluster of stars in the sky.

"Isn't it beautiful?" she asked finally.

"Yes," he said.

Although Freddy felt tempted to look at the beautiful scene in the sky, he had difficulty looking away from the woman. She looked just as he remembered Sadi at his last encounter with her.

"It can show you whatever you want," she said while keeping her gaze on the sky. Her words seemed like an invitation to make a wish, but then he wondered if she meant the swarm of lights above them or the crystal he faced in the real world.

"The real world," she said and then chuckled softly through closed lips.

"What is in the eyes of the spider?" he asked. "Why does it make me lose my memory?"

She turned from the sky and stepped very close to him, stopping with her face just a few centimeters away. Instead of meeting his eyes, she inspected his face from different angles, moving slowly from left to right. Her warm breath smelled of cinnamon.

"Am I upsetting you?" she asked.

Her lips almost brushed his chin, and his heart began beating faster again.

Although she appeared as a replica of Sadi Jacobsen, her eyes were not human, and he felt as though he was looking into the eyes of a dangerous predator like an owl or a hawk. A sinister creature stood behind those eyes. At any moment, her intoxicating smile might disappear, replaced by rows of sharp teeth.

"You do not upset me," he said while fighting the urge to step backward. The beating of his heart replaced the memory of his last question. "What do you want with me?"

She took a step backward. "I've been waiting for you."

"Why me?"

"Wouldn't you like to know," she said and her smile disappeared.

"I would like to know."

"You're unique," she said, making a slow orbit around him and arriving in front of him again. "And I think you're ready. That should be enough for now."

People usually called him *creep*, *retard*, or *freak*, but the way she said *unique* felt like a compliment. And ready for what, he wondered. She walked slowly around him again as though inspecting a statue at a museum. As she orbited him, he suddenly wanted to know her identity more than the reason for her presence. Maybe she would tell him that, but he also feared the answer.

"Who are you?" he asked with as much confidence as possible, hoping to conceal his anxiety.

She stopped walking and stood just behind his back. "That answer will just lead to more questions," she said in a mocking tone. Her warm breath on his neck sent chills all through his body.

"Will you answer me please?" he asked, using all of his frustration and fear to energize the request.

"That was very clever of you to use the computer," she said, walking around to the front of him again. "You deserved an intervention."

He waited and she filled the silence.

"The crystal is a beautiful gift. Is it not?"

"Yes, but what is it?" He also wanted to know how his sister had acquired the thing, but he could not ask all of his questions at once.

"Think of it as a mirror," she answered bluntly, "and a lens."

He thought for a moment. A lens focused light. A mirror reflected light. What did the crystal bring into focus and what kind of light did it reflect? The opportunity to contemplate some details of the situation suddenly helped alleviate the palpable tension of her presence.

"Am I the only one able to use the crystal?" he asked.

She continued looking into his eyes but without an immediate response. When she spoke again, she spoke slowly.

"You don't really want me to answer all your questions, do you?" she asked. "What's the fun of that?"

"You want me to have fun?" he asked, feeling disappointed.

"So curious," she said with sarcasm and then laughed. "You choose such tedious information over the experience I offered."

Instead of asking what she meant, he felt stupid. This new world he inhabited, whatever its meaning or location, was a singular experience and all he could think of doing was to ask questions. His imagination suddenly seemed extremely limited.

Freddy looked at the sky directly above him, at the beautiful lights. They shimmered and shifted into continually changing configurations, preventing Freddy from bringing the overall scene into focus. After some time trying, he abandoned the attempt. He sighed and decided to speak again.

"Okay, what do you want to show me?"

His question seemed to float in the space between them. While waiting for her answer, frustration for his lack of creativity transformed into excitement for whatever experience she chose for him.

Her next question was a frozen knife penetrating his chest.

"You desire this woman, don't you?" she asked, placing her right hand over her collarbone, drawing attention to her neck and breasts.

She seemed to be asking a simple question, but her words sounded like a statement, an accusation. She probably knew the answer already and just wanted a verbal confession. After focusing on the top of her breasts, his eyes grew wide and he gulped.

That is none of your business, he wanted to say. With considerable effort, he returned his attention to her eyes. His skin began to tingle with embarrassment.

"What does Sadi Jacobsen have to do with this?" he asked.

When she placed her hand on his shoulder, his embarrassment vanished. Her hand felt like a red-hot heating element and he imagined smoke rising from his shirt. But no pain or smoke accompanied the sensation. The heat was surprisingly comforting, and for a moment, he wished she would grasp him with her other hand.

"Go and find her," she said. After a tight squeeze, she released his shoulder. "Sadi is the next part of the journey."

Freddy opened his mouth to reply, but the woman suddenly looked like a lifeless statue, an inanimate object covered in real skin and cloth, and liquid eyes. When he took a step backward, her eyes failed to follow him. Whatever had given life to the object was no longer present.

While waiting for it to move again, he noticed the light around him beginning to fade and their shadows stretching away on the ground. He turned to the sky and watched the new star shoot back to its original position, shrinking to a single point and merging with the horizon. The other lights had also vanished, and the stone floor soon became the only physical sensation in the darkness.

Freddy regained his consciousness in the last position he remembered, sitting in the chair and staring at the crystal. The only light in the room came from the blinking LEDs of all his electronic equipment. Unlike the other blackout episodes, the time interval seemed much longer than a moment, more like an entire lifetime. He knew the whole experience had occurred only in his imagination, but it seemed too real for just a dream. It was a vision and the creature who had spoken to him did not originate from his mind.

He swiped his finger over the laptop touchpad and the monitor returned to life. His still image stared back at him and reminded him of staring at Sadi's lifeless face in the vision. After a moment of staring into his own eyes, Freddy turned the computer off.

When the computer screen turned black, he glanced down at the crystal again, making sure to avoid the spider's eyes and thereby falling into another trance. After enclosing the crystal in his hand, he walked to his dresser and inserted it under his folded tube socks, out of sight.

Exhaustion quickly swept over him. After lying on his bed, he just stared at the ceiling. The vision had exhausted his energy and left him feeling hollow. When he finally closed his eyes, images of Sadi began flowing as a stream past his mind's eye. He fell asleep in less than ten minutes.

Contacting Sadi Jacobsen became his last conscious thought. He spent the rest of the night dreaming about finding her and all of the things he could say, and do. He woke the next morning feeling physically refreshed and with the vision still alive in his thoughts. But unlike his dreams, the vision was linked to a physical object he could touch, the crystal.

Freddy needed additional investigation before he could attempt to contact Sadi. He left the house without encountering Mr. Smith's son, to his relief, and then spent several hours that day in the library and on the Internet reading about mind control techniques, hypnosis, and altered states of consciousness.

To explain the vision and the crystal, he would use the scientific method. Strange phenomena interpreted as aliens, demons, angels, or magic, all had a rational explanation. To begin, all he needed was a hypothesis—the crystal or spider had interacted with his mind and had caused a hallucination.

TWENTY

Gerald

When they reached Cesar's home, Gerald felt as though he stood before a Mexican royal palace, a small one at least. The front drive had four white arches, three meters high and leading to a large patio walkway in front of massive double doors. Several large pots with rose bushes filled the space with life. If he had felt sunshine and warmth, Gerald would have thought they were actually in Mexico, but the gloomy Seattle weather provided them with the usual drizzle.

A beautiful woman greeted them at the door. She had short black hair pulled back with an ornate gold and silver pin. When she focused her dark oval eyes on Gerald, they drew his attention away from everything else.

She wore no ring and Cesar introduced her as one would introduce a foreign dignitary. She seemed to share the same age as Cesar while retaining the beauty of her youth. Her name was Dominga Florez.

After leading them inside, Cesar excused himself to go and prepare something for them to eat while the woman led them to a large sitting room. Dominga sat on an ornate, single-cushion-backed chair with elegant and simple Queen Anne-style legs. All of the furniture appeared to have the same theme, a style Gerald might have chosen if he'd had the patience to spend the required time and money. During his first and only other visit to the home, Dominga had not yet arrived and the arrangements were not as nice. The woman had definitely brought her own style. In the chair, she looked as relaxed as a cat lying in the sunshine.

"I was unaware that we were having guests this early on the weekend." She spoke with a thicker accent than Cesar, as though she was much less unaccustomed to speaking in English. Gerald and Taylor leaned forward to focus all of their energy on listening. She laughed quietly before continuing. "You are lucky I was presentable."

Gerald could not imagine the woman in front of them looking anything less than pristine. He especially could not imagine her walking around in sweats and tousled hair.

"Yes, this was unexpected," Gerald answered after requiring a moment to process her words. "I hope we haven't intruded."

"Of course not," she said, her mouth bursting into a pleasant smile. "I love company. We get so few," she said and then paused while searching for the right word, "friendly visitors."

She turned to Taylor.

"Miss Taylor, Cesar called me on the phone and gave me some forewarning to your visit. He says you are the reason. How does your purpose relate to him? What could such a beautiful young woman want with my Cesar?"

The woman smiled affectionately and Gerald failed to detect any hint of jealousy, just curiosity.

"Does it have to do with business?" she asked.

Taylor paused a moment before responding and Gerald wondered if she suspected jealousy, but Taylor appeared undisturbed. "Yes, it's related to business. Cesar thought we could talk more comfortably at his house."

"Yes," Dominga agreed. "It is much more comfortable than that old shop of his. You will find Cesar to be the perfect host."

She turned to face Gerald again.

"My dear Mr. Foster, Cesar spoke of you before. I have wanted to thank you for helping him when he arrived here. Sorry, but my English can be poor sometimes."

"No, your English is perfect," Gerald said with a smile. "Did you know Cesar from Mexico, or did you meet him here?"

"In Mexico," she answered. "I am a friend of the family and arrived about six months ago. He was lonely and needed some company, more than just his infamous friend, Doroteo."

"I was looking forward to hearing about Cesar's history," Taylor said, smiling patiently. "He was going to tell me his story. What can you tell me about him?"

Dominga's eyes widened a bit at Taylor's abruptness, but her lips stretched even wider. "Cesar has had an interesting life, but in his later years it has unfortunately become a tragic one."

"That's true," Gerald agreed.

"Before he gets back, let me tell you what I know," she said and her lips closed tightly. "If you have gained Cesar's respect, he is a valuable asset. If not, then I would suggest you stay away from him. Many have made the mistake of taking his generosity for granted. If you are concerned about his, oh what's the word, *trustworthiness*, just know that Cesar will never betray his own sense of morality. If you come to understand that, then you will have nothing to fear. You will want him as a friend."

Gerald loved the way she said, *trustworthiness*. He fought the temptation to ask her to repeat the word.

Cesar entered the room again before Dominga could continue, carrying a large tray of fruit. He smiled and placed the tray on a coffee table in the middle of the room. In his other hand, he held a white bowl, full of dip for the fruit.

Another man followed Cesar into the room. While entering, he glanced briefly at Taylor then Gerald, and then returned his attention to the ground. Gerald thought he looked annoyed and unwilling to introduce himself. He carried a single silver tray with both hands, holding sandwiches, three glasses, and a pitcher of water.

Gerald thought the man looked extremely unnatural in the role of a waiter, and he felt as though the leader of a Mexican drug cartel from the movies was serving them. He had tattoos all over his arms, and his skin was stretched tightly over bulging muscles. He wore blue jeans with a silk button shirt and seemed unaware of the cold wetness outside. Gerald hoped the man would not harm Taylor's decision to trust Cesar.

"Sorry it took so long, Gerald and Miss Taylor, but good thing I had Doroteo here to help me, otherwise it would have been longer." Cesar smiled and nodded to Dominga. "Thank you for keeping them company."

"No problem. We were just talking about you."

The man who had helped Cesar bring the food, Doroteo, stood as if awaiting a command. Cesar turned to him with a pleasant smile.

"Gracias, Doroteo," Cesar said.

"De nada," the man replied then left the room with only a glance at Cesar, then Dominga.

As he sat down, Cesar noticed Taylor watching Doroteo leave the room. "Don't let his looks deceive you, Miss Taylor," Cesar said with a chuckle. "Let me assure you. He's more savage than he appears."

Dominga looked at Cesar with raised eyebrows in feigned shock, and then they both laughed. Surprisingly, Taylor laughed too and Gerald smiled in relief.

"I wasn't thinking he looked *savage*," Taylor replied, "just a little rough around the edges."

For the next several minutes they ate and talked about Dominga's relationship to Cesar and how they had met. Gerald felt relieved while watching Taylor interact with Dominga. They seemed to have a positive assessment of each other. The older woman's demeanor looked genuine and not just an attempt to be a good host and make Taylor comfortable.

After they had become better acquainted, Cesar brought the conversation to a more serious tone. He directed his words to Taylor, retaining almost exclusive eye contact with her, but he did glance occasionally at Dominga and Gerald.

"When I came to this country," he began, "I searched for a lawyer that I could trust, and I found Gerald. I don't know if he remembers, but when we first met, my English was very rusty, much worse than even now, if you can believe that. Anyway, he was very patient, helped me with my visa problems, and also helped me get set up with my shop."

Cesar cleared his throat then paused as though enjoying the memory.

"I will attempt to alleviate your concerns about me. At least, I will tell you everything you might want to know. I must admit, Miss Evans. You have my curiosity. For someone like Gerald and you to try to trick me before you reveal your true purpose, I believe that is worth my time."

Dominga looked from Cesar to Taylor and failed to hide the confusion in her eyes. She waited patiently for Cesar to continue.

"Miss Evans, you show strength of character not to base complete trust in others with something that must be very dear to you. You trust your own judgment more than your most trustworthy friend. You probably won't believe everything I'm about to tell you, but Dominga can confirm it all. You've probably never experienced anger and grief to the extent I have. Consider yourself fortunate. I wish no one had to experience what I did."

Gerald sat back in his chair and tried to get comfortable. Dominga crossed her legs and rested her head on her hand. Her dark eyes focused on Cesar and her face expressed admiration, deeper than mere affection.

TWENTY-ONE

Cesar

First, let me tell you that up until recently, I had a good life, an extremely blessed life. I grew up in wealth, and with it, privilege. My younger brother and I went to the best private schools and had everything needed for a fine education and a perfect future. With my parents, we toured all over the world, vacationed in the Caribbean, traveled all through Europe and Asia.

Believe it or not, even though I had everything a person could possibly want, I was always the good kid. My brother, on the other hand, was exactly what you'd expect a life of privilege can produce in a child. You'll hear more about him later. I don't give myself credit for how I turned out. It just happened. Maybe it is all genetics. I don't know, but either way, I was always a good kid.

My father was a wealthy man. He was a great man, intelligent and shrewd where money was concerned. But he didn't start that way. He started in the slums of Ciudad Juarez, not a very nice place to be. It's filled with violence, where the gangs and drug lords battle with each other and with the police. Fortunately, my grandmother was an amazing woman who knew how to keep her sons out of all that mess. Eventually, she earned enough money to move out and my father got a good job with a car parts manufacturer. Eventually, he moved up the ladder and became the CEO. It was the perfect fairy tale story.

As CEO, he doubled the company's revenue and profits in two years then he expanded the business. I wish I could say my father accomplished all this ethically, but sadly, I learned later that one factor in his success and the success of the company was due to their involvement in the drug war, or I should say, with the CIA.

I didn't learn of this until after I completed my formal education. My younger brother knew about it before I did. I'll get to that later.

My father wanted my brother and I to have a college experience in the United States, so he sent us to Stanford. My brother chose the school because he wanted to go to California. Like I said, I was a good kid and usually did what my father asked of us. Besides, it was Stanford, and I was not about to complain. Following my father's advice, my younger brother and I majored in business. I soon became bored with the subject, although I did stick with it.

Business classes did not require much of my time, so I started taking classes in mechanical engineering and focused on automotive engineering. This was partly due to my father's business where I planned to work. It just made sense to know more about that subject. Fortunately, I found it very interesting and I spent more of my time in those classes than my business classes.

My brother, on the other hand, spent all his time with girls and his fraternity brothers. We've always been friends, but our relationship was usually strained. At home, we were forced to spend our time together, but at school, our lives went in different directions. For him, every weekend was filled with alcohol and women. I wasn't opposed to extracurricular activities, but I was always blessed, you can say, with an intense curiosity about this world and could not be kept from trying to learn all I could. You can imagine that at Stanford, it was easy to get lost in my studies. It was just another step in my charmed life.

It took me six years to get both my business and engineering degrees. I have to admit that I put more energy into automotive engineering than business. It's funny because my brother and I graduated together. He got his MBA, and I got two Bachelor's degrees. One of his frat brothers was the son of a senator who was also a friend of the Mexican ambassador and my brother went to work with him as an aide.

My father was excited about this, to have a connection with a U.S. government official. After working for a couple of years with the ambassador, my brother went to work for my father.

I finished my M.S. engineering degree and wanted to continue for a doctorate, but my father talked me into coming back to Mexico to work for him. It wasn't that big of a disappointment because I figured I didn't need school to learn when I had all the resources for research back at home in my father's company. Maybe I just wanted the title of doctor? I was young, and things like that seemed to matter.

After working for my father for a couple of years, I talked him into branching out into motors, one of the only products he did not manufacture. We had the capital for it and I knew there was some market share we could capture. As you can guess, it was partly because I wanted to do some design work. We hired a friend of mine from school and some other local people and got our first few engines out in about a year. After three years the new engine division I started was contributing ten percent of our total revenue. A couple of years later, I offered to buy out the division as a separate entity. It was a good deal for both of us.

A year after I arrived back in Mexico, at one of my mother's frequent parties, I met the daughter of the governor of Chihuahua, the Mexican state where Juarez is located.

This girl was the most beautiful creature I'd ever seen. I had to see her again, and then again, and again. Six months later we were married and then a year later our first daughter, Sophia, was born. Those years flew by, and then four years later, my twins Max and Geraldo were born.

The business was going amazingly well, and I was still oblivious to the connection between my father's business and the CIA. I became suspicious when one of our pilots mysteriously died. So far, my father's company and my company were sharing some planes for shipping our goods to the United States and other places. When the pilot died, I became involved with hiring a new one. After looking into that side of the business, which I had previously let my father handle, I decided that it made more sense to buy my own plane and hire my own pilots.

Unexpectedly, I ran into a load of trouble when I tried to do this. Doroteo, who you just met, was in charge of security and discovered that a couple of the people causing us trouble were actually on the CIA's payroll. They coordinated the movement of some illegal material, and suddenly I was messing with that operation. They wanted to be the ones to choose the pilots as my father had always let them do. They needed special training and instruction.

You would probably be surprised to learn that Doroteo was a very close friend from my childhood. He was the type of friend anyone wanted. He wasn't the strongest kid on the block, but he was the toughest. Our lives separated for a few years when I went to college. He got a job with the police and spent much of his time undercover, fighting the drug supply chain, which also included some very corrupt government officials. Whenever that much money is involved, a lot of people want a piece of the pie.

When my business began to get going, I hired him as head of security. He would have figured out about our drug involvement earlier, but my father's company managed the shipping aspect. I always avoid this topic with him because he still blames himself for it.

We finally realized what was happening. Our products shipped by air to close cities in the United States, like Albuquerque, and then they would head to either Seattle, Salt Lake City, or Buffalo. Instead of a straight flight, they would stop in small airports where CIA agents would coordinate the transfer of their hidden stock of drugs. All of this had been coordinated for years, with the approval of my father, although he never did admit it.

I confronted my father with what I knew and he said they were merely cooperating with the law. I was very angry with the situation but also scared out of my mind. Doroteo said it would be better to leave it alone for a while, which we did. However, I was determined to eliminate our participation. Doroteo felt the same but knew that we were in a sticky situation and it would require delicate handling. The final decision was to buy a plane of our own and start by switching just some of our shipping to our management. We would transfer a little at a time until all of our merchandise was being shipped in our own planes and by our own pilots.

Doroteo said he would cut all ties to the drug trade and gratefully, I put a blind eye to his methods because they tended to supersede the law. In my mind, this was justified because the government officials from Mexico and the U.S. were working against us. My whole life, it never crossed my mind that the CIA would be involved with the drug war in this way. Doroteo can tell you more about it, but the money goes to very rich and powerful families who control the intelligence agencies. That is the reason why nothing has been done to end the drug war. All that matters is that the money keeps flowing. If anything gets in the way, it is soon eliminated.

After a year or so, we were shipping all of our goods and I thought the problem was solved. All would have been if my wife hadn't succeeded in persuading me into politics. When I turned forty-two, I decided to run for mayor of Ciudad Juarez. Part of me thought that I could do more good in government than I could as a business leader. In my mind, I owed it to the city that had given me so much. I decided to retire from the business and enter the political game. I stayed with the company as a board member but left the management to others.

My wife's father, who was no longer the governor of Chihuahua, had become a cabinet member in Ernesto Zedillo's administration. He guided me on how to win the election. Little did I know that the establishment already had their pick for mayor and it wasn't me. From the very onset of my public campaign, I got death threat after death threat. Doroteo became my security manager. He's the reason for my current heartbeat.

Yes, I owe my life to him, many times over.

So, not only was my life threatened, but the media tried to ignore me. If it hadn't been for my friends in the media, they wouldn't have given me the time of day. Yes, I had connections, and I owe them my victory. The media is key to getting elected and don't let anyone tell you otherwise.

It's funny and tragic, but before you become a political leader, you have this fantasy that you're going to change the system. What I found was that things were already well-established and politicians only have the power to keep the money flowing, not stopping or diverting it. You would not believe the number of bureaucrats that work independently from any elected official.

When I decided to run for a second term, that's when things started to heat up. During my time as mayor, there were the usual death threats, but nothing out of the ordinary. Of course, many of them were serious, but my security, as led by Doroteo, was flawless. Now that I look back on it, I think those that I thwarted the most as mayor were just biding their time until my term was over. Then they could go on as they were, making the public pay for all their programs, continuing to fatten their bank accounts. Up until that point, my family was relatively safe. Their lives were never truly in much danger.

Now that I look back at it, I was naive and stupid. Somehow, I felt that we were invincible. Like I said, I had a charmed life. Nothing bad had ever happened to me, every obstacle had been overcome, so why not this one? Now I don't blame anyone but myself, but at that time, I was angry and blamed everyone else.

TWENTY-TWO

Cesar

At the very beginning of my second campaign, my boys were kidnapped. I cannot describe the horror. It was like they always say, a waking nightmare from which there was no awakening. My wife collapsed many times with grief and worry. That was how bad it was. When that happened, I was actually jealous that she could escape reality for a while.

The kidnappers did not want money. Instead, they wanted me to promise not to run for mayor and not say anything about the kidnapping, or else the boys would die. They even threatened to kill one of the boys to show that they were serious.

At that point, I was willing to promise anything. That one act was all it took to break me. I lost the confidence that this would be overcome. My wife and I were a wreck, as I'm sure you can imagine. Every night during the ordeal, we slept with Sophia in the same room. It was the first time in my life when I felt that I could not rely on myself. I tried turning to religion, but that didn't help. Nothing did.

After a few days, there was a breakthrough. Doroteo found out where they were keeping the boys. I'll never forget the excitement and hope that information can bring. It was almost as good as if they were back at home. I imagined charging into their compound with Doroteo and the police, guns smoking, and saving the boys. It was the same invincible confidence I had before, scarred only by fear. I was confident that even if I died in the attempt, so would the kidnappers, and my boys would be safe.

Doroteo was the one who planned the rescue. He tried to forbid me from participating, but I could not be kept away. I was expecting the rescue to be like what you see in the movies, but instead, it was very anti-climactic. The boys were being held by only two men in a small house in a bad part of town.

I imagined killing the kidnappers a million ways, but when we retrieved the boys, all I could think of was getting them back to their mother, back to safety. I almost forgot about the men who held them. The two men happened to be just a couple hired thugs who were playing video games with my boys. After Doroteo put the fear of God in them, we let them go.

Even though I had promised not to run again, I figured that since we got the boys back, I could go back to my preparations for the campaign. A promise to someone threatening your family can be dropped. I would just be extra careful and have to worry about my family in addition to myself. Even Doroteo, who was usually more cautious than I am, was okay with our campaign preparations.

For a few weeks after getting the boys back, we didn't hear a thing about the kidnapping. It was as if the whole thing had never happened. It took two weeks before we were comfortable with the boys sleeping in their own rooms again. It seemed quiet, until a week after I had made the official announcement of my campaign plans.

I'm sorry, but what happened next I cannot talk about in much detail. It started when my wife and boys were in a car accident. My twin boys, who were fifteen at the time, died instantly. My wife was taken to the hospital in critical condition, but she died within an hour.

Before she died, she was able to tell me what happened. I would have thought it was just an accident. Apparently, she was being chased by a car with armed men and her driver lost control of the car. It had happened so fast that she didn't have time to call anyone. My grief, anger, and shock were too great to think clearly. In one day, most of my family was taken away.

My daughter was not with them when it happened, but my wife told me she was somewhere with her boyfriend. He was a great boy and I had always trusted him to keep her safe.

Frantically, we searched for her. She was all I had left. I could not accept the possibility that she could be gone too. That would have been too much, and I would have killed myself right there to stop the pain.

When I tried to call her to see if she was safe, I could not get a hold of her or her boyfriend. We searched for her for a few hours and eventually found her boyfriend. He had been beaten unconscious.

When we got him conscious again, he told us what happened. Some men had found them and took her. Naturally, he struggled to keep it from happening, but they overpowered him, and he was lucky that they didn't kill him. They only let him live to deliver the news to me. I was still in shock from what had happened to my boys and wife. Now that my daughter was missing, I felt like I was going to have a heart attack.

The only thing left was my daughter and getting her back kept me among the living. Her boyfriend was as distressed as I was. That experience bonded us. Despite my grief, what we shared gave me strength. I cannot describe it. To this day, I regard him as my son.

When the kidnappers contacted us, they told me it was my fault that my wife and boys had died. In a way, they were right, although, at the time, I could not accept it.

The instructions were similar to the previous time when my boys were kidnapped. If we told the media, my Sophia would die, so we had a quiet funeral while Doroteo went to work finding her.

Doroteo came to the rescue again. He was able to find where they were keeping my daughter. For the second time, I found myself in the role of rescuer. This time, Doroteo did not even try to keep me or my daughter's boyfriend from coming. At the time, my thoughts were that I was either going to die in the attempt to rescue her, or if she was dead, take my revenge out on as many of her kidnappers as possible. I did not care about what happened to me.

This time, it wasn't nearly as easy. She was not being held in some faraway place by a couple of nobodies. They were holding her at the compound belonging to the leader of one of the worst drug cartels. Even Doroteo had doubts about success. It was no secret about this man's involvement in the drug trade, but most people did not know he was one of the most influential men in all of Chihuahua.

Once we found out where they were holding her, we knew that they did not intend to let her go alive. She knew the place and the people. I knew the man and had been at political functions with him. We were never friends because of what I knew of him.

We left one night after midnight. Doroteo had a friend who had been in the military special forces. He was the one who planned the rescue and told us what to do. The compound was well guarded, but the guards were lazy and not expecting anything. That night, they were not ready for an assault. Fortunately, plenty of firepower helps provide a feeling of overconfidence.

The details after we got past the guards are a little fuzzy. I was too worried about my daughter to think about what we were doing. After a horrible time trying to locate her, we finally found her, but everyone had woken up and we were surrounded by his men. There was no way we could have gotten out of there alive. I thought all was lost, but luck was with us.

One of our captors was an undercover CIA agent. By some miracle, which I'll never understand, he decided to help us. It wasn't entirely because of any desire on his part to do what was right, but because they, the CIA, were planning to dispose of the cartel leader anyway. We just provided the perfect opportunity to do so. They could blame the incident on local political intrigue.

So, this agent turned on his compadres and killed them. We thought he was going to kill us next, but to my surprise, he turned to us and said we could take my daughter and leave. He told us several things, which I won't go into now. Let me just say that he gave us some warning that there was going to be a major upheaval in the country and it wasn't going to be safe for us. He told me that I had to leave the country, keep my mouth shut about what happened, and stay out of the media.

You can see the reality of it in the news even now, with the war between the government and the drug cartels and all the increased violence. The CIA decided that they didn't like the current drug trade administration. With the help of the US military, they are accomplishing their goals, but I better stop talking about it. I get too angry to see what is happening to my home. I cannot do one damn thing about it.

In the end, I could not persuade my Sophia to leave Mexico. She and her boyfriend fled to his relatives' home, far away in Jalisco. They plan to marry sometime this year. I am hoping to convince them to come and live with me someday. Eventually, I expect they will.

TWENTY-THREE

Gerald

When Cesar finished telling his story, Gerald looked at Taylor. She was shaking her head slightly as though in disbelief and amazement. After such a detailed explanation of horrible events, Gerald had difficulty keeping his good mood, but he knew the story already. Dominga had sat quietly during the entire discourse and acted as though watching a television program. Gerald wondered how she fit into Cesar's emotions. She had an obvious affection for the man.

Dominga rose from her seat unexpectedly. Before speaking, she looked at both of her guests. "Well, it appears that you have business to discuss with Cesar. I'll leave you to discuss, but you must not leave without saying goodbye."

Gerald also rose from his chair while the woman left the room. Cesar and Taylor remained seated.

"Mr. Sanchez," Taylor said once Dominga had disappeared from their view and Gerald had sat back down. She kept her gaze on Cesar. "I appreciate you sharing your personal history, more than you can know. I appreciate it and want to ask for your trust. I feel that I can trust you."

Gerald understood Cesar's motivation for sharing so much emotion. After such a display, Taylor would feel obligated to return the emotional trust.

"Before you tell me anything, should I be worried?" Cesar asked. "To keep your trust, will you ever require me to lie for you?"

"Honestly," Taylor began, attempting to sound sincere. "I don't know for sure, but such a possibility would be required only for your safety."

"Is it illegal?" Cesar asked, turning to Gerald.

Gerald acted offended but with a smile.

"Me, illegal? Come on, Cesar. You know me better than that. Even if our purpose was illegal, which it isn't of course, would I ever admit to it?"

Cesar laughed. He sat back and exhaled slowly.

"No, you wouldn't."

"Mr. Sanchez," Taylor said. "I trust Gerald completely, and I know that he trusts you, so I'm just going to tell you, bluntly, how you can help us, and ask for your participation. If you want no part of it, I won't mention it again. Just give me your word that this will be kept confidential."

Cesar leaned forward.

"Of course, go ahead."

"I've made a discovery," she said bluntly. "If we're successful in bringing it out in the open, the world will change, but certain people will not want that to happen."

She leaned forward, unzipped her backpack, and pulled out the black box. So far during their visit, she had kept the backpack between her feet. Both Gerald and Cesar stared at the box as though a rattlesnake had just appeared. After sticking the magnet to the surface with a loud snap, she handed the box to Cesar.

He turned the box over in his hand, examining its size and weight.

"Do I open it?"

"Flip the switch on the side," said Gerald, failing to control his excitement.

Taylor glanced at him in irritation but said nothing.

Cesar put the box on his lap, clicked the switch, and the box slowly floated towards the ceiling like a balloon full of helium. He jumped back in his seat and put his hands to his side.

"¡Cáspita!" he said in surprise.

Taylor laughed sharply and clapped her hands together and then looked a little embarrassed at the outburst. At first, everyone just watched the box float toward the ceiling, but Gerald jumped to his feet and grabbed it from the air, pushing the object back on Cesar's lap. The force against his hand felt quite unnatural.

"This is impossible," Cesar said finally, more to himself than anyone else.

After a few seconds, the older man seemed to regain his composure. His tense lips slowly relaxed into a smile. He placed his hand on the box and Gerald went back to his seat. Cesar let the box rise a few times and then pulled it back again to his lap. For several seconds after flipping the switch off, he kept his hand on the box and silently stared.

Gerald and Taylor waited for Cesar to speak. His mouth moved slightly as if chewing on a million thoughts. Finally, he turned to Taylor.

"You must tell me how this works."

"Would you have believed me if I would have just told you about it?" Her smile disappeared, and her usual inquisitive look returned.

"No," he said, laughing slightly. "I would have thought you were crazy. It appears to violate the conservation of momentum, but that cannot be possible!"

Gerald also felt curious about how the device worked but hoped they would not spend the entire afternoon talking about that. He glanced at Taylor and imagined seeing her mind preparing to explain the technical details. He spoke before she could.

"We can go over the technical details another time," he said quickly. "We came here to ask for your help with what we want to do with it."

"You definitely do not want to go public with this," Cesar said while staring at the box. "Agents from the government would be at your doors faster than the wind."

To Gerald's relief, they spent the next two hours discussing the plan he and Taylor had agreed to pursue the previous night. Cesar listened to their plan and the reasoning and seemed unsure about the idea of using the device to travel into space, but he did not immediately reject the idea. He claimed to have more interest in working with Taylor to develop the technology. They could use her invention however they wanted.

During the conversation, his tone of address toward Taylor changed. He acted impressed and almost afraid to argue with her as though he occupied the room with some famous scientist.

Cesar shared the same goal as Gerald and Taylor of establishing a better society, and they spent a significant amount of time discussing how her invention could help humanity. Releasing her invention to the world could potentially shift the military dynamics of all nations and ultimately decentralize the current power structure.

In Cesar's opinion, using the technology for space travel had too many obstacles. He thought there might be a better way, although he agreed that they would need a way to escape the government's grasp should the need arise. Like Taylor, he just needed more time to consider the idea.

"There is another option that you have not considered," Cesar said, sitting forward on the couch.

"What is that?" Gerald and Taylor asked together.

"It involves doing what we already agreed to do first, develop it. I'm sure we will think of a way to use this to make some money and eventually challenge the puppet masters. For example, asteroid mining has a lot of potential. What you've created may be able to economically accomplish that."

At the end of the discussion, they all agreed to start the project of optimizing the NMG design. Gerald felt another excitement growing inside him. He could now let them take control of the project while he could focus on other ways to help.

"Miss Taylor," Cesar said in a tone of cheerful insistence. "You must stay here with us. We will use my shop."

While he explained his reasoning, Gerald hoped that Taylor would agree to the proposal. Simply for security reasons, living with him was the safest and he had plenty of space in his home. They would start working as soon as Taylor could make the move. Gerald had expected this and wondered if she would feel comfortable with the arrangement.

At his request to live with them, Taylor sat back in her seat, rubbed her chin, and stared at the ground. After just a few seconds, she looked up at him.

"So, I wouldn't be an intrusion?" she asked.

"Of course not. The arrangement will also make Dominga very happy."

"You seem to already know what you want to do first."

"I do," he said with a devious smile. "You have indeed come to the right person."

TWENTY-FOUR

Taylor

"When can you move in?" Cesar asked without trying to hide his excitement. He acted like a child looking at a present, wondering about the contents. Taylor thought he looked adorable.

"As soon as you want," she said, unable to think of a reason to delay.

"I hope you don't find me too forward, Miss Taylor, but if you're going to live here, I would like to talk to Dominga and Doroteo about what you just showed me. They will need to know what is going on. You have my assurance that they can keep this confidential. I trust them with my life."

"I believe you," Taylor said then turned to Gerald. He looked like a spectator, rather than the driver. He seemed to be enjoying his position though, as comfortable as her mother's cat on the sofa. Without understanding why, Taylor felt good about the situation. After listening to the tragic story of Cesar's life, the man now felt like a relative.

"I suppose we should show them the NMG as well," she said.

Taylor wondered suddenly if having a baby felt the same as inventing something. Parents usually wanted to show off their creations and Taylor had difficulty hiding her pride and excitement. After showing Gerald and Cesar, she felt less hesitation to show others. When she had shown Gerald the previous evening, an overwhelming relief replaced her fear of the NMG failing to work, almost as if the NMG had only come into existence then.

She had definitely made the right choice of going to Gerald. She did have doubts about his plan, but he knew how to get things done. With a development as significant as the NMG, Taylor needed someone like Gerald.

Immediately after meeting Dominga, Taylor had already felt comfortable about their hosts, even the dangerous-looking one, Doroteo. She wondered how the man would react if she called him the name she felt tempted to call him, Dorito. Imagining his possible reactions caused a quiet chuckle.

"I'll go get them," Cesar said.

He seemed to share her excitement at showing the NMG. While waiting for Cesar to fetch his friends, she and Gerald sat alone in the room and admired the surroundings.

"It's like we've jumped into a raging river," Gerald said. "The current has taken us, and we're not getting out."

After a few minutes, Dominga followed Cesar back into the room and then Doroteo appeared a few seconds later. The dark stubble on his face and disheveled hair made him appear much darker than the other two. His demeanor made Taylor laugh to herself again. He looked like a man recently pulled away from an enjoyable activity and forced to participate in an incredibly tedious one.

Despite his intimidating presence, Taylor did not fear him but thought of him as a mystery in need of discovery. If she ever needed help in a physical fight, she would want to have Doroteo on her side. She decided to put some extra effort into developing a relationship with him. Making friends with a lion required special effort.

The man ignored both Taylor and Gerald until he sat in a chair, then he turned and shot a brief but threatening look at them. Taylor met his gaze and then casually turned to the beautiful Mexican goddess. She rushed to Taylor's side, sat down, and put her hand on Taylor's knee.

"Is it true you will come live with us? This is so exciting! Another woman in this house to keep me company. Tell me it is no jest."

Dominga's excitement caused the last of Taylor's minor reservations to evaporate, including the one about her being jealous of another female in the house.

"It is no joke," said Taylor, failing to suppress a smile.

"This is better in more ways than one," said Gerald in a more serious tone but smiling. "Taylor could use some female mentoring."

Both Taylor and Dominga glared at him.

"She needs nothing of the sort, *Mister Foster*." Dominga attempted to say Gerald's name with a country twang. The barely-passable English accent made Taylor laugh again. "But yes, the first thing we're going to do is some shopping. You've brought me a beautiful doll. I must dress her up."

Doroteo spoke for the first time since entering the room, but unfortunately for Taylor and Gerald, he spoke in Spanish and directed his words to Cesar who responded in Spanish. Taylor waited patiently for Cesar to finish his response then she spoke directly to Doroteo.

"You do speak English, don't you?" Taylor looked first at Doroteo then at Cesar and finally at Gerald, who began to sink into his chair.

"Of course," Doroteo answered quickly with an accent thicker than Dominga's.

"I think you might be interested in what Taylor has to show you," interjected Gerald in an attempt to diffuse the tension that only he seemed to feel.

Taylor cared little for the social tension in the room. She just wanted to see Doroteo's response. In her opinion, the man needed someone to challenge him.

"Do you want to see?" Taylor asked, directing her gaze to Doroteo and then Dominga.

"Yes," Doroteo answered blandly.

Did she detect a hint of a smile on his lips? She removed the black box.

"Who wants to be the first one to try it?"

Dominga and Doroteo looked at each other hesitantly and then Dominga motioned for him to go ahead. Taylor stood and held out the box, and when Doroteo stepped forward to grab it, she smelled a hint of pipe tobacco on him. The strangely pleasant smell made her pause momentarily.

After explaining what to do, she stepped back to her seat and watched. He activated the box without hesitation. After flipping the switch, Taylor noticed with delight his jolt of surprise. He muttered something under his breath in Spanish then he looked at his friends in the room with an apparent question on his face.

He released the box slowly and watched as it rose into the air. When the box had reached several centimeters above his head, he realized that it would continue without stopping. He put his left hand on top of the box and held it motionless for a few seconds before dragging it below his head again.

Dominga put her hand on Taylor's shoulder, keeping her gaze on Doroteo. "Ay dios mio!" she exclaimed with her eyes fixed on the NMG. "Where did you get this thing?"

"I invented it," she said.

For the next minute, everyone watched Doroteo play with her invention. For his final trick, he pushed it to the floor and then let go again, watching it move silently upward. He seemed oblivious to those around him and looked like a child playing with his first yo-yo.

Reluctantly, Doroteo relinquished the black box and let Dominga play with it. She held the object as one might hold a twenty million dollar vase, afraid of causing harm. Taylor waited long enough for their excitement to diminish, so they could continue their conversation.

—✳—

As Taylor and Gerald explained their thoughts and plans, their captivated audience listened intently. She expected them to have a lot of questions or objections about their motives, but when explaining the topic of promoting more freedom, they sat quietly and showed no signs of disagreement.

When they talked about the possibility of flying to space, Taylor felt some anxiety, preparing for Doroteo to scoff at the idea. Surprisingly, Taylor seemed to care more for his opinion than the others.

"Of course," interrupted Taylor after Gerald explained his desire to gather more people. "All this might not work out, so we'll have to take it slowly, but I believe it's definitely something to pursue."

"I don't think going into orbit is as easy to accomplish as you think," Doroteo said politely.

"Why do you say that?" Gerald asked. "They shouldn't have enough time to stop us."

"As soon as you are detected on their radar or infrared detectors," he began as though explaining to a group of children, "you will be considered hostile. Before you even see them coming, you will be destroyed by a missile or a fighter jet. You are fooling yourselves if you think you can outrun them."

"I think you're being a bit paranoid, Doroteo," Taylor said. "Not every centimeter of sky is monitored by radar. I bet there are plenty of unmonitored places to quietly ascend. Besides, we can make something more maneuverable than anything they can make, at least in the upper atmosphere and space. Once we make it high enough, we'll be out of their reach."

"Overconfidence, Miss Evans," he said, "will get you killed."

"I'll keep that in mind." Taylor smiled, challenging him.

She would enjoy their future interactions.

Dominga sat back in the chair next to Taylor. "I'm sure they've thought of this, Doroteo," she said. "We've got time to work things out."

"How do you plan to avoid bringing attention to yourselves?" Doroteo asked, ignoring Dominga's comment.

His use of the word *you* instead of *we* gave Taylor the impression that he considered himself outside of their confidential group, not a part of it. He seemed to disagree with that part of the plan, but she thought he might be testing them, to see if they had thoroughly considered all the issues. Despite his antagonism, she felt comfortable having him know their secret.

"Right now, I'm more concerned about the fuel issue," she said.

"What do you mean?" asked Gerald. "I thought your invention made it much easier to do?"

Before she could respond, Cesar spoke.

"Yes, Gerald, her device is a monumental achievement, but it still will take a lot of energy to escape Earth's pull. Acquiring enough fuel, discreetly, is going to be one of our biggest obstacles."

Even with his thick accent, Cesar's vocabulary impressed Taylor.

"Gerald, we didn't talk about it last night because it's just one of many things that need to be worked out before we can accomplish what we want."

"Well, I'm glad that you and Cesar can figure it all out." Gerald put his hands behind his head and looked out the window. "Like I always say—"

"Where there's a will, there's a way," Taylor said, finishing his sentence. She followed his gaze and noticed the gray winter light beginning to fade. "Yes, Gerald, we know, but you get the easy part. We've got to figure out *the way* part."

"That's what I love about this whole thing," Gerald said, smiling.

"This is an engineer's dream, Gerald," said Cesar. "I feel fortunate that you recommended me to Miss Taylor. I cannot wait to get working on this. The energy requirement, however, is going to be a huge obstacle, but there might be a possible solution."

"And what is that?" asked Taylor staring intently at him.

"Well," he said, returning her question with a smile. "You provided one part of the solution to the age-old dilemma, acceleration. I think I might know of the required energy source, but it might not be easy to find if it exists at all."

TWENTY-FIVE

Taylor

Only three days after their first meeting, Taylor transported most of her possessions to Cesar's home. In vain, her mother attempted to dissuade Taylor from the action but soon capitulated when she saw the futility of arguing. Taylor put more effort than usual in convincing her mother that she did not need to worry. An older woman would live with them and they would be working long hours on a time-sensitive project. Living somewhere else made no sense.

She neglected to tell her mother the specifics of the project, and her mother neglected to ask. Her mother rarely asked for technical details anyway and hardly ever understood when Taylor tried to explain. Usually, her mother felt satisfied knowing that her daughter was working on a project that might become profitable.

"This could be big, Mom," Taylor said in the hopes of instilling additional reassurance. "But I don't want too many people to know what we're doing. You can't spill any milk if your glass is empty, right?"

Cesar gave Taylor the room next to Dominga. Although she was delighted with the size of the room, the atmosphere was too feminine for her taste. The window curtains and bed had too much lace, and too many of the blankets and pillows contained excessive amounts of pink. But she never considered complaining over such trivial matters and decided to change some things, eventually.

For the present, she just wanted to keep Dominga happy. The woman had taken too much pleasure in furnishing the room for Taylor to say anything negative. Seeing Dominga's delight also helped curb the guilt she felt for receiving so much attention.

When Taylor finally felt settled, she wanted to start working immediately. But Dominga had other plans for her, and Taylor lacked the social energy to refuse when Dominga demanded that they spend the first two days shopping.

Despite Taylor's weak protests, Dominga managed to accomplish her overall mission and treated Taylor like the daughter she'd never had. Coming from her less-than-fortunate financial situation, as Dominga liked to say, Taylor felt uncomfortable receiving so much attention and gifts from the woman. But as she quickly learned, Dominga seemed to have no concern about money or price.

Dominga rarely looked at the price tag and only haggled over the price for amusement and a feeling of accomplishment. Taylor required only a few hours with the woman to appreciate her skill at manipulation while she kept her victim ignorant of the process. Dominga effortlessly maneuvered through difficult conversations, acting oblivious to tension and social barriers.

"When I discovered that Cesar was driven out of Mexico, away to the USA," Dominga said on their second day of shopping. "I told myself that I must visit him and help in the transition."

Taylor followed Dominga like a puppy through several clothing stores at a local shopping mall, places she would never choose to visit on her own. Expensive clothing went against her moral code, especially clothing made by cheap labor, enriching business owners she might otherwise despise. That much money could also be better spent on parts for her projects.

"Of course," Dominga continued, "he tried convincing me it was unnecessary, but that was only the polite way a gentleman would answer. I could tell from his tone of voice, however, that he had no real objections and most likely suffered from less refined company. Can you blame him? Imagine what it would be like to have Doroteo as your only companion. Yes, their friendship goes back to childhood, but can you imagine that man's effect on your spirit? Oh, I could not abandon Cesar to that fate."

"Of course," she said conspiratorially. "I have nothing personal against the man, you understand. It's just that he's a fish from a different pond. I have not had much luck engaging him in conversation. What little I do manage to squeeze out of him usually leads nowhere."

"I can understand that," said Taylor, smiling.

Dominga had several blouses slung over one arm, and with her other hand, she held a blouse to Taylor's neck to see how it looked. She did not bother to ask for Taylor's opinion. After gathering a few more items, Taylor followed Dominga to a dressing room. She put on the first pair of pants, looked at herself in the mirror, then took a deep breath and sighed before going out to show Dominga. She lost count that day of how many times she'd had to dress and then undress, a task she usually performed only once a day.

When she exited the dressing room, Dominga clapped her hands together in delight. "Those pants fit you very well, but I must say, the top is not as flattering as I imagined it. Here, try this one instead. Are you sure you won't try the skirt?"

Taylor had politely refused to wear any skirts and Dominga made no additional serious attempts to convince her. Pants felt more comfortable. Usually when purchasing clothes, if she could not see herself cutting or polishing metal or welding in them, she would put them back on the hanger.

During lunch on the second day of shopping, they ate in the mall food court.

"You must forgive me," began Dominga, "for stealing you away from what you came here to do. I understand that this is not exactly what you would do of your own choice."

"Not normally," Taylor agreed. She failed to think of a good reason to paint a false picture of herself. "Although, I am enjoying your company."

"That's good of you to say. I cannot say how enjoyable this has been for me. You are a gift from the gods, Taylor Evans. Now, it's overdue for me to shut up and let you talk. There are many things I must learn about you."

"Like what?"

"For one, I see you possess the same hatred of authority as Cesar and Gerald. For what they did to Cesar and his poor family, there is no forgiveness or reason. But the one thing I want to understand is the reason for *your* feelings. You are young and I cannot imagine what could have happened to make you feel the same way. Something must have happened! I am right, am I not? One of your main purposes is to escape our oppressive systems. But why? Cesar has told me of Gerald's reasons, but you are a mystery, Taylor. I must know."

Taylor paused for a few seconds and looked down at her food. At first, she could not meet Dominga's eyes. The woman seemed to have some magic, a spell to strip Taylor's reservations away. She also felt as though Dominga deserved to know her story. The older woman genuinely cared for Taylor and had devoted all of her time to making her feel welcome. Taylor decided just to start talking and ignore her usual reserve.

"When my older brother joined the army, I told him he was crazy. I knew the military works for big business and not for any ideology like freedom or the American way, whatever that is. He went anyway, and after a year, he returned broken. They sent him home for PTSD or some other bullshit excuse. He refused to talk about his experiences and then one day..."

She paused and looked up into Dominga's big brown eyes and realized her own had filled with tears, almost ready to slide down her cheeks. She'd never told the whole story to anyone, not even Gerald. He thought that her brother had died in the war, which is the story she allowed him to believe. She had hardly even discussed the matter with her mother. But before any tear escaped, anger returned and stopped the flood.

"I'm okay," Taylor said before continuing. "A few weeks after coming home, he committed suicide."

"Such a waste," said Dominga with a mixture of anger and sadness. She grasped Taylor's hand. "It takes courage to accept the truth of it, that they are unnecessary deaths, that they are the victims of hidden agendas of evil men. Most people try to console themselves by making the tragedy sound either patriotic or to fulfill some higher purpose."

Taylor felt no need to pause now that she had started talking. She felt good, surprisingly, talking about the tragedy that had affected her so much. Dominga had a way of making Taylor want to continue.

"I think of his death as a murder, really. I didn't start functioning until about two weeks after the funeral. My father never got over it. He was depressed and angry for two years. Then he got sick."

"And then he died too," Dominga said, figuring out the connection. Dominga's boldness surprised Taylor. She spoke as though completely unafraid of saying something offensive or anything that might trigger a negative emotional response. "Oh, my poor girl. Some people have too much sorrow in their lives, don't they? What has gotten you through it?"

"Can't let it control you," Taylor answered. "Besides, I'm the only thing my mother has left."

"I must meet her one day."

"Yes, you should." Taylor smiled.

"It must make you angry to think about it," continued Dominga. "Do you ever desire revenge?"

"Sometimes I daydream of an asteroid destroying the White House or the mansion of an infamous banking family." Taylor took a deep breath. "If there's no justice at the end of this life, that's when I'm gonna be pissed."

PART II

DISCOVERY

A ring of fire gold
Ready for a steady hand
In a wet bed of cold

TWENTY-SIX

Taylor

Before Dominga relinquished control of Taylor's time, Cesar had tentatively suggested, on several occasions, that Taylor begin working at the shop with him. But Dominga had dismissed him with a wave of her hand and a smile, and eventually, Cesar lost all hope of acquiring his new shop partner for the immediate future. Taylor noticed the impatience in his polite smile whenever Dominga told him about their plans for the day.

Despite her anxiety at postponing their project, Taylor enjoyed their time together getting better acquainted, and she pretended not to notice the private exchanges between Cesar and Dominga about the delay.

Although Dominga refused to reveal any romantic feelings for Cesar, Taylor suspected she had been in love with him for a long time and had spent her time there hoping for Cesar to someday reciprocate her affection.

From what Taylor could see, nothing romantic was occurring between them. Taylor suspected the death of Cesar's wife and sons was preventing any romantic activity on his part. Taylor had moved on after losing her brother, but she imagined that losing a wife and children was much more devastating.

After Cesar had suggested the possibility of another energy source, he sent Gerald on a quest to find it. Taylor still had serious doubts he would find anything, but for their sake, she had pretended to be optimistic. She remembered how excitedly Cesar had spoken about the possibility, which was her only reason to doubt that Gerald had gone on a fool's errand.

—✻—

"As soon as I heard news reports about the electrochemists at the University of Utah," Cesar said to Gerald, "and they claimed to have discovered cold fusion, I followed the story like you Americans follow your football teams. If it was real, I knew the people behind the Department of Energy would fight to stop it."

"But wasn't it disproven?" Gerald asked. "That's all I heard."

"There's a lot more to the story, Gerald," Cesar explained calmly. "Dr. Pons was the head of the chemistry department. Don't you think it a little bit suspicious that the head of a chemistry department at a major university would make such an announcement to the press if he hadn't verified it beforehand? That's something you don't take lightly. These were very intelligent people."

Gerald sat forward in his seat.

"I guess I didn't follow it all that closely. It happened in my *following-the-herd* years."

Taylor wished she could use Wikipedia to resuscitate her memory of the story highlights. Since Cesar and Gerald remembered watching the events on the news and in the newspapers, they were more aware of the details. For Taylor, the story existed with all the other countless historical curiosities. There were too many of them to investigate.

If the energy and finance industry had intentionally squashed the story of cold fusion, or whatever the chemists had discovered, then Cesar could be on the right track. A powerful energy source such as fusion could considerably simplify their task of space flight. Taylor listened with interest but did not want to elevate her hopes too high. Even though Cesar's explanation made sense and Gerald could probably reveal more of the true story, the solution seemed too easy and convenient.

Cesar smiled politely at Gerald's comment then continued.

"Right after the announcement was made, the Department of Energy, which everyone knows is controlled by the oil and finance industry, met with the president. They claimed interest in investigating the matter to see if it was true. All the evidence, however, shows that they were only planning how to bury the discovery and discredit the men who made the announcement."

"Sorry to interrupt you, Cesar," interjected Dominga. "But *why* would they want to disprove it?"

"For years," he said, turning to her, "governments all over the world have been pouring billions of dollars into high-temperature fusion. Billions and billions of dollars, and can you guess where all that money goes? To very powerful corporations.

"The recipients of that immense treasure want to keep the money flowing, but I believe there's a deeper reason. It requires big government. Since all that money goes to huge existing companies, it is a self-sustaining strategy. If high-temperature fusion ever becomes viable, it will keep the current power structure in place. Only the big companies will be able to control the energy production process, and those are the same companies profiting from all of the public spending. Of course, there's always the possibility that the research will never produce anything. They win either way and as usual, the public loses."

The more Cesar talked, the more excitement Taylor felt, so she interjected. "So, if something simple and easy to produce, as cold fusion seemed to be, was developed and viable, smaller companies could afford to utilize it. Local communities could provide their own energy needs."

Cesar finished for her. "Which would result in more local independence. And that's exactly what the big financial institutions don't want. They love big government spending. It keeps their accounts full. Those who have the power never want to lose any of the market share."

"Okay," Gerald said, trying to make sense of the new viewpoint. "If cold fusion was real, how did they keep it from being developed? Some company was bound to see the possibility and work on it."

"How familiar are you with how scientific research works?" Cesar asked.

"I've had no direct experience, so I probably don't know that much about it."

"The first thing you should know, it's like everything else in life. Funding is everything. Whoever controls the money determines what research gets funded and what gets discarded. The same people who control research funding also fund our politicians. All they had to do was to use the media to stigmatize Pons and Fleischmann.

"They made cold fusion a joke and then no one wanted to touch it. Those with a vested interest in hot fusion had a strong motivation to stop the research from going forward, and they have a limitless amount of money for the fight. Stop the funding of a thing and you stop that thing from development. It's like keeping sunlight away from the crops."

"Government agencies do control the majority of research," Taylor admitted, remembering how many of her professors were always focusing on their next government research grant.

"I've got something for you, Gerald, that may help you start your investigation. It's a book by a science reporter from MIT. He did a lot of research on cold fusion and was involved with how they tried to discredit it."

Cesar stood and walked from the room. When he returned, he handed Gerald a book entitled, *Fire from Ice*, by Eugene Mallove.

"So, I'm the one to investigate this?" Gerald asked, inspecting the cover.

"Taylor and I have to optimize the NMG designs and build an escape plan. If anyone can get to the bottom of something, it's you. Remember that if there's something to be found, it's going to be a secret. I believe that's what you love uncovering, right? I've been wanting to make my own investigation for a long time."

Gerald opened the book and began flipping through the pages. "Thanks for the vote of confidence. After reading the book, I might just visit the author."

"That would be a good place to start," said Cesar, shaking his head, "but it might be difficult."

"Why is that?"

"Eugene Mallove was allegedly murdered after publishing the book," he said sadly. "And just last year, the prime suspects in the case were acquitted. The whole incident could be a psychological operation, a diversion, but it is very suspicious and there's a chance it could be authentic. Either way, there's something to be found!"

TWENTY-SEVEN

Gerald

Gerald left Seattle and attempted to follow the last few months of Eugene Mallove's life. He read the book Cesar gave him along with all other information he could find about the man. While reading the police reports, court records, and media material, he knew that key information had been either missed or deliberately omitted. The lawyer who had defended the murder suspects had been a fool or worked secretly for the prosecution. Gerald considered visiting that attorney but decided it was too dangerous.

After consuming all of the evidence and court proceedings, he came to the same conclusion as Cesar. The man's alleged death had been much more than just a random act of violence. Most of Mallove's relatives and friends refused to discuss the subject with him, saying they had already told the police everything.

Gerald had made only one useful interview, an old woman who claimed to have known Eugene Mallove since his childhood. Old age had undoubtedly inflicted damage to her coherency, but Gerald had managed to extract one useful piece of information. Just before his murder, Mallove had returned from a trip to Utah. Gerald knew he would have to visit Salt Lake City next.

Before finishing the conversation with her, the ninety-three-year-old woman leaned forward, her eyes filling with sudden lucidity. She grabbed Gerald's arm with cold bony fingers. As she spoke, he fought the unexpected instinct to escape her grasp.

"They killed him, you know. Murdered him for what he knew and what he was trying to do. I told him to be careful, but he never listened to me. He thought that being a famous hotshot reporter would protect him. He was so naive and now he's dead."

After a few seconds, her firm grip relaxed and reverted to cold weak bones covered by loose skin. She smiled sweetly, but the gesture failed to erase his sense of foreboding. He would remember her last words with extra clarity, spoken with a trembling voice.

"Don't let them know where you've been. Cover your tracks!"

"I'll be careful," he told her.

Gerald thanked her and then quickly left her house.

He traveled next to Connecticut, to the apartment complex where Mallove was murdered. While standing at the place where they had found the dead body, Gerald wondered how other lawyers felt, the ones who defended or prosecuted people accused of murder. When they visited the crime scene, they had to imagine being the murderer. Gerald hated being so close to violence and felt glad to have chosen a different legal specialty, one where he mostly helped small business owners maneuver through the legal minefields that large corporations had lobbied congressmen to enact.

Gerald visited one of the older neighborhood residents who also knew about Mallove's final trip to Utah and even remembered the name of someone Mallove had visited, a man named Ammon. The unique name stuck in his memory.

Gerald returned to his hotel room and spent over an hour investigating the name, *Ammon*, and then found an interesting connection to a company in Salt Lake City named *Cerametrics*. One of the company executives had the first name of Ammon and had been a lab assistant to Dr. Pons at the University of Utah, the same professor who had announced to the world that they had discovered cold fusion.

After discovering the connection between Ammon and cold fusion, Gerald had difficulty keeping his excitement under control. He booked a flight to Salt Lake City that same day, and the next day he went to the airport and started his journey back to the West. On the flight, he wondered what he would find, either the final piece of the puzzle or a dead end. He had a feeling that Salt Lake City would be his final destination.

—✳︎—

When Gerald entered the visitor parking lot of the Cerametrics Corporation in Salt Lake City, he noticed freshly sprinkled salt all over the pavement. Remains from the recent snowstorm had just been cleared from the area. Huge piles of snow were deposited in the corners of the lot like some hastily erected fortress. The white snow would have been pretty, if not for the brown slush that stuck to everything. Just looking at all the frozen material made Gerald cold. He missed the warmer winter rains of Seattle.

He walked through the entrance and found a receptionist sitting at the front desk, staring at a computer screen. From the reflection on her thick glasses, Gerald could see her browsing the internet. When she noticed the stranger standing in front of her, she quickly clicked on the screen, erasing evidence of her indolence.

"Hello, sir," she said, her nasal passage slightly blocked by a cold. Her forced smile seemed as warm as the slush outside. She squinted to get a better look at him and sat up straighter, probably after noticing the suit and tie. "Who are you here to see?"

"Ammon Brown. He won't be expecting me today." Gerald leaned closer to the desk and put his hand on the counter between them. "Please tell him that Mr. Jones is here to see him."

Before arriving, he remembered his visit with the old woman back East when she had warned him to be careful with his name. Gerald hoped Ammon knew someone with the last name of Jones.

The receptionist sat back in response to his proximity. "Is this a personal visit?"

"No," Gerald said without elaborating.

The receptionist picked up her phone, dialed, and then talked so quietly that Gerald only heard a slight mumble. He failed to distinguish any recognizable words and tried to show disinterest, but he kept his eyes on her lips. After the call, she looked at Gerald with evident suspicion. He guessed that Ammon had very few surprise visitors.

"He'll be down in a few minutes. Please have a seat."

A few minutes later, a man came around the corner of the main entrance area. He stood shorter than Gerald by several centimeters while much thicker at the waist. He wore a button shirt with horizontal stripes and no tie. When he saw Gerald sitting alone in the lobby with only the receptionist, he slowed his pace and squinted in a blatant attempt to identify Gerald.

"Excuse me, Mr. Jones?" he asked after stopping in front of Gerald. "Have we met previously? Am I expecting you?"

Gerald extended his hand with as warm a smile as he could create.

"I apologize for coming to your place of employment, unannounced. I just wanted to know if I could arrange a time to meet with you, possibly for lunch this afternoon?"

From the corner of his eye, Gerald saw the receptionist look up from her computer at him, and he wondered if she would pick up the phone and call security. Then she turned back to her computer screen, probably enticed by a message on some social networking site.

The man had stopped smiling.

"What is this concerning?"

"I'd rather not go into detail here," Gerald said, leaning closer and lowering his voice so that only Ammon could hear him. "I have some questions about Eugene Mallove."

At the name of Mallove, the man's body stiffened and his eyes suddenly opened wider. He looked like a man attempting to make a difficult decision, whether to flee, melt on the spot, or start crying. After a moment, Ammon seemed to recover slightly.

"Whom, may I ask, do you represent?"

"Maybe I can take you to lunch, or we can just talk in your office?" In an attempt to calm the man, Gerald spoke as politely as he could. If Ammon experienced too much anxiety, he would be more difficult to handle. "Just me and no one else, at whatever place of your choosing. Today or tomorrow would suit my schedule the best. I hope you can spare some time."

"I'm very sorry, Mr. Jones," he said. "I have no idea what you're talking about. I know nothing about the man."

Gerald had hoped to act non-threatening, but now he decided that Ammon needed just a little additional motivation.

"Are you sure you want that to be your official statement, Mr. Brown?"

"Where are you from?" Ammon's voice seemed to contain some courage, but his body language contradicted his confidence. "I could call security."

"What's the harm in talking with me and me alone? If you want, we could go to your office and talk there, if it's secure. I am not from the government, or the energy industry, if that's what you're afraid of."

Gerald took one step back, to give the man some more room. Ammon ran his fingers through his hair and looked back the way he had come as though he still wanted to run away. He looked at his watch before answering and when he spoke, Gerald could barely hear him.

"Listen, I really don't know what this is about," he said softly. "I will meet with you today, but not for lunch. I can meet you later this afternoon around four pm. We can meet downtown at Temple Square, at the Christus statue. Just go to the North Temple Square entrance, and I'll meet you at the top of the visitor's center. You can't miss it."

Gerald looked up as though considering the location. He wanted the man to feel as though he was in control of the situation.

"That's fine, but what's the *Christus*?"

"It's the statue of Jesus in the North LDS Visitors' Center," Ammon said curtly. "It's a very prominent landmark. If you want to meet with me, that's where it's going to be. If you'll excuse me, I have to get back to work."

"Thank you," Gerald said as Ammon turned to walk away.

"I'll see you at four," the man said without turning.

Gerald watched Ammon until he disappeared from view. Before leaving the reception area and exiting the building, Gerald glanced back and noticed the secretary looking at him. When their eyes met, she did not look away or return his smile.

TWENTY-EIGHT

Gerald

When back in the warmth of his car, Gerald sat and wondered if he had ever heard of the Mormon Visitors' Center. He had never visited Salt Lake City before and knew only the general history of the city. According to his memory, the Mormons had been the first to establish the city and had made their headquarters there. Why had they moved there? Gerald did not know.

Since Ammon wanted to meet at the Mormon center, Gerald guessed that the man identified as a Mormon. Had Ammon expected to feel some sort of spiritual safety at that location or did he just want to meet somewhere crowded? Maybe both reasons were true.

Whether or not he could extract any useful information from Ammon, Gerald anticipated an interesting meeting. At the least, he might learn more about the city and its people. As a lawyer, learning about people and their motivation might benefit him one day.

Since Gerald had several hours to kill before the meeting, he decided to find the place, which was located in a large complex called Temple Square. He parked a few streets away from Temple Square, in the shadow of the Mormon temple, and used his iPhone to read about the city on Wikipedia. He learned about the founder of the city,

Brigham Young, and how he had wanted the temple to be the center of the city both psychologically and geographically. They had based the coordinates of the whole valley in relation to the temple and then built the Temple Square Visitors' Center.

He exited his car and looked up at the Temple. The immense granite building towered over the streets, cold, gray, and solid. While not the largest building in the city, it seemed like the most substantial and impenetrable, like an ancient German castle. A golden statue sat atop one of its six spires, shining brightly against the cloudy sky.

When Gerald got close enough to the building, he noticed strange symbols carved on the surface of the white marble walls. They looked like strange, astrological symbols and gave Gerald the impression that Mormons worshiped mythological beings other than what he knew from traditional Christianity.

While thinking about those who had founded the city, the persecuted group Wikipedia described, Gerald began to reflect on Christianity and religion in general. The topic rarely intruded on his conscious thoughts even though he worked with many people who identified as Christians.

Religion had never been a part of his life. His grandparents had identified as Presbyterians in name only but had failed to instill any religious beliefs in their children. As far as he could remember, his grandparents had never talked about their religious beliefs or encouraged him to participate in any religious tradition other than Christmas. During his adulthood, he often felt relief from his lack of religious indoctrination.

In his opinion, all traditional religions were nonsense. He saw no difference between believing in fairies and ogres and believing in angels and gods, beings who mysteriously and arbitrarily assisted humans in their lives. The concept seemed extremely contradictory. Invisible creatures helped humans but mysteriously left no evidence of that help. The behavior implied they were forbidden from being nice and acted in rebellion.

—✳—

After walking around downtown for a while and getting some lunch, he decided to go to the place where he would later meet Ammon Brown. But instead of entering Temple Square through the north entrance as Ammon had suggested, Gerald entered through the west entrance, which he found by chance. He had almost an hour before the meeting, so he decided to walk for a while and just explore the surroundings.

Despite his negative assessment of religion, the place instantly impressed him. The Mormon church kept the grounds very clean, and although many people walked around him, he had plenty of space. Little islands with cement walls were filled with different plants, mostly flowers and trees. Small piles of snow lay on the ground next to the walls. The cold air felt crisp and clean in his lungs.

A pair of young women approached him shortly after he passed through the gate. Initially, he thought they were from some international conference, but then he noticed the black name tags with *The Church of Jesus Christ of Latter-Day Saints* printed on them. The shorter woman looked like a native of Southeast Asia, and the taller one looked as though she came from somewhere in Latin America. He usually would have politely expressed disinterest in a religious discussion, but not when two beautiful women wanted to talk to him.

In two previous incidents, male missionaries from the Mormon church had asked to talk with Gerald. During the first encounter, he had politely asked them a few questions but with only mild interest. But when they had told him about their motivation for leaving home, to serve their church and God, Gerald had almost laughed at their rehearsed response and felt tempted to ask if they wanted to try again.

After that first experience, he had read some material about the church's history, about Joseph Smith, gold plates, and angels. Gerald had found their early history very interesting, especially as it related to the early American revivalist culture, but he wondered how the organization had survived. When the next pair of missionaries had asked to talk with him, he declined.

"Thank you, but I know everything I need to know about your religion."

The young women in Temple Square politely asked Gerald about his visit and seemed genuinely interested in him. They told him about some of the buildings and how Brigham Young had founded the city, including the temple.

When they started talking solemnly about the founder of the church, Joseph Smith, Gerald had to force himself to keep smiling politely. He felt sorry for the two beautiful young women. They most likely lacked any knowledge of the real Joseph Smith. They seemed happy to be missionaries though, so Gerald would not attempt to challenge their view of reality.

No matter what he thought about religion, Gerald had to admit that the Mormon church understood marketing. If the church chose to use their male missionaries in their visitors' center, they might drive people away rather than toward it. He sincerely wanted to talk with the girls more but wanted to arrive at the meeting place before Ammon. After a few minutes of talking, he asked them where he could find the statue of Jesus, the Christus.

"Enjoy your visit, Gerald," the taller girl said after pointing to a building behind him.

"Thank you."

On his short walk to the statue, Gerald began to understand the reason why Ammon wanted to meet him there. The trees, flowers, pensive statues of pioneers, and protective walls seemed to transport him into a different world, an oasis from the commotion of the city.

If Ammon expected supernatural beings to protect him, Gerald hoped he would also act less cautiously and maybe reveal more information than usual. The desire to meet in a safe place, protected by some deity, might indicate that Ammon possessed dangerous information, the same information that had led to the death of Eugene

Mallove, something not included in the book he had already published.

When he looked up at the two-story building, Gerald noticed the giant statue of Jesus in the window. *This is the right place,* he thought and laughed, remembering the quote from Brigham Young.

The statue of Jesus stood on the second floor in front of a large window, his arms outstretched. The statue suddenly reminded Gerald of an ancient Greek God, the one from his strange dream experience. If the statue had had black hair and a slightly sharper nose, he would have looked like the scary man from his dream. After shivering from a sudden chill, Gerald took a deep breath and then snapped a few pictures of the building with his phone. He hoped to look like a tourist.

His watch showed three twenty-five, just a little while before he expected Ammon to arrive, probably to look for him ahead of time. Before entering the building, Gerald searched the area for anyone suspiciously looking at him. He felt as if they were playing a game, with Gerald playing the part of a covert agent and Ammon playing the secret government scientist.

After entering the building, Gerald became conscious of the temperature again and enjoyed the transition from freezing to comfortably warm. Many more tourists were inside the building than outside, including several other young female missionaries. Most of the people dressed nicely as though waiting to take part in some formal event.

Gerald noticed some escalators going to a lower level and when he came close to them, he saw huge paintings on the walls below and felt tempted to visit them. But after a moment's thought, he decided against the diversion and reminded himself of his mission. He wanted to arrive at the meeting place before Ammon.

He followed a large winding walkway up to the second level, to the statue of Jesus. Huge paintings of planets, galaxies, and swirling cloud formations covered the ceiling and walls, and he felt as though he was walking through a planetarium dedicated to a fascinating combination of astronomy and Christian mythology. At the top of the winding walkway stood the Christus statue, arms outstretched in welcome.

Several people sat in the rows of benches between the statue and the huge circular windows. Gerald chose a seat in the back, where he could look from the statue to the people outside. After sitting on the soft cushioned bench, he took a deep breath and his body instantly relaxed.

While looking at the statue of Jesus, Gerald tried imagining how people felt centuries in the past, before Christianity. He wondered how they felt when visiting the temples of their gods and bowing down to their beloved stone icons. The common person probably had little experience with art and elaborate dwellings. The experience must have filled them with amazement and perhaps a good dose of fear and intimidation.

After his brief moment of contemplation, Gerald realized that the situation remained the same. Despite all of the information available to the common person, the majority still believed in what these monuments represented—the validity of their institutions.

Did people like the idea of someone more intelligent leading them? That thought did offer comfort, he admitted, for an omniscient being to be in control of everything. The concept removed all accountability from the individual and eliminated the burden of critical thinking. For a small moment, Gerald wished he could have that luxury.

"I still can," he whispered sarcastically.

He sat through several short presentations, given by two different female missionary pairs. The presentation included a recording of a deep male voice quoting biblical passages. After the first iteration, Gerald began watching the people sitting in front of him. Mostly, they appeared to be a mixture of Mormon tourists and local church members. Many families came with their children, and Gerald stopped counting how many times a parent shushed a child for a small disturbance.

After the third presentation, he watched Ammon ascend the walk-way and enter the large upper room. He looked around and did not see Gerald at first, due to a small group of young adults standing in his way. When their eyes finally locked in recognition, Gerald stood and smiled.

TWENTY-NINE

Gerald

Ammon shook Gerald's hand and then sat next to him. "We can talk here," he said, looking around the room suspiciously. The gesture made Gerald a little paranoid, but he acted untroubled.

"Excuse me for asking, but I'm just curious," Gerald said. "Why did you want to meet here, in this place?"

"This is as good a public place as any. I did not want to meet at a restaurant." Ammon took a deep breath and sighed as if emotionally exhausted after a long day at work. "Before we talk about anything, can I see some form of identification?"

"Of course," Gerald said and opened his wallet. He handed his driver's license to Ammon and then a business card. "You will notice that my name's not Jones, as I said at your work. I didn't want your receptionist to know my real name, but I don't care if you know. Just as you expect confidentiality from me, I also expect it from you. I work at a small law firm. You can look it up if you want. Are you still worried that I'm lying about my identity?"

Ammon looked at both pieces of identification, studying them for anything out of the ordinary. He did not seem disturbed by Gerald's use of an alias.

"One cannot be too cautious."

While Ammon inspected the license and business card, Gerald glanced over at the statue and then at a man facing them. The man was not looking at Gerald or Ammon but appeared to be looking out the window. While everyone else took pictures of the statue, the man seemed to be aiming his camera at them. Gerald had the distinct feeling of being watched, but then the man turned around and took a couple of snapshots of the marble Jesus. Ammon cleared his throat and handed the license back to Gerald and then put the business card in his jacket pocket.

Before beginning his prepared statement, Gerald rehearsed it in his mind again. Like most things in the real world, his story would contain elements of truth and fabrication, and he expected Ammon's story to be similarly composed. Gerald might be required to do extensive interrogation to gain an accurate understanding of the situation, but he did that for a living and usually got what he wanted.

"Let me start at the beginning," Gerald began, changing to a business tone. "Our client contacted us two months ago because he was being questioned concerning the death of Eugene Mallove. There have been no arrests made yet, neither has he been named as a suspect, but they're showing signs of getting ready to do so. We're preparing a defense against the district court's possible allegations of his involvement in the murder. You are aware of the case? Right?"

"Why do you say that?"

"Prior to the cold fusion announcement at the University of Utah, you worked as a laboratory assistant to Dr. Pons, and Dr. Mallove was one of the few defenders of cold fusion. He must have been around the lab where you worked. Did you ever meet him? What do you know about the murder?"

"I read about the murder of course, but what makes you think I have any special information about it?"

"Do you know what I think of it all?" Gerald asked, changing his angle of attack.

Ammon's brown eyes opened wide. "I have no idea."

"The original arrests they made in connection with the murder smelled of federal interference. Someone higher up wanted that case closed, and they didn't care if they got the right guys or not."

Ammon looked interested for the first time.

"What makes you think that?"

"After looking into the case, I saw nothing substantial to tie those guys with the murder. It was one of the flimsiest cases I've seen yet. Did you know, the two charged with the murder were exonerated just last year? Seems convenient, doesn't it? After the public forgets about the case."

"No," Ammon said. "I didn't know they were exonerated."

Gerald thought Ammon seemed more familiar with the case than he intimated. Before Ammon could continue, Gerald did.

"I read the book by Mallove too. He was quite the defender of cold fusion."

"I knew about the book," admitted Ammon. "He might have made some of the wrong people angry, for exposing what he did."

"I know about the conspiracy theories," Gerald said as though un-interrupted. He wondered if Ammon was starting to lower his defenses. "About how the oil industry doesn't want something like cold fusion being developed. I don't know if I completely agree. I think it goes to a higher level than that. Tell me, since you worked with Dr. Pons, what do you think about how the scientific establishment seemed to work with the media to discredit the claims? Were they really frauds?"

Ammon spoke more quietly, sounding offended but also worried. "Do you really think we would take that to the press without being absolutely certain of what we had found? Pons and Fleischmann spent years verifying the data!"

"If Mallove was killed for exposing a cover-up, why did they wait for him to publish the book?" Gerald gave no time for Ammon to reply. "I don't think they care as much about revenge as they care about letting the technology get developed. Mallove must have done something after his book was published."

"This is what I'm investigating now, tracking his activity before he died. If things go the same way they did before, concerning the murder suspects, I'm going to need hard evidence as to the motive for the murder. We need the correct motive, and that will keep my client in the clear."

"Seeking the truth, huh," Ammon said sarcastically. "And a lawyer too!" He laughed for the first time then glanced up to the statue of Jesus. "Lawyers were always fighting with him."

Gerald laughed politely, accustomed to lawyer jokes, but he felt unsure if Ammon was joking or being serious. He had expected the man to broach the subject of religion sometime in the conversation.

"The truth of cold fusion will get out, eventually," he said quietly. "God won't allow it to be suppressed forever."

"How do you think God will do that and when?" Gerald asked with a tone of sincerity.

"Seek and ye shall find," Ammon said gravely. "Someday, enough people will seek, and he will lead them to it."

Gerald suddenly thought of two questions: Why did God need enough people to seek to reveal the truth, and what was the magic number of people? Ammon looked up at the statue again and Gerald followed his gaze. Jesus appeared as though looking at them in disapproval and Gerald had to look away. The statue suddenly looked too similar to the dangerous man from his dream.

During the brief pause, Gerald wondered if he was ready to accuse Ammon of what he suspected, that Eugene Mallove had visited Cerametrics before his death. Or did Ammon need more probing? Gerald required only a moment to realize that he needed to divert the conversation away from religion, to more concrete matters where Gerald felt more comfortable.

"What exactly is the truth of cold fusion?" Gerald asked with reserved curiosity. "Is there more to it than what was presented in 1989?"

For the next few minutes, Ammon explained what he thought about cold fusion research. He attributed the absence of capital investment in research as the reason for the lack of progress. Even though several scientists at smaller institutions experimented with cold fusion, they did not have access to the funds necessary for sufficient development. To compound the problem, the media had effectively associated cold-fusion with lunacy and ineptitude, thereby cutting its financial umbilical cord.

If any scientist or researcher ever showed too much interest in cold fusion, they would be in danger of losing their jobs and reputations. Most of the public funds related to fusion were focused on hot plasma fusion. Ammon laughed bitterly about how hot fusion had failed to reach the break-even point yet, where the energy output equaled the energy input. In some of his experiments at the University of Utah, they multiplied the energy input by many times.

"Wait a minute," interrupted Gerald as if genuinely curious. "If that was the case, wouldn't they be using it to generate power commercially?"

Ammon stopped talking and looked at Gerald as if he had just crawled from some black abyss. For a moment, Ammon became speechless, and Gerald frantically attempted to think of the possible reason. From the look on his face, Gerald wondered if Ammon had said something unintended. When Ammon resumed speaking, he acted as if nothing had interrupted him.

"As with every new technology in its initial stages, the process was unstable and at times, unpredictable. At the time, we still hadn't understood the process. It's going to take a lot of money for the necessary research and development before they figure it out. I'm sorry I don't have anything to help you about the murder."

He turned to the window behind them and just looked outside.

Gerald continued, "Is it possible that Mallove was about to expose something new? Or perhaps he had something new?"

"Like I said. I don't know."

Gerald frowned. "You may be telling the truth, but I think you're holding something back. I'm holding something back too."

Gerald wondered what to tell him next, the truth about his real motives or what he knew about Mallove's visit to Cerametrics. Eventually, he might have to reveal both. Ammon turned from the window and looked directly into Gerald's eyes, silently waiting for him to continue.

"I know about Eugene Mallove's visit to Cerametrics," he said and then feared that his accusation would frighten Ammon too much. Gerald hoped that Ammon would think he also knew the reason for Mallove's visit when he had only a guess, a hope.

"If I found out about it," Gerald continued, "then there's a chance that government investigators will also stumble on it. But there's also a good chance that they won't, and if they do, they might put two and two together."

"Are you threatening us?" Ammon said, shifting uncomfortably in his seat. His demeanor suddenly transformed back to suspicion.

"No, I'm not threatening you," Gerald said, trying to suppress a smile. Ammon had not denied the accusation, implying the truth of it. "I'm just trying to find the motive for the murder."

"Yes, but your client is your top priority," Ammon said. He glanced up at the statue as if he expected Jesus to give him hand signals of what to do. "I know how you lawyers work, *save the client at all costs*. How do I know that you're not going to divert the investigation to Cerametrics? How do we know you are not working for the government?"

Gerald laughed loudly at this comment and glanced at a missionary at the base of the statue, talking on a microphone to the few people listening to her. At his outburst, several people turned to look at him.

"Sorry," he whispered silently then turned back to Ammon. "When you go home tonight, look up my name on Google and then my law firm. You'll see that the government and I are not exactly friendly with each other."

A simple search on Google would show his unsavory history with the government, or the FBI at least. Of course, Gerald's story could always be interpreted as an elaborate cover, an intelligence operation he would have difficulty proving false. But only a very few people thought that deeply, so he was not worried.

Gerald began to wonder if he should have fabricated the story of the client in the first place. Lying to Ammon in front of his god seemed the ultimate desecration. Did Ammon think that meeting in front of Jesus would prevent Gerald from saying anything dishonest?

"It's getting late," Ammon said. "Can we finish this discussion tomorrow?"

Gerald wondered if the time had come to bluff. He needed Ammon to tell him the reason for Mallove's visit to Cerametrics, but the man would probably keep that information secret. If Gerald had to guess about Mallove's visit, the reason might as well be what he hoped.

"Tomorrow, I need you to tell me what Mallove was planning to do with what you gave or showed him."

Ammon gulped, and to Gerald's surprise, he refused to deny the accusation, then he said, "I'll need a day to think about it."

THIRTY

Gerald

After agreeing to meet the next day, Ammon walked away without looking back, but he paused to look up at the statue of Jesus. "Probably gives him comfort," Gerald said to himself.

When Ammon disappeared from view, Gerald turned to look out the window one last time before leaving. The sun had set, and the scene looked much colder than before. He would rather stay inside in the warmth. But after a few minutes of sitting and watching the people outside, he reluctantly left the building.

On the return walk to his car, a tall pretty woman walking in his direction caught his attention and she gave him a friendly smile as she passed. Instinctively, he turned for a quick look at her walk away, but after turning, he noticed a man walking behind him. He wore a long black coat over a suit and tie. They made brief eye contact, and then Gerald faced forward again and continued walking. The situation could have been benign, but Gerald felt uneasy about it.

He heard the footsteps behind him for at least the next two turns of his path and kept his eyes ahead of him, trying to act casually. After the third turn, Gerald no longer heard his follower, so he quickly turned around for confirmation. After realizing that the man had gone, he sighed in relief.

Gerald had been followed before in his life, in Seattle and Kivu, a province in the Democratic Republic of the Congo when he had volunteered there with an aid group. During the most recent incident, undercover cops had followed him during his investigation of the Federal Reserve Bank break-in. He had tried confronting them, but they only denied his accusations, calling him crazy and paranoid. He remembered feeling foolish and frustrated. In the end, he decided just to ignore them and keep doing his business. Since he had nothing to hide, he let them waste their time and dealt with the situation as it progressed on its own.

As an aid worker in Kivu, soldiers sometimes followed his group. But during those incidents, the soldiers had made absolutely no attempt to hide their identity or purpose.

In the present situation, his paranoia rose to new levels. He tried to remain calm but could think only about the death of Eugene Mallove. To make the situation more complicated and dangerous, his current worries involved more than just himself. The lives of his friends depended on what happened. If Gerald noticed anything too suspicious the next day, he might have to delay the meeting until he felt safer.

After shutting the door to his hotel room and securing the deadbolt, he finally felt able to relax a bit. Once in bed, he had time to think. He missed the comforting sounds of his aquarium.

Since reality usually existed somewhere between two extremes, Gerald decided to assume the best possible case—he was suffering from baseless paranoia. But the best-case scenario rarely existed, unfortunately, so he had to consider the worst situation—clandestine government agents were watching and might kill him. If they existed and had kept Ammon under surveillance all this time, then Gerald would be under the same surveillance. In that worst-case scenario, he would need to make his visit to Cerametrics appear benign then quickly disappear and seek advice from Cesar and Doroteo.

After his concerns returned to baseline, Gerald considered an alternate situation, a much better possibility than the worst-case scenario. Perhaps one of Ammon's associates had followed him. Ammon was unlikely to have been working alone for this long of a time. Gerald had given him plenty of time to discuss the situation with his friends. If the positions had been reversed, Gerald probably would have had Ammon followed.

The next morning, Gerald stayed in his hotel room until ten o'clock then took a short walk outside. He wanted to see if anyone would follow him again. He saw no one suspicious. The bright light from another cold day helped him forget the paranoia of the previous evening. When he entered his warm car and shut the door, he felt better.

Nearly twenty-four hours after his first visit, Gerald returned to the lobby of Cerametrics. He encountered the same receptionist doing the same activity, pretending to work and shopping on *ubid.com*. He saw the website distinctly reflected on her glasses. After a few seconds of standing in front of her, she looked up.

"Hi, Mr. Jones," she began hesitantly. To his surprise, she had remembered his name. "Here to see Ammon?"

"Yes, I am. I'll wait for him here in the lobby."

"Okay, have a seat. I'll call him."

After a few minutes, Ammon entered the lobby wearing another forced smile, but he seemed less stressed than the previous evening. Perhaps the meeting at his religious sanctuary had helped him feel safer and more secure.

They shook hands and Gerald expected to be escorted to his office. But instead, Ammon said they were going on a drive.

"Where are we going?"

Instead of answering in the lobby, Ammon led Gerald outside to the parking lot. He spoke as they walked to his car.

"I discussed the situation last night with my friends and decided to give you the benefit of the doubt. I don't trust you completely, but I should know whether or not I can after today. Of course, it all depends on your level of cooperation."

Ammon opened the driver's side back door of his light blue Ford Escort and indicated for Gerald to sit. But instead of entering the vehicle, Gerald remained standing and held onto the top of the door.

"I need to know where we're going."

"Do you want to know why Eugene Mallove was murdered?"

"Yes," Gerald said, his excitement beginning to rise.

"Then get in the back and lie down. You cannot see where we are going. Understand?"

"You want me to lie down in the back?" Gerald asked while an irrational fear of wrinkling his suit passed through his mind. He had to suppress a laugh at such a superficial concern.

"Yes, or our meeting ends right here. If you prefer you can wear a mask, but that might look a little suspicious."

Gerald hesitated before getting in the back seat. "Can't I just sign a non-disclosure agreement?"

"Not good enough," Ammon said, failing to show any amusement at the joke. "Nothing bad will happen to you unless you're lying to me."

Gerald got in the back seat, but he sat erect. "And what if I'm telling the truth, but you still think I'm lying?"

Ammon sat in the driver's seat, shut the door then looked back.

"We'll know. Don't worry."

Ammon locked eye contact with him for a moment until Gerald relented and lay down. Either Gerald could follow their instructions, or he would have to determine another tactic. Even though the experience felt awkward, Gerald thought of the car ride as the final sprint to the finish line. How had Ammon and his friends downgraded the risk he represented? Had they made an internet search to verify his identity as he had suggested?

At the beginning of the ride, Gerald decided to keep quiet and just relax. But after about ten minutes, he tried asking Ammon about his family and personal life. The man kept his answers short and with little informative detail, so Gerald quit trying to make conversation. He also stopped attempting to keep track of all the turns. The whole ride took about forty minutes.

As the car slowed to a final stop, Ammon turned and extended a black stretchy hat over the back seat for Gerald to see.

"Here, put this over your head. We're going to get out."

Before sitting erect, Gerald stretched the hat over his head and eyes. The fabric was dense so he saw nothing but darkness. The experience reminded Gerald of Christmas morning as a kid when his father would lead them to the dining room, past the room with their presents.

When Gerald exited the car, the silence almost overwhelmed him. A light wind seemed to make the silence almost palpable, and the comforting sensation helped wash away some of his anxiety. He had only experienced that kind of silence in the Congo, but the cold created an entirely different experience. Gerald felt every ice crystal falling on his bare neck and hands.

As Ammon led him inside a building, Gerald had the distinct feeling of being watched by more than one pair of eyes. He instantly noticed the smells of mold and stagnant water. Without his sense of sight, the scent was much stronger. Ammon led him into a room and gently pulled him backward to sit on a chair. Surprisingly, he felt no fear.

"Can I take this thing off yet?" he asked after hearing the quiet click of a door handle.

Instead of answering, Ammon pulled the hat from Gerald's head and waited for his eyes to adjust to the light. Ammon stood before him in an empty room with a single light bulb hanging from the ceiling. Gerald quickly put his hand up to shield the light from his eyes, then turned to see the remainder of his surroundings. They had placed his chair in the middle of a large, empty room with old brick walls. He could see a window high up on the wall, but the glass was dark.

"Gerald," Ammon began, then paused to inhàle.

"I don't suppose you're going to tell me where I am?" Gerald interrupted.

"Not yet," Ammon answered while pulling a backpack over one shoulder. "Your location is not important. This is where we find out if you're being honest with us." He had attempted to speak confidently, but Gerald thought he acted as a man about to pull a bloody piece of meat from the mouth of a lion.

When Ammon removed a syringe from his backpack, Gerald scooted back in his seat. Seeing the cold metal made him shiver.

"Wait a minute, Ammon!" he said, his eyes opening wide. "I have no idea where I am, and now you expect to give me some drug? What's in the syringe?"

"Sodium thiopental," he said as calmly as possible. "It can be used as a truth serum, and it's completely safe."

Gerald turned around as though looking for a hidden camera. He wondered suddenly if a group of people watched him or if he should have felt afraid. When he returned to look at Ammon again, the man appeared completely harmless, and Gerald's anxiety decreased a bit. He would attempt to talk his way out of the situation, so he drew a deep breath before speaking.

"I am not letting you inject me with anything."

"You came here of your own free will," Ammon said. "I can take you back if you want, but this is the only way I can be satisfied."

"I cannot willingly consent to it," Gerald began, finally thinking of another valid reason to object. "It would be unethical. I have potentially damaging information, held in confidentiality for friends and clients. It would be unethical for me to put myself in a position to compromise their confidential information. I can't trust that you will attempt to extract only my sincerity and intentions. Therefore, I cannot let you inject me with that liquid."

"We may be at an impasse then," Ammon said while wiping his forehead. He looked deflated and unable to argue, and also a little impressed. "I am not the only individual who needs to trust you."

Gerald decided to use his last option, the truth.

"Listen, I'm willing to tell you whatever you need to know. I am willing to be completely honest with you."

"Completely honest?" Ammon asked with sudden suspicion. "Are you not who you say you are?"

"Not that," Gerald said and extended both hands in the air, palms toward Ammon. "I am Gerald Foster and a lawyer, just like I said I was. I was completely honest about that, but there is no client, or at least not the kind I implied. I have nothing, in any way, to do with Eugene Mallove's murder or any prosecution of it."

He paused to let the man comprehend the new information. Gerald anxiously watched his expression for any signs of anger. To his relief, Ammon reacted with curiosity.

"So who are your clients or friends then?"

"I am not at liberty to say," Gerald said, trying to sound reassuring. "But they mean you no harm in any way. They want to remain completely under the radar, anonymous like you. I haven't even told them about you, yet."

THIRTY-ONE

Taylor

While Taylor and Dominga shopped and explored Seattle, Cesar prepared for their work at his shop. He finished many of his current work orders or canceled them, and extended the remaining due dates. His single shop assistant chose to accept severance pay rather than wait until Cesar could hire him again, an indefinite amount of time. He also gave the man several referrals for other jobs. Taylor ignored her feeling of guilt for intruding on their lives, and she felt extra pressure to find success and not waste their time, or put them in any danger.

When Taylor and Cesar finally went to work, they were too busy to think much about Gerald and the status of his investigation. They only talked about the matter when Dominga or Doroteo asked about him at dinner. They were all waiting excitedly for Gerald to make his first progress update, Taylor probably more than the others. She considered the lack of updates to be either a good sign or a bad sign. Even if Gerald had no chance of success, at least the excitement of the chase would prevent him from getting in their way and keep himself busy.

"You have my undivided attention, Miss Taylor," Cesar had said during their first drive in the early morning darkness. "This is going to be an adventure."

"Yes it is," she had said, feeling excited for their first day at the shop. The yellow backpack had sat in her lap with the precious box inside.

Taylor spent the first couple of days teaching Cesar the technical aspects of how the NMG worked and the theory of operation. For a man of his age, Cesar surprised Taylor. He learned quickly and possessed an enormous capacity to accept and understand new concepts. She had expected him to fight the concept of the device's apparent violation of conservation of momentum.

Once Cesar was satisfied with his understanding, he wanted to start by making a more substantial prototype and incorporating better power couplings. Taylor found herself following his lead rather than what she had expected, leading the work. The older man had so many ideas, Taylor quickly gained a better appreciation of his talents and was even more glad for Gerald's suggestion to seek his help. His shop had nearly every machine they needed to build whatever they wanted. Her father's shop in Portland had a third of the space and only half the tools.

In just a few days, they made a test NMG device, bolted to the floor and connected to a force gauge to measure the output. No matter how many times they tested their creation, Cesar would shake his head in disbelief.

"If I had not seen it for myself, I would not have believed."

"Typical human response," Taylor said, laughing.

She enjoyed watching his reaction and working with him. For the first few days together, the experience reminded Taylor of the fun she used to have with her father, but it also reminded her of his death. The excitement of the work, however, helped drive the sadness away.

They spent many long days together and often complained of the shop time ending too soon. They never took more than fifteen minutes for lunch or any other break and usually only stopped when they had to go home for dinner. On many occasions, Dominga would call and complain about their dinners becoming cold.

After her first few encounters with Doroteo, Taylor began to wonder if he was intentionally avoiding confrontations with her, or if he just possessed a naturally elusive personality. If a sufficient opportunity presented itself, Taylor planned to corner him for a conversation. But they spent so much of their time and emotional energy at the shop that after returning every night, she only wanted to prepare for the next day and then sleep.

They first heard from Gerald more than a week later, from an email containing little information, providing only his location in the Eastern United States and his current objective, to obtain all the information about Eugene Mallove's affairs before his death. Gerald had no other concrete information to share, but he wanted to check some suspicious leads before he would give them any useful progress updates.

At the shop, time seemed to move too quickly for them to worry about Gerald. Although she was extremely curious about his progress, Taylor focused easily on their work. Even Cesar failed to initiate any substantive conversations about Gerald.

Five more days passed before they had any other contact with him. On that day, Dominga called just after noon and Taylor hesitated before answering. Dominga usually called a few times per day, complaining of their absence or asking if they would return home late for dinner. Before answering, Taylor used a cloth to wipe grease from her hands.

"Hello?"

"Taylor," Dominga said in an exaggerated tone of exasperation. "What are you and Cesar doing over there? Watching movies?"

"Of course not," Taylor replied, laughing. "We're working."

"Well, you should check your email, pronto. Gerald just called and said you need to answer his email."

"Why doesn't he just call the shop?"

"Do I look like Gerald's personal secretary?"

"Yes," Taylor teased then changed to a more serious tone. "I mean, of course not."

"For some reason, he doesn't want to talk about it over the phone. Maybe he's got sensitive information."

"Okay, thanks for calling, Dominga," Taylor said. "I'll check my email."

After cutting the connection, Taylor yelled to Cesar over all the machine noise, telling him of the news. She opened her email and saw the new message from Gerald. He had sent a concise message. After reading it, Taylor just stared at the computer screen. Her heart began beating wildly.

"What does it say?" Cesar yelled back.

"He says one of us needs to go to Salt Lake City to meet with him. He's not technically qualified to determine what he's found."

THIRTY-TWO

Gerald

"What do your clients or friends want?" Ammon asked. He sounded like someone playing Monopoly who had just drawn the card to go back to the beginning. "What is the real purpose of meeting with me?"

"They want the same thing Eugene Mallove wanted, what you gave to him."

Gerald's entire bluff depended on his guess being correct, that clandestine hired thugs had murdered Eugene Mallove for something in his possession, something Ammon and his associates had given or shared with him. If Gerald guessed incorrectly, Ammon would know and Gerald's mission might fail. A fusion power generator seemed too implausible, but so did the NMG. He had to make the attempt.

Ammon paused for almost five seconds, staring at Gerald's face but not his eyes. His next words sent a shiver through Gerald's chest.

"What do you think we gave him?"

"A fusion generator device," Gerald said without hesitation. For a moment, he feared Ammon would laugh.

"What do your friends want with a fusion generator?"

"It's not my place to say," Gerald said, trying to hide his sudden excitement. "But they know what will happen to them if they are caught with it. So you can see, it is in my best interest to fly under the radar, just like you."

"So how did you find me?" Ammon looked confused and worried. "Will others be able to follow the same trail?"

"We can discuss the details later," Gerald said as though details had little importance. "But I don't think you have any additional reason to worry. The whole cold fusion fiasco is part of history and no one is trying to open the case again. I am curious though, why do you think Mallove was murdered?"

"If you think about the alternatives," he began. "Destroying the technology was their prime objective. Murdering Mallove was a warning message to the world and to those who knew about it. They would not be able to eliminate everyone involved. Everyone knows that secrets will eventually be discovered. If a device was ever allowed to exist, it would escape their grasp at some time. Game over. Inexpensive and abundant energy isn't exactly in their best interest, at least not while the oil market is so lucrative." Ammon leaned up against the wall, below the window. "To tell you the truth, when we heard of Mallove's murder, we thought that we were going to get–"

"The same fate?" interjected Gerald.

"Yes. We took a huge risk showing him what we did, but we felt confident that Mallove would not willingly betray us. We just thought he would be more discreet with it. He planned to develop it, you know, get it into the right hands who could make it happen. Apparently, he made a mistake and took the information to the wrong people, or something else happened. We don't know."

"You're lucky to be alive," Gerald said. "I wonder if they killed him too quickly, before they learned about you? Have you ever considered the possibility that they know about you and are keeping you under surveillance?"

"After so many years," Ammon said. "We stopped worrying about that until I met with you."

"Of course, they could have faked his death and that would have had the same effect. Mallove could have been working for intelligence. They prefer controlling the opposition like that. But we'll never know, I guess. So, when do I get to see it? Is it here?" Gerald looked around the room, the one place he knew it was not located.

"It's not here," Ammon said while walking to the door. "I'd like you to meet my boss, Tom. He has a few more questions for you."

Ammon opened the door, revealing a tall man standing in a dark hallway. Light from the hanging bulb cast his features in an eerie glow. He stood probably four centimeters taller than Ammon and just as thick but with muscle instead of fat. He appeared to be in his mid-fifties with streaks of gray in his blond hair.

Before the man entered the room, he seemed to be inspecting Gerald for flaws. After a few seconds, he came to some conclusion and smiled thinly, with narrowed eyes. Gerald saw more confidence in Tom than in Ammon.

"Gerald Foster," Tom said, stepping into the room and shutting the door behind him. Gerald suddenly felt more imprisoned than at first. "I see Ammon let you into the club. We don't have any reason to worry about you, do we?"

THIRTY-THREE

Cesar

Cesar marveled at his luck to work with such a beautiful and intelligent young lady. As a younger man, he might have been intimidated or too obsessed with impressing her to get much work done. Sometimes when she looked at him, her green eyes made him pause with admiration, but he never felt any sexual attraction. After the death of his wife, Cesar felt no need to form physical relationships with other women, especially not young ladies like Taylor. At that point in his life, he focused more on enjoying the qualities of other people, male or female. Taylor made that task easy. Her confidence reminded him of his daughter and wife.

Having the friendship and trust of a man like Gerald Foster meant that Taylor was a good judge of character and shared the same traits. Intelligent people with integrity were usually drawn to others of the same or higher intelligence and not necessarily just those of the same interests.

When he had first seen Taylor and Gerald together, Cesar had wondered if Gerald had held a romantic interest in her. The younger man needed a strong woman in his life and they would be a good match, but Cesar thought that Gerald was destined for someone else. Given the opportunity, he decided to advise Gerald to maintain a completely platonic relationship with Taylor.

Cesar had enjoyed watching the growing relationship between Taylor and Dominga. His good friend needed a younger woman to love and pamper. She loved finding people like Taylor, someone who needed just a little polishing, someone who had not yet discovered the benefits of some vanity in her life. In Cesar's opinion, Taylor would never be truly converted, and that made her the exact person Dominga needed.

While working on the NMG, Cesar had thought their level of excitement could not rise any higher. Then Gerald had sent his message.

"I cannot believe it," Cesar said after joining Taylor at the computer and reading the message on his own. "Could he have found a fusion reactor?"

"He found something," Taylor said, brushing her thick red hair from her eyes. "He wouldn't be telling us this if he didn't think it was something important."

"To be honest," he said and felt suddenly as though confessing to a Catholic priest, "I never really believed in my heart that there was anything to find concerning cold fusion. It was pure hope, but I thought it would be good for Gerald to go on the hunt. He's like a bloodhound, only truly happy when he was on the scent of some poor wounded animal."

"I don't know what to think. It seems too good to be true." Taylor sat down in a chair and gave a long sigh. She looked tired.

"Yes," he agreed.

"All of this doesn't feel real," she said quietly.

"It's possible that there is something else going on?" he asked.

"What do you mean?"

"I don't know. He could be in trouble. His emails are encrypted, so why is he providing almost no information?"

"No," Taylor said abruptly. Searching for implications in his email probably required more time and effort than she was willing to give. "He thinks he found it, but needs us to verify it, as well as pick it up.

It's exactly how I felt when I called him about the NMG. If he was in trouble of some sort, he probably wouldn't have claimed to find anything. There's nothing to read between the lines."

"Maybe I just don't want to get my hopes up too high. But what if he found what we need?"

"If he has a fusion generator," Taylor said, smiling wide, "and it produces the kind of power it should, we can make a vessel they will have no hope of capturing."

Cesar suddenly wondered what Doroteo would say. He would probably lecture them about not proceeding too quickly, or at all. Later, Cesar would need to think of the best way to inform his friend. He and Taylor would continue their work on developing the new technology while Doroteo prepared for potential security issues.

"It also means we need to take more precautions against discovery," Cesar said and wondered briefly if they should abandon their quest. Several implications accompanied the new development and suddenly seemed like a group of hungry lions standing in their path. "This is getting even more serious than it already was."

Taylor's smile waned just a bit, but she retained the same confidence he had always seen in her, and her smile helped him feel better. In the following few seconds, they just stared at the computer screen in silence, and then another email from Gerald suddenly appeared in her inbox. Cesar glanced at Taylor before opening the email and they had to read his next cryptic note a few times to understand what he meant.

"They want a quarter of a million dollars?" Taylor asked incredulously. "In cash?"

"I was wondering when he would reveal the price tag," Cesar answered, attempting to sound reassuring. Taylor's reaction made him smile. The girl had probably never seen that much money in her life, but he considered the sum an insignificant compensation for what the scientists might be selling. "I expected more actually."

"Gerald can get fifty-thousand? Where the hell did he get that much money?" Taylor exhaled loudly. "Are you seriously considering bringing two hundred thousand?"

"I can bring the rest, no problem," Cesar said, shaking his head. "I won't let Gerald put that much of his own money into this. I will take care of this cost."

Cesar was relieved that they had not required more, and he also knew that Doroteo would attempt to change his mind. But despite Doroteo's likely protests, the relatively small price seemed like a good sign. Larger sums of money were more difficult to insert into the banking system, hinting that Gerald had encountered a small operation and not some larger, more dangerous organization. The financial investment seemed insignificant compared to his psychological investment.

At dinner that night, Cesar explained the situation to Doroteo and Dominga. When he mentioned the price, Taylor's expression worried him more than Doroteo's glare. Cesar knew the girl well enough now to recognize a weak attempt to appear casual about the situation. She probably felt guilty for not having the money to contribute to the transaction. If she still seemed troubled later, he planned to remind her about her incalculable contribution to their project. When he returned his attention to Doroteo, to his surprise, the man had no objection to the money.

"I'm going with you," Doroteo said, his tone allowing for no disagreement. Cesar saw no reason to argue with his friend, but he did have an alternate plan.

"What do you think about driving down with Taylor and accompanying me on the return trip?"

Cesar had been waiting for an opportunity for Doroteo and Taylor to spend some time together. Doroteo responded only with a *"hmm,"* giving Cesar time to finish his proposal.

"There should be no problems on the way there, or with the money transaction. I'm more concerned about getting the thing back."

"I'd feel more comfortable handling the payment," Doroteo said after a moment of thought. "It's not a good idea to do that by yourself."

"I know how to be careful, Doroteo," Cesar said, maintaining eye contact with his friend.

"Why does Gerald want you to drive to Salt Lake City?" asked Dominga incredulously. "Why on Earth won't you fly?"

"Dominga," Cesar replied softly, breaking eye contact with Doroteo. "If things work out, we might be returning with something highly confidential. We cannot take such a thing on an airplane or have it shipped. It is too dangerous. Someone must drive down there and pick it up, and only Taylor and I are qualified to verify what they claim it is."

"If it is too dangerous to fly, then you should not go. Cannot you learn how to make this thing and just do it here? Cesar Sanchez and Taylor Evans can make anything."

"We'll be okay," he assured her and laughed. "We should only be gone for two to three days and we'll come straight back here. Everything will be fine."

"So, Gerald will be driving back with you?"

"No," Doroteo said. "Since Gerald flew to Salt Lake City, he has to fly out. Otherwise, it will look suspicious if anyone investigates this matter in the future. There can be no link between Gerald, Cesar, and Utah. You should only use cash, and Gerald leaves the same way he got there."

Dominga scowled at all of them, especially Doroteo. Taylor kept her attention focused on her plate.

"And why does Taylor need to go at all?" Dominga asked with dangerous sweetness before Doroteo could argue more.

"There's no way I'm gonna miss this," Taylor said, placing her hand on Dominga's shoulder at her right and then her other hand on Doroteo's shoulder at her left. "Don't worry, we've got the man himself with us."

Cesar suppressed a smile at the sight of the girl being so affectionate with them, especially Doroteo who tensed almost imperceptibly and acted as though he had failed to notice the girl's hand on his shoulder. No one ever touched Doroteo, not even Dominga. Cesar turned away before his oldest friend could notice him smiling.

—✳—

When Cesar entered the kitchen at six-thirty the next morning, he was surprised to see Taylor sitting at the kitchen table, drinking coffee and eating toast. She looked up at him, smiling with obvious excitement in her wide eyes.

"Be careful on the trip and say hi to Gerald for me," Taylor said on his way out the door. "Let us know when we can come escort you home."

"I will," he said. "So you're heading into the shop?"

"Most definitely," she said, sipping her black coffee. "Without you there, I might get something done."

Cesar answered with a silent scowl as though offended, then he turned and left the house. He liked to wake early for a long drive and leave before sunrise. For some reason, beginning a long journey in darkness increased his excitement and helped the uncomfortable hours of driving to pass more quickly. As he exited the garage, he noticed Taylor waving from the front porch. The sight of her increased his excitement for the journey.

He expected the drive to the Salt Lake Valley to last about fourteen hours, more than enough time to consider all the possible problems he might encounter. The first eighty minutes passed as a dream as he watched the windshield wiper blades repeat the endless task of removing rain from the glass, and then snow after reaching Snoqualmie Pass. When he finally escaped the Cascades and began approaching Ellensburg, he enjoyed the transition from the wet Northwest to the dryer and colder Central Washington. He enjoyed the change of scenery and would miss the trees but maybe not the rain.

For most of the drive, he attempted to spend his time wisely by focusing on all of the ways to build the engine and how to incorporate the new power source for their craft. He was happy about their progress at the shop but knew they still needed much more work, especially if they got a fusion reactor. He tried to keep himself from getting too optimistic, just in case Gerald had not found what they hoped.

In the middle of his drive through Idaho, he received an email from Gerald on his iPhone. Gerald gave directions to the hotel where they would meet, and then they would travel together to see the device and the people who made it. When Cesar arrived in downtown Salt Lake City, the sky was beginning to darken and the whole valley began to glow with all of the artificial lighting. He would have to wait until the next day to fully appreciate the Wasatch mountains looming to the east. Seeing them at dusk had already made him feel small.

He drove directly to the hotel and instantly noticed Gerald in the lobby. When he saw Gerald's lips stretched into a wide smile, Cesar felt a flood of relief. He had unconsciously feared seeing concern or anxiety in the man's eyes.

"I think this is it," Gerald said after they had sat in the corner of the lobby, away from anyone else. "It required some maneuvering to get them to show it to me. They don't trust me fully yet, but I think you can help with that."

"So they showed this thing to you," Cesar said, stretching in his seat. After he had walked from his truck to the hotel lobby, his legs felt so much better. "How do you know it is what they claim?"

"That's why you're here, Cesar," he said with a laugh. "The device they showed me was amazing. They showed it to Eugene Mallove and planned to sell him one, but someone found out about it, and fortunately, they failed to make the connection to Cerametrics."

"This company, Cerametrics, they make and sell the device?" Cesar was amazed at the possibility. If true, how did they keep it a secret?

"Not exactly," Gerald explained. "The first guy I met used to be a lab assistant to Dr. Pons. He and his boss spent several years secretly developing the technology after he graduated. They use their company resources, but no one else knows about it, and his boss is the president. I met them both and they took me to see it."

"So they're trying to make money off it?"

"That was the original plan, but since Mallove's murder, they are scared to death of being discovered." Gerald sat back in his chair. "I had to threaten them a bit, for them to show it to me. For a moment, I thought they were going to kill me."

Gerald laughed quietly after the statement, but Cesar could see that he spoke with perfect sincerity. He liked Gerald and smiled while listening to him. Gerald was speaking as though they lived in an exciting movie.

Cesar knew they wanted money and would also not want to have a traceable transaction. "What do they want now?"

"Of course, they need money for it," admitted Gerald. "It's got some expensive components, they say, so they can't just give it to us, but they also want to introduce it to the world, just without the threat of death. That's probably why they are willing to take the risk on us, that and my amazing skills at espionage."

Cesar leaned forward and tried to retain his energy and concentration. Although he felt utterly drained, he could not relax just yet. "They don't know about us, do they? What did you tell them?"

"Just that I was working for some clients and could not disclose any of their personal information," Gerald said, then paused. A small family had entered the lobby and were walking to the concierge desk. The youngest child caught Gerald's attention, a girl about eight years old with long brown hair. She smiled at him, so he paused to return the gesture. Then he turned back to Cesar.

"I do, however, think they will be sympathetic to our cause if you think it's wise to tell them. Since we know dangerous information about them, we have some leverage. If we tell them about us, it will be in their best interest to keep it confidential. It might help them trust us."

Sitting back in his chair, Cesar thought for a moment. The reasoning helped to relieve his primary concern, the confidentiality of their secret work.

"We should discuss it with Taylor before sharing that with them." He smiled at the irony of needing permission from a girl less than half his age.

"Agreed. We don't want to risk making her angry." Gerald almost seemed more frightened of upsetting Taylor than their secret being discovered.

"What's your plan?"

"I told them you would arrive tonight," Gerald answered. "They said we had to do it at night, but I'll understand if you want to wait for tomorrow night. You must be exhausted from driving all day."

"I can rest later. Let's go see this thing." When Cesar spoke next, his tone gave no room for argument. "Oh, and I will be paying the entire sum myself. This is my way of paying you back for introducing Taylor."

THIRTY-FOUR

Cesar

"That's what I thought you'd say." Gerald smiled then exhaled. "I hate to ask this, but since we might need the truck, you'll need to drive. I can't drive a stick."

"No problem," Cesar said, failing to hide his disappointment. He had hoped to relax on the drive.

After Gerald called his contact at Cerametrics, they climbed into Cesar's truck and drove toward the west of the city, to the open desert. During the long car ride, they saw mostly snow and sagebrush. While passing the Great Salt Lake, the darkness prevented a clear view, but Cesar enjoyed seeing the reflection of city lights on the water. He hoped to have some time the next day to see the immense desert lake.

Gerald played the role of navigator on the journey. After nearly an hour of driving, they finally turned from the main road and onto a smaller one. Cesar figured that they had traveled about sixty kilometers away from the city.

"So, I take it that this is not the way to their company?"

"Oh, I'm sorry," Gerald said. "No, they keep the working prototype at an off-site property that one of them owns. As you can expect, they've become rather paranoid."

A crystal-clear sky accompanied the cold night. Cesar forgot the last time he'd seen the sky full of stars so clearly. During the winters in Seattle, he would often be lucky to catch a glimpse of the open sky, and lights from the city would drown much of the starlight.

After a short while on a smaller road, they parked behind a two-story brick building set off from the main road about two hundred meters. Cesar thought the structure looked like an old school building. A light shone from some of the windows of the first floor. When he stepped from the truck, the brisk desert wind hit him hard in the face. The cold penetrated his bones, and he instinctively wrapped his arms around his chest.

When they went into the building, the lack of wind felt like a heat source of its own. A taller man with thick blond hair sat at a long wooden table in the middle of a room surrounded by old brick walls. A shorter, stubby man stood by him as though ready to welcome them to his home. Cesar recognized them from Gerald's description.

"Ammon, Tom," Gerald said after closing the door. The men acted casually as though they already knew Cesar's identity. "This is Cesar, the client I was talking about."

Although both men were perfectly polite, Cesar could sense the anxiety in their body language.

"What line of work are you in?" Ammon asked.

For the next few minutes, they all became better acquainted. Cesar gave only a brief explanation of his history, including how he had fled Mexico. He assured them that their secret would be safe with him and his friends. They listened intently and without question. Cesar thought they looked satisfied after learning of his volatile relationship with the secret government.

When finished with the social proprieties, they led Cesar and Gerald down some stairs to a lit basement of brick and many exposed pipes. The space reminded him of the utility room of an old school. Cesar felt instant gratitude for the warmer air in the lower level. He could still hear the wind from outside, but the sound seemed more distant.

"We added this whole part of the room," explained Ammon as he showed them the large area filled with a random assortment of equipment. The walls of the new gray brick contrasted with all of the chips and cracks in the older walls. In the middle of the new area stood what he assumed to be the reason for his visit, a generator of some sort. Cesar's heart rate accelerated in excitement. The moment reminded him of when Taylor had shown him the NMG.

"We do some experiments at our work," said Tom. "But for the dangerous stuff, we come here. It's been easier to conceal the accidents."

Cesar noticed a small open closet, like the kind in a radiology office, where the technologist goes to shield himself from X-rays.

"What kind of accidents?" Cesar asked casually as he walked around the room.

The two men looked at each other, and Tom smiled. "Let's just say that we've worked out all the kinks for you."

Cesar felt an excited surge of cold blood fill his chest and his heart seemed to accelerate to keep the blood flowing. He turned to Gerald. "For us, huh." He was beginning to believe the view before him and what it implied. He stepped to the generator and extended his hand toward a piece of the stainless steel, then he put his fingers on the metal and slid them across the cool surface.

"So this is it? A fusion generator?"

Tom acted as though introducing his firstborn infant, nodding slowly with wide eyes. "Yes."

Cesar recognized only some of the components on the generator. He saw several small boxes with wire coils that looked like alternators. Shiny, flex pipes connected a group of segmented steel cylinders arranged in a circle, orthogonal to the floor. A large chamber sat in the middle of the cylinders, composed of ceramics, glass, and metal. Almost every piece had sensors connected to them. The other three men watched as he inspected the apparatus. A computer display showed digital readouts of several temperatures, voltages, charges, and energy flow. He noticed one readout indicating a steady, five hundred watts.

"It's so quiet," said Cesar, impressed that the device could run so quietly.

"The reactor only makes noise when it approaches maximum power," Ammon said with a smile full of pride. "Then it hums."

"And what is maximum power?"

Cesar wanted to start with a quick tutorial. He wanted to see the device in action. Tom rubbed his chin.

"We've got this one up to about five hundred kilowatts, but we're limited by our power transmission system. We could generate a lot more if it didn't melt the cables."

"That's good, right?" asked Gerald. He had a hopeful look in his eyes.

Cesar nodded and smiled silently. The power would be sufficient for a start. Then he wondered if he could understand it enough to scale it to their specific needs. He hoped they had an instruction manual.

For the next hour, they discussed the underlying scientific theory. Gerald stood and listened intently, but only as a spectator. He asked no questions and deferred all comments to Cesar. After just a few minutes of discussion, Cesar stopped trying to hide his excitement. To explain how their creation worked, Tom and Ammon spoke with equal energy.

Both of the men showed the same familiarity with its operation. Surprisingly, Cesar discovered that he understood almost everything, at least about its operation. By the end of the conversation, he had learned how the nuclear reaction proceeded, along with the by-products and the resultant radiation. They openly admitted to lack a full understanding of the operation theory and still had many unanswered questions.

But before Cesar became convinced entirely, he would need to see the device in action. Their obvious pride and excitement had successfully dislodged any suspicion of deception. He just needed to see for himself, as he had with the NMG.

"Can we have a demonstration?" he asked after they finished telling him about the heat transfer system.

"Yes, of course," Tom said rubbing his chin. "Even though this alone doesn't prove anything, take a look at the fuel level readout. For the past month, we've used only twenty-five grams, keeping this place warm basically. I understand if you need to see something more substantial."

"I'm impressed already," Cesar said, unable to stop thinking about the low fuel consumption.

"Okay," he said apologetically. "I'm afraid the most energy-consuming demonstration that we're set up to do right now isn't going to be very extravagant."

"What have you got?" He just wanted to see it working at a high power output. He wanted to hear it hum.

For their demonstration, they wanted to show the production of a copious amount of energy. They exited through a door in the basement to the back of the building where Ammon filled a fifty-five-gallon steel cylinder full of water. Behind the building, only the open desert was visible. After connecting a huge resistance heater coil to a heavy wire, he immersed the coil in the water. They covered the container with a makeshift lid, which looked like a giant spout.

"Interesting demonstration," Gerald said, shivering and holding his arms tightly across his chest.

"We don't want to draw attention to ourselves. Otherwise, we would make something really amazing." Tom held out his hands and motioned them to move back. He smiled. "We don't want to kill you two just yet."

The promised demonstration began about thirty seconds later. At first, steam began to escape into the air as a thick fog and then after about a minute, a three-meter jet of steam and water drops shot from the spout. All four of them stood in silence and watched the geyser spray high into the air. Even Gerald refrained from commenting and breaking the spell.

At the highest point, the jet spray rose ten meters into the air and the freezing wind quickly froze the water, forming ice crystals, which crashed back on the ground all around them. Cesar extended his hands toward the barrel to enjoy the heat like at a campfire. After just a short while, the water had all vaporized along with Cesar's doubts.

"Yes, I've seen enough," Cesar said with a frozen smile. "Let's get out of this wind."

—※—

When back inside and after Gerald had introduced the topic of the financial exchange, they explained the expensive costs associated with the materials and preparation of the components. The most crucial components contained a proprietary ceramic matrix, produced exclusively by Cerametrics, a mix of palladium and other expensive materials.

Of course, they wanted to be compensated for developing the generator, but their primary motivation was to see their creation replace petroleum and take its place as the primary energy source for humanity, as it already was for the rest of the universe. They also wanted the rights to it and the profits. Unfortunately, they knew the achievement of their ultimate goal lay far into the future, provided the intelligence agencies failed to discover it first. Cesar said he thought they had an idea of how to make that happen, but they would have to continue waiting.

"When we accomplish what we hope," he said to them. "Maybe we can work together on introducing it to the world. We'll definitely keep in touch. We're both treading on this dangerous ground now."

In the future, Cesar thought they might bring these two men into their full confidence, but he had to let Taylor help make that decision. Ammon and Tom's bravery and ingenuity had already gained his trust and respect, but sharing his other secrets with the two Mormons increased the chance of exposure for them all. For the present, conceal-ing the NMG was in everyone's best interest.

Ammon and Tom had taken a significant risk by trusting Gerald, and Cesar felt great satisfaction to have given the task to him. *Choose the right man for the right job,* his father had always said.

"I believe you asked for two hundred and fifty thousand dollars?" Cesar asked as confirmation. "Is this the one we're getting, or do you have the prepackaged item back on your shelves somewhere?"

"We have parts for several others," Tom said and smiled. "But we wanted to make sure we gave you a working model."

The two men accepted the money and only casually glanced at the contents of the large duffel bag before giving Cesar instructions on how to dismantle the equipment. Under Ammon's direction, Gerald helped Cesar take the apparatus apart and package the individual components. Cesar noticed the pleasure on Gerald's face to help with the process even when he showed an apparent aversion to getting his hands dirty or bruised. They provided several padded containers and got the whole package ready for transport in his truck, finishing just after midnight.

"If you ever need anything, please let us know," Ammon said after the truck started. "It might be a good idea to use Cerametrics for some of your other needs, just to throw people off the scent, if you know what I mean. Of course, maybe the less contact, the better. I don't know."

"Good idea," Gerald said from the passenger seat and Ammon nod-ded. Tom just stood with his arms folded across his chest as the wind tossed his hair like a salad.

Before they drove away, Cesar gave one last look at the building and felt a wave of solace about the whole event. When starting his own company, he had recognized it as the beginning of something big, and when he decided to run for mayor of Ciudad Juarez, he had thought that he could make a difference in the lives of many people, but that decision had changed his own life the most. It had cost him his family and country. In this new phase of his life, he had seemed to stumble upon Taylor and Gerald by pure chance. He hoped this part of his life would result in something better. He had much less to lose.

"Amazing," Cesar said to himself as they drove into the night.

As the building merged with the darkness behind them, he felt the historic aspect of the moment. The building might become a monument one day. He was tempted to stop and take a picture, but he just wanted to go home. He would return one day, back to the Utah desert.

THIRTY-FIVE

Taylor

Taylor went to work at the shop that morning but felt awkward spending time there alone. Thoughts of a possible fusion reactor fought for her attention. With the NMG and a high-power fusion reactor, they could build anything. No engineer or scientist on the whole planet could be as lucky. The anticipation of joining Cesar and Gerald almost paralyzed her, so at lunchtime, Taylor returned to the house and read a book to help pass the time.

After Cesar departed on his trip to Utah, Dominga became quieter and more reserved. She spent a lot of the time in her bedroom or on the couch, usually reading. On the night of Cesar's absence, Dominga did not prepare dinner, so Doroteo ordered pizza. And then when the email arrived the next day, Dominga read it before anyone else.

"Taylor, Doroteo," she yelled from her bedroom. "A message from Gerald and Cesar."

"Isn't it so cute how concerned she is?" Taylor said to Doroteo on their way to join Dominga in her room.

Taylor had spoken with exaggerated affection, hoping to spark some irritation. Amusement at his reaction might help calm her nerves. She felt as though a doctor had just emailed them with how long they had to live. Doroteo's grunt of annoyance helped, but not much.

"It's good news, I think," Dominga said.

Before he had left, Cesar devised a code for their communication about the event. If the message contained the phrase, *the next day*, it meant Gerald had found success and they would return immediately. If the message contained *they would return home soon*, it meant the whole thing had been a failure. In the email, Gerald said he would return home *the next day* and Taylor's heartbeat resumed beating when she understood the good news.

"So you will meet him in Boise tomorrow afternoon?" Dominga asked.

"That's the plan," Taylor said after taking a deep breath. She did not want to wait.

"We don't really have to go," Doroteo said as an afterthought, as though he had no interest in the whole affair. "I'm sure Cesar can make it back on his own."

"Doroteo!" Taylor said in exasperation, and then realized he had intended the suggestion to rile her. Instead of admitting to her gullibility, she pretended ignorance. "He's your closest friend and you are not worried? Don't you want to see the fusion reactor?"

Even though she felt safe in their secure location, Taylor lowered her voice whenever talking about the reactor. The information still seemed too unbelievable and insecure.

"I suppose," he agreed lazily.

Taylor had difficulty sleeping that night. She had wanted to leave already and not wait until the next day. The situation reminded her of her childhood at Christmas when her parents had always failed to successfully hide her presents. Waiting and keeping her knowledge a secret had almost ruined the fun of getting presents.

She eventually managed to fall asleep and then jumped out of bed without fatigue the next morning. After initially failing to see Doroteo waiting for her, she assumed he had overslept, so she knocked on his door. Since she had never previously attempted to wake him, she was curious about his possible reaction. She waited for several seconds without a sound, then decided to go and put all of her stuff in the car and wait. In surprise, she found Doroteo sitting in the driver's seat, his hands on the wheel and staring forward as if meditating.

"How long have you been in here?" she asked in exasperation. "You could have come to get me."

"Not long," he said without turning.

Without any other verbal exchanges, they started driving, and Taylor just watched as the wipers removed the heavy rain from the windshield. After a few minutes of silence, she decided to initiate a conversation, hoping to push Doroteo into an acknowledgment of her presence.

"I'm so cold. Can't wait for the car heater to get warm."

Doroteo made no response or indication of hearing her.

"Did you see Dominga before we left?" she asked while still looking forward.

Doroteo grunted something incoherent and she decided to interpret the sound as a negative answer. She wondered if Doroteo acted like this when tired.

"Do you think Cesar's nervous driving around with a fusion reactor all by himself?" She asked this question leaning forward and looking directly into his eyes. Then after positioning herself to face him better, she silently counted to three.

"Possibly," he said.

"Doroteo," she began somewhat forcefully. "This is getting ridiculous. I need you to talk to me. I cannot ride with you the whole way in silence."

He kept staring straight ahead for a few seconds and then spoke without turning his head. "What do you want me to say?"

"Okay, that was my fault. How about I ask it this way?" Hearing him speak made her feel a little better. She smiled and got more comfortable, as though preparing for a nice, long conversation with him. "How do you think Cesar *feels* about traveling with a fusion reactor, all by himself?"

This time, he looked at her but with the same blank expression. Taylor thought his eye sockets looked more deeply set into his face than usual. The whites of his eyes reflected the low light from the dashboard.

"I suppose he's not very comfortable with it."

"That's how I felt when I brought the NMG to show Gerald for the first time." She took her eyes off his, hoping to relieve any discomfort. She did want to have a conversation with him and not tease him the entire time. "I felt like I was going to get in a wreck and then an ambulance was going to come, pick me up, and notice what I had with me and turn it over to the authorities. If that didn't happen, I was sure to be mugged before I ever got to the Burgerville to meet Gerald, or else the police were going to see in my eyes that I was hiding something. Have you ever felt like that?"

His look of suppressed irritation told Taylor how much he preferred to drive in silence. She let ten long seconds pass without responding, a small present to him before her next barrage of conversation. She did feel a twinge of guilt for being so forceful, but she wanted him to feel comfortable with her, and talking seemed like the best way to accomplish that task.

"I felt that right after I joined the police in Mexico," Doroteo said suddenly, breaking the silence and surprising her. He began slowly, as though unaccustomed to saying more than one phrase at a time. While speaking, his eyes remained focused on the road. "I volunteered to go undercover, infiltrating the local drug dealers. Only a few of us were willing to do it. Back then I felt invincible."

"According to Cesar, you are invincible."

"Ha," he answered without mirth. "I soon became friends with one of the bodyguards of a low-level trafficker, and after only a few weeks,

I found myself in the middle of a meeting with one of the main cartel leaders. I always knew the dangers of the job, but that was the first time I realized they would kill me if they knew who I was. I remember being," he struggled for the right word, "frightened."

She would probably never hear him say that word again.

"What did you do?" she asked with genuine interest, forgetting the topics she had planned to broach. Before his confession, she had only wanted him to talk to her, to help pass the time more quickly. Now she was sincerely curious.

"I convinced myself that I didn't care if I died."

"How did you do that?"

He paused again before answering.

"There was a time in my life when I had to make a difficult choice, and I just went back to that moment."

A voice in her mind warned that if she wanted to have a good relationship with him, she should proceed carefully.

"I'll understand if you don't want to talk about it, but I would like to hear it."

He looked at her and paused again.

"Have you ever been in a fight?" he asked. "A physical fight? Wouldn't be surprised if you have."

If she wanted to extract information from him, he would require her to pay with an experience of her own. She smiled at a sudden memory.

"I threatened a couple girls before, but it never came to any actual violence, unfortunately."

"Well, have you ever thought you were going to get the shit beat out of you? Or, let me say it another way." He paused to gather his thoughts. "Did you ever *know* that you were going to get the shit beat out of you?"

Taylor was grateful for the answer to that question.

"No. I've never been privileged with that experience."

"It's at that moment that you can make one of the most important choices of your life. You can choose to cower, or you can choose to go down fighting."

"Most people lie down and take it," she said. "I would think."

"They don't think they have a choice. Those who do are lucky." He smiled for the first time. "Fighting back is the only way to survive. Even though you may not live to have another chance, people will think twice before they threaten you again."

"What happened to put you in that position, of fighting back?"

Taylor noticed a slight hesitation from Doroteo.

"I got the shit beat out of me, but my older brother never touched me again. That day, I earned his respect, but he never earned mine."

"It's okay if you don't want to talk about it, but what happened to your brother? I guess you two did not get along?"

"In English, if your brother tries to kill you, what would you call it? Not getting along?"

Doroteo turned to her from the road and waited for a response.

"Did your parents ever intervene?"

"My brother was a local dealer." He turned back to the road. "My parents were terrified of him, and so was I."

Taylor waited for him to continue, but they drove for the next three minutes in silence. Would he share any more information? She wanted to know more, but she might have to wait for more details. She felt fortunate to have gotten any information from him.

"I don't mean to belittle your experiences," Taylor began tentatively. "But physical violence is just one way to fight back. Look at Gerald. In a sense, he's been fighting for many years. At least he's not rolling over, and until now, we didn't even have a chance of making any progress."

"Does he even know what he's fighting?" Doroteo asked seriously.

"He knows better than I do, but he's just more optimistic. That's how he can be so happy, even with all this shit that keeps happening in this world. I just get so angry. Frankly, I can't understand how he deals with it."

She took a deep breath before continuing.

"If it weren't for my projects, my distractions, the injustice in the world would drive me crazy. I can't even turn on the news or listen to talk radio anymore. All they talk about is the housing market collapse. The worst part of it all is that everyone thinks it's okay to give the banks stolen money so that they can lend it back to us?"

THIRTY-SIX

Taylor

Taylor sat forward and took a deep breath. She needed a diversion for her growing anger, caused by her ranting. "So, what do you really think about what we're doing?" She had planned on broaching this topic sometime on the trip and that moment seemed as good of a time as any. "Don't worry about hurting my feelings."

"I like you, Taylor," he answered. "So you don't have to worry about me lying to you. I think what you're doing is dangerous, so I don't want to take any chances. The real enemy in this world is powerful. They control the most powerful militaries that have ever existed. They control the most powerful weapons and surveillance instruments. Their resources are limitless and they have billions of mindless and devoted followers."

"This world is full of people who don't want to fight back," she finished for him. "They take whatever is handed to them and with a smile. They're the cause of all this mess. Doesn't it piss you off? I don't care anymore about them. I'm in this for people like us. Who cares what happens to the rest of humanity. It's their own damn fault!"

"Do you feel better now?" he asked.

"A little," she agreed and smiled, then remembered that the *rest of humanity* included her mother and many other people she liked. Venting gave her a momentary reprieve from frustration.

"In my opinion," he began, "your chances are small. Why can't you just live your life? Bad things happen to people, things we cannot control. Life's not fair for most of us."

"And accept what is going on around us, without a fight? That's what you're saying?"

While getting on the ramp to I-90, he paused to focus on the road. Soon they would cross the bridge. They had another hour of night before dawn and would travel over dark waters. When he spoke again, he sounded apologetic.

"Yes, you are right. I'm just saying that you still have the chance to live your lives to the best you can possibly have. Instead, you're taking a dangerous road that might be very short."

"I don't look at it that way," she said, smiling. "For me, it's an adventure. We actually have a chance to do something significant. I've never felt so energized in my whole life. You can sense it as well, can't you? At least, you can see it in Cesar and Gerald, and maybe even Dominga."

"Yes," he agreed. "I can see it."

"So why are you choosing to be a part of it?"

He released the wheel with his left hand to scratch his chin and Taylor heard the scrape of fingernails over stubble.

"When Cesar was forced to leave Mexico, he asked me what I wanted to do. I could have stayed, but I was tired of the game. I thought that by following Cesar, I could take a break from all the fighting. I've been fighting my whole life."

"So..."

"Cesar," he said slowly as if still deciding to say more. "He needs my help. Friends help each other, right? Why am I even telling you all of this?"

"You like me. Remember?" She smiled and patted him on the shoulder then turned to face the road ahead. To give him a break from talking, she would continue filling the silence. "To be honest, I'm almost too excited to be scared. I get to work on something big and now with this fusion generator, I'm too shocked to believe it really, it's all got even bigger. Maybe I've been listening to Gerald too much. His optimism is rubbing off on me."

Thinking of Gerald caused her to smile. Doroteo laughed loudly.

"I thought Gerald was a crazy fanatic and couldn't believe Cesar would even listen to him. But now, I'm beginning to think he's either a genius or just extremely lucky. If this thing we're getting is a low-temperature fusion reactor, I'll never doubt him again."

"He's the biggest optimist I've ever known. It's contagious. If it wasn't for him, I wouldn't have found you guys, and I wouldn't have thought about going into space. That was all his idea."

She turned the radio on and then asked Doroteo if he minded listening to music. He showed no opposition, so she searched for an acceptable station to fill the background. Taylor liked music, but she never chose music as an activity by itself. Music had only one purpose, to help focus her mind while she worked. Unlike others in her age group, she rarely remembered the names of the songs she liked or the group who performed them. If she disliked what she heard, she turned the station, but her mind usually spent its energy processing other information.

They listened to the radio while the sun appeared behind the clouds on the horizon. Doroteo drove for a long time as though in a trance, always looking straight ahead. He never said anything about the music, or anything except as an answer to her comments or questions.

—✳—

They had planned to meet Cesar at a Home Depot store in Boise and so far, their only contact with him came from Gerald's email the previous day. Taylor agreed with the plan to refrain from cell phone contact. She also had doubts about the security of email, but they had to communicate in some way and paper moved too slowly.

"Dominga said your father was a machinist?"

Doroteo's unexpected question came after a long stretch of driving in silence. The last exit sign she noticed had indicated a place in Oregon called Baker City.

"Yes," she said, wondering what else Doroteo wanted to know. "He had a shop like Cesar's, but a little smaller. After he died, Gerald helped us transfer the ownership to my Mom."

"Was he part of the reason why you chose what you did?" Doroteo kept his eyes on the road. "What you wanted to study in school?"

When most people learned of her father's death, they usually said sorry or gave some other kind of condolence. The news made most people uncomfortable in her presence. Doroteo acted as though unaware of the social propriety, as though he'd already had extensive experience with death in his life, and chose to focus on those still living.

"If I had a different father, then I might have chosen something else." Thoughts of taking a different path in her life always caused anxiety. She hated the thought of her life being dependent on circumstance. "He always wanted to show me what he was working on and liked teaching me how to do things. It's probably mostly his doing, I'm sure, but I'm glad of it."

"I'm sure he wouldn't have shown you so much if you didn't reciprocate the interest. You must have been an interested student."

"*Reciprocate,* huh?" she said while laughing. "You're English is amazing."

"I never went to college, but when I was in Mexico, I studied English on my own. When I was working for Cesar as head of security, he had to work with some people who only spoke English, so it was good for me to learn."

"Well, you've got a heavy accent, but your English is great."

"Thanks!" He sounded genuinely pleased, which surprised her.

Two hours later, they entered Boise and took the exit that would lead them to the rendezvous point at the *Home Depot* store. They drove slowly through the parking lot for a few minutes in search of Cesar's truck. After failing to locate him, they parked at the back of the parking lot. Taylor began to worry.

"I wish we could use our phone to call him," Taylor complained. "It feels like we're in the dark ages."

"It was a different world without cell phones," Doroteo said wistfully. "Gerald was right about not using them. He should minimize evidence of visiting Utah."

"What did you do before cell phones?" she asked with sarcasm, intimating his old age. "It must have been annoying."

Doroteo did not respond.

THIRTY-SEVEN

Taylor

A few minutes later, Taylor noticed Cesar's truck as it pulled into the parking lot. In excitement, she exited the car and waved her hands. The cloudless sky helped the air remain crisp and bitingly cold, a welcome change from the eternal rain and cloudy skies of a Northwest winter. For the first time since leaving that morning, she stood on her own feet. Her muscles screamed with release from all of the caged tension. Blood flowed to her legs, flooding her entire body with endorphins.

While Cesar parked in the space next to them, the sight of his smile filled her with excitement—another sign of success. After opening the door to his truck, he greeted them with a simple, *"Buenos dias."* His beard seemed fuller than usual, and his hair looked as though he had just awoken. Then she realized how well he usually maintained his grooming.

She followed him to the back of his truck. Before he pulled the cover open enough for her to see, she quickly glanced around the parking lot for any spying eyes. No one else had parked in the back of the parking lot and the only other people visible were an older man and likely his son walking toward the store entrance.

Before seeing the reactor, Taylor had prepared herself to feel disappointed or just uninspired. They would have dismantled the apparatus and packaged it for protection during transport, and she expected to see just a bunch of boring parts. Her real excitement would come after assembling the reactor and seeing it in operation. But to Taylor's surprise, her heart rate accelerated with delight when Cesar removed the tarp.

"Is it true?" she asked, reaching into the bed and touching a metal cylinder. Although she was shivering from the chill, the cold metal felt good on her skin. "Did you see it working?"

"Oh yes, it's true," Cesar said proudly. "Gerald pulled through with this one."

Taylor put her hand on his shoulder and felt the warmth of his skin under his thin coat. Doroteo stood on the opposite side of the truck bed and looked at the contents with a curious expression. His dark eyebrows drew closer together, forming a sharp V.

"There were no problems?" he asked.

"Nothing I noticed," Cesar replied. "But I'm glad you came to meet me. Thank you."

"No problemo," Taylor said jokingly.

"No one followed you?" Doroteo asked.

"I don't think so."

"After you leave, I'm going to make sure," Doroteo said, not sounding convinced.

"Taylor, you can drive," Cesar began, holding his keys to her. "I'm tired."

"Of course," she replied, feeling glad to give him a break and talk about what had happened. She turned to Doroteo and smiled. "Do you think you can handle the drive back without me?"

"I'll manage," he said wryly.

—⁂—

For the first hour of driving with Cesar, Taylor learned all he knew about the device, and she enjoyed their roles being reversed. Previously, she had taught him about the NMG, but now with the fusion reactor, he became the teacher. Even though they had only a rudimentary knowledge of the fusion process, together they would have enough confidence to adapt the reactor to their needs.

She especially looked forward to reassembling the contraption, and the thought reminded Taylor of an experience from her childhood. When seven years old, she had disassembled her best friend's new binoculars and enjoyed learning how it worked. She remembered having as much fun reassembling it and seeing the relief on her friend's tear-filled face.

"I could not wait to tell you about it," Cesar admitted.

"Me too," she said while looking forward. After the drive with Doroteo, she felt emotionally drained. Their task ahead suddenly seemed more daunting than ever. "Tell me the story about how Gerald found it."

"In a past life, Gerald must have been a bloodhound," Cesar said and laughed. "He explained the story, but I do not understand how he traced it back to the company in Salt Lake City. I was too eager to see the thing. He left out a lot of the details. We can ask him when we see him next."

"Maybe we should start paying more attention to Gerald," Taylor said, laughing. Cesar looked confused.

"Do you not take Gerald seriously?"

"I take him seriously, usually, but sometimes his head seems to be in the clouds. I thought this was a wild goose chase, something to keep him occupied while we worked on the NMG. I won't ever doubt him again."

"He's an idealist," explained Cesar. "Many people use that as an insult, but it can be the highest compliment."

Speaking of Gerald reminded her of something she had wanted to discuss. "Sometimes I wonder if it's worth the effort. We're risking a lot on this."

"Freedom is superior to convenience," Cesar said as though repeating a pledge of allegiance to some flag. Then he turned to her. "Taylor, it's all about squeezing everything out of life. I could have accepted what circumstances gave me and lived the remainder of my life in comfort, but what would it have left me? Empty memories."

She took a moment to consider his words and was surprised when she had no desire to argue with him. She just wanted to hear someone else say what she already thought. When he failed to say anything else, Taylor looked through the window at the landscape of central Washington. In about forty kilometers, they would arrive in Yakima. While Taylor watched the scenery, she noticed a large barn on the left, sunlight reflecting off the shiny metal roof.

"Doesn't it feel like everything seems to be coming together?" she asked, using her left hand to shield the bright light. "Are we getting help from somewhere? I don't mean like from a god or any of that nonsense. But what's the probability of all this being planned? I mean, what's next, aliens? Did an alien give me the idea for the NMG?"

Cesar did not laugh at her joke and then spoke while looking through the passenger window. "If you're going to start talking like that, then all of human history would need to be re-evaluated."

He paused for a deep breath.

"Didn't Gerald say something about aliens? After acquiring a fusion generator and your NMG, expecting extraterrestrial help might be too much to ask of the universe."

"Do you think that's even a possibility?" she asked, turning and looking at him intently. "If an alien contacted Gerald, would he tell us or keep it a secret? How would you react if we contacted an alien?"

Cesar shook his head. "I really don't know."

"I've thought about this kind of stuff before, not just about aliens, but also about all the other bullshit like angels, devils, ghosts. Could we experience anything like them and have rational reactions? I don't think our psyche is capable of handling something so out of the ordinary.

"Sure, all that's in the movies and everything, but I think if anyone saw something remotely similar, their brain might refuse to acknowledge or accept it. We'd invent some lie as a rationalization. Our mind might attempt to explain it as some twisted version of reality, what we've already seen in the movies. Am I making any sense?"

"Not much," Cesar said and laughed. "Maybe we can talk to Gerald about it. I think I know where you're coming from, though. Maybe another influence exists that we don't understand."

"You can talk with Doroteo about it," she said and laughed with him. "I'll watch."

"That's fair," said Cesar. "How was your ride with him?"

"We had a good talk," she began. "Despite what you might think, I like the guy. He's tough inside and out, and I like that."

"I'm glad," said Cesar seriously. "I was worried."

—✳—

For the next hour, they drove without any other substantial conversation. Cesar seemed absorbed in thought, and Taylor was not surprised. They had a lot to do when they returned home. But if he wanted to work in the shop that day, she might get Dominga to make him stay home and go to bed instead. He looked too exhausted.

She looked forward to working in the shop again too, but other possibilities soon replaced thoughts of their work. While Cesar looked out of his window, her daydreams began. She imagined leaving the atmosphere and entering orbit in a craft she had helped to build. Taylor had always wanted to watch the blue light of the sky slowly transform into the blackness of space, and then for the stars to appear while it was day. After several minutes of those pleasant thoughts, the silence and streaming white lines on the road helped Taylor begin to drift in a river of her thoughts.

Taylor began to worry when she became conscious of her eyelids feeling heavy. She glanced at Cesar to see if he showed the same symptoms of drowsiness. He was sitting still with his eyes staring straight ahead as though in a trance. After looking back to the road ahead, she had to use all of her energy just to keep her eyes open.

In the distance, she saw a shimmer of light above the road, almost like a mirage. When they came closer, the aberration transformed into a huge hole in their lane. She tried to move her foot from the accelerator to the brake, but her body refused to obey the command. In panic, she watched the hole approach at more than a hundred kilometers per hour. As the distance between them diminished, she tried to scream, but only silent breath escaped her lips. She turned again to Cesar and saw no signs of alarm. His eyes were devoid of life.

The black hole in the road began expanding like a giant mouth, preparing to swallow the truck, its occupants, and its precious cargo. As they finally drove over the edge, Taylor only had the power to push back against her seat. Time slowed to a crawl and she felt as though they were falling down a dark mine shaft. They continued to fall until all light disappeared and then giant yellow eyes opened below them.

The horrible pounding of her heart wrenched Taylor back to consciousness. She felt pressure on her shoulder. She whipped her head around and saw Cesar, one hand on her shoulder and the other on the wheel.

"Slow down, Taylor," Cesar said calmly but with clear concern in his voice. "Are you okay?"

"What?" she asked in confusion and then blinked and shook her head. "I'm okay." She relaxed her hands on the wheel and pulled her foot from the accelerator. Their speed was more than a hundred and fifty kilometers per hour, and her heart seemed to be racing twice as fast.

"I think it's my turn to drive."

"Sorry for dozing off," she said in embarrassment, feeling guilty for interrupting his rest and almost killing them.

They pulled to the side of the highway and changed seats. Getting out of the car and feeling the cold again helped erase her drowsiness. While Taylor attempted to relax in the passenger seat, her mind remained fixed on the image of falling toward those yellow, alien eyes. She told Cesar nothing about her nightmare.

Taylor tried forgetting about the dream and especially about falling asleep while driving. She rarely experienced such problems while driving. All of their talk about aliens had probably influenced her thinking and weakened her state of mind. In the future, she would avoid thoughts about aliens and focus on her work.

PART III

INTERFERENCE

The summit finally reached
Enjoy the scene
Before the silence is breached

THIRTY-EIGHT

Gerald

While Gerald watched Cesar drive away with the fusion reactor, he felt a strange elation. At first, he attributed the feeling to the natural reaction of having participated in an event of historic significance. But that explanation seemed inadequate. Another human emotion dominated his overall feeling, a sense of entitlement.

Before his search for the fusion reactor, Gerald had only felt like an assistant to Taylor, helpful yes, but only in an auxiliary capacity. He never felt unappreciated though and enjoyed following Taylor's lead. He did not need more experience being in the lead. He got enough of that at his work.

He had happily acted as a facilitator to combine Taylor's genius with Cesar's resources and experience. But after delivering the other half of what they needed, he finally felt more like a partner. He now could make decisions on his own and felt less of a need to first seek Taylor's approval. Even with his new feeling of entitlement, he would never dare make any significant alterations to the group without consulting her first.

On his return flight to Seattle, Gerald concluded that they needed to recruit additional people to help prepare for the future. Although he trusted Taylor's and Cesar's judgment concerning scientific and engineering matters, he thought they should look at their options from other angles. In his opinion, all successful endeavors resulted from the efforts of a diverse team of talented people from multiple backgrounds.

After returning home, Gerald arranged a private meeting with Taylor to discuss his recruitment plans. For the discussion, he wanted a meeting without Cesar and especially without Doroteo who would likely disagree vehemently with the recruitment proposal. He felt confident prevailing in an argument with Taylor alone but not with Doroteo or Cesar supporting her.

The subsequent discussion he had with Taylor became more confrontational than Gerald had anticipated, even without Doroteo's or Cesar's participation. Taylor's first comment revealed how the rest of the conversation would proceed.

"Gerald," she said in exasperation. "You're like a little kid. You just can't wait to tell your secrets to all your friends."

But in the end, Taylor reluctantly agreed to let him recruit his friend, a retired botany professor from Germany, a woman named Gerda Schreiber. He refrained from revealing all of his plans and chose only to tell Taylor about Gerda. He assumed that Taylor would feel better about having an old retired lady know their secrets instead of someone still connected to the business or academic world.

On his drive to visit Gerda, Gerald reflected on everything that had happened since his rendezvous with Taylor at Burgerville. Of course, witnessing the NMG and then finding the fusion reactor had almost overwhelmed him, but the future seemed to contain even greater events than those discoveries. As usual, Gerald became lost in his thoughts while driving and almost missed Exit 253 to Bellingham. He eagerly anticipated seeing Gerda's reaction to his proposal.

Twelve minutes later, Gerald pulled into Gerda Schreiber's driveway and shut off his car. She lived in a small house in an older but clean and orderly neighborhood. While still in his car, the front door of the home opened and Gerda appeared. She waved at him from her porch and stood with a quizzical look on her old face. After smiling and waving back, he tried to remember ever seeing her smile.

"Hi, Gerda," Gerald said while running to her front door. In the short distance, the rain had soaked his head and neck, sending a chill down his spine.

"Come in, my friend," she said with a distinctive German accent. Her speech always reminded him of World War Two movies and the evil Germans. "Come out of the rain and get warm."

"Thank you, Gerda. It's a typical Northwest day, isn't it?"

"Indeed," she said while shutting the door behind him.

She took his overcoat and indicated for him to sit on a couch by the front window. Translucent white curtains allowed the gray outdoor light to fill the small room. He immediately noticed the various species of plants placed in every corner of the room and by all the furniture, not an unexpected sight in the home of a botanist, he supposed. Most of the vegetation had large leaves of various shapes and shades of green, yellow, and blue. The warm, humid air in the room offered comfort even though the plant life reminded Gerald of the cold Northwest forests.

While she went to the kitchen for coffee, he admired a painting of a beach at dusk, hanging on the wall above her black piano. The white caps of the waves contrasted sharply with the dark water and dangerous storm clouds in the sky. The artist had filled the space, between the black water and sky, with the brilliant blues, pinks, and oranges of a beautiful horizon. As the artist had most likely intended, the painting reminded Gerald of a bright future beyond the harsh forces of nature.

On the piano, a wooden picture frame showed a middle-aged man with the same blond hair, blue eyes, and sharp nose as his mother. Another picture opposite the man showed a woman of similar age with thick red hair. Her eyes appeared so light that Gerald could not discern any color, although he assumed they were blue. In between the two adults, sat a single picture of two blond, blue-eyed children, and an older boy with his arm around a younger girl. Gerald thought the children were between nine to twelve years old.

Gerda returned with a mug of coffee in each hand, steam rising into the air from the black liquid. She held the mugs with the steady hands of a much younger woman. She paused a moment to look at him through squinted eyes, as though searching for signs of ill health.

"If I remember correctly," she said while delivering the coffee and sitting opposite him, "you like it black."

"You have a good memory," he answered, genuinely impressed at her memory of their last encounter at a café, a year ago.

"Thank you," she answered as though annoyed to accept a compliment. "Now, I am extremely curious as to your visit. On the phone, you indicated that you were going to be up this way, but I cannot see any reason for anyone to visit Bellingham, so I assumed you came just to see me. As you know, I am only here, because my daughter got a teaching job at the University."

"Well," he said, pausing to sip his coffee, "I didn't want any phone record of a special trip just to see you."

"Interesting, considering some of your clientèle. Continue."

Gerald smiled appreciatively at her sarcasm.

"I want to include you as a consultant, of sorts, in a very sensitive project. But before I tell you the details, I feel the need to warn you."

"Warn away," she said and chuckled but without a crack in her serious expression. "I'm too old to fear dangerous consequences."

"I'm glad you feel that way."

Gerald took a deep breath, feeling immediate relief. On the journey to see her, he had considered the option of revealing his proprietary information without any warning of the associated danger, but that option would have stolen the choice she had in the matter. Gerald felt compelled to take the chance that she would refuse participation.

"I have a friend," Gerald continued, attempting to remember his planned approach, "who shares our beliefs about society. To put it simply, this friend of mine has invented a device that can transform the world as we know it."

—※—

Gerald continued with his exposition of the events Taylor had initiated. Gerda saved most of her questions for the end of his story, with only minimal interruptions for clarification. In the end, she peered at him with only thin slits for eyes, nodding slowly. After a few seconds, he began to wonder if she would explode into laughter or start swearing at him in German for telling such a ridiculous story.

"Hmm," she began slowly and opened her eyes wider, her light blue irises visible again. "I don't completely understand what you want with me. I don't have a great understanding of particle physics. What can I do?"

"Well, I'm mostly afraid of proceeding with tunnel vision, but I'm also concerned about the possible consequences of going forward with this. Remember what I said about escaping into space with this thing, to get out of their reach and make it visible to the entire world? Well, what if we have to escape into space for an extended time? What if we had to build a colony somewhere? As a botanist, your knowledge would be invaluable."

"Hmm," she said, leaning forward and excitement showing in her eyes. Although she looked directly at Gerald's face, she seemed to be looking through him. "Plant growth in a gravity-limited environment and artificial atmosphere. This area of research has always interested me. How far down the road do you see this possibility becoming viable?"

"At the moment, they are optimizing the integration of the two new technologies. From what Taylor explained, they will have the ability to go anywhere in the solar system, much faster than any vehicle currently available and with a fraction of the cost. All we have to do is keep it secret until then."

"Yes, I can see why she would be concerned about sharing this information. I almost can't believe your story."

"I had to see her invention for myself," he interjected. "I will try to arrange a time for you to see it too."

"That would be wonderful," she said and clasped her hands together, her first significant display of emotion since the beginning of the story. "While we've been sitting here, I've been fantasizing about what you said, about how government could have a very limited influence in space."

"Or no influence."

She and Gerald both smiled at that thought.

During the subsequent conversation, they reminisced. When Gerda had lived in Seattle, they had both been members of the Libertarian political party and Gerald had enjoyed talking with her at their social functions. After she moved to Bellingham, when her daughter-in-law had started teaching at Western Washington University, Gerda had withdrawn from political activity. She confessed to Gerald about losing faith in the political process and allowed old age to focus her thoughts on happier topics, such as her son and his family.

"Do you know anyone else who might be useful to join the team?" Gerald asked after a lull in the conversation. He had been waiting for an appropriate time to change the topic. "I'm looking for someone with a background in human biology?"

"Hmm," she said, sitting forward. "Let me think. As you already mentioned, this person would need to have the same belief system as ours. That's priority one."

"Yes," he agreed. "The last thing we need is someone who thinks a government agency should handle this."

"Unfortunately, all of my associates in that field are terminal collectivists, but I think my son may know someone in Portland." While trying to recall her memory, Gerda rubbed her left wrist. "She works at a pharmaceutical company there. She has a PhD in biochemistry I think. I'll have to ask him what her name is. He only met her a few times."

"That's great," Gerald said. "Let me know if you think of anyone else."

"Before you go, we can have lunch together." Gerda's eyes dared him to refuse. "I have some excellent homemade soup. It'll warm you up before you return to the cold rain."

During lunch, Gerald asked about her personal life and then spent the next hour looking at pictures of her son's family. He enjoyed taking a break from the topic of subversion, but seeing pictures of her grandchildren reminded him of how much his success or failure could impact the future of the next generation. His thoughts became another sobering motivation for how carefully he needed to handle the situation.

Before departing, Gerda asked for his preferred method of communication and he told her about the secure website channel he wanted to construct. He got the idea for it after having to arrange the physical meeting with Taylor when he should have been able just to call or email her. He wanted to avoid leaving electronic records of their correspondence and did not trust Google, Microsoft, or AT&T to protect their privacy.

"That's when I got the idea of having an associate of mine, a computer expert, build a website. He said he could have something up and running within a week."

"I will be excited to see it."

Before Gerald rose from the couch to leave, Gerda promised again to contact her son and get the name of the woman with the biology background. Then she would text Gerald with the woman's name. At the door, she hugged him unexpectedly and squeezed his arm. Her hand felt almost hot.

"Thanks for including me," she said before releasing her grip. "I am very excited about this."

"No, thank you."

After backing his car into the street, Gerald turned for one final look at the old woman and her quaint little home. Gerda was standing on her front porch with her hand extended rigidly in the air as though in salute. He smiled and waved then watched the elderly German woman disappear into her home.

—✳—

Before returning to the interstate, Gerald pulled into the parking lot of a small shopping area so he could contact his friend, Franklin Harvey, with the message to start working on the website. Gerald had already told his friend that he wanted to create the website, but he had wanted to wait until after his discussion with Gerda. If she had rejected his offer to participate, then perhaps the website would have had to wait.

If he'd had a successful meeting with Gerda, Gerald would send a secret code, per Franklin's request, to register the domain and start working on the website. Gerald remembered feeling amused at the young man's excitement. Franklin loved the opportunity to act covertly, even though he possessed limited information about the group and their secret technology.

Gerald typed the required text message on his iPhone and paused before tapping the send button. He smiled and shook his head at the absurdity of the secret code, but after hitting send, the message seemed mysteriously significant.

Remember your lunch and don't forget the punch.

Three seconds later, Gerald received Franklin's simple reply, a smiley face emoticon.

When Gerald had first discussed the website with Franklin, he'd told Franklin to devise the layout himself and create a simple, secure, and innocent-looking platform to communicate. Franklin would put more effort into the site, Gerald decided, if he devised the plan himself. Gerald remembered Franklin's contagious enthusiasm to begin working on the task.

"Cryptography is one of my specialties," Franklin had said with confidence, "and we can disguise it as an innocent website about something else."

Gerald had complete confidence in the young man's ability. He had met Franklin through one of his clients. During a visit to a small company he represented, he had seen Franklin, a young man of about twenty years, fixing a database issue. Gerald remembered noticing the words written on his cap, *Ron Paul for President*.

Gerald had introduced himself and had attempted to assess the young man's skills and capacity for independent thought. During their brief exchange, Franklin revealed a passion for the open-source software community, which he saw as a subset of the freedom movement. He spoke vehemently about how the government continually bureaucratized intellectual property and always seemed to shackle free communication with unnecessary regulations.

Franklin's attitude and intelligence had immediately impressed Gerald, more than the young man's program design experience. Gerald had never previously considered the open source community in that way, or in any way.

After sending the text, Gerald's excitement about the website began to mount. He decided to wait a couple of days before requesting an update but hoped Franklin would contact him sooner.

Gerald spent the remainder of his return journey to Seattle thinking about the best way to approach the next potential recruit. Hopefully, Gerda could get her name. He would have to do some research first and plan more carefully than he did for Gerda. Gerald needed to acquaint himself with her before trusting and involving her in their dangerous activities.

Just before pulling into his parking space at the office, his iPhone vibrated, a text message from Gerda. After clicking on the message, he shifted the transmission from drive to neutral and then stared at the name of her son's friend, the biochemist. Although the interior of his car was warm, he read the text message again and shivered.

Her name is Sadi Jacobsen, and she works at a place called Pantra.

THIRTY-NINE

Sadi

An hour after her daughter had gone to bed, Sadi Jacobsen made the mistake of lying on the couch to read, and then she fell asleep, an event which had become too frequent lately. Sometime later, her daughter's nanny, Jen, quietly turned off the lights and covered her with a blanket.

Shortly after midnight, Sadi awoke from one of her typical nightmares that left her fully conscious, eyes wide open, and staring at the front window of the living room. She thought the room looked darker than usual with only a sliver of the moon visible through the blinds. While wiping perspiration from her face, Sadi wondered if her nightmares would ever end.

As usual, her unconscious mind had tortured her with a slightly modified version of her son's death. He had died the previous November, the night before Barack Obama became the forty-fourth president of the United States. Even with her individualistic attitude, she had no personal opinion of the president, good or bad. But the timing of his election so close to the most tragic event in her life had put a stain on his name. The words, Barack Obama, had become a constant reminder of what had happened. No matter where she went, she

could no... e hearing his name in the news or everyday conversation. E... ...e seemed to either hate him or love him, but in her opinion, b... ...s like all of the other politicians, just another puppet, so she
refr... ed from talking about him.

...n her nightmare that night, she had found herself driving her car
again on the night of the accident. But instead of just her son, this
time her daughter, Helen, had also died. At the end of the dream, Sadi
had stood as a statue, holding two lifeless children in her arms while
the cold Oregon rain pelted her head and slid down her neck.

Since the accident, her nightmares had started to become less frequent. Although she was grateful for that, she also felt slightly guilty
for suffering less. While relaxing on the comfortable couch, Sadi
wished the dream would have been one of those bittersweet ones
where she could have experienced her living son, at least for a short
while before he died. Those dreams never left her feeling sick inside,
just sad.

The pain never went away during her conscious hours, but at least
in her dreams, she could still see her son. She used to try thinking of
him being with Jesus, but that offered no real comfort. The thought
reminded her of sugar. Although pleasurable on her tongue, sugar always left a bad taste in her mouth.

Before she had fallen asleep, she had been reading the American
Journal of Hematology. The magazine lay on the coffee table in front
of her, its outline barely visible in the dark. Her laptop sat next to it
and had long ago gone dark while she slept. Every second, a single
blinking LED from the computer power indicator illuminated the
table.

Her watch showed thirty minutes past midnight. Should she get up
and go to bed or stay there on the couch? She wished Jen would have
woken her instead of making her more comfortable. Sleeping on the
couch was happening too often lately. Since the accident, she'd focused too much on her work, staying up late. She needed to devote
more time to her remaining child, Helen.

"I need to get to bed," she whispered to the darkness, stretching her arms.

She began to remove the blanket but stopped after hearing the noise. It was the noise that had been absent for several months and that had haunted nearly every dream. Somehow, her dreams had managed to invade the real world, entering through the darkness.

In an attempt to banish any dream residue back to her subconscious, Sadi took two deep breaths and yawned. But after her senses recovered, she heard the distinct sound of a sleeping child again, just a couple of meters away from her. The sound seemed all too real and did not originate from her eight-year-old daughter or the nanny. Only a mother could distinguish the sleeping sounds of her children, and only her son had made that sound when he slept.

The noise originated from a recliner on the opposite side of the room, but from her position on the couch, she could not see through the darkness. "I must be dreaming," she whispered then closed her eyes with the hope of awakening in the light of the morning. Perhaps the past four months had all been just a nightmare about to end. But with her eyes closed, Sadi could still hear the slow, steady breathing of her sleeping son.

The calm breathing filled her awareness but offered no comfort. Such experiences only happened to people who'd lost their sense of reality. Sadi had spent the last four months convincing herself that she would never see her son again. While fighting back the tears, she imagined that a demon had entered the real world to torment her.

"Get a hold of yourself," Sadi whispered in an attempt to banish the sound.

Hearing her voice provided some emotional strength and gave her some time to think. Her sensations had an explanation. Her imagination had only modified some other noise. Sadi suddenly felt a great urge to stand on her feet. Her heart was pounding too hard inside her chest to remain motionless.

But then she remembered the funeral, the last time she had seen the body of her son. She'd never had a worse moment in her life, not even the day her son had died. She wished she'd never looked at the body. For a long time, she could not remember him alive, just a corpse in a coffin.

When her watch chimed, she jolted in panic as though the small noise had slapped her in the face. The time was one in the morning. For the past thirty minutes, Sadi had been listening to the sound of breathing, but it seemed as if just a few seconds. The breaths continued slow and steady as the waves on a beach.

Sadi reached toward the coffee table and the movement caused the laptop to spring to life. The soft glow instantly saturated her eyes and washed the remainder of the room in an even more impenetrable darkness. Sadi held her breath, wondering if the change in lighting would disturb the breathing, but it continued without pause.

Pushing back her fear, she tried speaking but could only whisper.

"Who's there?"

Silence.

Sadi tried adjusting her eyes to the light, but she could see only a dark haze beyond the illuminated laptop. She began to close the lid and then noticed a new email arrive in her Gmail inbox. Instinctively, she stopped and quickly read the message.

Lunch tomorrow? I'll text you. ~Gerald

At first, the message failed to register in her mind. A mysterious man had written to her, someone she knew only in cyberspace. But he would have to wait. The sound of breathing from her dream visitor superseded all other thoughts or considerations. She closed the lid of the laptop and waited for her eyes to readjust to the dark again. After a moment of gathering her courage, she spoke more loudly than before.

"Who's there?"

This time the sound of steady breathing stopped, replaced by the shuffling of a little body on the couch. A moment later, complete silence filled the room.

"Mama," said a soft voice, a voice not heard since the previous November.

—✳—

The word echoed inside her head like a hammer and froze the blood in her veins. Sadi felt completely paralyzed. The word was spoken exactly as she remembered. She listened to the sound of a child hopping off the couch and stepping in her direction. The outline of his tiny form quickly emerged from the darkness. Fear seemed to give Sadi enough strength to sit back against the couch until the cushions failed to compress any further.

The child stopped in front of Sadi and extended his hands for her to place him on her lap. A single tear fell from each of her eyes and they burned on their way down her cheeks. She knew he could not be her son, but he appeared exactly as she remembered.

"Hold him," said a voice inside her head. "Don't waste this time."

The voice in her mind seemed completely alien. The child waited patiently. His eyes reflected the low light in the room.

"Jacob?" she said tentatively. "How can it be you?"

Sadi extended her hands slowly and he melted into her arms, just as she remembered. For a long while, she just held him without speaking and all of the pain of the last few months quickly dissipated. A single tear slid down each cheek and fell on her arm. She remained silent.

"Mama," the child said as though preparing to say more.

Instinctively, she began stroking his head. After a few seconds, he tried to gently push away, but she refused to relax her hold on him. If she let him go, he might disappear. For the present at least, she would pretend the dream was real.

She eventually held him away from her, far enough to see his face. When she looked closely into his eyes, she noticed two infinitesimal specks of light and then wondered if she was seeing the moon's reflection or something self-generated. As Sadi stared at the lights in his eyes, she understood the reality of the child's presence. She could feel his breath on her chin, the warmth of his skin under her fingers. With sudden sadness, Sadi decided to accept the truth. The child in her arms was an exact copy, but not her Jacob.

Fear soon replaced the sorrow in her heart and she released her hold of the boy and leaned back on the couch again. As chills raced through her inner core, she hugged herself for warmth. For the next few seconds, they just stared at each other until she had gained sufficient courage to speak.

"Who are you?"

"I wanted to see you," he said in a perfect imitation of her son. "I wanted you to hold me again."

Attempting further communication seemed like insanity. To speak would confirm the child's existence, but she could not resist her instincts.

"You're not my son," she said more boldly.

Sadi should have continued to fear the thing before her, should have closed her eyes, and retreated into the darkness until the child departed. But she was beginning to feel calm. Logic was beginning to replace irrational thought. The child was not going to suddenly transform into some kind of monster. She felt no malevolence from him.

"Why are you here?"

"I miss you, Mother," the child said with sincerity.

"I'm not your mother. Why are you doing this?" she asked in desperation, holding back more tears. Sadi wanted to summon anger, but she felt only curiosity and sorrow. "Do you know where my Jacob is?"

The sound of a door opening upstairs suddenly hijacked her attention, and she realized her eight-year-old daughter, Helen, had awoken and was planning to use the bathroom or come downstairs. Just as she had known the sound of breathing from her son, Sadi knew the sound of her daughter's movement.

When the child moved closer to Sadi, she forgot briefly about Helen. The child standing before her put both of his tiny hands on her cheek and his face came within three centimeters of her nose. His hands felt warm and smooth as a normal child's hands. Without thinking, Sadi pressed her hands on top of his, and the touch wiped all thoughts from her mind.

"I need to go away again," the child said while stroking her cheek.

Sadi remembered her son performing the same action. While enjoying the pleasant sensation, she listened as her daughter walked softly down the stairs.

"*Helen*," the child said with thick affection, turning his head toward the direction of the stairs, just out of their sight. When he returned his attention to Sadi, she noticed the light deep within his eyes sparkling like sunlight on a stream.

When Helen had almost arrived at the bottom of the stairs, the child's eyes narrowed and returned to Sadi. Her daughter would soon come into view.

"When they come for you," he said. "Think of the future."

When Helen energized the kitchen light, the glow spilled around the corner into the living room and drove all of the darkness away, including the child. Sadi's hands fell onto her empty lap.

The eight-year-old blond girl stepped into the living room, rubbing her eyes. When she saw her mother on the couch, her eyes narrowed.

"Mom, what's wrong? Have you been crying?"

"I'm fine," Sadi replied as casually as possible.

When Helen came within her reach, Sadi pulled her close. For several seconds, she just hugged her daughter and stroked her hair while the conversation with her counterfeit son replayed in her mind. The experience had seemed too real for a dream, but Sadi could not explain the child any other way.

Other than blending all of her emotions and leaving her confused and emotionally drained, the child had delivered a message. Someone was coming for her and she needed to think of the future.

"I'm fine, Helen," she said, getting up from the couch. "Come on, let's get to bed. You can sleep with me tonight."

FORTY

Sadi

Sadi held a glass vial of blood between her thumb and index finger. As she shook the vial, a thin film of blood oozed down the wall. Although she worked with blood nearly every day, the beautiful red liquid still held some mysterious power over her, as though looking at the star-filled sky. The sight of blood always reminded her of life. She loved seeing it and was always amazed that such a beautiful substance could also symbolize pain and horror.

The film of blood on the glass container drained too quickly back into the dark red pool. The lower viscosity indicated an anemic donor. How many times did she have to complain to the screening guys? Too many blood samples came from anemic donors. The undesirable property should not affect her tests, but she hated the additional uncontrolled factors.

For the past three years, Sadi had worked for the pharmaceutical company, Pantra. She loved her job, especially her most recent position as the hematology project manager. The previous year, the company had promoted Sadi to the new position, which meant she had more freedom on her projects and reported to fewer people.

Sadi was currently focused on characterizing one of their new experimental anti-viral medications, Exdantrafir. For the past few weeks, she'd spent the majority of her time testing the T-cell response to an invasion of viruses the pathogen department had prepared.

She'd had difficulty concentrating on her work. The memory of seeing her dead son in her living room was eating some of her mental capacity. Her ability to focus seemed like a gyroscope with excessive precession. She had wanted to stay home, claiming illness, but she knew work would help keep her mind distracted from disturbing thoughts.

"Am I losing my mind?" she asked herself while shaking her head, the vial of blood still in her hand.

She placed the vial into the centrifuge and started the process of separation. Maybe she just needed time. Nightmares sometimes took several days to fade into more palatable memories. Before that happened, she still had to deal with the email that had suspiciously arrived at the same time as the child apparition.

On the drive to work, Sadi had received the man's promised text message. In as few words as possible, her new acquaintance had written where he wanted to meet her for lunch. She replied by text at a stop light.

c u there

To help her merge into reality again, Sadi needed to talk with another human, someone other than her young daughter or twenty-year-old nanny. She had become good friends with one of her coworkers, a woman named Zoya, and all that morning she had waited for an opportunity to talk with her. Although she could not reveal her experience with the child, she could discuss her lunch rendezvous.

Zoya, a native of Iran, had come to the United States with her husband for graduate school. After graduating, they'd had a daughter and then decided to stay. Only after becoming close friends did Sadi learn about her parents and how they were politicians in the Iranian government.

Zoya often complained to Sadi about the unfortunate situation with Iran and the tension between them and the United States. Sadi knew to avoid mentioning any of the anti-Iranian propaganda in the news and entertainment media. She felt sorry for Zoya and often wondered how she would feel living in a foreign country so intent on the invasion and oppression of her homeland.

Sadi could only share her deepest personal matters with a few people, Zoya being one of them. Ever since her son's funeral, her ex-husband seemed to lose all concern for their remaining child. Helen hardly knew him anymore. Although Sadi hated the man, she wished her daughter could occasionally spend some time with him. If nothing else, the time with her father could help Helen appreciate her mother more.

After their divorce, Sadi's ex-husband had become a symbol of her old life of drugs and apathy, the old Sadi. To be completely honest with herself, she did not blame him for the grief he caused. Ultimately, she had made the mistake of marrying him, just as her mother had unwisely married her father. People rarely broke or escaped their conditioning and often failed to change the course set by their parents, but Sadi prided herself on being one of the few who had broken her conditioning.

The process had begun when she chose to continue with college rather than quit. Then, when Sadi had given birth to her first child, Helen, she decided that Helen would live in better circumstances with a better example to follow.

Sadi only talked to her ex-husband when necessary, and fortunately, she'd rarely had to deal with him since the divorce. After the accident, he had stopped pretending to care about their daughter, and his absence had forced Sadi to arrange all of the funeral preparations herself. His family had tried to apologize for him, but his actions mattered little to her. He had acted as a jerk as a part-time father and had remained a jerk after their divorce. With him out of their lives, she finally felt free.

—✳—

Around ten o'clock that morning, Sadi found herself alone with her friend. "Hey, Zoya," she said. "I found something interesting on the internet."

The slender, short brunette sat in front of a computer screen on the opposite side of the room. Her ponytail spilled over the back of her white lab coat like a black snake on the snow. After a moment, Zoya turned from her computer screen and waited patiently for Sadi to finish.

"And..." Zoya said, an apparent question in her dark blue Persian eyes.

Having those beautiful eyes, darker even than her own, focused on Sadi brought a moment of appreciation. Before continuing, Sadi pushed a wisp of dark hair from her face. Sadi stood taller than Zoya by several centimeters, had fuller features, and was more pale, an obvious resident of the Northwest United States.

"Ever heard of the *Free State Project*?"

"Doesn't sound familiar," Zoya said, her smile stretching wider. "Did you join an LSD addicts anonymous group?"

Sadi smiled but refrained from indulging her friend by laughing. She wanted the conversation to remain quasi-serious.

"Close, but no. It's a group of people who moved to New Hampshire to create a free society. I found their website last night."

"Another freedom organization, eh," Zoya said and rolled her eyes. She spoke with a homogeneous mixture of humor and sarcasm but with eyes stained by concern. "Last year it was the *Libertarian party* then something called *Freedom Force,* and now this? You know you're on the CIA and FBI watch lists now, right? Has this, *Free State Project,* had any success?"

Sadi took another vial of blood. "I think they got someone elected to the legislature, but I haven't looked into it that much. I just think it's a cool concept."

"I doubt they'll get enough people to control an entire state."

"That's what I thought," Sadi agreed. "They're not exactly following the *baby steps* principle, but at least they're doing something."

"*Baby steps?*"

"Sorry. It's a reference from a movie with Bill Murray called, *What About Bob*. It's about starting small, taking manageable steps."

Sadi was always explaining American entertainment references.

"Oh," Zoya replied. "I haven't seen it, but Bill Murray is funny."

Sadi paused before continuing with the other topic she wanted to discuss. She knew Zoya would disapprove, but Sadi had to tell someone.

"I never told you about this person I met online, have I?"

Sadi tried to act casually as though she had simply forgotten to share an insignificant piece of information. But both of them knew the information had not been shared. Zoya shook her head in negative affirmation and opened her eyes even wider.

"What *person*?" she asked. "Is it a man?"

"Well you're right about the man part, but I have no reason to be interested in him *as a man* if that's what you mean. One of my friends, a lab assistant who worked here before you did, referred me to him and said he needed someone with a biology background. I've never actually met him in the real world. We've just been emailing each other."

"Does he have anything to do with the *Free State Project*?" Zoya asked. "Does he want you to move to New Hampshire or to donate something?"

"No, that was just one of the things he asked me about, but I don't think it's what he's really interested in. We talk about a lot of stuff. He sounds like a lawyer."

"So, he *claims* to be a lawyer," she began as if still deciding how to proceed. "What else does he *claim* to be? A millionaire just looking for some nice girl, like yourself, to share his vast wealth with?"

Sadi failed to stop herself from laughing and had to turn away to regain her composure. "Zoya, it's nothing like that. He really hasn't told me much about himself yet. And he hasn't claimed to be a lawyer. That's just what I suspect."

"Okay," Zoya said, and Sadi heard some relief in her voice. "So what does he want, do you think?"

"I don't know exactly what he wants, other than to meet with me," Sadi said tentatively, feeling like a gazelle drinking water from a pool with an alligator. "I got the impression he wants to get to know me more before meeting and revealing his true intentions."

Zoya shifted her chair to more easily face Sadi.

"Uh, is it a good idea to meet with him before you know what he wants?"

"Maybe not," Sadi admitted.

Even if Zoya doubted her judgment, Sadi trusted the friend who had facilitated the connection.

"So, don't do it," Zoya said in exasperation. "I don't know why you're telling me this. I know you're not going to listen to me."

Sadi disliked the frustration in Zoya's voice but unconsciously appreciated the diversion.

"Listen, Zoya, I know it sounds crazy, but I have a strange feeling about this. I just wanted to let someone else know about it so..."

Sadi paused and Zoya finished her sentence. "So that I would have something to tell the police when you are missing. You're not going anywhere without me. Where are you meeting this man?"

"Sorry, Zoya," Sadi said with real regret. "I can't bring anyone with me. But don't worry. I'm not dumb enough to meet him anywhere alone. We're going to meet in a public place."

"That is a good idea, but what if he is a crazy stalker? When he sees you, it will be all over. Don't let him follow you when you are done."

Sadi took a moment to mentally review her conversations with the man who had only given his first name, Gerald. The effort required less than a second to confirm her previous conclusions. Gerald had failed to exhibit the typical characteristics of a crazy stalker. The thought had initially crossed her mind, but she trusted her judgment.

Gerald had asked a lot of questions about her, as though just naturally curious, but he had seemed to know a lot already. That worried her a little. From his writing, at least, he had also seemed professional, well-educated, and polite.

He claimed to require her assistance for some kind of consulting but had refused to give any specifics over email. Did he want some incriminating information about her company? Due to its political tactics, Sadi had no love for the pharmaceutical industry, and she understood how often the industry wrote its own regulations and bought key politicians to pass them into law. But despite her personal feelings, she loved her work with immunology and had no intention of putting her job at risk.

If another pharmaceutical company or the government intended to initiate a lawsuit against Pantra, one of their lawyers might attempt to acquire evidence through its employees. The possibility of Gerald being an attorney for the government seemed unlikely. He had shown obvious signs of sincerely despising the government. He also could have gotten all of the information he claimed to need from an expert at the CDC. The government had plenty of its own experts.

If Sadi had learned anything from her formal education, she had learned to trust in evidence and make decisions based solely on the facts in front of her. So far, she had found no evidence to cause major concern.

"So when is your meeting?" asked Zoya.

"Lunch today." Sadi turned from her samples to face her friend again. "I promise to tell you all about it when I come back."

"Where are you going?"

"Not sure," Sadi said. "He's going to text me at noon about the place."

"Why do I get the feeling you aren't telling the whole story?" she asked, sounding somewhat offended.

"I've told you all I know," Sadi said as a meager offer of comfort.

Would Zoya attempt to follow her to her secret lunch meeting? If she did attempt to spy, she would need to sit inconspicuously but within hearing distance. Sadi would enjoy seeing the attempt. She doubted it would happen.

Sadi became consumed in her work for the rest of the morning. For a little while at least, she needed to forget about the experience with her son in the night and emotionally prepare for the next experience at lunch. Just before she left for her rendezvous, the topic of her clandestine meeting resurfaced. Zoya made Sadi promise to keep her phone handy and to call or text her if anything strange happened.

Zoya stopped Sadi just before she left. She squeezed Sadi's hand and held it while speaking.

"I'm sorry for being so nosy," she said with an unusually sweet smile. "It wasn't my place to pry. I know you wouldn't do anything *stupid*."

Zoya's sarcastic tone caused an involuntary smile to stretch across Sadi's lips. In her friend's not-so-subtle way, she sincerely wanted to prevent Sadi from acting stupid. On that occasion, she let Zoya have the final statement. She wanted her friend to feel as though she had some influence over the situation.

FORTY-ONE

Sadi

As Sadi walked to her car, she received the next text message from Gerald. He wanted to have lunch at the PF Chang restaurant, just ten minutes away from her work. On her way out of Pantra's secured parking lot, she waved to the security guard stationed there. On that day, only a few people left the site for lunch. Most employees preferred to stay on-site for their excellent cafeteria.

"Have a good lunch, Ms. Jacobsen," the guard said.

After turning onto the main street, she checked the rearview mirror to see if Zoya had followed her and then smiled when her friend failed to appear. She almost wished Zoya would have followed her. Although unafraid of the meeting, she would have appreciated her friend's opinion of the man.

At first, what she saw in the rearview mirror failed to register in her consciousness. After Sadi had turned onto the street, a dark green 2005 Mustang pulled out from the side of the road. Sadi took the next turn then glanced behind her again and noticed the same vehicle making the same turn, following her. Sadi shook her head and laughed at the sudden paranoia.

The air through her open window was cold but refreshingly dry and clear. Sadi welcomed the sunshine, a sharp contrast to an extremely wet Northwest winter where the dreary rain attacked them day after day after day. The cold air helped her appreciate the warm interior of her car and helped erase some of the strangeness of the night's experience.

To help distract her mind, Sadi energized the radio and turned the station to NPR. As she drove to the restaurant, she listened as the radio hosts discussed the global financial meltdown. During the first few weeks of the most recent man-made catastrophe, she'd listened intently to everything presented to her by the major media sources. And then after doing more intensive studying on her own, she'd become angry at the government for helping to facilitate the events.

Whenever the people on NPR talked about the subject, she fought the temptation to change the station. She never completely understood why she kept listening to people talk about the situation since she could not do anything about it. Perhaps she enjoyed having a specific target for her anger. Cursing the banks for their most recent round of plunder was easier than feeling angry at the universe for what had happened to her son. Perhaps if she'd had more freedom in her life, she would have chosen another road that night, and her son might still be alive.

When halfway to the restaurant, she looked behind her again just out of curiosity and noticed the same Ford Mustang traveling at about the same distance as when she had last looked. The man behind the wheel drove just far enough away to prevent her from recognizing his face. Had Zoya called someone to follow her, or had Gerald arranged the tail to assure that she came alone? The whole thing seemed too ridiculous, but she decided to test her suspicions anyway.

She knew of a gas station a few lights ahead and planned to pull into its parking area. After activating the turn signal, she kept her eyes on the rearview mirror and began pushing the brake pedal. The Mustang made no indication of turning. As the sports car drove past the gas station, Sadi noticed the driver looking straight ahead, but for one small instant, he looked at her. Even though warm air was blowing on her neck, the brief eye contact sent chills down her spine.

Sadi waited until the Mustang disappeared completely from her view, then she pulled back into traffic toward her destination. For a moment, she wondered if she should return to work and forget about the meeting.

"This is ridiculous," she said to herself.

Sadi noticed nothing else suspicious on the rest of her way to PF Chang's, and the dark green Mustang failed to make another appearance. As her memory of that disturbing experience quickly faded into the past, Sadi focused on the warm sunlight on her face and imagined meeting an interesting new person.

Unintentionally, Sadi found herself hoping to find Gerald in need of more than just a professional consultant. Whether lunch turned into a professional or personal meeting, however, Sadi hoped to meet with an unmarried man. Having lunch alone with a married man could make her uncomfortable, so she planned to watch for evidence of marriage. After the accident that had killed her son, she seemed to lose all interest in forming any new relationships, platonic or romantic. Perhaps this time she would feel different. She could use another friend who shared her rare and controversial perspective.

—✳—

After arriving at the restaurant, she realized they had failed to prepare for the problem of recognizing each other. Was he tall, short, fat, skinny? Should she carry a sign with her name?

In the restaurant parking lot, she felt the same uncomfortable sensation of being watched again. She looked around, half-expecting to see the green Mustang. After failing to recognize the vehicle in the lot, she told herself to stop worrying.

"I probably am being watched, you silly schizo," she said to herself. "He's probably watching me from inside the restaurant or his car."

Her paranoia reminded Sadi of being nineteen years old, the last time she had taken acid with her sixteen-year-old brother, Brian. As usual, they had taken the drugs while home alone and with all the blinds closed, so it was as dark as possible at five in the afternoon.

She remembered watching colors seeping through the blinds like smoke and then almost passing out from laughing. They had peeked from under a blanket, afraid of the creatures in the room with them, the creatures they had heard growling and laughing menacingly. She remembered thinking that when the evil creatures pulled the blanket away, it would be the end and they would die while laughing. She had looked forward to such an end.

Then Sadi remembered the horrible stomach ache following every experience with acid. Since then, the mere thought of doing acid nearly induced vomiting. Her reaction to the drug was one of the many reasons she had stopped doing it with him. Her brother probably still did acid every once in a while. Those thoughts usually made her sad, but at least her brother took care of himself and was an awesome uncle to her daughter.

After shaking the memory of her foolish youth, she entered the restaurant and pretended to act indifferent to the situation. At the entrance, a giant Chinese Terracotta warrior statue greeted her solemnly. While appreciating the piece of history it represented, a man tapped her right arm and addressed her.

"Ms. Jacobsen?"

Sadi turned and found a tall man standing next to her. He had dark hair, neatly combed to the side, and wore a dark blue suit.

"Gerald?" she asked, failing to hide her surprise.

The man stood taller than Sadi by several centimeters. He had enough thick hair to cover two heads but wore it just short enough to comb to the side. His dark blue suit hung on him as though he had lost five kilograms since its purchase. Overall, he looked professional and reminded her of a lawyer. His genuine smile helped ease her subconscious fear of encountering a crazy political activist.

"Thanks for meeting me here," he said as though they'd had lunch together often. Instead of waiting for her reply, he turned to the counter where a beautiful young girl greeted them with a smile.

"Yes, a table for two please," he said then turned back to Sadi. "I hope this place is good for you. I know it's close to your work."

"Yes, I like this place," she replied, somewhat confused at his tone of familiarity. She had prepared to introduce herself but felt awkward saying it now. For the moment at least, his disarming smile erased her confusion. She forced a smile of her own.

Gerald asked to sit in a remote booth instead of a table in the middle of the room where the hostess had wanted to place them. In uncomfortable silence, they followed the girl to their seats. On the short walk, Sadi looked at his left hand and noticed a naked ring finger.

"Sorry that I didn't introduce myself properly yet," he said confidentially after they were seated. "The name's Gerald Foster."

Until now, Sadi had never heard his last name. While looking through the menu, she noticed him inspecting their surroundings with suspicion. For nearly a minute of silence, the situation seemed like an awkward first date.

"So," she said somewhat playfully. "Have I guessed right that you're a lawyer?"

He looked up from the menu into her dark blue eyes and smiled.

"How did you know? Woman's intuition?"

"In your emails, you just sound like one. You write like one."

"If you mean I write like an above-average lawyer, then I'll take that as a compliment."

He set his menu on the table and the waitress almost immediately appeared to take their order. After the waitress walked away, the conversation continued as though uninterrupted.

"I suppose it's a compliment," she said. Sadi studied his eyes to see if they contained any emotion other than light sarcasm. So far, yes, but she probably had to know him better to see the difference. "I just like trying to figure things out on my own. So, let me see if I'm on the right track."

"Okay," he said as though he heard a challenge. "But I just want to warn you. I don't think you can even imagine my purpose for our meeting."

His comment made Sadi hesitate momentarily.

"Is that supposed to scare me?"

"No, I just like to get down to business," he said. "But let's see how close you get."

"You're interested in my work." She looked directly into his eyes again, squinting. "That's the easy part, considering all the questions you've asked me about it."

She waited for a response.

"Continue," he said.

"This next part, I'm not so sure about," she said and then sipped her water. "You either share several of my views concerning politics and history, or you're a damn good sociopath who's convinced me of it, to establish a sense of trust and solidarity."

He continued to smile but remained silent. If he meant to intimidate her, he had failed.

"Depending on the answer to that, you could be a government agent investigating Pantra. Or, you could be a lawyer for Bayer or another of our competitors, trying to steal proprietary information from me. If that's the case, I'll enjoy watching you squirm when I turn out to be uncooperative."

She raised her eyebrows in a challenge.

"Are you done?" he asked after taking a bite of his food and leaning back against his seat.

She thought he looked entertained, so she tried to sound indifferent.

"To be honest, I doubt either case. I think the more likely scenario is that you're working for some non-profit cancer research firm that dislikes working with that joke of a department, the CDC. My time is limited, but I'm willing to donate some of my time for a worthy cause."

"How about we start with what I'm not," he said as a polite interruption. "I may even tell you everything, but likely not today. You might not want to know everything. Ignorance is sometimes a convenient safety net."

"Okay, whittle it down some please." The way he stressed the word *safety* caused her to sit forward. When she found a more comfortable position, he continued.

"I'm not working for another pharmaceutical company, or for the government or a non-profit research group. Well, that's not true, I actually do occasional work for a few non-profits, but that has nothing to do with our meeting. I'll tell you about the group I represent, but I need to lay some groundwork first.

"Let me tell you what I know about you and we'll go from there." His smile transformed into a faint curve of his lips. "If that's okay?"

If he had failed to get her full attention already, he had it then. She slowly twirled her fork around some noodles, but kept it there on the plate, approving with silence.

"You were born and grew up in Portland, in a poorer part of town. Your biological mother died when you were ten years old, and you had to raise your younger brother, Brian, because your father was too busy with his job, along with his other activities, and his next wife was not very helpful."

"Not only did you go to college, but you stuck it out and even excelled. Very few people from your circumstances ever escape it. Not to give any credit to anyone other than yourself, but some of your courage and tenacity probably came from your mother's death. You look like her, you know. You must have been close. Her death may have made you angry. I don't know about you, but anger can be a strong motivator. That's one of the problems with people today. They aren't getting angry, about the right things at least. But whatever the reason for your strength, you definitely have my respect."

He did not wait for her to respond or validate any of his words. In their email correspondence, she had told him some of her history, but not even half of what he knew. He continued with her story as a boat cutting through the waves.

"You married while working towards your undergraduate degree in chemistry and graduated with honors, even after having a daughter. You and your husband separated near the end of your graduate school at the University of Washington. While there, you earned your PhD in molecular biology where you focused on infection and immunity. I read your first publication in the Journal of Hematology. To be honest, much of it was beyond me, and I only finished it so that I could look intelligent for reading it, so don't try to discuss it with me."

Gerald paused as if trying to decide to go further. When he spoke again, he started cautiously and became quieter.

"After the death of your second child, you and your husband finally divorced."

Gerald leaned forward and focused on her eyes. He seemed prepared to stop speaking if she displayed signs of anger or sadness.

"I know your son died last year. I was sorry to learn of it, and I'm very sorry to mention it. After his death, you've probably started thinking seriously about all you've been told, by your religion, by the government, and by society in general. I think you've realized that almost nothing can be taken at face value, and usually, it is almost the exact opposite. As you and I have discussed online, the truth can sometimes be horrible, but it must be faced and should not be ignored. Your emotional strength and the fact that you're an expert in microbiology are just what I am looking for. I think you can make a great contribution to the group I represent."

Sadi felt as if he had just invaded her home and looked through her underwear drawer. But she did not feel angry, just insecure and vulnerable. To be privy to that kind of personal data meant he either had connections or just knew how to dig for information. Being a lawyer probably helped too. In the short pause, she planned to speak, but he continued.

FORTY-TWO

Sadi

"I just need you to know that we've done our homework on you," Gerald said, eyes wide. "And I want you to take me very seriously. I believe you can be trusted. It's my job to help you trust me."

Sadi thought of seeing her son early that morning and strained her eyes to keep them dry. Did that experience prepare her for this meeting? Did the experience relate to Gerald in any way? The thought was too improbable to take seriously, to suggest out loud.

"Okay, you have the upper hand," Sadi said finally, glad to keep tears from her eyes. "I didn't even try to figure out who you were. Your first name was good enough for me."

Sadi laughed to herself and forced a smile. In an attempt to appear as unconcerned as possible, she sipped her water.

"You're probably wondering why I needed to know so much about you."

"You want me for some kind of consultancy, something secret?"

"Yes," he answered. "We need you for your technical expertise, and if you decide to help us, it needs to be kept confidential."

"So why all the personal information? Why do you care about my political views?" That seemed to be his key factor in choosing her. He could have picked from thousands of experts in her field. Sadi leaned forward and lowered her voice. "Why do you care if I know about all the lies everyone seems to be swallowing? That can't have anything to do with my educational background."

Gerald leaned away from her as though her proximity made him nervous. She watched his eyes as they moved from her face to the rest of the dining room. Was he worried about something and trying to hide it? He suddenly seemed frightened. Before resuming eye contact, he continued speaking.

"What did you think about that group I told you about? The *Free State Project*?" After he finished scanning the room, his eyes locked back on hers.

"The *Free State Project*?" she said in unfeigned frustration, a bit too loudly. "Oh my God. That's what this is about! I'm not moving to New Hampshire if that's what you're getting at."

"Why not?" he asked, an amused tone in his voice.

Her heart sank with sudden disappointment. The whole situation made little sense. Why would this man, who appeared so intelligent and wrote so eloquently, go to all that trouble for just one person when the Free State Project needed many thousand to make a difference? Did he think she would make a large contribution? She hated the thought of being solicited and wasting her time.

In the next few seconds, Sadi realized a more personal cause for her sudden disappointment. Subconsciously, she had let herself hope for the meeting to include the possibility of a romantic connection. And then his physical appearance and obvious intelligence had helped her become vulnerable to the natural need for a personal connection. He had also violated her sense of independence, which she'd spent so long to re-establish.

As he sat there with eyebrows raised and silently waiting for a response, all of her negative emotions became directed at him. She had difficulty concentrating on his question.

"Why won't I move to New Hampshire?" she began. Talking gave Sadi an emotional release, and her internal anger transformed into words. "First, they're trying to free an entire state. There aren't enough individualists who know what's truly going on in the world, and who give a damn, to fill a county. Second, even if we were numerous enough for a whole state, the government would come down on us harder than they did on the South during the Civil War."

Instead of shock at her anger, Gerald seemed amused by her arguments. "Yes, but if they were successful? Would you do it?"

"I'm not itching to move to the cold Northeast, but sure, in your very hypothetical world, I'd do it." His failure to recoil at her emotional outburst had damaged her confidence. Before finishing, she unconsciously clenched her left fist on the table. "Only if I thought they had a chance."

"Even if they couldn't eliminate all of the artificial laws, wouldn't it be nice just to live in a community of people who share our views?"

The argument made sense to her. If she'd had more than just a few days of casual thought on the subject, she probably would have more fully considered his postulate. Unfortunately, she had only looked at their website a couple of times. His arguments made no difference. Part of her wanted to stay angry at him, and emotional momentum helped too.

"To be honest, I would rather stay away from many of the people who claim to be interested in freedom." The disappointed look on his face gave her a slight sense of guilt for speaking rudely. "But yes, I do like associating with true individualists."

His tone became more serious then and his smile disappeared.

"How much would you be willing to sacrifice to live in a place like that? Twenty thousand dollars? Fifty? A hundred?"

Her anger quickly returned to its previous level. *How could I have been so stupid?* Even though she had refused to move to New Hampshire, he still wanted her to donate money anyway.

"You can't be serious," she said. "I can't believe you're asking me for a donation."

He sat back in his seat and the amusement returned to his eyes. "I never claimed to be associated with the Free State Project, and I'm not asking you for money. These are all hypothetical questions."

Sadi sat in stunned silence for several seconds. Her anger slowly turned to a feeling of relief for being wrong in her assumptions. Then she felt foolish for being so angry, and she would require some time to relax. Would her ridiculous hope return? Hope for a possible romantic connection? All of the emotions of the past ten hours suddenly left her physically exhausted. At that moment, she felt as though Gerald had sent her back to the beginning of a board game.

"Now I feel stupid for being so angry," she said in mock anger. "You seemed to enjoy watching me vent."

He laughed uncomfortably.

"I apologize for putting you through that. I really did not intend to make you feel any negative emotions."

"It's been one of those days," she said in apology. "Normally, it would have been fine."

"Good. Now, you did not answer the question. Hypothetically of course, how much would you be willing to sacrifice? I'm sorry to put a dollar amount on sacrifice, but I think many sacrifices can be measured in dollars or at least a percentage of one's bank account."

"There are plenty of other things to sacrifice," she said and paused to take a bite. "I don't believe that what you're proposing is even possible, not now at least. Even if a free society like that existed, it would not exist for long. They'd find a way to destroy it before the world realized that it actually worked.

"First, they'd send intruders to stir up trouble, create some fake terrorist act or another kind of event, and claim that the free society was responsible, reinforcing the misconception that it would never work and was a horrible system and harbored criminals.

"Once they had the justification to eliminate us, it would be all over. I'm sure you can imagine how many missiles they can launch, how many tanks they can roll over us. Remember what they did to Hiroshima and Nagasaki? Remember how many people they killed, people like you and me who were just trying to make a living? Remember what the Russians did to Chechnya? What China did to Mongolia? What the North did to the South? How many kids they killed in Waco Texas? I could go on and on. If I remember right, you even wrote something similar in one of our email conversations."

"Yes," he said dejectedly and the look on his face reminded Sadi of when she had revealed the true identity of Santa to her daughter. He continued, more somber. "You're probably right. History is filled with tragic events. Or at least, that's what we've been taught. But it wouldn't surprise me at all if some of the Free State Project leaders worked for the intelligence agencies. They don't like waiting for grassroots organizations to form on their own."

FORTY-THREE

Sadi

"Now, Sadi," he said more cheerfully. "I don't want you to be angry with me, but I cannot tell you everything today. First, for your protection, and second, because you will need to consider the implications of your involvement. However, what I have told you needs to be kept confidential. I need you to promise me that this conversation stays between you and me. Do I have your word?"

"Sure," she said without pausing. "You have my word."

"Even if you get questioned by a government official?"

She gulped but nodded. "You still haven't told me anything."

"If anyone asks you about this meeting, tell them that I decided not to tell you anything. You did not want to continue our conversation. Understand?"

"I understand about acting ignorant, but let me get this straight. You're talking about establishing a free society? How is that even possible? I think you're sincere, but *think* is not good enough. I don't know if I'm willing to sacrifice my security and comfortable lifestyle for the small chance of a free society."

"Like I said, I'm not going into details today, but you're almost on the right track."

Up until that point, Sadi thought of freedom as just an abstract thought, an idea existing only in fantasy. Of course, she wanted to live in a land of freedom. Of course, she would fight for her daughter to have a better future. Even though she thought the Libertarian party had a minuscule chance of success, she had joined them. At least, she thought her vote meant something.

Had her choices carried too little risk? The government had no reason to fear Libertarians, or Anarchists even. Being so few, they had little or no real power. The overwhelming majority of people supported the establishment, either the Democrat or the Republican face of the beast. The majority believed everything the news told them. She liked Gerald's view, the concept of living with others who wanted true freedom. How much would she be willing to invest? How much of her daughter's future would she risk? She needed time to think.

Suddenly, Sadi remembered the Ford Mustang on her way to the restaurant and then when Gerald was suspiciously looking at the people around them. For the first time during the meeting, she became more conscious of the people in the restaurant. A group of three college-age guys occupied the booth behind her. They spoke rather loudly, and she doubted if anyone could hear her conversation over their raucous chatter. Sadi spoke in a whisper, just in case.

"Do you think we're being watched?"

"What makes you say that?" he asked with an unexpected smile.

"On my way here," she began, "I thought someone was following me, a man in a dark green Mustang. I pulled into a gas station, and he passed me, but I was sure he had been looking at me."

Gerald sat back.

"You probably haven't spotted him here, am I right?"

"No, I haven't, and there was no Mustang in the parking lot when I got here. I checked but forgot about it until now. Do you think he was following me, or was it just my imagination?"

"I'm afraid it might be true," he said, shaking his head as though he considered being followed a mere annoyance. "Sometimes they have a guy following me. I think they're trying to build a case against me, because of some previous issues that I really don't want to discuss at the moment, but it's unrelated to the topic we've been discussing. I apologize if they give you any trouble. Just remember that the law does not require you to talk to them. I can be your lawyer if anyone asks."

"Who are they?"

"The Federal Bureau of Investigation," he said while putting a piece of steak in his mouth.

"Okay?" Sadi asked tentatively. "You're going to have to tell me about it. If you want me to trust you, I can't think of you as an outlaw."

"I understand," he said. "I didn't want to talk about it because it's kind of embarrassing, but I guess you do deserve an explanation. A year or so ago, some acquaintances of mine broke into the Seattle Federal Reserve office or were caught attempting to. I really had nothing to do with it, but I pissed off the FBI when I chose to be their defense attorney, pro bono. I didn't let the FBI take advantage of them and then I exposed one of the undercover FBI assets. You can verify the story if you don't believe me. It's all public record."

"I'll take your word for it. For now."

His explanation had failed to quell some of her doubts. She already had too long of a list.

"If you decide not to get involved, then you have nothing to worry about. Your record's clean and the FBI will find no interest in you."

"Well that's good," she said. "I guess."

He smiled again.

"After work tonight, go home and think about a future where you own your life without coercion. I think it's worth the risk. If you want to know more, please contact me. I'm pretty excited about what's going on and wish we could go over all the details now, but as I said, you have to make the decision first."

"I'm sorry, but you've got to give me more than this." Sadi could not make an informed decision on what Gerald had revealed. "At least, tell me how I can contribute to your group. Why did you choose me?"

From the look in Gerald's eyes, Sadi knew he had hoped to avoid this question. Before he answered, the experience with her son that morning rushed into her memory again.

"I guess this was inevitable," he began. "The answer might not be acceptable to you, but I chose you because I think we might need you."

"You *might* need me? Why not wait until you know?"

"That's hard to explain without telling you confidential information. But maybe I can reveal how I found you."

He looked above her head and slightly to his right, as though attempting to recall a memory. Sadi tried to remember what *looking to the right* meant in psychology. Was it searching for the correct answer or inventing one? He continued before she could remember.

"An old coworker of yours, Paul, introduced you to a friend of his and his friend described the encounter to his mother, a woman named Gerda Schreiber. His mother is an old friend of mine. When I asked if she knew anyone with a background in biology who also believed in individualism, Gerda gave me your name."

"Yes. I remember you telling me that."

"Well, what I didn't tell you was that when I heard your name, I just knew I had to contact you, even before I learned more about your background in biology. I don't usually base my decisions on feelings, but in your case, I couldn't ignore them.

"I hope that doesn't scare you, and I'm not making up some sort of black magic pick-up line. Please don't take it the wrong way. When I learned more about you, I just knew you were the right choice. All that I can say is that we want people to look at things from several different angles."

While he finished his explanation, the memory of her son in the night nearly overwhelmed her awareness of their surroundings. Before responding, she picked up her glass and poured some of the cold water down her dry throat. A deep breath helped restore her composure.

"If I decide to get involved, how do I let you know? Through email?"

Gerald looked relieved by her response.

"No, email is too insecure. Log into our secure website. That will be your answer."

"Even if I want to learn more, I can still decide not to get involved?"

He nodded and then looked at his watch.

"Well, our hour is up. It was very nice finally meeting you, Sadi, in person. I do hope you consider the next step. Even if not, I hope we can still keep in touch. There are too few of us."

"Sure," she said and then wondered if she had responded too quickly.

He removed a business card from under his suit coat, wrote on the back for a few seconds then handed it to her. His card reminded Sadi of her divorce lawyer, the kind of man she did not particularly want to remember. She quickly read the name of his law firm, *Foster and Fowler*.

She turned the card over and saw what he had written: the address of their website, a username, and six random words. Before Sadi visited the website, he told her to make several different web searches, sign into several websites, and then do an internet search for three of the six words on the back of the card. A search of any three words from his list would deliver their site in the top ten choices. He did not want her to type their website directly into the web browser. In addition, she could only log into the site within a specified time of the evening. The extra precautions seemed extreme and unnecessary, but Sadi agreed to follow them if she chose to proceed.

As they exited the restaurant, Sadi thought of more questions but knew he would not answer them. Before going their separate ways, she searched the parking lot for anything suspicious and noticed nothing out of the ordinary, especially not the green Mustang.

"I hope we meet again," he said while shaking her hand.

"It was good meeting you, Gerald."

After reaching her car and grasping the door handle, she turned for one last glance. Gerald was standing in the same spot and watching her. He smiled and raised a hand then turned to his black Ford Taurus and disappeared inside.

FORTY-FOUR

Sadi

When Sadi returned from lunch, she had difficulty concentrating on work again. Although she had failed to learn much of what Gerald wanted, her mind raced through the countless possibilities. At least, she no longer suspected him of being a government agent.

The memory of being followed by the man in the Ford Mustang continued to haunt her and filled her with a sense of violation. Just thinking of their brief eye contact sent chills through her system. Whether the man worked for the FBI or another organization, Sadi had no clue. At that time, the employer made little difference.

"So how did your meeting go?" Zoya asked with a teasing smile. "Was it a romantic connection? Are you interested in him?"

Even though the possibility of a romantic relationship had been one of Sadi's secret hopes, the mere suggestion caused a flare of annoyance. Sadi wanted to blame her friend for placing the thought in her mind, but she could not. For the sake of confidentiality, she would pretend to play the game even if the act caused embarrassment. Failing to deny the accusations might cause Zoya to continue believing the wrong assumptions.

"Lunch was good," Sadi began. "He was not married, or at least he wasn't wearing a wedding ring."

"Was he handsome?" Zoya's knowledge of the English language contained only limited vocabulary about sexual attraction. She often used the word *handsome* to categorize men.

"Actually, he was handsome," Sadi said before she could consider her response and then remembered Gerald watching her in the parking lot.

For the present, Zoya asked no other questions, and neither of them discussed the topic again for the next few days. Sadi regretted mentioning the meeting in the first place and hoped to avoid the topic in the future.

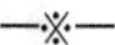

Two nights later while falling asleep in her room, Sadi had the distinct feeling of being watched. After opening her eyes and looking around at an empty bedroom, the sensation remained. She tried to ignore her perception, closed her eyes, and concentrated on falling asleep again.

A tornado of bright colors eventually formed in her imagination and replaced the feeling of being watched, and she soon forgot about lying in bed. The colorful tornado slowly dissipated and became replaced by a view of her kitchen with her brother sitting at the dining table. She missed seeing her brother, Brian. In the dream, he had not visited for several years.

While she watched him at the table, her brother wrote studiously on a piece of paper, oblivious to her. A hazy yellow light obscured the paper and his hands so that Sadi could not see them clearly. The light seemed perfectly normal in her dream and raised no alarm for breaking any laws of physics.

After some time of watching Brian, people began walking through the kitchen, people from her memories. Some of the people were admiring the beautiful kitchen while others reminded Sadi of shoppers at a grocery store. Most of the shoppers stayed only briefly and no one seemed to notice her.

Sadi knew some of the people intimately and the others only by sight. Occasionally, a famous actor, politician, or news anchor would appear. Donald Trump and John Wayne walked in together with her dead grandmother. The old lady looked confused as though deciding to approach Sadi to ask a question. But before Sadi could talk to her, the old woman turned and walked from the room. Sadi had no memory of ever meeting that grandmother, just seeing her picture.

During the entire episode, her brother wrote furiously on the paper and paid no attention to anyone around him. The fuzzy yellow light remained over his hands and the paper.

Strangers eventually replaced all of the familiar people, and they suddenly stopped and turned to face one direction, to a space between the counter and the refrigerator. She also noticed other people's faces peering through the windows, all looking in the same direction.

Sadi followed their gaze and saw a young boy, maybe twelve years old, sitting on the ground in the small space with his back to the wall. Although Sadi knew him, she could not recall his name. Of all the people who had walked through the kitchen, only the boy was acknowledging her existence.

After staring into the boy's eyes for several seconds, she realized the reason for all of the interest in him. He was the only living person in the room. All the rest of the people were ghosts, creatures in another realm, including her brother at the table. Everyone was staring at him, mesmerized by the light in his eyes, the blazing light of life.

The boy was scraping his feet against the ground, attempting to push himself farther into the corner. The sight of him suddenly filled Sadi with sadness. As a child, everyone had rejected the boy. Only Sadi and her brother had given him friendship. The fear in his eyes felt like a stab to her heart.

In the next instant, all of the strangers in the kitchen exploded into puffs of smoke and Sadi could not see anything for a long time. After the smoke dissipated, only Sadi and her brother remained with the boy. Sadi looked at the windows and saw only darkness beyond the glass.

Sadi suddenly remembered the boy's name, and she knew strangely how to banish his fear. She had only to grab his hand then speak his name. But as she stepped forward, the boy cringed in terror again and she paused in temporary confusion. She took two more steps before noticing that the boy had somehow gotten farther from her. And then she noticed the hazy yellow cloud covering her brother's hands. The cloud was growing.

"I'm not going to hurt you," Sadi said after returning her attention to the boy and extending her hand.

The yellow cloud in her periphery continued to consume her brother and would soon consume her and the boy. She had to hurry and touch his hand before the cloud overtook them, but after two more steps, he was already too far away. The cloud finally enveloped her too and she saw nothing else, only hazy yellow light. She could not see her feet, hands, or any other part of her body, and for a while, she wondered if she even existed. But that did not seem to matter. She soon forgot about everything, including her brother and the boy. And then she forgot about gravity and the cloud of light.

Sadi was now alone in endless space, with no Sun, Earth, or anything but the distant stars in her view. But instead of causing panic, her isolation was comforting. Everything from her life was too far away to matter anymore.

—✳—

At first, the bright blue dot just looked like all of the other stars around her, but when the Earth had grown to the size of her fingertip, she recognized it as her home planet. As the surface features became more discernible, she realized that she was speeding toward the planet and her return to Earth meant death. The giant orb was racing to meet her and she would burn up in the atmosphere and become a beautiful shooting star, a child's wish before bedtime. Her destiny seemed almost poetic.

When the Earth filled her entire view, she expected a quick end. Her body would soon vaporize, her ashes to remain in the upper atmosphere for eternity. She had no time to despair, no time to regret the loss of time with her daughter, brother, friends, and career. But instead of vaporizing in the plasma wind, Sadi continued unscathed through the atmosphere.

The speed became incredible. She was flying faster than a bullet through the clouds. After ripping through them, she saw a line on the Earth, stretching as far as she could see in both directions. The line transformed into a road with a dot on it. Then the dot transformed into a man. He was just standing there, looking up at her.

Right before she crashed into him, she recognized the man. Gerald Foster was standing there, arms held wide as though preparing to catch her in a warm embrace. She noticed his smile and the lack of fear. She held her hands forward like Superman, an absurd attempt to cushion the impact. And then just before her momentum obliterated them both, she jolted awake.

In the dark of her bedroom, Sadi sat up in bed and wiped cold sweat from her face. Without light to distract her mind, she kept imagining Gerald's face crashing into her, followed by the vague memory of a boy cowering in her kitchen. The dream seemed like a message from something other than her subconscious.

FORTY-FIVE

Sadi

While sitting in the darkness, Sadi continued to imagine Gerald's face rushing toward her at lightning speed. To stop the assault, she had to get out of bed, exercise her muscles, and enter the light. She needed to replace her imagination with reality.

Sadi would have usually slept ninety minutes longer, but getting up at four-thirty in the morning seemed a small price to pay for relief from her dreams. As Sadi walked through the hall toward the stairs, she stopped by her daughter's open bedroom door. Helen was lying under the covers with only her blond hair visible. A pink glow from the night light filled the room with softness, and the sound of Helen's steady breathing added to the tranquil atmosphere.

She forgot what time Gerald had said to log onto the website, but she did not care. After finding his business card, she opened her laptop computer in the kitchen and brought the machine to life. While waiting for the operating system to wake up, she prepared coffee.

As instructed, Sadi chose three of the six keywords on the card for the internet search and the target website appeared as number four in the list of several thousand search results. She clicked the link and a cartoon-style drawing of a rocket leaving the Earth filled the main page. From the other pictures and text, a random visitor would think they had landed on a site dedicated to astronomy, although the purpose of the site was not explicitly defined. The page contained an impressive array of star charts, constellations, and cartographic depictions of the Earth with velocity vectors and scientific formulas in beautiful calligraphy. Sadi was instantly impressed.

Sadi's fascination with the website allowed the girl approaching the kitchen table to escape her notice. When her daughter's twenty-year-old nanny cleared her throat, Sadi jumped in surprise.

"Oh, I'm sorry," Jen said and yawned. "I heard a noise and came down to see if Helen was awake. God, I'm tired. Sorry, Sadi."

Sadi thought the girl looked more ragged than usual, even after just getting out of bed, then she remembered the rock concert Jen had attended with her friends the previous evening. She'd returned home after Sadi and Helen had fallen asleep. Sadi considered advising the girl to take a shower to wash the dried sweat and tangles from her dark brown hair and the smeared mascara from under her eyes, but she refrained and suppressed a laugh at her appearance.

"Sorry to wake you, Jen," Sadi said as she turned the computer screen away from the girl's view. "How was the band?"

"Awesome," she said with a wide smile and then rubbed her eyes. "Your brother sure had the crowd going. I think he even noticed me."

Sadi understood Jen's infatuation with her brother, Brian, an affliction that hundreds of other young girls had also suffered. Usually, Sadi would indulge the girl by letting her talk about the experience, but she just wanted to get back to the website.

"Let's talk later," Sadi said and smiled. "You should go back to bed. From my viewpoint, you could use a few more hours."

Jen ignored the teasing insult. "What are you doing up this early?"

"Bad dream."

"That's too bad," Jen said, attempting to see past Sadi to the computer screen.

Sadi leaned closer to the computer and let the awkward silence become an indication of who would win the contest to see the website.

"Alright," Jen said with a small frown. "I'll just get back to bed."

Sadi smiled while watching the girl walk away. She loved Jen as a sister and trusted her completely. Jen had turned into the perfect nanny for Helen. She always put her job above everything else in her life and loved Helen as if she were her daughter or little sister. Sadi also liked having another woman in the house.

In some ways, Jen acted as a typical teenager. She obsessed over music and went to a concert with her friends nearly every month. She liked staying up late and sleeping in late. But she also loved just hanging out with Sadi and Helen and could discuss any topic with either of them. Sadi had the impression that the girl was trying to compensate for the disinterest and lack of attention from her parents and siblings.

After discovering Sadi's relationship with the attractive lead singer of a local band, Jen bought all of their albums and became their biggest fan. When Brian had come over to visit for the first time after she had started as the nanny, Jen had almost fainted with excitement. The memory of that event always made Sadi smile.

And then a few months after hiring Jen, Sadi had confronted her about the familiar smell of marijuana on her clothes. Although afraid of being fired for the offense, Jen had told the truth about the situation and her bold admission had impressed Sadi.

Sadi took a more pragmatic approach to drugs than the general population. If Jen could do her job well, why should Sadi care about what Jen did during her off hours? Since Sadi cared for the girl, she did her best to warn Jen about the dangers of drugs, especially the more harmful ones, and to stay away from them in general. They were forbidden in her home, but due to her stupid actions as a youth, Sadi refused to let the situation scar her opinion of the girl.

Sadi also enjoyed talking about the music Jen liked. Their musical tastes overlapped in several areas. At the beginning of their professional relationship, Jen had asked Sadi to attend a concert with her. Although the offer had tempted Sadi, she'd wanted to keep a bit of a professional boundary between them. Sadi had no problem smoking a joint every once in a while by herself, but going to a concert and possibly becoming tempted to get high with her employee seemed like a bad idea.

Sadi had attended enough of her brother's shows anyway and wanted to distance herself from his type of friends, although she still shared a love of music and enjoyed discussing the topic with him.

—✳—

After Jen had walked back up the stairs to her bedroom, Sadi waited and listened until all indications of movement ceased. She turned back to her laptop screen and noticed the login box under the address bar. While holding Gerald's business card, she read the username he wrote and typed it in uppercase letters, IRIS.

Had Gerald produced the username just for her, or did the word simply indicate a recruit? Although she preferred to choose her username, the word either referred to the flower or part of the eye, and she considered each option as a compliment. After yawning, she signed into the site as IRIS and a prompt asked her to create a password. A welcome message appeared after she hit ENTER.

Welcome IRIS, please read this page and answer the question at the bottom. By signing in and continuing further, you agree to keep what you learn strictly confidential. Thank you for your willingness to participate!

Sadi required only a minute to read through the information on the new page. The text failed to include anything definitively related to the group's true purpose but instead explained how the website should be used as a secure medium to communicate with other members. The text also included random references to drugs and sex, including how a rocket was a phallic symbol, giving her a completely different impression of the front page.

At first, she was confused then realized that the text was likely intended to mislead the reader. Either that or Gerald had wanted her to join a site devoted to helping people cope with addictions to sex and drugs. The clever prose was probably intended to lead interlopers into believing that the members of the site wished to hide embarrassing personal information.

After chuckling for a moment, Sadi began to feel better about joining. The bottom of the page contained three options.

Want to proceed?

Still need more information?

Not interested!

After selecting the first option, Sadi positioned the cursor over the *Confirm* button and rested her index finger on the *Enter* key. She paused for several seconds. Did she have enough rational reasons for accepting the invitation? Her mind answered with a *no*, but her feelings told her to just hit the key. Her decision to proceed seemed to flow from the vision of her son the other night and her most recent dream.

Although Gerald had failed to mention the subject of compensation, Sadi wondered if participation offered anything other than the opportunity to be part of something important, such as human freedom. Would her actions help increase her own freedom or Helen's? Was that worth the risk?

After clicking *Confirm*, some new text appeared, which gave her instructions about the next step. She needed to log into the site again after twenty-four hours.

"Great," she whispered. "More waiting."

Sadi wondered again why Gerald had chosen her name as IRIS. When not satisfied with any of the options that her mind presented, she closed the computer and attempted to rest from thought for a while.

FORTY-SIX

Sadi

After deciding to join Gerald's group that morning, Sadi had another difficult day concentrating on her projects at work. Her mind kept returning to all of Gerald's possible reasons for wanting her participation. Although the website had instructed her to wait twenty-four hours, she decided to hurry home after work and log in anyway. Gerald would not ban her from the site for such a small infraction.

As Sadi was scrambling to finish her final task of the day, compiling her latest test results in Excel, Zoya walked into her office and began talking to her. Sadi was watching the computer screen, entering data, and pretending to participate in the conversation. When Sadi sensed Zoya's sudden excitement, she stopped typing and looked away from the monitor.

"I'm sorry, but what did I just agree to?" Sadi asked.

"Don't try to get out of it, Sadi," Zoya said, shaking her head. "Your mind has not been here with the rest of us today. You need to relax with a drink. Who knows, maybe you'll meet someone."

Sadi desperately wanted to go home, so she could begin the next step in the process with Gerald and his group, but she also felt an obligation to Zoya for ignoring her all day. A drink with her friend was tempting, just not socializing with unfamiliar men. She disliked the idea of making a romantic connection at a bar.

Zoya did not let her go home first, claiming that Sadi might change her mind. Zoya followed Sadi to the closest pub and they sat together at the bar. After getting their drinks, Zoya initiated the conversation by complaining about her child's teacher and how her husband did not agree with her poor assessment of the school and the curriculum. Sadi mostly just listened and tried to avoid thoughts of Gerald and her strange dreams. While sipping her drink, she avoided eye contact with any guy who happened to look in her direction. During their conversation, Zoya nodded toward several different men, her eyes wide with the question: *What about that guy?*

After Sadi shook her head at the fifth suggestion, Zoya rolled her eyes and sighed in exasperation. Sadi smiled sweetly, as though trying not to laugh.

"Are you ever going to tell me what happened with your secret rendezvous with that man?" Zoya asked.

"Didn't I already tell you about that?"

"You told me he was a lawyer and needed a consultant for one of his clients," she said and met Sadi with wide eyes. "You left out more information about the most important part, the part that I *wanted* to hear. He is single and handsome, and..."

"Yes," Sadi answered and remembered Zoya asking the same question already. Sadi sipped her drink to avoid saying more.

"Hmm," Zoya said and paused for a second. "When are you seeing him again?"

"I don't know."

"You're enjoying this aren't you?"

"What do you mean?" Sadi asked, tilting her head slightly. She almost lost her composure and laughed, but she somehow refrained from smiling.

"Stop laughing at me," Zoya said, acting hurt. "Promise me you'll tell me if anything happens. I need a promise!"

"You'll be the first one to hear anything," Sadi said and then decided to be nice to her friend and give her something juicy. "He is *very* handsome, but I'm not expecting anything to happen."

—✳—

Sadi arrived home early enough to put Helen to bed for the night. Helen had wanted to see her mother, so Jen had let her play the Wii to pass the time.

"Mom!" Helen said after Sadi walked in the front door. She jumped from her perch on the couch where she was playing Mario Kart.

Helen loved that game more than all the others, one of the only things she seemed to enjoy doing lately, other than drawing. She threw her arms around her mother's waist.

"Welcome back," Jen said sarcastically from where she sat at the table. She looked up just enough to acknowledge Sadi's arrival.

"I was waiting for you forever!" Helen spoke while yawning. "Where were you?"

"I'm sorry, hon," Sadi answered. "Zoya made me get a drink with her. She had some stuff she wanted to tell me."

"Were you looking for a man?" Helen asked loudly while running back to the couch to continue her game.

Jen snorted with a laugh from the table. Sadi ignored her.

"No man tonight, dear, just a drink." Sadi sat on the couch next to her daughter and watched her play the game. "You're in third place. Good job!"

"I was in first," she replied angrily. "Waluigi just pushed me over the cliff. He's always undermining me."

Where did her daughter learn the word, *undermine*? Did she even know what it meant? Helen often used random new words that she heard from various sources. Sadi turned to Jen and mouthed the word, *undermine*?

"She was falling asleep on the couch," Jen said and shrugged. "So, I said she could play the Wii until you got home."

Sadi stood, walked toward the kitchen, and noticed a thick opened textbook and several papers scattered across the kitchen table. While Jen was working on her schoolwork, she drank orange juice and ate toast. Jen liked toast with butter and nothing else. She often ate the same food to begin and end her day.

"Thanks, Jen," Sadi said sincerely then changed her tone to one of playful seriousness. "All those carbs are going to catch up to you when you get to my age."

Jen answered by taking a large bite of toast, smiling, and then returning silently to her work. Helen finished her game five minutes later, ten minutes after eight in the evening. After her game, she followed her usual bedtime routine, bathroom, a drink of water, and two short books that Helen insisted Sadi read to her.

As she bent down to kiss her daughter goodnight, Helen put her skinny arms around Sadi's neck.

"I love you, Mom!" she said with a huge smile and a tone full of exaggerated drama.

Helen liked to put extra emphasis on most displays of affection. Sadi loved that part of her personality, but she hoped the behavior would fail to transform her daughter into an excessively dramatic teenager.

"Love you too," Sadi answered while trying to pry Helen's hands from her neck. Sadi laughed and imagined her neck snapping under the pressure from such tiny hands. "Okay, you can let go now."

"Is this our home?" Helen asked after releasing her mother.

"Of course, this is our home," Sadi answered. "Why would you ask that?"

"Hmm," Helen replied as though considering a complicated philosophical question. "I had a dream last night about moving to a new home, but I don't remember where."

"Do you want to move?"

"Oh, I don't know." Helen yawned and rolled onto her side, facing the wall. Her words became a whisper. "It might be exciting. Good night, Mom!"

Usually, when Helen had finished participating in a conversation, the other participants should abandon all efforts to keep the conversation going. Sadi ignored the urge to ask another question and patted the covers over her daughter. While leaving the room, she left the door slightly open and glanced one last time at the lump under the covers.

Sadi went downstairs and took her laptop to a chair with its back against the wall in the living room where a nosy Jen would have difficulty spying on her. After logging into the website with her username, Sadi discovered a completely different style than the other pages she had seen. Overall, the site looked simpler. Gerald and his friends had put a lot of effort into making security tight.

At the top of the screen, a blinking mail icon indicated that Sadi had a message from Gerald. In the note, Gerald did not attempt to hide his excitement at her decision to join. For the next hour, while Jen stayed at the kitchen table, Sadi sat in the living room with her laptop, reading the website content.

FORTY-SEVEN

Sadi

A few days later, while Sadi was preparing Helen for bed, the phone rang. She would have let the call transfer to voice mail, but Helen lifted the receiver before Sadi could stop her.

"Hi, Uncle Brian!" she said excitedly then held the phone out to her mother with a pout. "He wants to talk to you, Mom."

Sadi sighed and knew she had to talk to him. Conversations with her brother sometimes lasted a long time, and she'd just wanted to put Helen to bed and relax. He usually called earlier in the evenings, or would just visit unexpectedly. Before taking the phone, Sadi tried to remember the last time she'd talked with Brian. It had been longer than two weeks since he'd called last. She should have called him on her own.

"Hi, Brian," she said, keeping the impatience from her tone. "How's it going? Sorry, I haven't called. I've been distracted lately."

"I've been too busy to notice," he said laughing. "You won't believe who contacted me."

"Who?"

"Freddy called me yesterday," he said and paused to let her recognize the name. "And he wants to get in touch with you, but don't worry. I didn't give him your address or phone number or anything yet."

"Freddy Carlson," she said, and the memory of him from her dream made her heart skip. She knew no one else named Freddy. "Is there a reason why I wouldn't want to talk to him?"

"No," her brother said and then paused. "It's just...you remember how fond he was of you. I thought I'd give you the choice."

"Did he say what he wanted?"

"He just said he needed to see you, but he wouldn't tell me why. You know Freddy. He's in his own world."

"Well," she said and paused for a moment to give an impression of consideration. Yes, she definitely wanted to see Freddy. "Give him a call and see if he wants to visit here, but you're coming with him."

—⁎—

The next night, when the strange car pulled into her driveway, Sadi watched anxiously from the window. The darkness and rain obscured the faces of the driver and passenger, but somehow she recognized the shapes of her brother and Freddy in the front seats. She felt some anxiety to see Freddy walk through the door with her brother. It seemed like her past trespassing on her present.

Sadi took one last look outside and realized something. She assumed Brian would drive Freddy to her house, but her brother sat in the passenger seat. Freddy had driven some luxury sedan that her brother would have never chosen or been able to afford.

"Too pretentious," he would have said.

Sadi had difficulty imagining the strange boy from her youth driving an expensive car. They had been just a bunch of poor kids from the bad side of town, and Freddy had come from an even worse situation than she and Brian. Then she remembered Freddy being an intelligent and nice kid. So, why would he not have a good job and a nice car? He deserved it. She was happy for him.

She held no grudge against Freddy, just anxiety at seeing him again. She had liked him as a friend. If they had met by chance at a grocery store or somewhere, the encounter would have been a pleasant one. They would have talked for a long time, perhaps set a time for a meeting with her and Brian. On this night, circumstances were completely different. Freddy had actively sought her, and after she dreamed of him and her association with Gerald Foster, the encounter seemed like an ill omen.

While waiting for her uncle, Helen sat on the couch and played the Wii, totally oblivious to everything. Her tiny hands were holding tightly onto the controller and moving it violently from side to side.

Jen joined Sadi at the window and looked over her shoulder at the car.

"Who's that?" she asked. "Are you expecting anyone?"

"Oh, sorry. I forgot to tell you. Brian's coming over with an old friend of ours."

Due to all of the strange emotions Sadi was experiencing, she'd neglected to tell Jen of the planned company.

"That's Brian? Brian is here *now*?" she asked somewhat in shock. "Why didn't you tell me? I look horrible."

Jen raced up the stairs to the bathroom by her room. Sadi would get a lecture about her negligence later. Jen never admitted to being infatuated with Brian, but she never hid her excitement at seeing him, either. Too many times in the past, Sadi had seen other girls fall into the same trap of her brother's confidence and charisma.

Almost immediately after the bathroom door had slammed shut upstairs, Brian rapped on the door once and then opened it.

"Come in out of the rain," Sadi said before saying hello. "Put your coats over here, on the rack."

Before she had time to say anything else, Helen slid off the couch and ran in front of her.

"Uncle Brian, Uncle Brian," the little blond girl screamed as Brian removed his coat.

Sadi had taken his coat just before Helen smashed into him. While he pretended to suffocate, she hugged him hard and laughed wickedly as if intentionally trying to kill him.

"Choking," Brian gasped in a whisper. "Need oxygen! Can't breathe!"

"Hi, Sadi," Freddy Carlson said as he awkwardly placed his coat on the rack. "Thank you for letting me visit. It is great to see you."

"Good to see you too, Freddy." Sadi stood motionless, about to hug him, but he held out his hand to her, and they greeted each other like a formal business introduction. "How long has it been?"

"I believe," he said, gathering the right words. "It has been eight years."

The sounds of Brian and Helen momentarily drew their attention away from each other. Brian had grabbed his niece and spun her over his head. After making her do a backflip, she landed on her feet and then fell back on the couch. But before he let Helen relax, he plucked her from the seat again and presented her to Freddy.

"I forgot to introduce you," he said and became more serious. "This is Freddy Carlson. He used to hang out with your mother and me when we were younger, but older than you."

Helen tilted her head up to him and gave Freddy a silly look.

"I'm Helen," she said in a high, squeaky voice, acting like a living doll whose string had been pulled.

Sadi rolled her eyes.

"Oh come on, Helen. Act normal for once."

"Hi there, mister," she said with a new, deeper voice, too deep for an eight-year-old.

"Hi, Helen," Freddy said, smiling. "It is good to meet you. Thank you for letting me come to your home."

Sadi liked the dichotomy between her daughter's informality and the proper address from Freddy. At that moment, Jen came down the stairs and around the corner and acted surprised to see people in the house. Sadi smiled discreetly. Her brother would easily recognize Jen's performance.

"Hey, Brian," she said as casually as she could. "What a surprise. Sadi forgot to tell me that you were coming. I saw you at your show a couple weeks ago."

He turned to her and smiled, and Jen preened like a cat in the sun. "Hey, Jen. I saw you, but I lost sight of you. Otherwise, I would have come over to say hi."

"Don't lead her on, brother dear," Sadi whispered to herself, hoping he could hear her thoughts. She wondered if their blood relationship allowed for telepathy. Probably not.

"Race me," said Helen, running back to the couch and grabbing a Wii remote. She offered the controller to Brian, and he looked from Jen to Sadi then back to his niece. "I think," he said hesitantly, "that you can't stop me from playing with you."

"This is an old friend of ours, Freddy Carlson," Sadi said, turning to Jen, and then to Freddy. "And this is Helen's nanny, Jen. She lives here with us."

"Good to meet you, Freddy," she said then promptly excused herself to sit on the loveseat to watch Brian and Helen play the Mario Kart game.

"Sorry, Freddy," Brian said while steering the virtual car with his Wii controller. "I'll be over here for a while. I take orders from this one here."

"So, what have you been doing the past eight years?" Sadi asked as they walked to the dining table in the kitchen. From their location, they could hear everything from the video game participants in the living room. "I want to hear about what's been up with you."

—✳︎—

As Freddy and Sadi talked, Brian played the video game, but he also attempted to participate in their conversation. Helen kept scolding him to keep his eyes on the virtual road and accused him several times of not concentrating on driving. Jen sat opposite them on the loveseat, totally engrossed with the game. She kept cheering for Helen and clapped her hands when Brian crashed his virtual vehicle.

"Throw that shell at him," Jen yelled at Helen every few minutes.

Sadi kept Freddy talking for most of the conversation. He told the story of how he came to work for his employer, Mr. Smith. While learning of his good fortune, Sadi felt extremely gratified. She knew the horror of his childhood all too well. Except for the loss of her son, the problems in his life made her challenges seem easy.

"Freddy's not telling you the best part," Brian yelled from the living room.

"What's that?" asked Sadi, turning to Freddy.

"I do not know," Freddy said in a puzzled tone.

"This guy he lives with, his mansion is in the Sylvan Highlands, and Freddy has access to all his money!"

"I only use it to get what I need," Freddy said defensively. "Sometimes he tells me to get other things I do not need. I would never steal from him."

"Of course you wouldn't," Sadi said and put her hand on his wrist. "I am so happy for you, Freddy. Sounds like things are finally looking up for you. You deserve it."

"I think providence is smiling on us both."

"So how's school going?" Sadi asked. "You're going to Portland State?"

"Yes, and I will be done next year with my bachelor's degree."

Freddy told them of his plans to attend graduate school and wanting to major in something related to cellular biology. He still needed to decide on a major but felt torn between all of the different fields. Sadi advised him to enter graduate school in the department he wanted but to keep an open mind and explore the possibilities before making his final decision.

"There's no hurry. You're in a good position," she said and smiled wide. "You don't have any kids or an idiot spouse to distract you."

"I am sorry you had to deal with that," he said gravely, not laughing with her as she had intended.

"That was the past," she said. "I think we're both looking at brighter futures."

During their conversation, Freddy seemed able to relax and feel more comfortable, but he still seemed socially awkward. Sadi felt sorry for him. He would probably never feel entirely comfortable in social situations. Sadi decided to focus her thoughts on his improved personal life.

Sadi was also impressed by his knowledge of biology, and science in general. Judging from his questions about graduate school, he had a good understanding already of biochemistry. He also seemed technologically savvy. Being removed from all of the former drama in his life had probably given him time to focus on learning. With access to everything he could ever want, his talents could only blossom.

During the next pause in their conversation, she wondered about the real purpose of his visit. When talking about graduate school, she thought he had just wanted advice. Then she remembered her dream of him and falling back to the Earth. She probably needed to talk with him with more privacy.

FORTY-EIGHT

Sadi

"Time for bed, Helen," Sadi said when the time reached nine-thirty. "No complaining. I've let you stay up."

Helen would have argued with her uncle visiting, but Brian said he would put her to bed. After Jen followed Brian and Helen up the stairs, Sadi turned to Freddy. He suddenly looked concerned.

"So you haven't mentioned why you wanted to see me," Sadi said after a sigh. "It's been fun to see you again, but your visit was not to get advice about graduate school, was it?"

"No," he said, avoiding eye contact and looking at the table. "It was not the purpose of my visit. I have something to show you."

Freddy stood from his seat and walked to the coat rack by the front door where he had hung his coat. He removed something from an inside pocket and returned to the table, his hand clasped over a small object. Sadi briefly imagined him returning with a weapon and held her breath.

"I think I am supposed to show you this," he said while sitting and placing his right hand on the table between them.

"What is it?" Sadi asked, taking her first breath. She saw the sides of flat glass in his closed palm and could feel her heart rate accelerate. A strange thought occurred to her. The object in his hand was connected to everything else strange happening in her life recently.

"Sadi, I do not know how to say this," he said with a glance at the stairs. "So maybe I can just show you and see what you think."

He slowly opened his hand to reveal a flat piece of rectangular crystal. Its surface shimmered with refracted light, but Sadi could still see the embedded spider inside. At first, the object reminded her of a piece of acrylic encasing a real creature, but upon closer inspection, the spider looked like a flat piece of rock and the glass looked too intricate and perfect to be acrylic. After recognizing the spider, she remembered the time when she had invented his secret code word, the trick to help Freddy identify people when he could not see their faces. She wondered if he still used the *spider* code. When Brian had talked to Freddy on the phone, had he said the word, *spider*? Although a trivial matter, she decided to ask her brother later.

"It's beautiful," she said finally and felt a strange desire to take the object from his open palm. "What is it?"

Freddy paused as though not understanding the question. "I have no idea what it is," he said finally in a whisper.

For the next few seconds, they just stared silently at the crystal.

While admiring the beautiful object, several questions came to her mind. What did he want her to say? Was it a gift? Was he still infatuated with her? He might still be infatuated with the memory of a younger Sadi, but he surely could not still feel the same now. Time had probably buried his childhood obsessions or maybe enhanced them. Before she broke the silence, Sadi wondered if he felt any disappointment at seeing her again.

"It's very intricate," she said and gently lifted the crystal from his palm. After turning the object in her hand to see the other side, she was slightly surprised. The encased spider looked identical on both sides. "The detail is amazing. Where did you get it?"

"My sister gave it to me, but when I asked her about it later, she did not remember giving it to me."

"That's weird," Sadi said, frowning at the memory of his horrible sister, Wanda. "I don't think she would give you anything this interesting on purpose. Was she drunk when she gave it to you?"

"No, she was sober," he said, not laughing at her jest, then he pointed his index finger just above the crystal surface over the spider's head. Sadi noticed how he averted his eyes, as though avoiding a bright light. "What do you see if you look at the eyes of the spider?"

Sadi attempted to focus on the rows of glimmering eyes lining the head, but her vision blurred and she had to look away. She wondered if her eyes just felt tired. But after looking away from the eyes for a few seconds, she decided that her eyes were operating normally. She rubbed her eyes and made one more attempt to focus then shook her head in irritation.

"It hurts my eyes to look at it," she said, feeling confused and a stronger curiosity. A list of possible experiments came to her mind, the result of her long experience doing scientific research. "That's very strange. Do you have any idea how it does that?"

"It does the same to me," he said without looking away from the crystal. "I also tried taking a close-up picture of the eyes but had the same problem trying to focus the image. I do not know the reason yet."

While he spoke, Sadi thought he looked less timid and more like a detached researcher, seeing the situation objectively.

"I also had the same problem when I tried using my microscope," he said. "I read a lot about optical illusions but could not find any phenomenon similar to this."

"An optical illusion." Sadi rubbed her chin while staring at the crystal. "I've never had an optical illusion hurt my eyes like that."

"The refresh rates of video can induce seizures," Freddy said bluntly. "Especially at rates less than 50 hertz. I cannot imagine that this has any kind of refresh rate, but I was thinking it may cause our eyes to refocus at the same frequency, which might produce the same effect. I read about some companies making light-emitting devices for the military that can make people sick. That might be disinformation though, meant to scare the public."

"Do you think this thing was made by the military and your sister found it by mistake?" she asked.

"Or it could just be from a private company, some prototype."

Before responding, Sadi looked at the crystal with a new appreciation and then dread. If the military had created the crystal, why had his sister claimed to have no memory of giving it to him? Was she lying? Sadi had no difficulty believing his sister was capable of lying, especially if someone had paid her to give the crystal to Freddy. But there had to be more to the story.

"This isn't everything is it?"

"No, it is not," he said, sighing and lowering his voice to a whisper. "Please do not think I am crazy. This object also put me in a trance and gave me a strange vision."

He looked down at the table as though embarrassed.

Sadi remembered meeting her dead son several nights ago, then her dream of Freddy and Gerald. The memory sent a chill through her entire central nervous system. At that moment, she knew the crystal and Freddy were linked to all of her other strange experiences. Could the crystal show her son again? Were she and Freddy the subjects of some psychological operation of the CIA or FBI?

"What happened in the vision?" she asked, trying to remain calm with her heart rate suddenly increasing.

Her question seemed to have a physically draining effect on him as though she had just punched him in the stomach. He shifted in his seat before responding.

"A strange woman appeared and talked with me and showed me things. It was not a typical dream. At the end of it all, she said to find you."

"Did this woman say why?"

"No," he answered.

"Can I see the crystal again?"

Sadi rubbed her chin and took a deep breath as though preparing to dive underwater. She wondered if he had expected her to have the same vision when she first looked into the spider's eyes, to fall into the same trance. From the look in his eyes, she saw no reason to suspect ulterior motives. The Freddy from her past would have never intentionally harmed or manipulated her.

Freddy returned the crystal to Sadi, and she began a more thorough inspection, one with a new respect and without looking at the eyes. While inspecting the rectangular crystal, she marveled at its beauty and detail. She wondered who could have possibly made the object, other than some sophisticated company. An alien? Was the crystal a religious relic? Had Jesus or Buddha held it once? Her imagination began offering several other explanations.

"Maybe the eyes contain a subliminal trigger that initiates a related storyline when you go unconscious. Just a guess. Maybe you can do it again and see if you have the same experience."

"Yes, I thought of that too," he said, taking a deep breath. "I am planning to make another attempt later. For the moment, I do not want to assume the military made it. I do have a hypothesis about how it works. Maybe the eyes are positioned so that I cannot focus on any one of them, and my eyes will simultaneously attempt to focus on the next and the next and then come back to the first."

"Like an unending computer program loop," she said, impressed by the concept. "Interesting."

Freddy smiled before responding.

"I took a video of myself when it put me into a trance."

"You took a video?"

Sadi sat back, looking at him with curiosity. For just a moment, she wondered if he had acquired some other mental condition during their long separation. Obeying strange people in dreams was usually risky. But during her conversation with Freddy, she had sensed a higher level of maturity. He no longer seemed like the lost and lonely boy she'd known as a teenager.

"Yes," he answered. "I wanted to verify that it was not just in my imagination."

"That was smart," she said, feeling genuinely impressed and then a little awkward at his instruction to find her.

"I brought the video with me. If you have a computer, I can show you. It is evidence. I feel the need to show someone."

"Okay," she said.

Did she really want to see the video?

—✳—

Freddy opened the palm of his hand to reveal the crystal again. At the same time, Sadi heard steps on the stairs and the sound of Jen laughing. Freddy closed his fingers around the crystal again. When Jen and Brian returned to their view a moment later, he looked at them with wide eyes.

Sadi quickly intervened.

"Could you guys leave us alone for a few more minutes?"

Brian quickly scanned her face and nodded.

"Come on, Jen," Brian said in a tone of sarcastic mental anguish. "Obviously, we're not wanted."

Jen followed Brian through the kitchen like a puppy and they disappeared into the hallway. From her peripheral vision, Sadi had noticed Jen's lips stretched into a wide smile. She knew Brian would expect Sadi to reveal the parts of the conversation he had missed. She would usually tell her brother whatever he wanted to know, but in this instance, she might retain some of the details, at least until she could invent a good way to exclude information about Gerald's group. She still had not told him about them or the vision of her son.

After Jen and Brian had disappeared from view, Sadi stood and retrieved her laptop from a hidden drawer in a dark wood cabinet in the living room. The cabinet served as their entertainment center and could hide the presence of electronic equipment such as the television set. She placed her laptop on the kitchen table, and then Freddy gave her a portable flash drive containing the video file.

As Sadi watched the video, she stared in disbelief and shock as light from the crystal splashed onto Freddy's face. The mixture of beautiful lights and the eerie, motionless state of his facial features made Sadi pull her arms tightly across her breasts to fight the sudden chill. The entire evening seemed like another dream, and in a small way, she hoped the experience was a dream. Then she could wake up and continue with her normal life.

At the end of the video, Freddy removed the flash drive and closed the program so that no one could watch the video again on her computer. Sadi understood why Freddy had feared losing his sanity. She would have had the same reaction. In some small way, she felt psychologically prepared to hear his story and watch the video. The experience helped to validate her own recent incredible experiences. She suddenly decided on her next action. She would introduce Freddy to Gerald and show him the video.

Sadi turned from the computer screen and looked into his eyes, but he quickly returned his gaze to the floor. He waited for her to respond.

"One thing's for certain," she said, taking a deep breath. "You're not crazy, Freddy. There have been some strange things happening to me lately too. Strange dreams, new people. Might be related. Let me get back to you about this."

Although the idea sent chills down her spine, Sadi knew the crystal and Freddy's vision were related to Gerald's secret technology group and probably the vision of her son. But before continuing with her plan and introducing them, she had to check with Gerald first. He would help her make the decision.

When Freddy looked at her again, Sadi thought she saw physical and emotional exhaustion in his eyes, but also some relief. Sharing the burden of his bizarre experience might have lifted a weight from his mind. For a moment, she was tempted to share the vision of her dead son, but she promptly changed her mind. The thought of sharing that incredibly personal experience filled her with a strange anxiety. She did not want to begin crying in front of him.

"I am glad you let me show you," he said.

FORTY-NINE

Sadi

When Sadi's brother called again the next day, he wanted to know what Freddy had wanted, and Sadi gave him a reason she knew he would reject.

"He just wanted to see me again," she began. "To confess his former love for me."

"Yeah right," Brian answered, and as she had expected, her brother laughed. "Freddy'd never admit to that. He's still too shy about it. We had a good talk in his car. Wow, can you believe his luck? The personal servant of a millionaire who doesn't care how much money Freddy spends on himself. Come on, what's the real reason he came to see you?"

"Can't tell you yet," she said. "And that's the truth."

Brian paused before answering.

"Okay, don't tell me," he said in resignation. "So what does this mean? Is he going to be in our lives again? Is he going to be in *your* life?"

Sadi laughed into the phone.

"Like I said, Brian, I can't say anything about it now, but I'll fill you in if anything happens."

She wondered if her brother could hear her forced and insincere laughter. If Brian thought Freddy had caused her any anxiety, he would have continued asking her questions until she'd told him everything.

Since meeting with Freddy, her memory of that strange and disturbing experience mixed with all of her other recent experiences, and they overwhelmed her. At first, she'd accepted Freddy's visit and his news, but the memory of the video became more frightening the more it replayed in her mind. The experience reminded her of when she had taken Helen on a hike to the top of Beacon Rock in Washington. For the entire following week, Sadi had dreamed of the hike and of Helen falling from the narrow trail to her death. The nights after Freddy's visit, she would close her eyes and the blue and orange lights would shine from the spider's eyes, then reach for her. In some of her dreams, crystal spiders crawled all over her bed, shooting bright orange webs of light at her face and trapping her.

Her imagination kept supplying explanations, which increased her sense of unease, so she attempted to avoid thinking about them. She concentrated on her plan—transfer the investigation to Gerald and let the lawyer find the answers. All of the strange things in her life had begun after meeting Gerald and his secret energy group.

After two days of considering her situation, she decided to finally email Gerald about what had happened. He told her to use their website's secure chat environment.

Sadi: *Something happened, but I don't know what it means. I think it's related to the group.*

Gerald: *okay, what is it?*

Sadi: *I'd rather not say over the internet.*

Gerald: *Can you tell me anything?*

Sadi: *You probably wouldn't believe me if I told you anyway. I need to talk to you in person. It's kind of urgent. When can you come back to Portland?*

Gerald said he would visit Friday afternoon, just two days away. After giving him her address, she'd felt great relief, almost as if her mental suffering had already come to an end. She held onto the irrational feeling that Gerald would take care of everything.

—※—

She took Friday afternoon off from work to meet Gerald at her home and arrived ahead of time at an empty house. Jen was still at the community college and Helen was still at her elementary school. Sadi always felt strange being home alone. Usually, she would have enjoyed the hour to herself, but other emotions were competing for her attention, including the new thoughts of occupying an empty home with an attractive man. When she saw his car pull into her driveway, her pulse intensified and seemed to skip a few beats.

When he entered her home, she first noticed his suit and professional demeanor. He had a laptop bag slung over his shoulder and his hair was held perfectly in place, in almost the same position as when she first met him at the restaurant. She felt under-dressed, wearing blue jeans and a blue button blouse. They had been in communication for a few months already, but she still felt a little uncomfortable seeing him in person. And preparing to share an important and confusing secret had failed to alleviate her anxiety.

"How was your drive down here?" she asked after sitting at the kitchen table. She felt a sudden sense of déjà vu. She'd heard Freddy's story from the same position at the table.

"Nothing out of the ordinary happened," he said and then laughed uncomfortably. "For me, that's saying something."

"Are you still being followed?" Sadi asked, mildly curious. Being watched by the government seemed trivial compared to what she planned to share. "Is it something you ever get used to?"

"I haven't noticed anything since we met," he said. "That's probably a bad thing, assuming that if they don't want me to see them, I probably won't."

"I guess that's a good thing," Sadi admitted. She felt unprepared to talk about the purpose of his visit just yet. "Does anyone suspect what you're, I mean, what we're doing?"

"I'm pretty confident no one knows what we're doing," he said convincingly. "They're only interested in me for my past affairs, and I think they're running out of steam."

"That reminds me," she said, attempting to appear irritated. "You haven't told me everything yet."

"Okay, but first why don't you tell me why I needed to drive down here? It was urgent, right?"

"I want to know exactly what's happening in the group first. I need to know why so many strange things are happening to me. Maybe I won't *want* to share what has happened. Maybe it's related, maybe not."

He thought about her words for a moment, inspecting her face for clues of her intentions, and she stared back with eyebrows raised. She wanted to see how he reacted to an ultimatum.

"Of course, of course," he said in apology then drew a deep breath as though preparing to confess a crime.

She smiled discreetly with satisfaction.

"You deserve to know everything. I'll just tell it plain and simple. I have a friend who invented something. It can take us anywhere we want to go, and I found a secret energy source for it. We're creating a small multidisciplinary team to help in the development."

"My God," she said while locking eye contact. From the look on his face, she wondered if he expected to receive a demand to leave. "How can I help with that?"

He looked relieved by her response.

"We need a few experts in different disciplines, to help see the task from different angles, those like us who–"

"Like us?"

"I mean," he began in clarification. "People like you and I, those who can see what's going on in the world. The energy industry will do anything to retain energy *dependence* and the military will fight any new technology that might threaten the system. I am hoping you can help us figure out the best way to utilize this opportunity. It's a dangerous task though."

While Gerald waited for her response, she stared at him with narrow eyes. She responded slowly.

"I really don't know what to say right now," she said with total sincerity. "I know what you mean, though. Energy is the key to control. Who is your friend who invented this thing?"

"She's a friend from college," he answered casually. "We met when I was in law school at the University of Oregon. She called me in January and wanted to show me something."

Sadi wondered how he felt about the girl, but his tone seemed to indicate nothing more than a casual friendship. Before her curiosity could proceed any further, she scolded herself for worrying about any of his romantic connections. She had more important sources of concern.

For the next ten minutes, she listened to the condensed story of how he had found the fusion reactor and of its delivery to the girl and their Mexican friends. Listening to the story helped Sadi forget about human relationships, for a little while at least, but it only added to her anxiety. The story failed to explain why she had seen her son, why a woman in a vision had told Freddy to visit her, and why she had seen the video of the lights emanating from the spider's eyes. Too many unanswered questions.

"I need a drink," she said then stood and began walking to the refrigerator. Cool liquid slid down her throat and the short pause might help restore her mind to reality. As she walked, she could feel his eyes on her back. "Do you want anything to drink?"

"Sure, whatever you're having."

"You were right, Gerald," she said after returning with two glasses half-filled with dark purple grape juice. "That's an unbelievable story, and I think you're crazy to tell anyone about it. Perhaps after I explain why I wanted to see you, you will feel the same way about my story."

"I can probably handle any story now," he said with a chuckle.

FIFTY

Sadi

“A couple nights ago, an old friend of mine came to visit me,” she began and realized the similarities of their stories. Gerald’s story had begun the same way. “I haven’t seen him for over eight years. In that time, we haven’t spoken or had any communication. He was a childhood friend of mine and my brother’s. I don’t know what psychological condition he’s got, but he’s different. He’s got some form of autism or something, but he’s high-functioning, very high-functioning.”

“What are his symptoms?” Gerald asked. “Is he a savant?”

“I don’t think he’s a savant. When you talk to him, he’s almost normal. He makes eye contact. He listens to what you’re saying.”

She sat back and considered again how to continue.

“There seems to be some disconnect in his brain in some ways. He lacks the ability to connect things. He can’t connect voices to names, actions to reactions. On top of it all, he’s had loads of other problems to deal with, like growing up through the foster care system and all the abuse that came with it.”

“Poor guy,” Gerald said with sincerity. “It’s good that he had you as a friend.”

"Yeah, we were his only friends. The only ones I knew of."

"So why did he contact you after all this time?"

"He said that he was instructed," she said then paused, "in a dream to find me."

"Let me guess," he said with a wide smile. "It wasn't just some random dream, or a subconscious desire to see you again."

She continued as if uninterrupted.

"He acquired a strange trinket, a crystal with a stone spider inside." Sadi paused when she noticed Gerald's pupils suddenly expand. She quickly continued. "If he looks into the spider's eyes, it can put him in some sort of a trance. When he visited me, he brought the crystal to my house and showed me. He knew how crazy the whole thing would sound, so he captured it on video."

"He captured his vision on a video?"

"No," she said. "He recorded himself going into a trance. I saw it for myself. There were strange lights coming out of the spider's eyes. It was disturbing to watch. It frightened him, so he came to me for help."

Gerald sat back in his seat and sipped his juice.

"He might have made the video to trick you, but you would have considered that and not felt the need to call me. What about this experience made you think it was connected to our group?"

"It was too much of a coincidence with my involvement in your group," she said, trying to hide her feeling of confusion. "There's no other reason for him to visit me unless it was related."

"Wow," he said, shaking his head. Gerald set his glass on the table and ran his fingers through his thick brown hair. "We have to visit this guy. I'd like to see this video for myself, and the crystal."

"I know you haven't had any time to consider this, but what do you think it might mean?"

She almost wished he had no explanation. She might not want to know the answer. While looking at him, Sadi recognized the opposite reaction from what she had expected. He seemed excited about the news. He had an almost instant response.

"Lately, I'm more open to strange hypotheses," he said and scratched his chin. "This crystal seems like an advanced mind control device, something the military would be interested in. What do you think? You're the scientist. Do they have the capability to make such a device?"

"I don't think so," she said, instantly disliking the direction of his question. "When I looked into the spider's eyes, I could not focus on them. It felt very strange, but I saw no vision and I cannot account for the lights."

"If the object can do what you say," he began as though talking to himself, "then it must have been made by something else. Aliens? Some other intelligent life on Earth that we don't know about? So, you said he was instructed in a dream to contact you?"

"It's got to be your group, I mean the group."

"Wait a minute," he said. "We may be taking this too much at face value."

"What do you mean?"

"You say you haven't seen Freddy for a long time, and he has mental issues? How do you know he's not being manipulated? I'm not saying you shouldn't trust him, but sometimes people like that can be taken advantage of. What if the video was created by some graphics expert and then your friend was made to believe the story? But then the question changes. Why would someone want to do that?"

"To mislead the group?" Sadi suggested. She found some comfort in the alternative explanation but also disappointment for failing to find a link to her other experiences.

"To undermine what we're trying to do," Gerald said, laughing and shaking his head. "I like the alien explanation better. This could be a bad turn of events. There's only one way to find out. Let's give your friend a call and make a visit. Is that what you had in mind?"

"I didn't get that far," she admitted. "He did give me his phone number and told me to call some day." Sadi stood from the table and found her phone by the refrigerator. "Should we call him now?"

"Sure."

—※—

She felt anxious calling Freddy, but Gerald's presence offered some comfort. After learning about his living circumstances, she wanted to see where Freddy lived and meet his boss, the wealthy old man.

After a single ring, an elderly man answered the phone.

"Hello," the old voice said, filled with concern and fragile as rice paper.

"Uh, hi," she said and cleared her throat. "I'm looking for Freddy Carlson?"

"He's not here. Who is this?"

"I'm a friend of his, Sadi. I–"

"Friend?" the old man replied with a tone of disbelief and suspicion. "He's never mentioned your name, Sadi. What kind of friend? How do you know him?"

His angry and accusatory tone caught Sadi by surprise. She looked at Gerald and shook her head in confusion.

"I'm an old friend from when we were kids. He came to see me a few days ago."

"He did?"

Sadi listened to silence for several seconds. When the old man began speaking again, his tone had softened.

"Sorry, I didn't mean to be rude. May I ask why he visited you?"

"I'm sorry, but he might not want me to share that. Can I speak with him first?"

"He can't come to the phone right now. What do you want from him? Are you one of his sister's friends?"

The old man was growing impatient again.

"No, I'm definitely not friends with his sister," Sadi said and thought she understood the old man's concerns. Freddy had a horrible sister. "Like I said, my brother and I were practically his only friends, a long time ago. He just wanted to see us again."

The old man paused again, and she listened to the sound of his breathing.

"This may sound forward," he said. "But what do you do for a living?"

"I am a biologist at a pharmaceutical company," she said.

Sadi despised people who loved to flash their credentials, so she spoke diminutively about her position. She worked with some of those people. She suddenly had an idea.

"One of the reasons why he came to see me was to ask for advice about graduate schools. He's interested in biology and knew about my line of work. I wanted to come and see him, tonight if possible. Would that be all right?"

"To tell you the truth," the old man answered and his tone transformed again, back to concern, almost panic. "I don't know where Freddy is. Do you have any idea where he might be?"

"What?"

"He's missing. He never came home last night."

"Oh my God," Sadi said, shocked.

"It's never happened before," the old man said with desperation leaking into his tone. "The police won't do anything. I have a private investigator looking for him, but he doesn't have any good leads yet."

Sadi covered the phone with her hand and turned to Gerald.

"He's missing, and his boss is frantic."

She suddenly had a new fear. If the old man refused her request to visit, she might never see Freddy again or have her questions answered. Then she felt guilty for worrying about her own concerns, rather than her friend's safety.

"Let us come over. Maybe we can help."

"If you help me find him, I will be in your debt."

FIFTY-ONE

Sadi

After the old man gave directions to his house, Sadi sent Jen a text message, saying she might not be home until late and to bring Helen home from her gymnastics class. At five in the afternoon, Sadi and Gerald left her house in his car, the sun only a vague blur behind the dark clouds. As they drove through the light rain, Sadi wondered if they could help find Freddy and if the old man would blame them, and what Gerald really thought about her story.

They entered the driveway where Freddy lived and had to wait for the gate to open before they could drive to the tall archway covering the entrance. On the short drive, they saw the old man peeking through the windows at them.

Sadi knocked and Gerald stood slightly behind her to the left. His calm presence helped Sadi feel less anxious. She wondered what he felt about her, and how much she cared.

The old man opened the door while she was knocking and introduced himself as Bill Smith, Freddy's employer.

"Hi. I'm Sadi Jacobsen, and this is my friend, Gerald Foster."

Before arriving, Sadi considered claiming Gerald was her brother. If she introduced him as her lawyer friend, the old man might be suspicious about their true motives, although he would never be able to guess them. The man looked suspiciously at Gerald for only a few seconds before letting them into the home. He asked no questions about Gerald's identity or profession.

"Come inside."

He led them into a large sitting room with a piano and some simple furniture. The furniture seemed too small for such a spacious room. Sadi and Gerald sat on a small couch, and the old man chose a Victorian chair opposite them. He quickly explained how Freddy took care of the house and most of his affairs.

"I have come to depend very much on that boy," he said, his old voice cracking. Sadi wondered whether he would start crying or coughing.

"He spoke very highly of you, sir," Sadi said.

"He's grown on me," the old man said and looked at Sadi with clear eyes. "I'm worried because he's never stayed away overnight. If he ever did, I know he'd tell me beforehand, or at least he'd call me. I know he would. Was there any other reason why he came to visit you the other day? I've been unable to reach his sister. I wouldn't be surprised if she were involved."

"If his sister was involved, what do you suspect she might have done?"

"I don't know," he said. "It's the only lead I have to go on. She wouldn't want to disrupt his position here with me because it benefits her. She would not want to jeopardize that."

When Sadi first saw the thin old man, she had expected him to be slightly incoherent. To her surprise, he acted and spoke confidently although with the frailty of old age. His sharp eyes seemed to notice everything before them. She liked him instantly, and when she made eye contact, she decided to be completely honest with him. Lying to him seemed like a foolish decision.

Up until that point, Gerald had remained silent and had let Sadi handle the conversation. He sat forward then.

"What were the very last things you remember him saying to you, Mr. Smith?"

"Nothing out of the ordinary," he began and slowly pounded his leg with his fist. "He was going to his college class, then he had a lab scheduled. He usually arrives home by two or three. If he planned to come home later, he would have told me."

"Do you know how to get in touch with his lab teacher?"

"Already had her contacted," Mr. Smith said, his voice filled with disappointment. "He attended the lab as usual and finished early. According to her, Freddy acted the same as he always did."

"So your private investigator talked to his lab teacher?"

"Yes. He also went through the downstairs rooms, the ones Freddy uses, looking for clues. He is checking on some things, he says, but he doesn't have any solid leads. He's going to check on Freddy's sister. I told him not to let her know we can't find him."

"Do you mind if we have a look through his things?" Sadi asked before she had time to consider the propriety of the question. "Sorry, if that's too much to ask."

He stared at her like a cat preparing to pounce on a bird. Had she just ruined the opportunity to help? Would he kick them both out of his house?

"Freddy didn't visit you just for your advice about graduate school," he said finally. "Did he, Ms. Jacobsen?"

"Not entirely," she said quickly and smiled at allowing an old man to intimidate her. "What I mean is, that was only part of his reason, but I wouldn't feel right about sharing everything unless I had his permission first."

"Now you're worried about his privacy?" asked the old man. "You just asked if you could go through his private things. If you cannot tell me everything you know, at least tell me something."

"It's very different," said Gerald, "than what you might think."

The old man sat back in the chair and smiled for the first time.

"I know Freddy, probably better than anyone on this Earth. I wouldn't be surprised by anything you'd have to say."

Sadi felt the need for a private conversation with Gerald about what they wanted to tell Mr. Smith. On the drive, they had neglected to prepare for the possibility of telling the old man everything that had happened to Freddy. She and Gerald made eye contact, and then she wondered if he had the same questions. They all waited for her to speak.

"Mr. Smith," she said slowly, still not fully knowing what would escape her lips. "Freddy was having strange dreams, dreams in which he was instructed to find me. That's the truth, but I know it sounds weird. Has he said anything about that lately?"

The old man leaned forward farther in his chair.

"He hasn't said anything about dreams, but he *has* seemed more worried than usual. I just assumed it was due to his classes. Could his dream have been stress-induced?"

"This was no normal dream," Gerald interjected. "It was more of a trance, externally induced possibly."

"Now you're making even less sense," the old man said in frustration.

"I know it doesn't make sense." Sadi tried to sound comforting. "He took a video of it happening and showed me. Otherwise, I wouldn't have believed it either."

"If that's true, there must be a reason why he was told to meet you. What are you and Gerald involved in? What's the connection between you all?"

He suddenly reminded Sadi of a judge trying to settle a dispute.

"Gerald's just a friend," Sadi said quickly. "He was going to help me figure this thing out. That's all."

Mr. Smith looked at them both with obvious distrust. Before he could interrogate them further, Gerald turned to Sadi.

"Tell him about the ornament that Freddy showed you."

"What ornament?" Mr. Smith looked from Sadi to Gerald and then back to Sadi again.

She had doubts about revealing the crystal with the embedded stone spider, but Gerald had given her no other option now, except to lie.

"Freddy brought a crystal to my house to show me, a little bigger than the palm of my hand. It had a flat spider made of rock inside it. I don't suppose he ever showed it to you? I know it sounds crazy, but I saw the video he took, with my own eyes. Light was coming out of this crystal thing. He believes the crystal put him in a trance and showed him the vision. It might be a clue that will lead us to him."

"No, he has not shown this thing to me," Mr. Smith said in anger. "How am I supposed to believe you?"

"You're not," said Gerald with sympathy. "Were we to find this crystal, it might be more believable for all of us, including myself. Like you, I just have Sadi's word to go on. I just came here to help her find her friend. Perhaps you could search through his rooms for this crystal for us?"

Gerald's words seemed to appease Mr. Smith. The muscles in his face relaxed a little. He placed his cane on the floor in front of him and started to stand, so Sadi stood and extended her hand to help him.

"Thank you," he said without emotion, accepting her hand. "Now, you two please stay here while I go look for this thing."

After the old man had left the room, Gerald stood and walked to the window. "What are we going to do if he doesn't find the crystal orna-ment?" He stared through the window and into the night. "Any ideas?"

"I'm wondering what we're going to do if he does find the crystal," she said.

She tapped the fingers of her right hand on the chair arm, then looked up to Gerald at the curtains. Would she have been able to per-suade the old man this far by herself? Gerald was more experienced with investigations involving people. At her work, she had become an expert in investigating the world of microbiology. Hopefully, she could contribute something to the search.

"The future holds too many possibilities to plan for them all. Let's just go with the flow and see where it leads." Gerald spoke while looking out the window, and then he returned to sit next to Sadi again. "Maybe we can fit together what's going through Freddy's mind. You said he was worried. What would a person like Freddy do if he was worried?"

"When we were younger," she said, attempting to remember Freddy from the past. "He probably would have hidden somewhere, but now he seems more proactive. He's smart and is probably trying to figure this thing out on his own. If Mr. Smith doesn't find the crystal, Freddy may have it. Maybe he discovered something and went to investigate and then got into trouble?"

"Did he think it had anything to do with aliens?" Gerald asked. "If so, how would he go about verifying it?"

"Hmm," she said. "I'm more inclined to think it's from the military, but if he thought it involved aliens, maybe he went to a place where he thought an alien could contact him. Somewhere high and isolated?"

"Good thought. A peak might be a good place to start. I'm not really dressed for hiking, but I can be flexible. I really would like to see that video," Gerald said, shaking his head.

"Don't laugh," Sadi said as a new thought materialized. She doubted they'd find the video. "Could it be some kind of ghost?"

He looked at her strangely as if preparing to ask about her sanity.

"I don't believe in ghosts."

Experience as a researcher had taught her to always consider every possible angle and do tests before dismissing any possibility. She hated the idea of making a type one error, rejecting the actual truth. Of course, she also hated to accept a falsehood, but that meant abandoning the truth right in front of her face. After the death of her son, she refused to believe that a human life ended with the death of the body.

"This world has a lot of unexplained things in it and especially after seeing that video, I'm willing to entertain any idea."

"A ghost huh," Gerald said, breaking eye contact. "Hmm."

Sadi waited while the synapses in his brain worked to determine his next action. She turned and stared at the curtained windows. The silence ended abruptly when Mr. Smith's voice called to them from the hallway. He soon entered the room and aimed his cane at them. Sadi suddenly felt like a child again, when her teacher would tell the class to open their books.

FIFTY-TWO

Sadi

"Come with me downstairs," the old man said. He waited only a moment before turning and disappearing into the hallway. "There's a strange light coming from under Freddy's bedroom door, and it didn't feel like a good idea to enter by myself."

Gerald stood first then extended his hand to help Sadi stand. She accepted his help and watched Mr. Smith walk away, wondering if she really wanted to enter a room with strange lights. As they followed the old man through the halls and then down the stairs, Sadi imagined finding the door already open. She shivered at the thought.

After reaching the bottom of the stairs, a new realization temporarily replaced her anxiety. If Freddy claimed the whole lower level as his own, he had more space than her whole house. The realization made her smile. In the large lower level, they entered a long dark hallway with several rooms on either side. A faint blue and orange light shot from under the last door on the right, as though from a low-frequency strobe light. Mr. Smith extended his cane again, aiming the instrument toward the light.

"I didn't notice the light until after I had looked through some of the other rooms down here. My eyes are not as good as they used to be."

Sadi and Gerald stopped behind the old man, waiting for him to make the next move. As he lowered the cane, Sadi noticed his hand shaking, from age rather than fear. He used his cane like an invisible laser pointer. After a moment, Gerald stepped forward.

"I suppose we can't just stand here."

He stepped past Mr. Smith and slowly approached the door. After reaching the door, he leaned forward and listened for a moment, his eyes on the floor. Silence filled the next few seconds as they watched Gerald begin to extend his hand slowly toward the handle. Before making contact, the light under the door disappeared. Mr. Smith looked at Sadi and then at Gerald who had turned to face them both.

"Maybe we should call the police," Sadi whispered and placed her hand on Mr. Smith's shoulder.

She felt a strange need to connect physically with another human. Did her fear originate from inside her mind or from what lay beyond the door? With her hand on his shoulder, Mr. Smith seemed to gain the courage to start walking. After reaching the door and Gerald, he hit his cane against the solid wood. The hard sound destroyed the silence.

"Who's in there?" the old man asked in anger, and they waited several seconds for a response. The sound of the knocking seemed to echo in her mind, and the echo soon transformed into silence again.

"Is this Freddy's room?" Gerald asked.

"It's the room he sleeps in," the old man answered. "All the rooms down here are his. I don't come down here much."

"Well," Gerald said unexpectedly, placing his hand on the door handle. "Here goes nothing."

He turned the handle and then slowly pushed the door completely open. After waiting a moment, he leaned forward to see into the room and then slowly stepped inside. Mr. Smith followed at a tentative but steady pace, extending his arm for Sadi to hold. For a moment, she felt like the stereotypical frightened girl walking behind the men, the men who had not seen Freddy's disturbing video.

Mr. Smith flipped a switch on the wall to energize the lights, and the large room was suddenly less frightening. Sadi noticed a bed immediately to her right and small windows on the wall ahead of her and to the right. Several tables lined the walls, each table holding some piece of equipment. She noticed two microscopes, several computers, and other instruments she failed to recognize. Freddy's room was very tidy.

"I don't see anything," Gerald said after inspecting the room for several seconds.

"Where was that light coming from?" Sadi asked.

"Well, we all saw it," Mr. Smith said. "Perhaps—"

His voice stopped abruptly when a blue light drew all of their attention. The light originated from inside the top drawer of a dresser next to the bed. The light shone through the cracks and flickered like a candle.

Gerald used both of his hands to slowly pull the dresser drawer completely open, holding his face away as though a creature inside prepared to jump out at him. Sadi felt more curiosity than fear. If the drawer contained a ghost, it was a tiny one.

Gerald placed his right hand inside the drawer and removed the crystal with the embedded flat spider. He raised the object in the palm of his hand to eye level, blue and orange light shooting from his hand to the ceiling. As he tilted the crystal sideways, to see the source of the light, Sadi shot her hand toward him and grabbed his wrist.

"Don't look into it, Gerald," she said, remembering Freddy's warning not to look into the spider's eyes.

"The light is coming from inside the head," he whispered as though talking to himself.

Despite her hand on his arm, he turned the crystal sideways and the light illuminated them all. Sadi felt as though an invisible force was pulling her head so that she also faced the crystal. Intense curiosity overpowered her futile mental resistance.

PART IV

INTERLOPER

When by the tiger chased
Better find somewhere safe
Or your life, soon erased

FIFTY-THREE

Taylor

While standing around their prototype engine, Taylor made adjustments and Cesar typed into one of the computers, which was connected to all of the sensors. They kept the engine on the operation table, as Taylor liked to call the large bench, but the apparatus looked nothing like an engine. It looked more like a random jumble of unrelated equipment. White tubes and copious multicolored wires encased several stainless steel cylinders twenty centimeters in diameter.

"What's the output now?" Taylor asked while adjusting a set screw. She looked over to the computer where Cesar sat, but he had the screen turned away from her.

"Just another quarter turn and we should be at the maximum," Cesar said in excitement. "There you go. Keep it right there. It's modulating around seventy amps. Let's see how long it can hold."

From his wide smile, Taylor assumed that Cesar was enjoying the successful experience. Taylor was also enjoying herself, meaning she had a look of deep concentration rather than a smile.

"What does the temperature monitor read? I want to make sure temperature control is holding steady as well. That's probably more important than power, at least for now."

When she saw the temperature, she smiled at last but only briefly.

"When we're coming back into the atmosphere, you can worry about overheating, and I'll worry about power output," Cesar said, half teasing but with a serious tone. He reminded Taylor of her father.

She turned to the sunlight streaming through the window high above them and then jumped at the sight of Doroteo right behind her.

"Holy shit, Teo," she said out of shock but then attempted to appear calm. "Will you stop sneaking up on me?"

She expected to see the general satisfaction he felt at catching her off guard. A few days after she had started sharing his home, Doroteo had said he would try to teach her basic survival skills. He never asked for permission.

But instead of showing any sign of victory, he waited for Taylor to regain her composure. He stood silently as though waiting to make some announcement. Cesar concentrated on the computer and ignored them both.

"Hey," Doroteo said finally.

Taylor held steady eye contact with him, preparing to reply, but he discreetly handed her a piece of paper. She took the paper from his leathery grasp.

Someone's listening to us now.

Doroteo turned away and approached the operating table and then pretended to inspect the engine. After Taylor read the note, she felt the blood drain from her face and her skin felt even paler than usual. She walked calmly to Cesar, handed him the paper, and went back to the engine to stand by Doroteo. Cesar glanced at the paper and paused for no longer than half of a second.

"Let's go get something for lunch," he said. "I'm starving."

Taylor looked at her watch and saw the digital readout turn from ten fifty-nine to eleven. They usually ate lunch after twelve. For the next five minutes, they brought their tests to a stop and waited for the power-down procedure to complete.

Doroteo extinguished all of the lights in the shop and motioned for her and Cesar to stay by the exit until he rejoined them. A single ray of light shot down from a window near the ceiling, and the light made the dust particles in the air sparkle. In the lower light level, Doroteo removed what looked like a handheld stun gun from his pocket.

Taylor leaned close to Cesar's ear and whispered.

"What's he doing?"

"After we leave," Cesar said while keeping his eyes on Doroteo.

Doroteo had removed a small instrument with a red LED light from his pocket and held the object in his hand. The LED blinked with a frequency that changed with his location in the shop. As Doroteo walked casually around the large shop area with the small instrument, the scene reminded Taylor of the movie, *Ghostbusters*, when Egon was searching for ghosts with his handheld device. Taylor felt an unexpected irritation at failing to remember the name of the device from the movie. After a few minutes of inspection, Doroteo stopped at a bench where their radio sat.

After a moment of staring at the radio, Doroteo walked back to Taylor and Cesar. She followed him outside while Cesar locked the door. They all climbed into Doroteo's dark blue Dodge Ram truck, and as usual, Taylor sat in the extended cab.

"Is this secure?" asked Cesar after shutting the door.

Doroteo looked angrier than she had ever seen him.

"Of course," he said with a thick accent.

Taylor never knew what to expect from Doroteo's manner of speaking. He often alternated between using an almost unintelligible Mexican accent and sounding like a typical native suburbanite.

"Teo, what did you find?" Taylor asked.

As they pulled onto the road, Doroteo kept his eyes focused ahead of him.

"I didn't find anything at the shop," he began, and Taylor heard no more anger in his voice. "I just wanted to make sure the place was clear before we left."

"What made you suspect the possibility?" asked Cesar.

"While driving up just now, I found a car parked down the street," he said, his anger returning. "I made eye contact with the man inside right before he looked away." Doroteo shook his head and slowly blinked his eyes, possibly as a sign of frustration. "At that moment, I knew. The man drove away while I was parking."

"Who was it?" Cesar asked.

"FBI," Doroteo answered with certainty in his voice.

Cesar nodded his head in agreement.

"Made eye contact eh," Cesar said and smiled. "Losing your touch a bit."

Doroteo grunted under his breath but said nothing.

On their way to Taylor's favorite sandwich shop, they discussed the worst possible scenarios. By Doroteo's estimation, the agent could have been listening for two to three days at most. At first, Taylor was afraid of her secret being discovered, but after recalling the past few days, she remembered saying nothing incriminating.

If the FBI heard them talk about the NMG device or the fusion reactor, they would still have had no direct evidence of their activities. They only talked about topics such as power transfer, computer control, and efficiency optimization. Their conversations and work had focused on the specific design details, not the overall picture or science behind the new technology. They never used the term fusion, only generator and engine.

Despite her attempt to consider the situation optimistically, Taylor felt sick inside. Being investigated by the FBI caused enough concern even if they had no evidence, yet. How long before the FBI raided their shop and confiscated all of her hard work? Why did the FBI show interest in them?

As the best-case scenario, Doroteo had caught the agent at his first attempt at surveillance. Another possibility involved the CIA. Taylor remembered Cesar's story about how the CIA had warned him to stay out of trouble. Maybe they were just checking on him. Even in that benign situation, the CIA still might have heard something and decided to investigate more. She decided to stop thinking about the possibilities and let her friends handle the situation. They had much more experience.

After arriving at the restaurant, Cesar and Taylor ordered a sandwich, but Doroteo just sat with them and had water. He tried to look bored while also probably watching for someone snooping nearby. They ate at a booth farthest away from all of the other patrons and spoke quietly about the possibilities.

"We can talk all day about what we think they have on us, but how do we figure out what they *do* have on us, or what they suspect?" Taylor spoke while chewing a large bite of her barbecue chicken sandwich. "How are we going to do that?"

Doroteo looked at her without emotion.

"We capture him and make him tell us. That's how."

Cesar frowned but remained silent. Before continuing, Taylor quickly finished her bite.

"Capture an FBI agent?" she whispered in disbelief. "And then what? Kill him when we're done?"

"If you want," Doroteo answered in perfect seriousness.

"What's your plan?" Cesar asked as though simply trying to determine what movie to see that night.

"Wait a second," interrupted Taylor. She looked at the two men as though they were two hitmen planning a murder. "We can't capture a government agent. That's kidnapping. Besides, if we do capture him and we get the information, then what? We let him go and warn him not to include it in his next report?"

Cesar reached over the table and put his hand on hers, and Taylor realized how loudly she had spoken. She looked around the restaurant to see if anyone had turned to watch them. When Cesar finally spoke, he talked to her gently, as a father to a child, and she wondered if he now thought of her as a daughter.

"Taylor, remember who you're talking to here. Doroteo and I have been in much worse circumstances than this before."

"Yeah, but you were the government."

Instead of providing comfort, their nonchalant attitude caused her to feel more impatience and paranoia.

"There are bigger sharks in the ocean, Taylor," he explained. "Little fish in the government can be eaten just as easily, and often more frequently. Remember, government officials don't usually make the important decisions."

His words failed to placate her.

"How are we going to get the information out of him?" she whispered even quieter. "Torture him?"

Doroteo leaned closer.

"Is that how you think I get information from people?" he asked almost threateningly.

Another person might have cowered before those four, dark eyes on them, but Taylor knew to hold steady eye contact with both men.

"I haven't really thought about it until now, so you tell me."

"It won't come to that, Taylor," Cesar said. "But it may not be pretty either. Just trust us. Let's listen to Doroteo's plan."

"Wait a moment," she said in surprise. Among all of her other questions, she had neglected to ask the most obvious one. "If they had no bug in the shop, how do you know they were listening to us? Did they have something in the phone?"

"Our voices are vibrations aren't they?" Cesar said. "Vibrations transmit through walls and windows that can be electronically enhanced. They have many ways now."

"Unless you can prove otherwise, they can hear you," Doroteo said while pretending to casually people-watch.

They spent the rest of their lunch break discussing all of the possible problems with the plan. Taylor mostly listened and reserved many of her concerns for later consideration. After a while, she began to feel a little better about the situation. She had never participated in anything like what they were considering. The movies had always made her laugh at how unrealistic their surveillance and intelligence activities appeared. The movies looked fun.

FIFTY-FOUR

John

Agent John Pratt of the FBI had thick dark brown hair, naturally tan skin, and dark brown eyes. He liked to keep his hair short, his fingernails trimmed, and his skin tight through exercise. When people looked at him, he always appeared happy and pleasant. He spoke politely to people, and everyone thought he liked them, but he kept his real feelings deeply hidden. In reality, only a few people held his respect. Those who found themselves on the other side of his facade knew his domineering, critical, and manipulative side, the aspects of his personality that made him an effective FBI agent.

Agent Pratt sat at his desk staring at all the papers strewn over its clean surface. If anyone came by his desk, they would see him reading, diligently working. In reality, he only stared at the closest paper while attempting to suppress the memory of the previous twelve hours of his personal life and invent an escape from his current predicament. During the past several nights, he had only slept for a few hours. His new girlfriend's three-year-old child had chosen the night to cry, ask for drinks, watch movies, basically everything but sleep.

Before he had allowed them to move into his apartment, his girlfriend had accepted full responsibility for her child. He had informed her that he would not be a babysitter or handle the child's needs. He had lied about liking children, at least her child, and always invented an excuse to avoid responsibility. At that time in his career, he could not allow himself to become emotionally attached to children. They would make him soft, and he needed to be hard, as the criminals he hunted.

Like an idiot, he had assumed his girlfriend would take their contract seriously. After they had moved into his apartment, he'd discovered the woman's true irrationality. Her agreement basically meant nothing, and she secretly expected him to do everything he had verbally refused to do. There was high tension whenever he failed to obey any one of her subconscious expectations.

If he only had known how annoying the kid would become, he never would have let them move in with him. Every day, he waited for the perfect opportunity to end the relationship, and whenever he failed to find a good excuse, he imagined possible scenarios where they just disappeared, like death or abduction. He could only hope.

Agent Pratt worked in the Counterterrorism Division at the Seattle, Washington, FBI field office, the second assignment in his eight years at the Bureau. He loved many of his job duties but hated writing reports and analyzing data for other people. He spent twenty percent of his time collecting data, the fun part, and eighty percent in analysis and writing reports, the mind-numbingly boring parts.

The top papers on his desk related to his most recent case, the two anarchistic, extremist college kids. The papers contained information such as pictures, college transcripts, and their most interesting email messages. Both of the kids attended the University of Washington and had different majors. As far as Agent Pratt knew, they had never met each other.

He spent much of his time recently, gathering information about several other similar suspects, hoping to group them somehow. They crossed into the terrorism radar by all of the time they spent searching the internet for explosive devices. Unfortunately, judging by their grades and types of classes, none of them had any understanding of science. In Pratt's opinion, none of them showed any indication of possessing sufficient motivation or intelligence to carry out a violent attack, no matter how much they bragged about it to their loser friends.

Pratt's boss wanted information about as many anarchists as possible, in the hopes of catching one of them with homemade explosive devices. If Agent Pratt had any luck, he would apprehend those vermin extremists in the act of exploding something or at least a failed detonation. In his other fantasies, explosives destroyed one of their all-night beer and porn bashes, leaving the world with fewer losers. In that case, he would miss the pleasure of sending the kids to jail, but the senseless destruction would feel better than nothing. So far, his efforts were showing absolutely no possibility of any future accidental detonations.

After his most recent reconnaissance operation, Agent Pratt began contemplating the next phase of his strategy. He wanted to use FBI resources to help one of the kids acquire explosives. But were any of them worth the effort? The FBI had to be careful. Such tactics could backfire. His superiors would not tolerate another fiasco like the 1993 World Trade Center bombing when the FBI had infiltrated a terrorist group and supplied them with explosives and then got caught. The FBI received terrible publicity from that incident when the explosion took place. He still did not understand why his superiors had allowed the news outlets to report the information since it had given the CIA more reason to taunt them.

If Pratt had handled that case, the public would never have discovered the truth. Not that the exposed truth mattered anyway. As long as the mainstream media never validated the story through exposure, the public would never believe the story when an independent source eventually exposed it.

Agent Pratt despised the typical arguments against such tactics. He believed the rationale adopted by the intelligence community. Instead of allowing criminals to recruit potential terrorists, the FBI and CIA should proactively control the situation recruit the extremists first.

When Pratt had suggested his plans to the director of the Seattle office, they had failed to become part of the agenda. His boss wanted something more low-level, something to give the office a good image without the possibility of bad press, and besides, the FBI head office was not pushing for anything at that time. Pratt had little hope of success with these small-time losers, but he did find some hope in a new case he had acquired. His boss did not need to know that he was going to follow his plan anyway.

His phone rang and he recognized the phone number of his boss. A phone call usually meant a request for Agent Pratt to visit his office. Otherwise, the director would have used email. Without answering the call, Agent Pratt rose from his desk and went to meet with the director.

"What's up, Jason?" Pratt asked as he entered the office.

"Shut the door and have a seat."

FIFTY-FIVE

John

Pratt shut the door as requested and sat in one of the chairs in front of the director's desk. The Counterterrorism Division Director, Jason Smithson, had been heading the department for five years now. Before he was appointed the director, he had worked as a special agent, the same as John. They remained good friends since his promotion. He had blond hair, and light green eyes, and was wearing a white shirt, stretched tight against his muscular arms.

"I've been reading your update on the college kids," Jason said while looking at his computer screen. "You've got to have more on these guys than this. You're my best agent. I'm counting on you. I'm not sure if you've been using our informants to their full potential."

Agent Pratt sighed and sat back in his chair.

"It's probably true sir, but I really don't think these kids have it in them. I'm getting sick of reading their pathetic emails. To tell you the truth, I hate these kids more than I hate Muslims."

"All the more reason to get the little shits, wouldn't you say?" the director said and smiled. "From their emails, it sounds like they do have it in them. You need to give me more. Figure out a way to push them over the edge. I cannot include this lack of progress in my report. You know how it goes."

The director stared at his friend, waiting for a response.

Agent Pratt met the intense gaze of his boss without flinching. Only Agent Pratt could have had that kind of exchange with Jason Smithson, at least the only agent at their office. Even more than their friendship, John Pratt and Jason Smithson shared a common cause. They both intended to rid the world of extremists, anyone who fought or would fight against them, against the establishment. While the other agents scrambled to discover how to please their boss, Jason and John read the same page from the same book. If Smithson was upset with the lack of progress of a case, John Pratt was upset too.

"Sir," he began. "Some of the problem is because of the time I've spent on Gerald Foster lately."

Agent Pratt waited for a response and expected an angry one.

"Good old Gerald," Jason said while shaking his head. "I know it's good to keep tabs on that guy, but he's been a dead end for a long time now, ever since he exposed your contact and you failed to convict him."

"I know, I know," Pratt replied in response to the blunt rebuke. "But, let me tell you what I haven't included in any of my reports yet. He's been talking a lot to our old friend, Cesar Sanchez, and there's something new, a recent college graduate, a genius in mechanical design, another extremist he's been talking with."

Jason Smithson sat forward and looked interested.

"Oh, they'd love for us to bring that guy down," he said.

Agent Pratt imagined the director licking his lips.

Ever since Gerald Foster's indirect involvement in the Federal Reserve office break-in, he had been on *the list*. But unfortunately, Gerald had become a dormant volcano since the incident. He still had great extremist potential, but he knew how to keep a low profile. Pratt had been following Gerald Foster in the same way the Japanese sought the blue tuna.

"The girl who moved in with Cesar Sanchez is quite a beauty," Pratt said while imagining what he could do with her. "But she's a smug, little bitch. She works in his shop now and seems to be just like Gerald, another fucking extremist. Her brother committed suicide after coming back from Iraq. She's pretty pissed."

"Perfect," Jason replied sarcastically. "Sounds like the birth of another tumor on society. Can't she just blame the terrorists like everyone else?"

"There's been a lot of secret communication between them all."

"I don't doubt it," said Jason. "Gerald's smart and knows we're watching him. What makes you suspicious of Cesar and this girl?"

"I've been at their shop, and they're up to something." John sat back in the chair and glanced over Jason's head at the picture of him with Bill Clinton. "I'm not sure what they're making, but I'm going to find out. Are you ever going to tell me about Cesar and why we're not supposed to touch him?"

"I can't say because I don't know. It's classified, over my head." Jason Smithson turned to his computer and punched some keys. Then he took a deep breath and cleared his throat, a sign he planned to change topics. "I also wanted to talk to you about the Hezbollah case. In your report, you did not give me an update on your lead of their funding source."

While they talked about other cases, John Pratt's mind kept drifting into fantasies of placing Gerald Foster into a military detention center for interrogation. If he only could have the chance to interrogate him, what would he learn? The fantasy seemed like too much to hope. His experience with Foster as a new lawyer proved the man's skills and his understanding of how the legal system worked, including all of its loopholes.

The Law Firm of Foster and Fowler had several suspicious clients, including an Islamic trust fund and some remote business operations on Native American reservations. He seemed to be supporting all the people Agent Pratt hated, namely anyone involved with un-American institutions.

A successful prosecution of Gerald Foster would add a negative stigma on those anti-government groups, not to mention revenge for exposing their man in the End-The-Fed group. Pratt needed to make an example of him, send a message to others involved with those groups that Gerald loved. They and all of the goddamned Muslims were enemies of the USA.

Sometimes, Pratt would find himself daydreaming of shooting Foster. He would find a back alley somewhere, dark and alone then shoot him in the stomach. And then before all of his blood had escaped the punctured aorta, Pratt would finish the deed with a bullet to the head. His body would never be found, only some blood.

That kind of end seemed too easy for Foster. People needed to know what happened to him. Agent Pratt had fun fantasizing about killing him anyway. The act would leave Pratt with nothing other than personal satisfaction. But he needed recognition for the indictment. To get complete satisfaction and advance his career at the Bureau, Pratt had to follow standard procedure and put Gerald Foster behind bars.

Pratt hoped to use the new development in the Foster case to learn more about Cesar Sanchez. He had been the governor of Ciudad-Juarez in Mexico and had somehow managed to escape the drug cartel upheaval and relocate to the United States. From the reports he had found in the media, Pratt knew Cesar should have been assassinated as his wife and sons. Something suspicious had happened to prevent his death.

—※—

At the end of their conversation, Agent Pratt left Jason Smithson's office with more assignments, probably intended to divert his attention from what he wanted to do, investigate Gerald. He would need to spend more time at work. Would his new girlfriend get tired of never seeing him and move out of his apartment, and take her obnoxious kid? That little girl always seemed to ruin their fun nights together.

He spent the next few hours cleaning up the mess on his desk and preparing to close some loose ends. He needed to schedule another trip to the University of Washington campus to follow up with the fanatical anarchists. Before leaving, he would need to acquire some petty cash for one of his informants, a janitor who had access to their dorm room. While thinking of his inevitable conversation with the janitor, Pratt prepared for frustration. If a grenade sat on the table in the kid's apartment, the idiot would lift the grenade to look for anything interesting underneath. For this reason alone, John only accepted pictures from the man and never his assessment.

Pratt had only one thing he could trust in the world, money. The average human obeyed money, the only devotion Pratt could expect from them. If he spent sufficient time, he could always find someone to do what he wanted, for the right price. Money also ensured discretion. The janitor knew that if anyone ever discovered his underhanded dealings, he would look like a creep no one could trust or believe, and the money would stop flowing.

Before he left for the university the next morning, John Pratt visited their surveillance device expert, or as they all affectionately referred to her, the bug girl. When people came into contact with Charlie, the short and solid woman, they first noticed her hair. Perfectly straight auburn bangs stopped just above her eyes. Her hair always reminded him of a waterfall, frozen in time.

"Charlie, remember that little favor?" he asked.

"Depends on whether you're gonna dump the girlfriend or not," she said and smiled, her clear braces glistening in the light.

John ignored the impulse to gag at the thought of any romantic connection with the woman. He smiled instead.

"How many sexual harassment charges do I have to file, Charlie?" John smiled and laughed convincingly, punching her in the right arm.

"So are you ready yet for me to make that placement?" she asked in a serious tone.

"We need to hold off on that, for a while."

"What happened?" she asked.

"Unfortunately, I've already got what I need," he said in a regretful tone of losing the need for her services.

He had no intention of telling her or anyone else what really happened, that Cesar's friend, the rough-looking Mexican thug, had caught Pratt spying at their machine shop. From that brief look into the man's dark eyes, Pratt knew he had to be careful and back off for a while. After investigating Doroteo's profile, Agent Pratt decided to change tactics and use a more sophisticated approach when dealing with a former chief of security.

After he finished talking with the bug girl, he left for the university. On the drive, he imagined several possible confrontations with Doroteo, the Mexican. The man would probably pose an interesting challenge, but Pratt felt confident in his abilities to prevail in almost any conflict. Success all depended on mental and physical preparation. Perhaps he would have the pleasure of a confrontation one day.

FIFTY-SIX

John

On his way home from work Friday night, Agent Pratt stopped at one of his favorite pubs. He liked to go by himself and avoided becoming too familiar with anyone there. He enjoyed the anonymity. If he ever recognized anyone, he would try to avoid eye contact and sit somewhere far away.

He liked to look at the women, the pretty ones, have a few drinks, and watch whatever game happened to be playing. When he had the opportunity to talk with an attractive woman, he usually invented a unique name and occupation he thought would interest her the most. Most women responded positively to his strong and confident demeanor more than his fabrications, but they usually bored him in the end, and he would politely let them know to get going. If no female caught his attention, he stayed less than an hour before going home to his girlfriend. He resented feeling obligated to spend time with the woman and her kid, who had severely damaged his sex life.

On that night, he met an interesting woman. She wore an expensive strapless dress, dark blue, and tight. The fabric strained to contain her feminine form, especially her large breasts. She was the one to approach Agent Pratt and seemed sincerely interested in learning everything about him. He had difficulty inventing a fictional persona when her scent and golden skin intoxicated him more than the alcohol in his scotch. His immediate physical reaction to her felt like a separate heartbeat.

After an enjoyable thirty minutes of conversation, she claimed to need fresh air and suggested going somewhere more private, but she failed to mention any place specific. The location seemed an unimportant detail to Pratt. He could easily handle going anywhere with her, for a few hours at least.

On the way to his car, he began experiencing some difficulty walking and thinking simultaneously, and for the last few steps, he even required her assistance. He looked up at her and felt like a puppy being inspected by a little kid who wanted to buy it.

"Whoa there, big guy," she said, laughing at his drunken behavior and leading him to the passenger door.

The door seemed to open at just the right time, just before he fell into the passenger seat. On his way down, he hit his head. She laughed at him again, her mouth opening so wide he thought she would swallow him whole. He laughed at the strange and frightening sight, but he really wanted to close his eyes and just cry. By the time she had shut his door and opened hers, his laughter had transformed into quiet snoring.

"Barely made it to the car," she said to herself, then sighed.

She looked around the vehicle to see if anyone had noticed, but no other human came into her view. A taxi drove past and then there was quiet. The woman stared at Agent Pratt for a few minutes, searching for evidence of consciousness. After feeling assured of the drug's effectiveness and her safety, she retrieved his wallet.

Careful not to leave any fingerprints, she made sure to follow the Mexican's instructions and wear gloves. She removed all of his money and credit cards from his wallet. In disappointment, she found only fifty-five dollars in cash, but the Mexican had given her seven hundred dollars for the job, so she was not that disappointed. He told her to take the cards and then cut them into pieces later and discard them far away in a public trash receptacle. After taking the cards and money, she put his wallet back in his pocket.

No one watched as she drove away and no one would have cared if they did. On the drive, she removed her wig and tried to ignore the feeling of anxiety about her final task of the night, meeting the Mexican and receiving the rest of her money.

John Pratt dreamed of a disturbing trip to his dentist's office while wearing grease-stained overalls. As he lay flat on his back in the dentist's chair, the dentist and his assistant probed, poked, drilled, and talked. John tried to follow their conversation, but a large rubber dam separated his upper and lower teeth. He could barely manage to concentrate on breathing let alone listening. The dentist and his assistant acted as though they were working on a car engine.

After the dentist and his assistant had faded to nothing, John watched as a thick, nebulous fog rushed past him like a river. Different colors of black swirled above him. He had never experienced such a sensation. For what seemed an eternity, he floated in the beautiful new colors, and then after another long time, he began to enjoy it. Nothing could disturb him.

After floating for a long while, his environment began changing again. An increasing physical pressure began to squeeze him from all directions. He'd never felt such amazing pressure. In the darkness, he smiled, and that action added to his euphoria.

The pressure and his euphoria intensified and almost brought him to the point of oblivion, but then the shaking began. A light began to fill his vision and coalesced into vague shapes, like figures from a Picasso painting. The main character, a tall, skinny wizard wearing a pointed hat stood in the center of a congregation containing millions of people.

The wizard stood much taller than all of the people surrounding him. A glowing fog of bright green spewed from the tip of a staff in his left hand, the source of all the light. The people swayed around him as though with some invisible current, illuminated by the green fog above them. Part of the fog swirled above the old man, part swirled around the crowd, and the rest ascended into the black sky. The entire congregation focused on the wizard, and also John who watched from far away.

"John," said a voice from the sky, a whisper too loud to ignore. "Shoot them. Kill them."

John looked above him to the source of the voice, but he could only see the green fog ascending into the sky.

"Who said that?" he asked in a whisper, suddenly afraid of attracting the wizard's attention.

The wizard turned toward the sound and his angry, yellow eyes shone like a bright laser. John wanted to pull some of the darkness around him and shield himself from the light.

FIFTY-SEVEN

Taylor

It was Friday night just after dark. While Doroteo went to acquire the FBI agent from his contact, Taylor and Cesar waited in an empty foreclosed home at the end of a long private road, in the dark. If all went according to plan, Doroteo would arrive with the unconscious government agent, or else he would arrive alone. He told them not to use their phones, since their call records could be used later as evidence against them should the FBI suspect their involvement. Taylor spent the time attempting to build confidence in her friends' plans.

According to Doroteo, a set of illegal drugs would help them extract information without the need for physical violence or coercion. That gave her some comfort, but the information failed to erase her shock at the plan itself. Any mistake could destroy her future. Any piece of evidence left exposed might lead Taylor and her friends into the comforting embrace of a federal prison. Would she be sent to the infamous prison in Guantanamo Bay? Maybe she should study Islam to prepare.

"Will you please explain to me again why they won't suspect us?" Taylor asked. "I know Doroteo seems to have no concern about the plan, but I'm still not used to kidnapping people and drugging them."

Cesar sat down on a chair that had been left in the upstairs bedroom, but Taylor remained standing at the window. While waiting for him to answer, she tapped her left shoe with the heel of her right shoe.

"The FBI is a government agency," he began. "Is that enough or do I need to give more explanation?"

"Normally, that would be all I needed to hear, but with our safety on the line, I need more."

"Okay, so you're not convinced," he said and laughed. "To give them credit, FBI agents are good at what they do, offense. They have the money, the manpower, and all the other required resources to plan effective offensive strikes. Fortunately for us, they have a huge bureaucracy to weigh them down. It's very effective at making them ineffective, especially at defense."

"I'll have to take your word for it."

Taylor could feel him looking at her, but she could not see his eyes in the low light. When she heard him exhale, she knew he had more to say.

"The most successful private companies, which aren't subsidized by the government, are usually led by the skilled and ambitious people who rise to the top. In the FBI and other government agencies, those in leadership are usually those with the best connections and not necessarily those who are most qualified. It's mostly politics, who-you-know, what you're willing to do. Their priorities are set by political agenda. Their organization was designed to protect the top criminals, the people who control the money and capital. The bureaucracy won't expend the time required to find out what happened to one agent stupid enough to let himself get caught. Doroteo thinks the guy will be too embarrassed to tell anyone about it, especially if he ever wants to get promoted."

"Yes," she said impatiently. "I get that, but this guy won't remember any of it right, because of the drugs?"

"Taylor," he began quietly. "You've never taken any illegal drugs in your life have you?"

"Of course not!" Taylor looked affronted. "I kind of like my brain."

"All this media attention about the government torturing people for information, the debate if it is ethical or not," Cesar said then paused, tapping his foot on the wooden floor and the noise seemed to replace the darkness. "A bastard's trick, a red herring. That's all it is. If they want real information, they'll use drugs."

"I know. Psychological warfare."

"Doroteo's got his own special concoction of hallucinogens and other drugs to keep this guy in the perfect state for us. He'll tell us everything we want to know." Cesar laughed slightly. "He'll even sell out his mother and father if we wanted him to, but I'm afraid it won't be as dramatic as the movies. Sorry, but at least it should be entertaining."

"So he's not going to remember anything?"

"Not much. Just remember what we told you and what he does remember will not include us."

Eventually, they heard a car driving slowly down the gravel driveway. They listened to a car door opening and closing and then footsteps toward the house. When the door opened downstairs, Cesar put a finger to his mouth. They both stayed in the room and kept the door closed. When the intruder began ascending the steps, Taylor became conscious of her heartbeat pounding loudly in her chest. The motion felt loud enough to be heard in the stillness, but Cesar appeared calm. Even though she knew Doroteo was walking up the stairs, only the sight of him entering the room would remove all of her doubt.

The noise stopped outside the door, followed by two quiet knocks.

"All is well," Doroteo said quietly from the other side. "You can open the door."

After Cesar opened the door, Taylor stopped breathing and thought a giant humpback stood before them. She stared at them in horror until the giant mass became distinguishable as Doroteo and another man slumped over his shoulder. Doroteo stepped forward and gently unloaded the man on the cot in the middle of the room. Taylor took a deep breath. Had she actually become an accomplice to an abduction? In disappointment, she had expected to be more excited than afraid.

Cesar closed the door and joined Doroteo at the cot. For the next few seconds, the two men just stared at the unconscious man. Doroteo was taking deep breaths as though he had just run a marathon. In the dim light, Taylor noticed a dark bag covering the man's face. She stood several steps away, afraid of interrupting the scene and waking him. If he woke, Cesar or Doroteo would have to handle the situation, not her.

Cesar removed a small LED lamp from his jacket and energized it, casting the room in a soft bluish glow. Doroteo sat in a chair and exhaled loudly.

"Just give me a moment. I'm not so young anymore."

"You and I both, my friend," Cesar said, patting Doroteo on the shoulder.

FIFTY-EIGHT

Taylor

Taylor took a tentative step closer and stared at the unconscious man. He wore jeans and a polo shirt, which looked blue, but in the dark, she had difficulty determining the exact color. While inspecting the man, Taylor realized how heavy he must have been for Doroteo to carry.

"You carried this guy up the stairs?" she asked quietly with a new respect for Doroteo. "He must be over a hundred kilograms."

"I could not have done it," Cesar said.

She turned to Doroteo and spoke as quietly as she could.

"What if this guy wakes up but pretends to be asleep and he's listening to everything we say?"

"Yes, we'll have to be careful about that. From what he was given, we have about another hour, give or take, before he'll even start to regain his senses, but they won't all come back at once. He'll be disoriented and not able to think clearly for several hours."

Taylor took the last step to the cot and stood directly over him. The only way to overcome her fear was to stare at the cloth covering his face. She listened to his shallow breathing and watched the slight rise and fall of his chest. The scene seemed like a group of vultures waiting for an injured animal to die.

They had to wait about thirty minutes before they could continue with the plan, the injections. If they administered the drugs to him while still asleep, Doroteo said it could be dangerous.

"Have you discovered this man's identity?" Cesar asked.

"Not yet," Doroteo answered. "But he's our man. I recognized his face."

Cesar slid a pair of gloves over his hands and reached inside the man's back pocket. After retrieving a wallet, he opened it and the man's badge reflected the LED light in Cesar's hand.

"Special Agent John Pratt," he read. "Just as I thought, from the Counterterrorism Division. That narrows it down a bit. At least, they don't think we're committing some sort of crime."

Both men laughed, but Taylor gulped.

To pass the remainder of the time, they discussed the FBI Counterterrorism Program. Doroteo argued with Cesar about the real goals of the FBI. They disagreed on small points but agreed on their primary objectives, to legitimize the war on terror by keeping it in the news and causing a lot of smoke. Building an effective illusion required the injection of money, manpower, and activity.

"What is the drug we're going to use on this guy, on Agent Pratt?" she asked. Taylor wished the man's name had remained a mystery and wondered if she could convincingly deny knowing his name if the police ever questioned her about him.

Doroteo turned from the FBI agent.

"We will first give him a drug called Amobarbital. You might have heard of it. It's not the best stuff, but it's easier to acquire than what the intelligence community uses, and it works. I've also added a trace amount of LSD. This combination works well."

Hearing Doroteo talk about illegal drugs made her laugh. She had begun to associate Doroteo with almost every illegal activity. After purchasing a dangerous and illegal nuclear reactor, they kidnapped a government agent. Next, they would inject LSD into their victim. What was their next crime?

"Wait a minute," she said. The truth serum part made sense, although it reminded her of a cheap mystery novel. But why the LSD? "Is the LSD supposed to help him talk to us, or forget?"

"Both," said Doroteo as he tried to hide a smile. "LSD is just to make it an unbelievable experience, to distort his memory if government psychiatrists ever attempt to uncover what we've done. I've got another drug to help him forget almost everything."

"Taylor," Cesar began. "You know this is how real information is forcibly extracted from prisoners, don't you? This is how I got them to tell me where they were holding my daughter."

"Will there be permanent damage to him? I mean, I've heard these kinds of drugs can change a person."

"Probably not, but what does it matter?" Doroteo asked with some impatience. "We have to find out what he knows. He could ruin all your work, your future, and mine. Stop worrying about this man, and worry about what you need. He may be just doing his job, but we have a responsibility to defend ourselves and our friends."

Taylor almost allowed herself to continue arguing with Doroteo, but she felt unqualified for the task and decided just to let the professionals do their work. She gritted her teeth in capitulation.

"You're right, Doroteo."

"I know," he said with expressionless eyes.

His irritated tone reminded her of their dangerous situation. Despite how calmly he talked, she could see anxiety in his kinesics. Never before had he ever acted so irritated toward her. Did the stress of the situation reveal his real feelings? She shrugged. Maybe she would talk to him later about it.

No one spoke for the next few minutes as they watched the man for signs of consciousness. Cesar noticed the first body movement, from the agent's fingers.

"He's almost ready to receive the next dose. Don't worry, Taylor, he's not close to being conscious yet, but we should proceed soon."

Doroteo spoke and his tone had returned to normal. "Let's go over what we're going to do next."

For the next minute, they explained Taylor's role again. She would do all of the talking in a whisper. Her native accent had a smaller chance of being remembered than a Mexican one. Having a female interrogator would also help him feel more relaxed. Taylor suspected another motivation from the two men, to give her the experience. She felt like their daughter on her first hunting trip and they had handed Taylor the gun.

"Oh, one other item," Cesar said.

He opened his backpack and removed an electronic metronome. He started the device at a slow setting, twenty beats per minute. The rhythmic tapping chimed quietly in the room and Taylor imagined the sound as a mouse hitting a cowbell with a little rock. They listened to the steady tick of the metronome for about thirty seconds and no one said anything.

"This helps me concentrate and might help him feel relaxed," Cesar said.

"Wow," she whispered in amazement. *How many times have they done this?*

After ten more minutes, the first signs of consciousness became apparent. In the dim light of the LED lamp, they could see the man's fingers begin moving more, and then he started moaning with his head slowly turning left and right. All three of them hovered over the cot as though inspecting a patient ready for surgery.

Taylor switched her attention between Doroteo and Cesar, waiting for one of them to intervene before the FBI agent awoke or said something. She fought the urge to throw her elbow into them so that they would begin. She imagined the agent jumping off the bed, pulling his gun, and shooting like a crazy outlaw from the Wild West.

In the next moment, he groaned loudly and Taylor thought she heard words from under the cloth covering his head. Cesar and Doroteo leaned forward to listen, and Taylor took a step backward.

"I think it's time," Cesar whispered to Doroteo.

When the agent's hand slowly began moving toward his face, Doroteo reached out and stopped his hand from going any farther. Cesar stepped close to Taylor and whispered in her ear.

"You're up, Taylor."

She felt like an actress who had suddenly forgotten her lines. Cesar must have noticed her hesitation.

"Tell him everything's going to be all right," he continued. "That we're going to take care of him. Remember, you're our voice, and you'll be his whole universe."

"Okay," Taylor whispered, her heart pounding. Cesar scooted her chair next to the cot and Taylor sat down then leaned closer to the FBI agent.

"Everything is okay. Just relax." After speaking to the man, she instantly felt more confident. Cesar nodded in approval.

"Where am I?"

After Agent Pratt asked the question, he mumbled something else that Taylor failed to comprehend. She waited in silence for the man to respond, but he seemed to fall back asleep.

Doroteo stepped over to his bag on the floor and retrieved a syringe and vial. With only Cesar by her side, she felt more exposed to the government agent who might jump off the cot and strangle her. When Doroteo returned to her side, she felt better. He gently pulled her away and whispered in her ear.

"I'm going to give him the Amobarbital now. It will start working in just a few minutes. Then we'll be able to question him. As long as you keep him talking, he'll tell us whatever we want to know, but it might be hard to keep him focused and awake. Just keep him talking."

When Doroteo stuck the needle into the back of the agent's thigh, he jerked and made a weak attempt to pull his leg away, but he lacked the strength to resist fully. Taylor placed her hand on his shoulder and cringed upon contact, not from fear but an instinctive and personal dislike for him. The man on the cot had spied on them and fought against their freedom. She wondered suddenly if a rabbit placed a paw on a sleeping coyote if it would have felt the same.

FIFTY-NINE

Taylor

"It's going to be all right, Agent Pratt," Taylor said softly. "You should feel better soon."

They wanted her to call him Agent Pratt so that he would focus on his role as an FBI agent. A few minutes later, the man appeared relaxed on the cot again and Doroteo moved his chair to the other side of the agent, opposite Taylor. Cesar sat at the agent's head with Doroteo and Taylor on his sides. The scene reminded Taylor of a group of friends warming themselves around the flames of a fire.

"Hey," the agent said suddenly, shattering the quiet scene. He spoke in a voice louder than any of them had used since entering the house. "Hooo issss therrrr?"

Taylor heard him smack his lips together as though trying to prevent saliva from escaping his mouth. To understand him, she would need to concentrate. His voice seemed to have difficulty penetrating through the cloth.

"Where'm I?"

"You're safe," Taylor whispered. "How do you feel?"

"How'd I feel?" he asked in a tone approaching laughter. "Greaeaeaeaeat. What ya gave me? Give me moooooooore!"

"It's the medication. When you fell, you hit your head pretty hard."

"Head dos'n hurt," he said with sudden confusion. He reached for his head, but Taylor stopped his hand at his chin.

"Don't touch," she began, but a cry of panic interrupted her.

"Oh my god!" he almost screamed. "I can't see. Where's th'light?"

"You can't see because your head is bandaged," Taylor said and had to suppress a laugh. "You shouldn't touch it."

"Oh my god! I'm blind! I'm blind!" In his panic, he had failed to comprehend her words. "I'm neverrr gonna see again, am I? This is the end for me."

"Don't cry," Taylor said. "It's going to make your head hurt more. Listen to me. You're not blind. Your head is bandaged. That's why you can't see. Your eyes are fine."

"I'm not blind?" he asked in a tone of disbelief.

The next instant, he spoke with relief and started laughing. "Ahhhh. Thank you, doctor. Thank you! Ha ha ha. I owe you my life. Whatever you want, just name it."

"You're welcome," she said and smiled at his promise to give her what she wanted. "We'll get to that later. For now, I just want you to relax."

"My head dos'n hurt," he said in more relief. "I'm healed! You fixed me!"

"No," she said sternly. Her responses came easily and instinctively. "Your head does hurt."

"Alright," he said in quick agreement.

While fighting the temptation to laugh, Taylor regretted not being able to video record the experience for future enjoyment. That was probably the greatest injustice. A video could be used against them in court.

"Try to stay with me," she said. "Just keep talking. It'll help. Can you do that?"

"Shore, alright. Am I in a hospital?"

The agent suddenly jerked his head to the left, aiming his face somewhere above Doroteo.

"Whoa! Whoa! What th'hell are you?"

He spoke with fear in his voice, as though a frightful creature had appeared above him. He reached up and grabbed at the air, at some LSD-induced horror. Taylor was not prepared for hallucinations and looked at Doroteo and Cesar for guidance. They just smiled and nodded for her to continue.

Taylor paused to regain focus. The rhythmic dinging of the metronome filled the silent gaps in the conversation and made time flow like a marching band.

"What have you been doing lately, Agent Pratt?"

"Going to college," he said, snickering and swatting in the air. His fear had disappeared. Taylor moved her hand to his forearm. If he decided to fight her, she lacked the physical strength to restrain him. "Gonna get the kids. Gotta get 'em."

"What are the college kids doing?"

"Planning a bomb," he said, and his tone changed to foreboding. "Gotta catch 'em in the act. Oooooh, it's gonna be good."

"What else have you been doing?"

"Checking on my old friend," he said. "We're not good friends really. No, not really."

"Who is this friend who's not really a friend?"

"Watching," he said and trailed off into a whisper. "Keepin' tabs on Foster."

Taylor squeezed his arm to keep the words flowing.

"Lisssning tooo..."

"Listening to what?"

"His friend, good old Sanchez, and some girl. Tlayer's her name I think, like Tlayer Slift. Ha ha ha. Funny name, pretty girl. Yes, very pretty girl. Would not mind a night with her, nope. Probly shood'n be saying that to nother woman. Ha ha ha. Are you jealous?"

His comments about them and especially her, transformed her amusement to anger and embarrassment. She took a deep breath to calm herself, but before she had a chance to respond, he continued.

"Hey, I'm not supposed to be tellin' you this? I am Eff Bee Ayee, don't you know? Fe..der...al Byo...row...of–"

He enunciated the words as though chewing them.

"I know," she interjected. "I'm an agent too."

"Knew it," he said and nodded his head triumphantly. "What's your name? Not fair you get to know mine, and I don't know yours."

"We'll get to that later. What else have you been doing lately?"

He continued speaking about his leads on some Islamic terrorist cases and how he needed to trace all of their funding sources. He hated that part of his job, mostly due to associating with Muslims. He hated them, but his superiors wanted to crack these kinds of cases. They would give more publicity.

Extremists and potential domestic terrorists from the United States interested him more than the stereotypical Islamic terrorists. Taylor had a hard time understanding his feelings and opinions. They consisted mainly of hatred and anger, much more than any desire to protect the public or bring criminals to justice. Her indignation against the government originated from horrible experiences in her family, so maybe Agent Pratt had experienced something similar. Most likely though, the media had conditioned him that way.

"So what do you have on these little shits?" she asked, mimicking the way he talked about them. "Gonna stick 'em in jail if all goes well?"

He laughed again, annoyingly.

"Hey, you're my kind-a-girl, I think. You're gorgeous, aren't you? I get the feeling you are, probably gotta boyfriend too."

"I'm nothing special," she said, shrugging and looking at Cesar across the bed.

He smiled while shaking his head in disagreement and she felt her cheeks flush.

"Nuh-uh," Agent Pratt scolded her, shaking his head under the sheet. "You are one hot agent. I can tell. Ha ha ha."

He spent the next several minutes talking about his progress on other cases while continually asking about her physical appearance. Whenever he strayed from her chosen topics, she could usually redirect the conversation. Eventually, she returned the discussion to Gerald and his friends.

"Tell me again, why do you hate Foster so much?" she asked as casually as possible.

"Gerald Fucking Foster," he said with contempt, the first instance he seemed serious. "Foster's an extremist like all th'others, maybe worse. For what he did, he should be in jail. We'll get him."

Agent Pratt waved his index finger from side to side.

"What did this guy do? I already don't like him."

"He wants to eliminate the Federal Reserve. Wants to take out the money supply. Can you believe that? Not much worse you can do."

He spoke next in sync with the metronome.

"What."

"A."

"Shit."

"Lots of shitheads want that," she said and smiled.

She felt the same as Gerald on that topic.

"Foster planned the Federal Reserve building break-in, the whole damned thing, and got away with it. He let his friends take the blame."

"How did he do that?"

"Cause he's an asshole lawyer. That's how." He suddenly stopped talking and grabbed at some invisible thing in the air. Taylor let him grab at nothing for a few seconds. "Whoa, come back here you. Come on, just a little closer."

"What else did he do? Is he up to anything now?"

"Don't know," he said and left his hand suspended in the air. He finished his thoughts only after Taylor pushed his hand back down to his side. "But he must be. Gotta find out what his friends are doing at that machine shop."

"So, what are they up to?"

"I've been liss'ning," he whispered, still chuckling. "They don't even know."

"For how long?"

"Long enough to hear some strange shit."

"What kind of shit?"

Her tone had suddenly turned to anger and Doroteo put his hand on her shoulder.

"A jet engine that's not a jet. Too quiet." He put a finger on the cloth covering his face. "Shhhhhh"

"That doesn't make any sense."

"It doesn't make any sense," he sang. "No sense, no sense, no sense. Gotta keep lissssennninnng!"

Taylor kept silent for a few seconds and Agent Pratt quickly fell asleep. This time she let him sleep. She sat back, and Doroteo leaned forward.

"Very good, Taylor," he said. In the low light, she could see the outline of his smile. After the brief display of praise, he patted her on the back. "I'm going to give him the next drug now. It's going to be harder to talk to him, but it will erase the remaining memory of the night."

Doroteo rummaged through his backpack for another vial of liquid. When he inserted the syringe into Agent Pratt's other leg, the man only flinched but remained asleep.

The metronome marched forward.

Tick

Tick

Tick

Cesar stood and motioned for Taylor to come with him into the hallway. Once out of the room, Cesar leaned close to her and spoke with a tone of relief.

"He doesn't know anything," he said.

"Sounds like it, but I still want to know two more things. What exactly has he heard, not just what he thinks he's heard, and what he plans to do."

"Never satisfied are you?" he asked, looking directly into her eyes.

Suddenly, they heard talking from the room, so Taylor turned to go back. But before she reached the door, Cesar grabbed hold of her arm.

"Just don't put too much emphasis on our true interests."

After returning to the room, she found Agent Pratt calling for her. Doroteo was holding onto his arm.

"Pretty lady, pretty baby. Talkin to you. Yoohoo. Talkin tooo yoooo hooo. Why sooo quiet?"

Taylor quickly sat down and patted his shoulder.

"Don't freak out. I'm right here. You were telling me about what you heard in that machine shop."

"No more talking, until you say sorry...and why am I floating in the air? Not fair. Hey, fair, air. Ha ha ha. I'm a damned poet. What a trip!"

"Stop being such a bastard," she said in the hopes of getting his attention. "I have nothing to be sorry about."

"Bastard," he said and licked his lips. During the brief pause, Taylor imagined the word as a sucker in his mouth. "Hmmmm. Give me one second. Rastard, no that doesn't work. Lizard, no no no. Hey, I got it. Conjastard! Ha! Conjastard rhymes with bastard."

He laughed in triumph and continued laughing until he started to cough.

"Listen to me, Agent Pratt," she said once his coughs had subsided enough for him to hear. "You need to stay focused for just a few more minutes, okay? Just finish your story, and we'll be done. You can get back to sleep."

"Not tired anymore," he said while yawning. "Not tired at all. You are one amazing nurse agent. I feel all better now. What time is it?"

"Don't interrupt me," she said barely louder than a whisper. Impatience told her to yell at the man, but she feared to break the stillness. "What exactly did you hear in the machine shop?"

"Ha," he said loudly. "Don't know what they made really, but they'rrrrr excited about it. Talking about space a lot. Sir Space-a-lot, like from the legends. Oh mannn. I am on a rolllll. Are you writing this down? This beautiful poetry just keeps flowing out of my mouth like a damn river. I should have been a cyclist, no I mean a lyracal, you know one of those guys who writes music, a lyracle. Damn it all to hell. That's not it!"

He raised his hand and began conducting a silent symphony to the metronome beat.

"You mean a lyricist," she said impatiently.

"Oh, thank you, pretty agent nurse. Thank you so much," he said and started crying. "You saved me! Now I can be a leereesist, just like I always wanted."

While he cried great sobs of relief, she waited to talk again. All of his irrational behavior stopped being funny and had become only an annoying and embarrassing spectacle.

For the next twenty minutes, Taylor attempted to discover what he planned to do. But no matter how nicely she asked or how much she threatened him, he refused to tell her his plans. No one ever irritated Taylor that much without severe repercussions. Eventually, he agreed to tell her, but only if she let him whisper the secret in her ear.

Agent Pratt said that their discussions about freedom and the absurdity of the government made him too angry to hear anymore, so he planned to break into the shop himself someday. He admitted to being intimidated by their security guy and even had doubts about finding anything incriminating. He only cared about putting Gerald in jail somewhere and had no real interest in the Mexicans or Taylor.

After hearing his plan, Taylor returned to the topic of his target Muslim groups, her final act in their performance. Doroteo said that people remembered the beginning and end of conversations more than the middle. If Agent Pratt successfully recalled any part of their interrogation, they wanted him to remember the end, which excluded them.

When Agent Pratt began repeating a little poem he called, *Allah and the dollah*, Taylor decided to end the conversation. Under any other condition, his poem would have made her laugh.

"Okay, Agent Pratt," she said. "That was a beautiful poem you sang about. You're going to be a great lyricist. I bet you're thirsty, yeah, really thirsty."

He stopped repeating the poem.

"Yes, I am."

"I bet your throat feels like a cactus, doesn't it?"

"Oh my god, yes! Please, just give me something to drink."

Doroteo reached inside his bag and removed a small glass vial of liquid. After removing the lid, he handed the container to her and she stared at the liquid in the LED glow for a few seconds. The sedative would become an unimpressive end to a strange evening. She dreaded the thought of lifting the cloth from his face and helping him take a drink.

"I'm going to be real gentle," Taylor said as she slipped her hand under his head and helped him lean forward to drink. When the cold liquid touched his lips, he breathed deeply. He needed only one gulp.

"Oh yeah," he said after licking his lips. "Oh yeah!"

"I'll give you more in a minute," Taylor said and returned his head to rest on the cot. "We don't want you to have too much too fast."

"Anything you say, doctor agent."

Taylor heard no more from him. After a few more seconds, his left hand slowly slipped off his chest to hang motionlessly at his side. They stared at the body in silence until he became completely still and was breathing quietly. Taylor felt herself relax. Her friends would bring the remainder of the show to a peaceful end.

"So you're going to take him outside some bar?" asked Taylor in the dark. She stood at the window, looking at the trees that surrounded the private drive.

"He's going to be confused when he wakes," Doroteo said. "It'll be a while before he begins to suspect that anything strange happened. Hopefully, the woman from the bar will help provide a convenient and pleasant answer to his lost memory of the evening."

While Doroteo put his things away, Taylor watched outside. After a minute, she noticed a distant light through the trees. In a panic, she recognized a car rolling slowly down the long drive.

"Um, guys. Someone is coming."

SIXTY

Taylor

"What?" both men asked in unison. Their eyes were completely submerged in shadow.

"Someone is driving towards the house," she said and ran to extinguish the LED light.

"¡Mierda," Doroteo said in anger then joined Taylor on the opposite side of the window.

Together, they watched a small pickup truck moving slowly down the drive. Doroteo's car sat in the driveway, just out of their view. Cesar had parked on the street, beyond the trees that he and Taylor had passed on the way to the house.

"Probably just some stupid kids," Cesar said.

"Wait here," Doroteo said. "I'll take care of this."

He left the room and Taylor heard him run down the stairs in just a few steps. Cesar stopped the metronome and joined Taylor at the window. The absence of the metronome ticking momentarily disoriented her. What was Doroteo going to do?

Taylor tried to appear calm and ignore the annoying sensation of her throbbing heart. From the outside, the window must have appeared dark with no occupants, but Taylor felt exposed and trapped.

The timing of the truck's arrival also seemed like too much of a coincidence. The vehicle could have appeared during the interrogation when no one was watching.

"What's he going to do?"

"I have no idea," he answered, and Taylor thought she heard a bit of amusement in his tone.

"Worried?"

"A little," he admitted, looking straight into her eyes. "But, let's let Doroteo worry about it."

They returned their attention to the oncoming pickup truck that looked like a Ford Ranger. The truck stopped about thirty meters from the house.

"Damn it!" Taylor whispered. "They see the car in the driveway."

"Look," Cesar said and pointed.

The truck resumed its forward motion and stopped again at the edge of their vision. The lights in the cab suddenly burst to life, revealing a teenage boy and girl. The boy opened the door and stepped out while keeping his hand on the door. Taylor heard their muffled voices through the window.

"No one's home," the boy said.

"But the car," the girl said, pointing through the windshield. "Someone's here."

"Too dark for anyone to be home," he responded. "The real estate agent left a car here to make it look like someone was here, to scare people away. Come on. It's more fun this way anyway."

The girl swore before exiting the truck and when the door shut, the cabin light turned off. The girl joined her boyfriend as he approached the house and they vanished from sight. The girl said something else and Taylor wondered if she heard the words correctly.

"Hey, that looks like an undercover cop car?"

"You're just paranoid," the boy replied.

Cesar walked slowly to the door but stopped when the floor creaked. He motioned for Taylor to approach the door from another angle.

"You weigh less," he said barely audibly.

She took a couple of tentative steps and heard no squeaking from the floor. In the quiet, she heard every noise, her boots softly tapping the floor, her breathing, her heart beating. She opened the door to the hallway and listened. The teenagers were whispering just outside the front door of the house.

In the silence, they waited. Cesar stood like a statue in the middle of the room, afraid to move and make the floor squeak again. She could hear Agent Pratt breathing softly and rhythmically.

If the kids came up the stairs, she would let Cesar take control. She felt confident in his skills and instincts in dangerous situations. Taylor only feared being discovered, not scaring the kids away. She hoped Doroteo could resolve the situation without hurting them.

The sound of the failed attempts to open the locked front door suddenly replaced all other sounds. When the noise stopped, the kids would probably try the back door or leave. But thirty seconds later, Taylor heard the door in the back of the house slowly open and close. While holding her breath, she watched for a light to appear from the bottom of the stairs, but the house remained dark. As she listened to their conversation, her anxiety began to decrease.

The teenagers spoke quietly about where to *do it*. They failed to define explicitly what *do it* meant, but it obviously involved some sexual act. The girl just wanted to hurry and then leave. Taylor shook her head and laughed inaudibly.

Stupid teenagers might ruin her plans, because of sex.

A bright light suddenly shone through the window behind her and from the bottom of the stairs. Taylor turned toward the window and extended her hand to shield her eyes from the intense light.

"Shit, shit, shit," the boy said in a panic.

"Oh, God. Is it the cops?" the girl asked. "If my dad finds out, he's going to kill me."

Taylor heard them walk quickly to the front of the house to look out the window.

"What the hell!" the boy said in a tone of surprise and anger. "It's my truck lights."

"What–" the girl began to say, but a loud noise from the back of the house interrupted her.

Taylor and Cesar listened to a loud scraping sound and heavy footsteps from the back of the house. Even though Taylor knew that Doroteo was making the noises, a sudden fright raced through her. She had a momentary fear that one of the teenagers would have a heart attack. She turned to Cesar and noticed his mouth stretched into a wide grin.

"That'll do it," he whispered.

"Holy Jesus," the girl shrieked in dread.

The boy said something with a similar alarm, and then soon afterward, the front door opened and slammed shut. Within seconds, the truck drove away, down the road and out of sight, leaving the house in darkness once more.

PART V

PROBE

Specters from the sky
Take you for a ride
How high can you fly?

SIXTY-ONE

Gerald - Sadi - Bill

Gerald lay on the couch of his childhood home. While staring at the ceiling, he watched as random patterns in the popcorn ceiling shifted into strange creatures and faces. The scene looked like a demonic, cloudy sky. Thousands of faces showed different expressions, some showing fear, some crying, and some laughing. He watched in mild curiosity as they floated in and out of recognition.

His fever of a hundred and three degrees Fahrenheit was fighting a raging infection. To help combat his fever, his mother had given him a large dose of acetaminophen. Then an hour after the first dose, she gave him another large dose of ibuprofen. While watching the faces above him in the ceiling, he listened to the muffled phone conversation between his mother and grandmother. He did not understand what they were saying. Although his skin felt like fire and the air felt hot inside his lungs, the possibility of death no longer produced fear. He just wanted to fall into an abyss of numbness.

The faces in the ceiling appeared to shift as though they were watching invisible activity in different locations of the room. Some of the faces talked silently with each other, probably sharing frightening secrets. Occasionally, they would pause and look down at Gerald, but only for a brief moment before returning to their private conversa-tions. The whole experience felt extremely strange and disturbing but was partly a comforting distraction. While his body fought the infec-tion, the faces in the ceiling consumed nearly all of his attention.

Twelve-year-old Gerald was attempting to remember the most re-cent events in his life and why they had seemed so important: his school project due the next week, his best friend moving to another state, the prettiest girl in school showing no interest in him. His mem-ory felt far away as though his experiences in school had occurred sev-eral years in the past. Nothing in his life mattered to him anymore. For the remainder of his life, he was content to lie on the couch and just watch the ceiling of faces.

The heat emanating from his skull soon became his only sensation, the only input from the outside world. The heat spread from the top of his skull to the rest of his body but stopped before reaching his cold hands. Young Gerald touched his forehead with cold fingers and en-joyed the sensation. The cold had become the only remaining physical pleasure in his life.

Eventually, he slept and dreamed of a pleasant car ride with an old man and a beautiful woman with dark hair and blue eyes. No one spoke as they drove on a country road in the middle of the night. While they traveled, he enjoyed watching the windshield wipers re-move small streams of rainwater from the glass.

While her newborn son squirmed in the bed next to her, the hours seemed to flow past as a river of maple syrup. Sadi attempted to recall a longer night in her life. Perhaps the memory of a longer night would give her hope for an end to the current one. But for the present, her only memory became the previous uncomfortable moment and then the next. The tiny new human in her arms cried every few minutes and would only stop when Sadi rubbed his back and pulled him close.

When exhaustion had finally overpowered her senses, the action of rubbing his back became automatic.

Sadi loved her infant son more than anything in the world, but the reason for that love was temporarily eluding her awareness. Would her love endure through the night? Could she function as a mother without that emotional connection? Fear of losing the connection to her son consumed her thoughts when conscious and haunted her dreams when she slept. As she alternated between the conscious state and sleep, she imagined herself trapped in a continually revolving door, unwilling or unable to exit.

While sleeping, Sadi dreamed of a pleasant car ride with an old man and another man closer to her age. No one spoke as they drove on a country road in the middle of the night. While they traveled, Sadi enjoyed watching the windshield wipers remove small streams of rainwater from the glass.

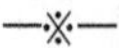

As he lay in the hospital bed after his heart bypass surgery, Bill Smith thought about how close he had come to dying and wondered how many more years he would live. Every few hours, a nurse would visit and examine his physical condition. They kept him heavily sedated, medication for pain and sleep. The burning pain in his chest would occasionally feel like an explosion, imprisoning all of his thoughts, and then the nurse would come and increase his pain medication, and he would sleep again.

At one point, Bill heard the voice of a familiar man asking questions, and he opened his blurry eyes to see his son standing by his bed. But when he tried to respond, he forgot the question and no words escaped his open mouth. After a while, his son vanished, leaving Bill with only his thoughts for company.

Several times, a woman wearing a brilliant white dress would appear by the bed. She looked like his wife at their wedding, but since she had died a long time ago, he doubted the validity of his senses. A daughter could look like the woman at his side. Did he have a daughter and had just failed to remember her? He asked why she had come to him and what she wanted, but she would just smile serenely. While looking at the woman, he could also see the lights on the ceiling through her face. He missed his wife.

Sometimes the room darkened and his eyes dimmed, and he could see the inside of a car sliding smoothly over a country road in the night. He sat with a younger man and woman, their stone faces forward, motionless. When he looked through the window, he saw dense trees moving quickly past his view, soon replaced by other trees. In the car, he felt calm and peaceful. In the car, the pain of surgery vanished.

SIXTY-TWO

Sadi

"Sadi," a voice said, bursting from the darkness, ripping her from the dream. "Wake up."

Sadi paused for a moment before opening her eyes, fearing what she might see. Did Gerald lie beside her in bed? Was she dreaming still? What had happened after Freddy's bedroom?

But after inhaling the scent of new leather and feeling the soft crunch of her seat, her fear vanished. With no memory of how she had arrived in her present position, she somehow found the courage to open her eyes.

Sadi saw a dark forest through a car window. She extended both hands forward and squeezed the steering wheel in front of her, flexing her arms and enjoying the sensation of endorphins entering her bloodstream. She had somehow driven an unfamiliar car and parked on the side of an isolated road in the forest with Gerald Foster in the passenger seat.

LED lights from the dashboard cast a soft glow on the new leather interior of an expensive car. Sadi turned to her right to see Gerald sitting in the passenger seat and then glanced to the back seat where Mr. Smith sat, his head tilted back, either sleeping or dead. Her sudden panic soon passed after she recognized signs of the old man beginning to regain consciousness.

"What are we doing?" Sadi asked, staring at the old man for a few seconds before returning her attention to Gerald.

"I have no idea where we are or how we got here. I woke up to find you and Mr. Smith asleep."

Before Sadi could respond, she heard movement in the back seat. She and Gerald turned around and watched as the old man opened his eyes and began inspecting his surroundings in an attempt to assess his situation.

"What are you doing driving my car?" he asked in irritation and obvious mistrust, reminding Sadi of an abduction situation. "Where have you two taken me?"

His quick recovery surprised Sadi. He seemed more aware of his surroundings than she or Gerald.

"We both just woke up too," Gerald said, turning to Sadi. "I don't remember how we got here, and that's the truth. Do you remember anything, Sadi?"

"You were awake before I was," she said to Gerald, an instinctive attempt to defend herself from the old man's accusations.

"Okay, I don't mean to accuse you both," Mr. Smith said as though interrupting two children in an argument. "We were in Freddy's room, looking at that crystal thing. Does anyone have it?"

"I do," Sadi said before consciously considering the question. She did not remember taking the object, but somehow, she knew its location. "It's right here."

She could feel the object on the seat between her legs. She lifted the crystal carefully into everyone's view, holding the object away from her. The crystal surface scattered the LED light of the dashboard onto the ceiling, but the orange and blue light was no longer shining from inside the object.

"Don't look at it," Gerald said in warning. "That's when my memory ends and everything else went fuzzy. We need to determine our location."

Gerald turned to look through the front window as though he could determine their location just from the view. In the following silence, Sadi listened to the soft vibration of the engine and the sound of light rain hitting the windows. The sensations helped soothe her anxiety. After a moment, Gerald reached his hand to the steering column and energized the headlights. The bright light illuminated tall evergreens on either side of the narrow road.

"Does anyone have a phone with them?" Mr. Smith asked.

While holding the crystal out of her view, Sadi looked at her feet, then her lap, and all over the car for her purse. She suddenly imagined a frantic Jen, unaware of her location or time of return.

"I don't have my purse with me," she said in frustration. She always carried her phone in her purse.

"I don't have my phone with me either," Gerald said.

"We drove here for a reason," Sadi said, trying to calm herself. "We need to figure it out."

"Ms. Jacobsen," Mr. Smith said and leaned forward. "You're the one in the driver's seat. What do you remember?"

Sadi returned her hands to the steering wheel and closed her eyes. She remembered the dream of lying in bed with her newborn son, but she did not want to talk about the experience. She answered him with her eyes closed.

"I can't even remember getting in the car."

"I remember having a very vivid dream," Gerald said. "I remember being sick when I was ten or eleven. My mother gave me a ton of painkillers to fight a fever, but all the drugs just made me hallucinate. I remember staring at the ceiling and seeing faces there. I don't know if it means anything, but I was the first to wake up."

"Maybe we should drive a ways to see if anything shows up," Sadi suggested. "Maybe we're pointed in this direction for a reason."

"Maybe we stopped here for a reason," Gerald said. "I'm going to get out and have a look around."

"Do you think that's a good idea?" Mr. Smith asked.

"We came to help you locate Freddy," Gerald answered and opened the glove box in front of him. He lifted several papers and eventually found what he wanted. "Oh good, a flashlight. You two stay here until I get back."

"I'm going with you," Sadi said. She expected Gerald to protest, but he just nodded and then opened his door. After opening her door, small drops of rain began hitting her hand and wrist. She turned to the back seat and saw Mr. Smith looking out the window as though contemplating joining them.

"Don't worry," Sadi said before stepping out of the car. "We won't go far."

"Thank you," he said while staring out the window.

Sadi had difficulty determining his tone. Sarcastic? Grateful? She suddenly felt like a servant.

On their walk to the front of the car, Sadi shivered from the cold air and rain hitting her arms, head, and neck. Too bad she had failed to bring a hat. While holding her arms tightly against her breasts, she watched as Gerald scanned the area with his flashlight. Out in the cold and rain, she would last maybe one to two hours before hypothermia set in. The thought of Freddy out there somewhere in the cold wetness caused her to shiver even more than her physical reaction to the cold.

"This is insane," Sadi said. "Even though I already saw this crystal thing in action on Freddy, this surreal experience is hard to handle."

"I'm trying not to think about it and focus on finding Freddy," Gerald said while shining his flashlight off the side of the road and into the thick undergrowth of the forest. "Poor old man thinks we've kidnapped him."

The forest sloped upward on the left side of the road and downward on the right. Sadi saw nothing but moss-covered trees, a forest floor of ferns, and if either of them stepped off the right side of the road, they would tumble about five meters and crash into thick blackberry bushes.

"I'm not going to lie, I'm kind of scared," she said and attempted a weak laugh. "And not just for Freddy."

"Do you think Freddy's out here somewhere?" Gerald aimed the flashlight at the blackberry bushes below them and clutched his chest for warmth with his left arm. "Are we supposed to go looking for him, through that?"

Sadi could feel Gerald's growing frustration. Up until that point, Sadi thought he was acting as a boy scout on an adventure. Sadi had no experience with Boy Scouts, however, or camping.

"There's nothing here," she said and walked to the passenger door. "We should start driving again. I think you should drive though."

"See anything?" asked Mr. Smith after they returned to the warm interior of the car.

"No," Gerald began. "I think Sadi had the better idea. We're going to drive a little until we see something."

—※—

When Gerald started driving, he kept their speed at a slow twenty kilometers per hour. Sadi wanted to suggest he drive faster but decided to just watch out the window. After less than a minute, she noticed a dirt road maybe fifty meters ahead on the right.

"A road," she said, pointing. "Look."

An old mailbox at the beginning of the dirt road indicated a private drive with only a single destination. The mailbox leaned sadly to the left and appeared unused for many years. Recent car tire tracks led down the road though, slightly washed away by the rain. The single set of tracks indicated one car's entry without a return trip.

For some mysterious reason, Sadi knew they had arrived at the right place. Gerald entered the road without comment. In any other circumstance, trespassing on private property would have caused her to feel awkward, but their current situation seemed different.

As they moved slowly down the long road, no one spoke. They traveled a couple thousand meters while looking through the windows for signs of life or evidence of Freddy's presence. When they arrived at a ninety-degree left turn in the road, Gerald stopped the car and extinguished the headlights.

"Look up there," he said, pointing to the trees to their left. "I thought I saw a light."

Sadi turned to look, and Mr. Smith sat forward squinting.

"What kind of light?" Mr. Smith asked.

"I don't know. I don't see it anymore."

"I think it's a barn," Sadi said after her eyes adjusted to the absence of the headlights. She saw the outline through the trees, but there were no lights. "It might be time to get the police."

"No," Gerald and Mr. Smith said simultaneously. Mr. Smith continued, "I don't have any reason to believe you two, but I do. We were brought here for a reason. It seems to me that if whoever delivered us here wanted to kill us, they could have driven us off a cliff."

Against her will, Sadi agreed with his argument, so she did not protest. She had instinctively suggested to involve the police, but she knew they had to resolve the situation themselves. She had a daughter to consider and would act irresponsibly by risking her own safety. Gerald chose to remain silent about his motivation and probably wanted to keep out of the spotlight, no matter how small.

"You're right," she said finally. "I was just getting scared."

"We'll be okay," Gerald said, looking into her eyes. "I have a good feeling about this. Well, that's not exactly true. At least I don't have a bad feeling about it anymore."

"Yes," said Mr. Smith from the back seat. "I think Freddy's here too."

For the next few minutes, they watched the barn for signs of movement before deciding to drive onward. For the remainder of the road, they drove slowly and without headlights. Despite his claim otherwise, Gerald looked frightened, and only Mr. Smith seemed unaffected by any feeling of foreboding. Maybe after such a long journey in life, he possessed less fear of the end.

The road ended in a clearing with several hundred acres of open field behind the old barn. From what she could see in the dim light, the crop resembled alfalfa. In the dark of night, the barn stood silent and wet.

"Looks like this is an entrance to that road over there," Gerald said, pointing to the small road winding to the right from the barn. His finger followed the direction of the new road and then to a speck of light on a hill far away. "Looks like a farmhouse way over there. Must have been the light I saw. This barn's probably used as extra storage. Doesn't look very inviting, does it?"

Gerald parked directly in front of the barn, and then he killed the engine.

"So what do we do?" Sadi asked.

Of course, they needed to check the barn, but that action had an obvious problem. From what Sadi knew, they had no weapon or object they could use for protection other than a solid flashlight. What if an angry farmer discovered them? Being shot by a farmer with a shotgun seemed like a pathetic end to her less-than-illustrious life. On the other hand, what if they found nothing in the barn? That possibility felt almost as frightening as physical danger. Freddy would still be lost, and they might have to consult the crystal again.

Before Sadi gave any indication of being mentally prepared, Gerald opened the door. He walked around the front of the car and opened Sadi's door for her. Before exiting the car, she slipped the crystal into her right pocket. With the crystal out of physical contact, Sadi felt more vulnerable.

"I don't think anyone wants to be left behind," Gerald said while holding the door for her.

The light rain restored the chill instantly to her core. She hoped the cold wetness would not make the old man sick.

"Thank you," Mr. Smith said when Sadi opened the door and helped him stand. "Seems to me that we should be looking for Freddy's car. I don't see any other car here."

"Where did those other car tracks lead?" Sadi searched for signs of the car tracks they had seen at the beginning of the road. "Does anyone see them?"

Gerald shined his flashlight down the road where they had come, and it revealed two sets of tire tracks. Their pair of tracks stopped where Gerald had parked. Sadi watched the flashlight beam illuminate the other set of tracks leading to the back of the barn.

"If that's Freddy," Gerald said and then shined the light on the face of the barn, "then he parked around the back, probably to avoid being seen?"

"That's got to be him," Mr. Smith said quietly and with a tone of relief. He lifted his cane in the air, pointing to the barn door. "We should look in the barn first."

"I think you're right," Gerald answered. "Let me go first."

SIXTY-THREE

Sadi

They followed Gerald silently through thick wet grass to the barn door, the sounds of their movement mixing with the sound of the rain on the leaves around them and the slight breeze in the trees. After stopping at the door and putting his hand tentatively on the old and rusted latch, Gerald handed his flashlight to Sadi then placed his other hand on the door frame.

The latch unclasped with a loud, resounding click. At the harsh sound, Sadi's heart seemed to skip a beat and Gerald froze in place. He recovered a few seconds later and continued to open the door with the loud squeak of the rusty hinges. After opening the door just enough for him to step inside, the creaking stopped, and the ensuing silence seemed to repair the damage to Sadi's nerves.

"Hand me the light," Gerald said.

He shot the narrow flashlight beam into the barn and swept it left and right, but from his position, only he could see inside. While Sadi and Mr. Smith waited impatiently, Gerald suddenly stopped moving and just stared into the barn. After waiting several seconds, Sadi placed her hand on his shoulder and wondered if he was afraid of something.

"Gerald, what do you see?" she asked. "Is Freddy in there?"

"Don't move," he answered quietly. He spoke so softly, Sadi could have mistaken his words for occurring only in her imagination. When he spoke again, his voice increased in volume. "I think he's in there, but he's not alone."

"What do you mean, not alone?"

"What's wrong?" Mr. Smith asked loudly, causing Sadi to cringe and squeeze Gerald's shoulder.

She turned to face Mr. Smith, placed her hand on her lips then shrugged and shook her head, hoping to indicate her ignorance. Immediately after facing Gerald again, he extinguished the light from his flashlight. He slowly backed away from the door and turned to face his companions again. As they huddled in the dark and the rain, Gerald spoke so quietly that Sadi feared Mr. Smith would be unable to hear him, but the old man acted as though he understood.

"I believe that your friend is in there," Gerald began, addressing Mr. Smith. While speaking, he paused twice to turn and check the door. Sadi felt her anxiety grow during the time required to explain the situation. She followed his gaze both times and almost expected a dark apparition to fly from the interior of the barn.

"The floor's covered with hay and he's asleep in the middle. The problem is," Gerald paused again to listen.

"What the hell is in there with him?" the old man demanded.

"There's a bear sleeping next to him," Gerald said, smiling awkwardly, but his attempt to downplay the situation lacked any hint of comfort. He gulped before finishing. "He's next to a bear cub too, I think."

"What kind of bear," Sadi asked before taking time to consider if the detail made any difference. "Let me have the light."

"Does it matter what kind of bear?" Gerald asked while handing her the flashlight.

"I don't know," she said in irritation. The situation seemed too ridiculous. In the low light, Gerald must have misinterpreted his senses. "Is it a big bear, small, or what? This whole thing is crazy. I know there's no polar bears around here or grizzlies. But for all I know, it's a panda bear."

"Okay, okay," he said, taking a deep breath. "It was dark brown, maybe not as big as a grizzly, I don't think. My experience with bears is very limited."

"A bear?" Mr. Smith said to himself. His grip on Sadi's arm tightened. "I don't know if we should shine the light in there again."

"If you want to look," Gerald said, "shine it on the floor, close to the door."

Sadi stepped ahead of Gerald and Mr. Smith followed her with his cold hand on her arm. She shined the flashlight at her feet and then moved the beam across the entrance threshold. To her amazement and horror, she saw Freddy huddled into a massive creature, a bear with thick brown fur and a smaller bear lying on the other side of him. For several seconds, she felt paralyzed by fear and dared not move. She imagined the bear waking at any moment.

A new desire overpowered all of her other senses, the desire to run and keep running. Sadi had never experienced such a strong urge, but she found difficulty tearing her eyes away from the strange scene. Although the adult bear hid part of Freddy's face, she recognized his blond hair. For the next extremely long seconds, she just watched, the light rain falling on her unprotected neck and sending shivers down her spine.

After taking a deep breath, Sadi resumed some control of her senses. Freddy and the bears were making no indication of waking. She extinguished the light and stepped back to discuss their options.

"Yes, definitely bears," she said, turning to Mr. Smith and shaking her head in disbelief. "And Freddy."

"We could drive the car to the barn door," Mr. Smith said while Sadi was wondering what to do, "shine the high beams on them and blast the horn. Maybe that'd scare the bears away."

The old man's words surprised Sadi. The slow movement of his physical frame and weak voice had continued to betray a quick mind.

"It might put Freddy in danger," Gerald responded with concern.

"Is it possible to wake him without waking the bears?" Sadi asked with little hope for an answer in the affirmative. Wild animals possessed more sensitive hearing than humans and would certainly wake with less disturbance. "If only we had some kind of weapon. I've got pepper spray in my purse, but I don't have my purse."

Gerald looked suddenly above Sadi and Mr. Smith to the forest behind them, his mouth open, his eyes wide, and a soft-white light illuminating his face. When Sadi turned and saw the light, her blood seemed to freeze in her veins. Instinct commanded her to run, but she felt like a tree, firmly attached to the ground.

A bright point of light, high in the trees, was moving slowly toward them. The light was far away but still bright and flickering when the branches blocked the view. Sadi imagined someone holding a bright flashlight and drifting through the air toward them. She feared the light much more than the bears, an irrational fear she could not describe.

"What the hell is that?" Sadi whispered. "It's coming our way."

"It's something tall or floating," Gerald said and placed a protective hand on Sadi's shoulder, slowly pulling her close. "We should get back in the car."

"We're not leaving Freddy," the old man said defiantly, but he also appeared frightened. "We've got to get in the barn. If those bears haven't hurt Freddy, they shouldn't hurt us."

With his frail hand on her arm, Mr. Smith pulled Sadi toward the barn entrance and pushed the doors open wider. The hinges squeaked loudly in protest, making Sadi cringe but not stopping her. After they entered the dark interior of the barn, the cold hand on her arm became the only reminder of Mr. Smith's presence. The physical connection provided some comfort. If an old man was not afraid, Sadi would at least feign courage.

Without looking away from the light, Gerald stepped backward into the barn and then slowly shut the door. The old hinges squeaked loudly again and Sadi imagined the bears waking, but when she looked at them, they remained motionless, still sleeping peacefully.

The light from outside shined through the seams between the wood panels, creating long lines of white light on the floor.

Gerald stayed close to the door and watched through the cracks, the light illuminating his face. As the light intensified, Sadi saw the barn interior more clearly and their danger felt more palpable. The scene suddenly seemed like a twisted horror show with Sadi and her companions as the imminent victims. Had some nonhuman entity set the scene for its amusement?

While Sadi attempted to breathe in silence, an unpleasant smell began assaulting her senses, a mixture of rotting hay and wet animal hair. The smell contrasted sharply with the scent of fresh air from outside. Sadi had never stood so close to bears, not even at the zoo. Her imagination alternated between being eaten alive and the mysterious light approaching through the trees. The light became a mixture of irrational fear and curiosity, which overpowered all other instincts, even the urge to flee.

The light through the seams in the barn walls continued to intensify and Sadi felt tempted to follow Gerald's example and look outside, but she managed to stop herself. Gerald was standing motionlessly as though in some kind of trance, a narrow band of light illuminating the right side of his face and crossing his eyes. The bears suddenly seemed insignificant compared to whatever was approaching outside through the trees.

"Gerald, what is it?" Sadi whispered.

Gerald did not respond, so Sadi pulled his sleeve to get his attention. But he remained motionless and looked like a statue in the bright light illuminating part of his face. Sadi released his sleeve and then turned away from the barn door, from the white light shooting through the seams and cracks. Would the light put her into the same trance? She turned to Mr. Smith who appeared conscious still.

"What's going on?"

"I don't know," he answered flatly. "Are there people coming our way?"

"That's not a normal light," Sadi said, frantically searching for any other explanation. "And it's high in the air, so I don't think so."

The experience felt too real, not abstract enough for a dream. She found the old man's hand and clasped it firmly.

SIXTY-FOUR

Sadi

When the light source began moving higher up the walls, Sadi and Mr. Smith just watched, but Gerald's head tilted upward robotically. Then Helen's face flashed through Sadi's mind. Would Helen ever see her mother again? The thought almost made her head ache. In panic, she grabbed Gerald's arm and shook him.

At her touch, Gerald finally showed signs of consciousness. He turned from the light and glanced at her, then at Mr. Smith, his eyes squinted and full of questions. A new sensation grasped her attention, a vibration at the base of her neck, which seemed to resonate from her brain stem. The sensation urged her to look upward and refocus on the light. The bright white light was traveling slowly over the barn roof, illuminating a loft with hay spilling over the edges.

"It's moving towards that opening," Gerald said.

He pointed to the wall above the loft to an open window near the arched ceiling. While watching the light, Sadi understood what Gerald had experienced. The light consumed her entire focus, displacing all concern, worry, and anxiety. She had no more desire to look elsewhere or run away.

Like an audience in a movie theater, all three of them watched as a bright object traveled through the empty window space. At first, its intensity blinded her, but after a few seconds, her eyes adjusted and the features became discernible. The levitating object resembled a giant, polished chrome bullet with an extremely sharp tip and just large enough to fit through the window. At first, Sadi thought she was seeing white fire from the back of the object, but then her eyes resolved brilliant white strands, thousands of glowing filaments, which looked like white hair suspended in fluid. The glowing filaments gently waved in the air as though responding to an invisible current. After passing through the window, the object turned slowly toward them and began to descend, the sharp end pointing in their direction and the back end disappearing from view.

Freddy and the bears continued to sleep, oblivious to the bright light illuminating the entire barn. The cylindrical object floated halfway between Freddy and Sadi, stopping three meters above the floor and then becoming completely motionless. Even the strands of light behind it had stopped flowing. Sadi imagined the scene as a photograph, a single snapshot in time.

The tranquil scene lasted only a few seconds before the object began to descend again, the sharp tip facing Sadi who stood between Gerald and Mr. Smith. During its descent, the strands of light extended farther and reached Freddy's face behind it. The old man tightened his grasp of Sadi's hand but said nothing.

The filaments of light approached within centimeters of Freddy's face and ears, and for a moment, they seemed to touch him affectionately. The mother bear moved her giant paw slightly.

When finished examining Freddy, the object began moving slowly toward Sadi. She no longer felt like the member of an audience. Instead, she felt like a patient on an operating table, naked and without anesthesia. Her heartbeat intensified as the distance between them narrowed. When the sharp tip stopped within several centimeters of her face, her heart seemed ready to explode. While the tip hovered motionlessly at eye level, she imagined the thing rushing forward and piercing her head. Then the filaments of light began stretching from the back of the object toward Sadi, Gerald, and Mr. Smith, immersing their faces in light.

the back of the object toward Sadi, Gerald, and Mr. Smith, immersing their faces in light.

SIXTY-FIVE

Sadi

After several seconds, Sadi lost her fear of the sharp tip and began admiring the strands of light that hovered only two centimeters from her face. Each one glowed with a slightly different color than its neighbor and from a distance they combined into a brilliant white. Sadi's fear quickly transformed into a deep appreciation for the perception of color. For the moment at least, Sadi felt content just to stare into the light.

After several seconds of appreciation, or maybe an hour, Sadi could not tell, the fine tendrils of light began to ripple like waves around her nose, eyes, ears, lips. They danced like the trace of an oscilloscope and simultaneously flowed as beautiful hair in the wind. The waves increased in amplitude and frequency until the light coalesced into an object, a familiar face.

The face appeared as a topographical map at first and then transformed into the more detailed image she recognized, her daughter. Contour lines of color became finer and finer until they disappeared altogether and Helen's face became real, and then Helen's whole body seemed to be standing before her. Watching the construction of an artificial Helen was disturbing at first and Sadi's mind refused to accept the final three-dimensional object as her real daughter, but she also failed to recognize any difference.

A new background materialized around Helen and the barn quickly became only a memory. Sadi now found herself standing before the front steps of an immense Catholic cathedral, a place of cold and gray with Helen standing at her side. The familiar building caused a flood of memories to nearly overpower her. One set of memories hit harder than the rest, her mother's lectures about having faith in Jesus. If she could only let Jesus into her heart, he could save her from the horrible, wretched fate of her sinful life.

Helen was holding tightly onto her mother's hand, afraid of being lost in the crowd, which flowed past them up the stairs and into the cathedral. Sadi enjoyed the warmth of her daughter's hand, a stark contrast to the cold of her surroundings and the stone faces of the people. When Sadi looked down, away from Helen, she noticed her gray dress falling just past her knees. She hated getting dressed up for church.

Sadi turned to see a long line of people behind them, and then when she tilted her head to the sky, she saw cement gargoyles watching lazily from their perches high on the cathedral walls. The frightful demons watched the people like birds of prey, ready to descend at the first sign of weakness or death.

After taking their first step on the stairs, they had no choice but to continue following the crowd. They soon passed through the hungry cathedral doors and entered the warm building, but despite leaving the view of the gargoyles, Sadi found little comfort. The interior smelled old, stale, and she could taste on her tongue the perfume and cologne of hundreds of people.

"Stay close, dear," she said to her daughter.

"Don't let go, Mom."

"I won't."

As they walked slowly down the main aisle, Helen faced forward with her head down, and Sadi searched for two empty seats. Huge murals lined the walls, most of them showing Jesus with his twelve apostles. Almost every scene included a depiction of Jesus in agony and unbearable suffering, too graphic for children to see. One showed Jesus with thorns covering his head, digging into his flesh, and blood flowing down his head. Others showed Jesus praying under a tree or on the cross with his eyes toward heaven. In one of the paintings, Jesus reminded Sadi of a gargoyle outside.

Sadi found space for them to sit on the right side of the front row. None of their neighbors exhibited any acknowledgment of their presence, keeping their heads bowed to avoid disturbing the stillness. The large white pulpit stood several meters in front of them and had a golden cross painted on the front. A white-robed priest sat on the right, his hood resting on his shoulders. He reminded Sadi of a character from a horror movie, a man with dark eyes, which sucked light from his surroundings.

After the priest rose from his seat and stepped to the pulpit, he smiled ceremoniously and then grabbed the edges with both hands. As he scanned the immense room, his smile widened and his eyes seemed to connect with every member of the audience. When he made eye contact with Sadi and Helen, he paused momentarily and his smile vanished. But then his smile returned after moving to the men and women next to them. Helen squeezed her mother's hand tightly.

"My brothers and sisters," the priest said as he slowly backed away from the pulpit. "The time has come!"

The man turned so that he could see both the audience and the stained glass window behind the pulpit, and all eyes turned from the priest to the colorful glass. As Sadi peered into the light, the glass rippled like a reflection on wavy water. The immense window showed Jesus in the clouds, angels by his side, and demons below his feet. When the figures in the glass came to life, the crowd gasped with delight.

A living Jesus emerged from the glass and entered the great hall of the cathedral, levitating high in the air. Behind him, Sadi noticed the crowd of angels who had remained in the glass, and the small figure standing with them, her son Jacob, who looked the same as the day he had died. Jesus suddenly looked down at Sadi and smiled as though he felt sorry for her. When he turned back to the crowd, Jesus called to them all with outstretched arms.

"Come, follow me!"

At the sound of his voice, the crowd exploded in cheering and rejoicing. People rose to their feet, triumphantly shaking their hands to the heavens. Her small child in the glass smiled wide and looked directly at her.

"Hallelujah!" the crowd said in unison.

"Praise the Lord!"

"Oh, blessed Jesus!"

Everyone except for Sadi and Helen began moving toward Jesus and the stained glass window. For a moment, Sadi felt only fear. She held tightly onto her daughter's hand, to stop her from disappearing into the crowd. When Sadi returned her attention to Jesus, he started floating backward in the air until he entered the window and then disappeared. The people ascended the steps to follow Jesus and soon vanished with him into the glass.

When Sadi saw the people enter the window, a single thought solidified in her mind and replaced her fear. She could follow them and finally reach her son who was standing just on the other side. Jacob would be with his sister and mother again. Her little boy smiled wide and reached his right hand toward her, the tips of his fingers stopping on the other side of the semi-translucent barrier. Sadi and Helen moved forward with the masses, Helen holding onto her mother's right hand and Sadi extending her left hand toward her son. She grasped his tiny hand, and he began pulling her through the barrier. But when Sadi finally stepped into the window, her son and the heavenly host vanished in a blinding flash of light.

The bright light quickly dispersed and Sadi found herself in an arid mountain range, on a dry and dusty road. All kinds of trees lined the road, oaks, junipers, cottonwoods, and cedars. Dust from the road hovered in the air around them, moving lazily in the breeze. The dust stung her eyes and sand crunched between her teeth.

Sadi walked with the same crowd from the cathedral, but instead of their nice church clothing, all of the people wore their casual attire. She failed to see her son or Jesus, just the long and dry road, so she kept walking, squeezing Helen's hand from fear of losing her. While walking, Sadi began to wonder if the masses were traveling in the right direction and if Jesus was leading them.

The people around her spoke in hushed tones, and Sadi tried to distinguish what they were saying. But she understood only one word, reverently repeated.

"Jesus, Jesus, Jesus…"

While listening to the people chant the name of Jesus, the memory of her son drifted further into the past, along with the memory of the cathedral and the wet Northwest winter. And then after what felt like an eternity of walking, Sadi lifted her eyes from the ground and saw a massive cliff wall a hundred meters ahead, which seemed to ascend into space. Sadi wanted to stop and consider her surroundings, but the flow of people on the road acted as a strong river current and kept them moving forward.

When the dark hole at the base of the cliff wall came into view, Sadi was afraid again. The opening in the rock resembled an old mine shaft, and the people disappeared inside, consumed quickly by the dark. Sadi began resisting the forward motion of the crowd. Helen squeezed her hand harder, and all of Sadi's thoughts focused on her daughter.

"Mom," Helen said. "I don't want to go in there."

"Jacob was with Jesus," Sadi said in desperation. "We have to follow him."

Helen released Sadi's hand, and several people instantly filled the space between them. The crowd swept Sadi along with them, leaving Helen standing still and out of her sight. Sadi yelled for her daughter to follow her, but Helen did not answer. With some effort, Sadi stopped and pushed against the crowd until she reached Helen again.

She wanted to scream at her daughter but somehow retained control of her emotions.

"Helen, what is wrong with you? We've got to follow Jesus."

"I'm scared, Mom," Helen said and put her hand over her eyes to hide the tears. "I didn't see Jacob, and I don't want to go in there."

Sadi crouched down, forcing people to walk around them.

"He was there, standing with Jesus," Sadi said. "Jacob was with Jesus. I saw it."

"Jacob was with Jesus," Helen repeated, attempting to please her mother. She forced a smile through her tears.

"Yes, Jacob was with Jesus." Sadi lifted her daughter to rest on her hip. "Here honey. I'll carry you, so you won't have to walk on your own."

For the moment at least, she had the strength to carry her daughter. Walking again felt good. Returning to the flow of the crowd and succumbing to the current required so much less effort than fighting the current or even standing still.

When they reached within twenty meters of the mine shaft, Sadi noticed an ornate wooden frame surrounding the entrance, beautiful carvings of smiling angels and grimacing demons. The people entered without hesitation, believing those ahead of them were doing the right thing. Sadi felt a similar comfort, but the idea of entering the darkness without a light caused a brief panic.

"Got to have faith," she said to herself just before entering the tunnel, and exiting the light.

SIXTY-SIX

Sadi

Once inside the tunnel, Sadi enjoyed watching the reflection of the daylight on the crowd ahead of her, but their outlines grew fainter with every step. The sensation of noise soon replaced the light, the shuffling of feet, and the muffled words from thousands of mouths. The light of the world behind them quickly shrank to a smaller and smaller rectangle, and after only a few minutes, the light had become a pinpoint of light, a single star in the darkness.

The air in the tunnel became colder, and the smell of wet clay intensified, causing Sadi to shiver and hold her daughter more tightly. Holding Helen provided the only warmth. The hard ground provided the only connection to the world.

"Jacob is with Jesus," Sadi said quietly every few minutes to remind herself.

When Helen began repeating her words, Sadi received the emotional strength to continue moving forward. She walked for a long time in the tunnel, feeling like a refugee from the world outside, the world of the sun. To occupy her mind, she focused on the concept of community, being a member of the group, sharing the same experiences with the people around her, the same struggles. But after a while, doubts began to infect her conscious thoughts again.

Where were they going and why had Jesus disappeared after they exited the cathedral? Why did Helen deny seeing Jacob? The people around her would have the answers. They would not have entered the tunnel without something more concrete as motivation. Sadi extended her hand toward the person in front of her.

"Excuse me?" Sadi said after feeling the shoulder of a shorter person, a woman with a small frame. "When will we reach Jesus? How far is he?"

"We have to push through the darkness," the woman said while still facing forward. She spoke as if addressing a child. "When it is the darkest, when we're on the brink of despair, then Jesus will appear."

Sadi could not see anything. She wondered how the tunnel could get any darker.

"How do you know?"

"Each must follow their own path."

Sadi considered asking the woman another question but thought she might have better luck with someone else. She turned to her left and felt the elbow of a tall man. His arm was thin and weak.

"What are we doing here?"

"Everyone must follow Jesus," he said with a comforting and gentle tone, as a loving grandfather.

"Yes," she said in relief at hearing a more friendly response. "But where are we going?"

"It's not the destination but the journey."

Although his tone sounded empathetic, he spoke without turning his head, as though speaking to an audience rather than a single person. The woman to their right spoke next, unsolicited.

"Fear and doubt are of the devil!" she said angrily. "Don't let him inside your heart. Praise the Lord!"

"Praise the Lord!" repeated several other people around them.

Instead of providing comfort, a sudden fear wrapped its cold fingers around Sadi's heart, temporarily stealing the warmth of her daughter. The mention of the devil made the hairs on her neck stand erect. Had the devil put fear in her heart? Did he hide somewhere out there, in the darkness of the cave?

"No," she said more loudly than she had intended.

The word felt like a water hammer in her veins. The source of the fear came from the realization of her predicament, not from the devil. She slowed her pace and people had to push past her. The darkness of the tunnel suddenly seemed absolute, as though it surrounded each molecule.

"We're inside a mountain," she said to herself. "And without a light."

Her arms were so tired from holding Helen, but when she considered the possibility of setting her down on the ground, Sadi felt a more horrible panic. The thought terrified her more than the darkness or a possible demon just centimeters from her face. If Helen wandered away, she might be lost forever. Sadi pulled her daughter more tightly against her ribs. The fear infused additional strength into her arms.

Where had Sadi taken her daughter?

Sadi came to a complete stop and then turned to look behind them but failed to see any point of light. The light of the shaft entrance had diminished to nothing or was hidden behind the people.

"What's wrong, Mom?" Helen asked.

"I don't think we should be in here, Helen."

Sadi no longer felt comfort from sharing the same predicament with those around her.

"What do we do?" Helen asked. "Please don't let me go."

"Where's your faith?" a voice asked from her imagination, a faint whisper in her ear.

"Faith in what?" Sadi asked, but she received no response.

Sadi paused for a few seconds and tried to think rationally. The first and easiest option had an uncertain outcome, just follow the crowd and see where they led. The situation reminded her of dominoes and she suddenly felt like one. Everyone was placed in a line and had only one purpose, to fall.

Another option had more certainty but also required much more effort. Going against the crowd would lead back toward the cave entrance. She knew the entrance existed, just not its exact location without the light.

As the people pushed to get past her, she recalled her experience in the cathedral with Jesus and her son. If she left the crowd and returned, would she ever find Jacob again? Returning to the world of light was abandoning her faith. Her son might be lost forever.

"No," she said to herself. "By turning back, I am not abandoning Jacob."

"What was that, Mom?" Helen asked.

"Helen," Sadi said then took a deep breath. "We're getting out of here."

Sadi extended her right hand and began pushing against the current of the crowd. At first, she had difficulty moving while also attempting to avoid doubts about her direction. To help focus her mind, she concentrated on her one conclusion. If she ever wanted to see the light of day again, she had to push against the crowd and keep moving.

After what felt like an eternity of pushing and struggling, a faint star finally appeared in the distance. At first, the light flickered when heads blocked her view, but it soon became a constant source of light. Sadi had never experienced such a feeling of relief. The star grew larger and larger until the light also became heat and began to burn her face.

When they finally reached the entrance, Helen began to cry and warm tears fell onto Sadi's hand. They hugged each other as the light welcomed them back. And then the light grew too bright, and Sadi had to close her eyes.

SIXTY-SEVEN

Sadi

Sadi opened her eyes and found herself back in the barn, staring at the bright light from the glowing filaments. Hot tears were sliding down her cheeks. She still felt immense relief from escaping the tunnel, as though the memory of the vision with Helen originated from a real experience. But the memory failed to warm the chill of the cold barn air.

The beautiful filaments of light soon began to pull away from her face, returning into the back of the shiny hovering object, and for several seconds, she just watched them. Then slowly, she began regaining awareness of her surroundings. Gerald stood by her side, facing the object without expression or movement. Sadi wanted to nudge him in the ribs to see if the action would get his attention, but she feared to move. After a few more seconds, she had gained enough courage to turn away from the object, and she saw Mr. Smith crouched down by Freddy's side. He was still lying in the middle of the barn floor, but he was now looking at Mr. Smith and there were no bears in sight. To her relief, Freddy's open eyes indicated life and awareness, and Mr. Smith seemed unharmed too.

When the strange object suddenly began to ascend into the air, the action seemed to jolt Gerald back into awareness. His eyes opened wide and he glanced at Sadi, and then at Freddy, and then returned his attention to the object. No one spoke as it ascended slowly above the loft. While watching, Sadi assessed her strange fascination with the lights. A beautiful painting or the eyes of her child always caused the same wonder and amazement.

The object stopped its ascent a meter above the loft, and Sadi held her breath as it just hovered motionlessly. While wondering what would happen next, the object quickly rotated and then disappeared from her view, leaving a streak of light burned onto her retinas. The streak of light looked like the trail of a shooting star and then slowly vanished. The sudden collapse of air made a loud snap and she jolted at the sound.

As her eyes readjusted to the dark, Gerald turned to her.

"Are you okay?"

"I'm fine."

She wiped the tears from her eyes, hoping he would fail to notice the evidence of her emotional state. For some reason, she felt embarrassed. The experience of the tunnel was too personal and traumatic. A moment later, Sadi energized the flashlight and noticed the look of exhaustion in his eyes. No tears slid down his cheeks, but his face glistened with sweat and he looked as though he had been running from a pack of hungry wolves.

"What happened to you?" she asked, concerned.

"I don't know," Gerald said then turned to the old man in the middle of the barn, crouched beside Freddy. Gerald spoke loudly, so Mr. Smith could hear. "How's your friend?"

Before responding, Mr. Smith glanced at Sadi, and she saw the countless questions in his old eyes. What just happened? What was that thing?

"You both were staring into the lights," Mr. Smith said from his position beside Freddy. "For about five minutes straight, neither that thing or either of you moved. I've never seen any living thing remain so still. If I had stayed there, the same thing probably would have happened to me, but I moved away when those strings started reaching for me. What did you see?"

She saw fear and distrust in the old man's eyes.

"I saw my son," Sadi said quickly. "He died last year."

He looked at her for a moment then shook his head.

"I'm sorry."

"What happened to the bears?" Gerald asked, and Sadi felt relieved to discuss a different subject.

"They left about a minute after those strings tried to get me," Mr. Smith said. "It was very frightening, and strange. I was counting on them being afraid of the lights, but they just woke up and left without looking back. I've been trying to get Freddy to respond ever since."

"Is he okay?" Sadi asked and quickly joined Mr. Smith on the other side of Freddy. While staring at Freddy's face and into his open eyes, she noticed the smell of wet animal hair again.

"I don't think he's hurt," Mr. Smith said. "He's just not responding. Maybe if we try to move him? I want to get out of here."

Sadi helped the old man pull Freddy into a sitting position. He gave no opposition but just looked at them with blank eyes. Gerald stayed in the same position by the wall, watching them.

"Gerald," she said quietly to get his attention, but he took a moment to look at her. "Gerald, are you okay?"

"What?" he asked then sighed. "No, I'm okay."

Before Gerald could move to join them, a noise from outside stole her attention, the snap of a twig and the rustle of leaves. Even Mr. Smith heard the sharp sounds. Sadi continued staring at Gerald, listening for more noise, evidence of some creature out in the darkness. Did the bears wait outside for them? The thought made Sadi shiver and pull her arms tightly across her breasts for warmth. She wanted to run to the door and hold it shut so that nothing could come into the barn, but she stayed motionless, afraid to make any additional noise.

After a few more seconds of silence, Sadi heard what sounded like a human running away from the barn door, then more running down the road. She felt relieved knowing the sound originated from a human rather than a bear, but then her relief transformed into fear again. Who had been watching them?

Gerald turned and peered through the seams in the barn door, and then almost immediately, a bright light appeared through them, illuminating Gerald's outline and reminding Sadi of the time before the strange object's arrival. Only now, the light quickly diminished instead of growing brighter.

A noise from the floor at her back returned her attention to Freddy. The light had restored him to awareness. He jumped to his feet and ran to the barn door, pushing Gerald out of the way, then throwing the door all the way open and escaping into the night. Before her mind could offer a logical course of action, she just listened to the sound of Freddy running in the same direction as the mysterious person outside. She looked from Mr. Smith to Gerald.

"I'll go," Gerald said then stepped through the open door. But before running after Freddy, he turned back to them. "Stay with Mr. Smith."

SIXTY-EIGHT

Sadi

After Gerald disappeared from her view, Sadi stepped closer to Mr. Smith. He had placed his cane on the ground in preparation to stand. While she helped him to his feet, he looked up at her with confusion in his eyes. He was probably wondering what she wanted to know. What could have caused Freddy to move so fast and without warning?

"Should we go after them?" Sadi asked. "They might need our help."

"Yes," Mr. Smith said, holding onto Sadi's arm as they moved toward the barn door. They traveled at a faster pace than she thought possible for the old man. While they walked, a million thoughts fought for her attention, but she attempted to focus on what they would do after finding Freddy and Gerald.

At least, she still had the flashlight. As they walked, she pointed the beam ahead of them. Once outside, she looked up at the overcast sky and felt the light rain on her face again. The cold sent a sharp convulsion through her body, but she welcomed the familiar sensation and the fresh air. The water helped reconnect Sadi to the world she understood. When she attempted to listen for sounds of running, she heard only the light patter of rain.

"Go ahead without me," said Mr. Smith. "I'll catch up."

"No, I'm not leaving you. We'll go at your pace."

"I don't suppose Gerald left the keys?" said Mr. Smith as they walked past the car.

"I doubt it," she answered.

She considered asking for his opinion about why Freddy had run away, but she decided to focus on the path ahead. They walked in silence, listening intently for any noise other than their own. Although she was concerned for Freddy's safety, she felt more worried about Gerald and the old man. From Freddy's most recent behavior, Sadi had the inexplicable impression that he knew exactly what to do.

After the turn in the road, the barn disappeared behind them, and Sadi could see a dull red light through the trees, far away. The light appeared different than the light from the mysterious object, probably originating from a car's brake lights. Strangely, she almost wished to see the beautiful, multicolored strings of light again. Would she ever?

"What's that light?"

"It looks like car brake lights," Sadi answered.

Sadi mentally prepared herself to pull Mr. Smith into the trees at the first sign of danger, making sure to keep a good hold of him. The thought of entering all the spider webs, wet moss, and ferns of the Northwest forest almost seemed like a worse alternative than encountering the object again. Then she remembered the bears. They lurked out there somewhere too. She decided to extinguish the flashlight, and when the light had disappeared, Mr. Smith gripped her arm more tightly, but he said nothing.

After considering all of the horrible possibilities, Sadi almost stopped and ran back to the car to wait for Gerald and Freddy to resolve the situation. She felt afraid but not the same panic as she had felt inside the barn. That kind of fear had paralyzed her. But with Mr. Smith depending on her, she felt the courage to keep moving.

The road had one last turn before they would reach the red lights, about fifty meters away. Then without warning, a white light burst to life through the trees next to the red lights. The mysterious object had reappeared. The brilliant white light illuminated the forest and then began ascending from the ground. Sadi and Mr. Smith stopped briefly to watch as the light ascended. And then in the next instant, the light disappeared into the sky and Sadi heard the sharp snap of collapsing air again. She returned her attention to the road in front of them and waited until her eyes readjusted to the night.

"Was that the same object?" Mr. Smith asked.

"I think so," Sadi answered and started pulling him forward again. Until that moment, she had not considered the possibility of there being more of them. "I hope it's gone for good now. Come on, we should keep going. We're almost there."

Mr. Smith resisted enough to stop her from moving.

"I can't see very well, especially at night. We shouldn't take any unnecessary risks. If they're in trouble, it might be good not to let them know we're here."

"Okay," she said. "We'll go more slowly and quietly."

Sadi let Mr. Smith lead the way, and they slowly approached the final bend in the road before coming into view of the car, the source of the red light. Sadi stopped and faced Mr. Smith.

"I can see better than you," she said. "Wait here while I have a look."

She left Mr. Smith on the side of the muddy dirt road and then crept closer to the turn so that she could investigate the scene. At first view, her mind struggled to interpret the chemical signals from her eyes. She saw a large SUV with red brake lights illuminating the trees on the side of the road, then she saw Gerald and Freddy. Gerald turned and made eye contact with her. He waved and began walking to meet her, so she ran back to Mr. Smith.

"Gerald's coming," she said and held onto his arm again. "It appears safe. Let's go."

"Freddy's with him?"

"They're next to a car," she answered while leading him around the turn.

—✳—

They met Gerald after stepping into the red light.

"What happened?" she asked, looking past him to the dark blue vehicle, what looked like a Ford Explorer.

The light from its red tail lights flooded the scene in an eerie glow. The passenger door was open, a leg dangling out the side, along with an arm. Through the open door, Sadi noticed another man in the driver's seat. Freddy was leaning over the unconscious man and appeared to be searching for something.

"When I got here," Gerald said and began leading them toward the vehicle, "these guys were in their car, ready to drive away, but that flying thing from the barn suddenly appeared over their windshield and shined strange lights on them, which knocked them unconscious. Then that thing grew really bright and started floating up above the trees. It got so bright, I had to close my eyes."

"Do you know who they are?" Mr. Smith asked.

"I don't know," Gerald said. "Freddy's been looking through all their things. He won't talk to me. I don't know what he's looking for. Maybe you can talk to him?"

Mr. Smith walked slowly past Sadi and Gerald and approached the vehicle where Freddy was bent over the unconscious driver. But while Mr. Smith was still walking, Freddy backed out of the car, holding a gun in his right hand. Mr. Smith stopped and waited, and Sadi held her breath. When Freddy turned to face them, he pointed the weapon to the sky.

"Freddy," Mr. Smith said slowly. "What's going on?"

Before he answered, Sadi realized the rain had stopped.

"Do you know who these men are?" Freddy asked and glanced briefly back to the car. He spoke more confidently and forcefully than usual.

"I have no idea," the old man said.

"Do you, Mr. Foster?" Freddy asked, turning to Gerald. While waiting for him to answer, Freddy maintained steady eye contact.

"They're probably the FBI agents, keeping track of me," Gerald said defensively.

"Do you know that they can ruin all your plans, and put some of your friends in prison, or worse?"

Sadi noticed Gerald's body become rigid while answering, but his tone remained casual.

"Yes, I know."

"These men are in a position to take away our freedom," Freddy said, glancing at Sadi and Mr. Smith then returning his attention to Gerald. "That is certain."

"Unfortunately, they always have that option."

Freddy pointed the gun at the unconscious man's head.

"We would be justified in taking their lives."

Freddy closed his lips tightly, and Sadi saw his index finger tighten on the trigger. She gulped, her eyes opening wide.

"Freddy," she said. "What are you doing?"

"That may be true," Gerald interjected, ignoring Sadi for the moment. "But you're the one with his finger on the trigger."

"We are all in the same predicament," Freddy said.

He kept the gun steady.

Mr. Smith turned to Gerald and Sadi, the red brake lights highlighting every wrinkle on his face. He spoke with anger in his voice.

"What is going on here? Who are you two with?"

Gerald ignored Mr. Smith and kept his focus on Freddy.

"That is not our only option," Gerald said desperately, as though Freddy was pointing a gun at one of his friends. "If we kill them, it would be difficult to remove all traces linking us to their deaths. Their car probably has a tracking device on it. They would be led right to this spot, and they'd find evidence linking us to them. We don't have any credible alibi."

"But it might give you enough time to accomplish your goal."

"There's got to be another option," Sadi said.

As much as she abhorred the idea of killing the unconscious men, she experienced difficulty disagreeing with Freddy's conclusion. If someone threatened her freedom, she had the right to defend herself and her daughter. But Gerald had made better points.

"Fortunately for them, we will spare their lives," Freddy said, smiling strangely. After lowering the gun, he wiped the trigger and grip of the gun with his sleeve then reached over the men and put the gun back in the car glove box. He turned back to Sadi and sighed as though he had held his breath too long. "Sadi, give me the crystal."

Sadi approached the car slowly and then saw the face of the other unconscious man in the passenger seat. Both men lay against their seats, facing forward with closed eyes. They wore jeans and t-shirts. In the low light, their features were only slightly discernible. As she came closer, she suddenly felt afraid of making any noise and had to fight the urge to run the other way.

She removed the crystal from her pocket and held it in her open palm for Freddy to grab. After taking the crystal, he held the object close to the man's face, two centimeters from his nose. Sadi stepped back when blue and orange lights shot from the spider's eyes. The man immediately opened his eyes and sat forward as the intense beam of light shined steadily for about twenty seconds.

The man sat motionless until the lights stopped shining, and then he fell back into his seat again, unconscious. Freddy moved around the SUV to the next man and performed the same operation on him. When the lights disappeared and the man fell unconscious, Freddy remained motionless, staring at the dark crystal in his hand. Mr. Smith stepped to the open driver door, holding onto his cane for support.

"Freddy?" he asked. "Are you okay?"

At the sound of Mr. Smith's voice, Freddy turned from the crystal and stared at him, blankly. He no longer had the same look of confidence and authority, and when he finally spoke, he sounded exhausted.

"Mr. Smith, you should not be in the cold like this," he said. "You will get sick."

Freddy went around the vehicle, closed the driver's door, and then returned to the passenger seat. He gently lifted the unconscious man's hand and leg into the vehicle, then shut the door.

"Freddy," Mr. Smith said quietly. "Will you explain to me, to us, what is going on?"

"I will try to explain it all but after we get out of here." He placed his hand on the old man's upper arm and began walking with him back to the barn. "We should not be here when they wake up."

Sadi and Gerald followed Freddy and Mr. Smith on their slow pace back to the barn. Sadi wanted to ask Gerald about what had happened, but she decided to postpone her questions until they could talk more confidentially. On the walk, no one spoke, and Sadi listened carefully for evidence of the bears. She wondered if the others were doing the same.

"I parked at the back," Freddy said after reaching the barn.

He led them to his car, a Subaru hatchback. He opened the passenger door for Mr. Smith.

"We'll just follow you," Sadi said.

"Come back to my house," Mr. Smith said before letting Freddy shut the door. "We all need to talk about what happened here tonight."

After they began following Freddy on the dirt road, she finally felt safe. She was sitting in a comfortable vehicle, out of the rain and cold. The bears and FBI agents could no longer harm them. The vision of the cathedral and the tunnel soon began replaying in her mind, and Sadi wondered if they would see the mysterious object again. What else could it show her?

SIXTY-NINE

Sadi

For the first few minutes after getting in the car, they drove in silence and enjoyed the comfort of being on the dry, warm side of the windows. She enjoyed watching the trees flying past the car and water drops sliding sideways across the windshield. But as they got closer to Mr. Smith's house, Sadi just wanted to go home, see Helen, lie in bed, and wait for the next day to consider all of her questions. She felt emotionally and physically exhausted.

"Well, we know one thing," Gerald said, breaking the silence first.

Sadi detected a bit of triumph in his voice.

"What is that?"

"We're not dealing with ghosts here."

He turned to her, and his smile soon vanished. Sadi gulped.

"So what are we dealing with?" she asked instinctively, not really wanting to hear his answer.

"That thing was not from Earth," he said. It was a statement and not conjecture.

"Some kind of alien spacecraft?"

"They're either tiny little guys," he said, chuckling. "Or that thing was some kind of probe."

"It couldn't be a military thing? Could it?"

She doubted the government had any device so advanced and sophisticated. If they did, she would have to reconsider her entire perception of reality, again.

"It's probably a safe assumption," he said. "If the government had that sort of thing, they wouldn't need regular humans tracking us as well."

"Unless those guys were the ones controlling it," she said gravely.

"Then why would it chase them to their vehicle and knock them unconscious?" he asked as though he had already considered the question. "I saw it. They were scared to death."

"Good point," she agreed then tried to decide what option frightened her more, aliens or their fellow humans. "Any ideas about what it wants? For some reason, that probe or whoever controlled it wanted us there."

"From what you told me of Freddy, the spider in the crystal was designed specifically for him, something he couldn't resist. I feel like we're being used. Okay don't laugh, but I have a strange question."

"I'll try not to," she answered with a smile.

"All this has a scientific explanation, right?" He drew a deep breath, keeping his eyes on the road. "I mean, we're not dealing with magic or the supernatural are we?"

Sadi considered how to answer without hurting his pride. She stared at the road ahead and took a few deep breaths. Despite her limited experience with Gerald, she sensed an insecurity about his ability to grasp scientific topics.

She felt sorry for Gerald, the typical victim of public education, which forced children to memorize formulas, dates, and details about scientific celebrities rather than teaching underlying principles. Then while the public education system erased their natural curiosity, the entertainment industry filled their confused heads with stories of zombies, angels, and magic. In the end, people depended on artificial authority figures instead of trusting their own reasoning.

"There are a lot of mysteries in the world, Gerald," she began finally. "I don't pretend to understand them all, but everything has a logical explanation. That spider and the probe can integrate with the human mind. It's very advanced, but it's not magic."

"I know," he said with relief. "Sometimes I just need a reminder."

"Especially in this situation," Sadi said, smiling.

He turned from watching the road and made brief eye contact. "What is Freddy usually like?" he asked. "Does he always have multiple personalities?"

Sadi recalled Freddy holding the gun to the man's head.

"He's normally shy and timid."

"That's not what I saw."

"After Freddy put the gun away," she said, trying to remember. "He looked scared, almost normal."

"Well he seems to know where we are," Gerald said after a moment of silence, and then she and Gerald looked at Freddy's car in front of them. "Maybe he has GPS? I still don't know where we are. Do you?"

"Not yet," she said and tried to laugh, but failed. "I'm still trying to figure it out."

Sadi desperately wanted to go home, hug Helen, see Jen, feel normal again. She looked outside, seeing only trees and a black sky. Eventually, she would see a sign and know their location.

Sadi considered asking Gerald what he had seen under the influence of the probe's beautiful lights, but then she might have to tell him more of what happened in her vision. She did not feel ready to share such a personal experience. But after a moment, she decided to ask anyway, despite what he might think of her.

"What happened to you in the barn, after that thing confronted us?"

He glanced at her, then turned back to the road. He spoke slowly as though searching for the right words.

"I had a dream, a very disturbing dream. I did not like it."

"Do you remember it well?" she asked casually with her eyes on the road ahead of them. "I'll understand if you don't want to talk about it."

"I really just want to forget it," he said and smiled. "Let's talk about it another time."

"I can understand that."

"You had one too?" he asked. "About your son?"

"Yes. I don't want to talk about it either," she said and laughed. "But what do you think the dreams or visions meant? Did that thing make the dreams or was it just a natural reaction to the light?"

"I think it was testing us," Gerald said, tightening his grip on the steering wheel. "Freddy was testing us too, I think."

A new thought hit her mind like a hammer, an idea inspired by a television show she used to watch. In the show, creatures took people into the water, killed them and made clones, and then returned the clones to society. At first, the clones felt confused and disoriented, unaware of what happened to them, just as she felt now. Was she now a clone?

She remembered enjoying the show but cursed herself for filling her head with such irrational ideas, which dug their claws into her mind and interfered with her capacity for rational thought. She needed to remain rational for Helen.

"A test huh," she said, pressing her lips together. "I'll have to think about that."

"Have you ever thought about us being guests here on Earth?" he asked after a few seconds. "Maybe our real home is out there somewhere?"

"Are you talking about religion?"

"Not really," he said. "I'm talking about the origin of our species being from somewhere else."

"The thought might have crossed my mind once or twice. I'm inclined to think it began here. The grass isn't always greener on the other side." She tried laughing but only managed to snicker. Memories of the cave and the joy of her escape inspired her next question. "Are you religious?"

"That's kind of a vague question," he said. "What's your definition of religion?"

"That's an even better question," she said, pausing for an answer to form in her mind. "I guess it's the belief in a higher power. Wait, that sounds stupid. Let me rephrase that. Do you believe in a greater intelligence than humans possess? Intelligence is a certain power, I suppose."

"Then yes," he answered immediately. "I am religious, but I hate the classical definition of God. I believe in creatures out there with higher intelligence, but from what I see in the world, I don't think they are benevolent. What about you?"

"There's too many unexplained things in the world, but I really don't know what I believe," she answered honestly. Sadi usually avoided thoughts of religion and disliked talking about the subject due to its effect on her sense of reality. Religion always brought painful memories. Her father had often used the lethal weapons of religion—guilt and fear—to get what he wanted. "My parents are Christians, and I used to consider myself one. We would go a few times a year, but my brother and I stopped when we moved out. The last time I went into a church was for my son's funeral."

"Not a very good association, I would guess," he said after a moment of silence. "Religion puts a bitter taste in my mouth."

"My brother and I used to joke about being anti-Christian," she said in an attempt to lighten the mood. "You probably wouldn't understand."

"I can understand that," he said and smiled. "I used to be anti-establishment, or at least that's what I thought. It was exciting going to protests, fighting the evil corporations, the greedy capitalists."

"That's funny," she said. "Now you're a lawyer, defending them. Just kidding. If you weren't anti-establishment back then, what were you?"

"Just someone in search of purpose I guess, like most of the young. The real leaders of the world always provide the young with an idol to follow. But most people end up joining what they're fighting against. It would be nice if more people could look just a little deeper than the surface."

"Reminds me of watching the news lately," Sadi said, glad for the change of topic. She still felt unprepared to discuss the events of the night. "It's all about the protesters blaming Wall Street and wanting the politicians to write more regulations, but Wall Street was just following the laws they paid the politicians to write. It's frustrating to watch. I usually have to turn it off. What made you change your views?"

"I went to work with an international aid group in Kivu, the Congo," he began. "That experience really opened my eyes."

He paused and Sadi wondered if he planned to continue.

"What happened?" she asked finally.

"I saw reality," he began. "The media shows the destitute from third world countries being fed and clothed by rich westerners, but they never show the root cause of the problem, why they're so poor in the first place. The corrupt regimes of the third world are supported by our government and corporations in exchange for their resources. Their people get just enough to eat so they don't revolt while the governments get all the financial support they need.

"Keeping the people in a state of poverty keeps production costs small and increases profits for corporations. That's the truth I discovered, and then it went downhill from there, to the history of our country, the history of religion, and learning about those who control the money supply. The whole thing used to make me so angry. Now I just try to focus on making a better future by trying to help the small, local companies not involved with the corruption of the system."

"Yeah," she said, lamenting with him. "And our government takes our money to pay for it all. I don't like thinking about it either."

In the following silence, Sadi attempted to focus on seeing Helen and Jen again, to restore some form of normalcy to her life. She could never return to the fantasy world again, a world where decent people in the government labored to keep her family and friends safe from terrorists, murderers, rapists, and human traffickers.

"You and I can't stop it," he said sadly. "Those who try to stop it are ridiculed, marginalized, and even killed. People are fools to think we can stop it. *If we can just educate the masses*, they say. I'm sick of trying to educate people. We need to take more immediate action. We need to band together. I want to live in a society with people like you and me. If we build it, others will come."

Sadi made no answer, just nodded.

On the remainder of the return trip, they traveled in silence. Sadi watched lights, trees, and buildings flying by. Her mind returned to the events of the night and then what Freddy might reveal to them. Finally, they pulled onto a familiar road, highway twenty-six heading southeast. They would soon be passing the road leading to her house. As they passed the turn, she wondered when she could go home.

SEVENTY

Sadi

They arrived at Mr. Smith's house at twenty minutes past midnight. Sadi and Gerald went inside and waited in the same room where they first had waited when the evening began. Sadi found her purse on the couch. She had ten messages on her phone, four from her brother and the rest from Jen. She dreaded listening to them, so she decided just to call instead.

She excused herself from the room as she entered the number to Jen's cell phone. While waiting to hear the sounds of a connection, she hoped Jen had not chosen to call the police, and thus make an official record with the authorities of the abnormality. Jen answered the phone immediately.

"Oh my God," Jen said with panic. "Sadi, where are you?"

Sadi was too exhausted and made no effort to invent a story.

"We're fine, Jen," she said quickly and then slowed her speech, hoping to indicate a stable situation. "Everything's okay. Sorry to worry you, but I can't talk about it now. I'll tell you the story when I get back."

She had no intention of telling Jen the story or even a tiny part of the real situation and would concoct a plausible explanation on the way home. As a lawyer, Gerald could help probably engineer an acceptable cover story.

"Okay, I'll wait for you to get home," she said with relief. Before Sadi could respond, Jen continued more excitedly. "Your brother called several times. Have you called him yet? Want me to call him for you?"

"Yes, that would be nice." Sadi felt a strong urge to return to the room with the others, but she could not cut the connection yet. "Is Helen asleep?"

"Yes," Jen said flatly.

"You didn't call the police did you?"

"I was going to give you another hour then I planned to call."

"I should be home in a couple of hours, so just go to bed, and we can talk in the morning."

Jen would probably wait for her anyway, Sadi assumed. When she returned to the room, Gerald was still alone, sitting erect and breathing steadily as though his energy had returned. Sadi hoped her appearance did not reflect how tired she felt.

"I wish I felt like you look," she said. "I'm exhausted, but you look like you just took a shower and are ready for the day."

"It's kind of exciting," he said and smiled. "Now that we're out of the elements, back in a warm and comfortable place, I feel better. To think we actually came in contact with an alien, and it didn't kill or abduct us! That's pretty lucky."

"An alien is not the only explanation," she said, amazed that he had found humor in the situation. "It's a likely explanation, but we should keep our minds open to other possibilities."

"Agreed," he said, still smiling. "But for now, let's just go with the alien explanation because it is the most likely, in my mind at least."

"Okay, so where does it lead us?" she asked. "What does it want?"

"Well, it's not the typical alien invader you see in the movies, the ones where they want to kill humans and take our resources." Gerald shifted in his seat. "At the time, I was scared. I have to admit. Scared out of my mind. However, thinking back on it, the probe did not threaten us. Did you feel that it was malevolent in any way?"

Sadi considered his question. Her dream or vision felt more like a test rather than an experience meant to intimidate, scare, or manipulate her. Her dream involved familiar experiences on Earth and of humanity, not of space and alien creatures. When she had decided to escape the tunnel and move toward the light again, she felt as though she'd had a purpose in life. Escaping the darkness had seemed as though she was passing a test, accomplishing an important feat. She smiled at the memory of entering the light but then remembered the anguish of seeing her son. He always tormented her dreams, just out of her reach.

"No, I don't think it was malevolent," she said finally.

"Since it used Freddy to contact us, I think..."

Gerald stopped talking at the sound of Freddy and Mr. Smith approaching from the hallway. He and Sadi turned to watch the room entrance. The old man entered first, followed closely by Freddy. He looked exhausted, more than Mr. Smith even. They sat next to each other on the same couch. The scene reminded Sadi of a parent bringing her child to a store clerk to return a stolen piece of candy. Freddy looked embarrassed. She felt pity for him. Her doubts about his identity evaporated.

"We've discussed it," Mr. Smith began. "Tonight is not the night to discuss everything. I think we're all too tired, especially Freddy."

"We understand," Sadi said in total agreement.

"Okay, but before we go," Gerald said abruptly. "Freddy, can you tell us quickly what that thing was? We can discuss the whole thing in more detail tomorrow."

Sadi, Gerald, and Mr. Smith turned to Freddy. Before responding, Freddy looked at the ground.

"I am very sorry that all this happened," he said then looked up at each of them. He opened his hand and stared at the crystal on his palm. "The crystal was a gift from my sister, which I could not refuse because I desperately wanted it. Perhaps if I had refused the temptation, all this would not have happened."

"Don't blame yourself, Freddy," Sadi said. "There's no way anyone would have expected this."

"Like Mr. Smith said," Gerald said, speaking compassionately but also with a bit of impatience. "We can discuss all the details and conjecture together later. We all just want to know what you think that thing was. Sadi and I are calling it a probe."

"Something controls it, controls this," Freddy looked at his palm again and gently transferred the crystal to his other hand. "It is not human, but I do not know if we can call it an alien. I do not know what it is or what it wants."

After Freddy stopped speaking, no one answered immediately and the silence in the room felt like a barrier to further conversation.

"Do you remember what happened?" Sadi asked, leaning forward. Curiosity had overpowered her desire to leave. "Were you being controlled by it tonight?"

"It did not control me. It is hard to explain," Freddy said, looking briefly into her eyes. "After waking up in that barn, I could see our predicament in perfect clarity, the probe and the FBI agents outside. I saw the entire situation from every angle imaginable. I had all the information I needed to make an informed decision. Your thoughts and potential actions were all in front of me."

"Were you given any information about the group I represent?" Gerald asked. "What do you remember?"

Freddy kept his gaze on the crystal and seemed unaware of anyone else in the room.

"I felt like a different person, but it was me. It was me. I do not know what to think. I am sorry."

"Do you know anything about my friends?" Gerald asked again. "Please, whatever you know needs to be kept confidential."

"I'm sorry, Mr. Foster," Mr. Smith interrupted. "It's time for you to go. Freddy needs to rest. We'll call tomorrow, and we can arrange another visit. Come on, Freddy. It's been a long couple of days hasn't it?"

Mr. Smith placed his cane on the floor and Freddy helped him stand. Before Gerald could say anything else, Sadi stood to her feet.

"Of course," she said. "We understand."

"Goodnight, Sadi," Freddy said and paused as though wanting to say something else. Then he changed his mind and began walking from the room without looking back. "Goodnight, Mr. Foster."

After Freddy disappeared into the hallway, Mr. Smith began leading them to the door. "I'm just an old man," he said, holding his cane for support and Sadi suddenly remembered walking on the road with him and the cold rain on her neck. "My time on Earth is nearly over, so I don't plan on getting involved with what you're doing. That thing we saw is obviously something for the young to handle. I don't know what your group is involved in, but you better not hurt Freddy. He's all I've got."

"We don't want to hurt anyone, especially Freddy." Sadi put her hand on his shoulder. "Believe me. He's a good friend of mine, and I would never hurt him."

"I believe you," Mr. Smith said. "Let's talk tomorrow. Have a good night."

SEVENTY-ONE

Sadi

Sadi woke up at nine the next morning to a bedroom full of the diffused light of a hazy outside. The warmth and comfort of her bed contrasted with the cold, wet memories of the previous evening. She never slept that late, not even on a Saturday. When Gerald had delivered her home, she had offered for him to stay the night, but he'd insisted on returning to his hotel room. He'd already paid for the night and did not want to impose.

She hurried down the stairs to the ground floor and saw Jen with her laptop computer opened on the bar in the kitchen, and Helen sitting in front of the television in the adjacent living room. Helen saw Sadi first.

"Hi, Mom," she said without showing any concern or curiosity about her abnormal activity from the previous evening. Jen had successfully kept Helen unaware of her mother's long absence, and Sadi felt grateful for that.

"Good morning, dear."

Sadi knelt on the ground in front of Helen and hugged her for longer than usual after just a night's separation. While holding her daughter, Sadi remembered the experience in the cave and shivered at the thought of releasing Helen's hand in the darkness. Thankfully, eye contact with her daughter was helping to melt the horror of the experience. The memory of her son tried forcing its way into her conscious thoughts, but she immediately pushed that thought away. She lacked the mental energy to think about her son or what the dream or vision might mean. She needed food.

"Gonna tell me what you were doing last night?" Jen asked, looking up from her laptop. "Did you forget your phone or something?"

Sadi had already prepared a story, without Gerald's help, an explanation containing much of the truth.

"I'm really sorry, Jen," she said apologetically. "Freddy, the friend that visited on Tuesday with Brian, went missing. His employer was really worried and asked for my help. A friend of mine and I met at his house and then went out looking for him. Both Gerald and I left our phones at his house, and his employer did not have one. We didn't think we would be gone that long."

Sadi wanted to include as much of the real story as possible. Although the possibility of two adults simultaneously forgetting their phones seemed highly unlikely, they really did forget their phones. And since she also planned to spend more time with Gerald, she needed to let Jen know about him. Her story needed to include him and stay consistent with any future activities.

"Who is this Gerald guy?"

"He's a lawyer," she said. "I've done some consulting work for him. And I also thought that I might ask him for some legal advice for Freddy who was a former ward of the state. Freddy's mother and sister might make trouble for him, so he might need some legal representation."

To complicate the situation, and hopefully divert Jen's attention, Sadi had added the legal information, which should help shift the focus away from the events of the previous night. Jen held Sadi's gaze for a few seconds before acquiescing and returning attention to her laptop. Sadi stared at the back of Jen's head for a moment, pondering several questions. Did Jen question the completeness of her story and just lack the strength to challenge her? Should employees question the motives of their employers? Why did she care so much?

—✳—

For the next couple of hours, Sadi followed her usual routine in an attempt to forget about the previous evening. She needed a break from the memories, needed to put them in the back of her mind and heal from the damage to her sense of normalcy. She could resume trying to understand the implications of recent events when they visited Freddy again.

When she checked the website just after eleven, she found a message from Gerald.

Call me whenever, or just respond and I'll be over.

Before responding, she considered one obvious implication of his visit. If Jen met Gerald, the girl would undoubtedly have more questions about Sadi's true intentions. Jen would see Gerald as a romantic interest to Sadi and he would probably become a frequent topic of conversation. After a long sigh, Sadi responded by text.

While waiting for Gerald to arrive, Sadi washed a load of laundry. As she chose the wash settings, Jen appeared in the laundry room, excitement showing in her wide, brown eyes.

"Sadi, you have to come see this. It's amazing."

Sadi started the wash cycle and then followed Jen from the room. At first, her heart raced with panic at what might have aroused such excitement. Her mind began to associate excitement with recent events, strange metal objects hovering in the air, centimeters from her face.

"What is it?" Sadi asked after arriving in the kitchen.

"It's a video of this amazing singer in the UK," Jen said. "Her name's Susan Boyle."

Sadi sighed in silent relief and smiled. Jen would often experience tremendous excitement when she discovered an interesting video on the internet. Sadi usually gave her best effort to appreciate them and refrain from criticizing them too much. Jen's laptop lay open on the bar and the Firefox internet browser showed a YouTube video on pause.

Sadi watched as a man named Simon Cowell, a judge on a talent show, introduced a slightly overweight woman on a stage with maybe a thousand people watching in the audience. Sadi enjoyed the singing performance, but the melodramatic reactions of the audience and judges provoked a strong urge to laugh. She shook her head slightly and tried to smile as though the performance had impressed her half as much as it had impressed the audience.

"Wow!" Sadi said when the video stopped. "She was good."

"Isn't she? Look how many hits this has gotten so far."

"Doesn't really sound like your kind of music," she said, hoping to divert attention from the reaction of the crowd. "Are you going to buy anything from her?"

Jen turned her attention from the screen.

"No, but that was awesome, right?"

"Pretty amazing," she said flatly, but she smiled wider.

"You're not impressed," Jen said, frowning and rolling her eyes melodramatically. "Alright, spit it out. I can see that you want to ruin this, like everything else I get excited about."

"No, I really do think she's a good singer, but don't you see what they're doing?"

"Let me guess," she said sarcastically. "She's not actually singing? It's a recording?"

"No, but you are being duped." Sadi failed to completely conceal a smile. "Her performance is real, but how they're showing the reaction of the crowd and judges is to manipulate your reaction. The show could have chosen any decent singer and put them in the same position, and you would have had the same reaction. It's just a marketing strategy to sell a product. That's how the entertainment industry works. They give this woman a lot of exposure to make her famous and then a bunch of people will buy her songs."

"Well, I think she's a good singer," Jen said indignantly.

"Come on, push play. I want to hear it again." Sadi laughed affectionately and placed her hand on Jen's shoulder.

"No, you don't," Jen answered, faking emotional damage but failing to hide a smile. Jen clicked the play button and they listened to the song again without Sadi making any other comment.

Sadi usually noticed attempts by the media to manipulate the public, and she was even more sensitive to them after meeting Gerald. Correspondence with Gerald had increased her skepticism of the world. She now suspected ulterior motives in almost everything. Would her paranoia grow out of control after the alien encounter? Would she begin making false conclusions, or see false connections?

—※—

Gerald arrived a few minutes before two in the afternoon. When Jen heard the knock on the door, she came downstairs from her room and pretended to look in the refrigerator for something to eat. Sadi knew her true intentions, to assess her new male friend. While living together, she and Jen had become almost like sisters, more than the usual employee-employer relationship. Sadi knew how Jen thought.

Jen stepped next to Sadi as she opened the front door.

"Hi, Gerald," she said and then turned to Jen. "This is Jen Andrews, Helen's nanny."

While Jen gave Gerald a rather long and comprehensive visual inspection, Sadi looked away to hide the roll of her eyes.

"Good to meet you, Jen," he said. "I'm Gerald Foster."

As Gerald walked through the doorway, Jen nodded in approval, smiling deviously. Behind his back, she stuck both thumbs in the air for extra emphasis. Sadi said *shut up* with tight eyes and a shake of her head.

"I hope you don't mind," he said loud enough for Jen to hear clearly. "I called Mr. Smith an hour ago, and he is expecting us anytime. He says Freddy is ready to talk now. Oh, and we shouldn't eat before we come over."

"Oh good. Let's leave now then."

Sadi smiled appreciatively, but inwardly she felt a small annoyance that he had called Mr. Smith. She held more of a relationship to the situation than he did. Did she feel a need for more control over the situation or did she just dislike the idea of following his lead?

"I was hoping to meet your daughter, Helen."

"Of course," she said, and the request instantly dissolved her annoyance. She turned to Jen.

"I'll go get her," Jen said and ran toward the stairs. She returned almost a minute later with Helen hiding behind her back.

"Why are you being so shy?" Sadi asked. Helen peeked around Jen and looked at Gerald with irritation. Jen had probably forced her to leave some activity.

"Hi, Helen," he said, smiling and crouching down to her level. "Wise choice to not trust me. I'm a lawyer."

His joke failed to earn even a small smile. Helen strained to keep her lips as straight as possible. Sadi waited impatiently for her daughter to say something embarrassing.

"You're not funny," Helen said without emotion.

Sadi frowned, but Jen snorted with amusement.

"Well it was nice to meet you too," he answered without showing any indication of emotional damage. He remained crouched. "Do you know what I love about kids?"

"No," Helen said, curious. "What?"

"Because children always tell the truth. In my line of work, that's very refreshing. I always have to wonder if people are lying to me."

Helen looked at him then at her mother.

"I guess it was good to meet you," she said then began walking slowly backward, toward the stairs.

SEVENTY-TWO

Sadi

At Freddy's house, Mr. Smith opened the door just as Gerald began knocking. The sight of him restored all of her memories of the previous evening. Sadi had begun thinking of the night as a dream, as the cave, but at that moment, the reality of the memories felt like a slap in the face.

Mr. Smith led them through the hallways and into the dining room and then shut the doors so that Sadi felt isolated from the rest of the house and even the world. A large platter of food sat on the huge table in front of her containing raw vegetables, fruits, sandwiches, and several dips. The setup looked a bit unbalanced, a simple spread of food set in a lavish dining room. Freddy asked what they wanted to drink and then quickly filled their ornate crystal glasses with their drink of choice.

"I dispensed with my cook and the other staff a few years before Freddy came," Mr. Smith explained. "After retiring from the government and my other activities, I found it unnecessary to keep them since it was just myself, and I didn't care about impressing anyone anymore. You must forgive Freddy for this inelegant assortment. He thinks more about substance than the presentation."

"Most people like sandwiches, and vegetables are good for you," Freddy said, looking to Gerald and then Sadi. His eyes lingered longer on Sadi.

Sadi sat by Gerald on one side of the table while Freddy and his boss sat on the other side. The setup reminded her of a job interview but with food instead of paperwork between them.

"Thanks for lunch," Sadi said.

"Yes, thank you," Gerald quickly agreed. "It looks good, and I'm hungry."

"It is the least I can do after what you all went through last night, for me."

"What exactly did happen last night?" Gerald asked before they could continue with more chitchat. "I mean, how did it all start?"

"What do you mean?" asked Freddy. "How did I get to the place you found me, that barn?"

"That's a good place to start."

"I finished with my lab," he began and set the flat rectangular crystal with its encased spider on the table in front of him. The surface shimmered with a rainbow of refracted color.

While waiting for him to continue, everyone just stared at the crystal. Sadi suddenly wanted to see the head of the spider, to see the blue and orange lights again. If she looked, would she wake in a strange place? Could she see her son again? She had to use all of her strength to look up from the table and focus on Freddy. In her peripheral vision, she saw the closed doors and then wondered if they could prevent the probe from appearing.

"I wanted to know what this was all about," he continued after the pause, still looking at the crystal. "So I thought that maybe if I went to a place, far away from civilization, something different might happen. It was just a feeling I had."

"What were you expecting?" Gerald asked.

The scene reminded Sadi of those television shows where police detectives interviewed suspects in an interrogation room. She wondered if Freddy felt uneasy with so many eyes focused on him.

"If I was away from everyone else, out somewhere by myself, perhaps whoever or whatever controls this thing would come to me."

"That's a pretty brave thing to do," Sadi interjected. The thought of entering the barn with the probe and the bears put a chill in her blood and caused Sadi to shudder, even in the warm room. "I wouldn't have dared try that alone."

"Not very smart if you ask me," said Mr. Smith with the hint of a scolding tone, "but, we already had that discussion."

Freddy looked at his hands on the table as though Mr. Smith's words had caused him to feel ashamed, but he quickly continued, his eyes fixed again on the crystal.

"I could not keep this from my thoughts. Every time I closed my eyes, it was all I could think about. It told me to visit you, Sadi, so I did, but I was afraid to show you, Mr. Smith. I wanted to find some answers first."

"Did you get answers?" Sadi asked.

"I drove west, past Buxton," he continued. "I felt strange while driving, like being put on cruise control and seeing the car steer by itself, only I remember steering. I can only describe the journey as walking in the dark with only a single step ahead illuminated."

"So, it led you by controlling the available information." Gerald was speaking more to himself than to Freddy. "That's interesting."

"It was dark when I finally got out of the car," Freddy said, undeterred by Gerald's comment. "I walked alone into that barn, and then the probe appeared, right in front of my face. That is when my vision went black. I do not remember any bears."

Freddy looked up from the table and made eye contact with Sadi. She recalled the time when he had stood outside, next to the Ford Explorer, pointing the gun at the government agent's head. The memory caused a shudder. She wanted to ask about the bears but soon forgot about them.

"It took me on a journey in my mind."

"Where did it take you?" Gerald asked, leaning forward.

"We traveled toward the sun," he said, and his eyes grew wide. "We went to Mercury, I think, to some structure and then crashed into it, into a black tunnel filled with light. I cannot accurately explain the experience."

"Does this structure actually exist?" Sadi asked and shivered at the mention of a dark tunnel. "Because when the probe came to me, I had a dream, at least Gerald and I did. Nothing in my dream was real."

"I do not know," he said. "I think it is real though."

"Were you told why? Why you?"

"I do not know. I think it wants me to go there. I think that is why it wanted me to visit you, Sadi, so that I could come into contact with your group."

Mr. Smith sat forward as if Freddy had given him the baton to lead the conversation.

"Before we go any further, it's your turn to talk."

Gerald and Sadi looked at each other for a moment then returned their attention to Mr. Smith.

"I don't have a choice, do I?" Gerald asked, smiling weakly.

"I don't need too many details," Mr. Smith said, "but you need to give me something."

"Okay," he said. "First, you have to promise to keep this confidential. Our lives depend on it."

"Of course," the old man said automatically.

"She's gonna kill me," Gerald said quietly to himself and then took a deep breath. "A friend of mine came to me with an invention of hers. It can take us into space and will revolutionize the aerospace industry."

"They're looking for people who share the same beliefs," Sadi interrupted before Mr. Smith could ask another question. "People interested in ending our oppressive system."

"If you haven't noticed," Gerald continued. "The Earth is run by some dangerous people, and there's no place to escape their influence."

Gerald sat back against his chair and let the information sink into the minds of his audience. During their brief explanation, Mr. Smith had listened intently, and Freddy kept shifting his attention between them and the crystal on the table.

"After what Freddy told me, what you say fails to surprise me." The old man chuckled as he talked. "So am I right to assume that you need to keep this from the government, from the military I imagine?"

"Exactly," said Gerald. "I'm only telling you because of this alien incident. Now, we all share dangerous secrets."

"We don't know it was an alien," Sadi interjected.

"You wouldn't have told me," the old man said, and laughed again but with more sarcasm, "if you knew my identity."

"Your identity?" Sadi asked. When she turned to Gerald, she saw the same confused expression that she felt. "Are you someone different than who you told us?"

Mr. Smith's eyes narrowed.

"I did not lie to you. My full name is William Benjamin Smith."

He paused after speaking and silence filled the room.

His name meant nothing special to Sadi. Gerald touched his chin with his right hand and looked up at the wall, but he made no verbal indication of recognition. After a moment of waiting, Mr. Smith continued.

"I am the former Secretary of Agriculture for the federal government, part of the presidential cabinet. I'm one of the dangerous people you mentioned, at least I used to be."

"Really!" said Sadi in surprise, feeling a momentary panic as though she had just confessed all of her secrets to the chief of police. His calm expression, however, erased the sensation of panic.

"Your name does sound a little familiar," Gerald said, "but what do you mean, you used to be one of the dangerous ones?"

When the old man sat back in his chair, Sadi knew he planned to give them a more detailed explanation. She and Gerald sat in silence while listening to him speak. His story had a similar trance-like effect as the multicolored lights of the probe.

—✳—

After many years in different government positions, William Smith became the Secretary of Agriculture and acquired a lot of money in his positions due to all the government subsidies distributed to farmers and corporations, which included those he owned. He grew proficient at enacting programs and laws that transferred vast amounts of money from the general public. He had acquired friends almost at the same rate and had helped them receive a disproportionate amount of government handouts.

Mr. Smith owned thousands of acres in North and South America and his son currently governed most of the business and planned to take complete control when his father finally died. His son eagerly waited for that day.

"If I could, I'd sign it all over to you, Freddy, but you'd never survive my son's wrath or the wrath of his friends. You would literally be dead in less than a month."

Mr. Smith shook his head in disgust, but Freddy appeared untroubled by the announcement. When the old man spoke again, he addressed Gerald.

"Yes, you are correct, Mr. Foster. There are very dangerous people running this world."

Mr. Smith then described the guilt he had experienced from the years of stealing money from the public to give to his friends, his relatives, and the friends of his fellow politicians. He had required several years after leaving government service to finally accept the real purpose of his political work, transferring money from the general population via the government structure to the wealthy families who run the intelligence agencies and to those who supported them.

"For almost a year," he said. "I was so depressed that my health started degrading. I spent several years afterward trying to think of ways to undo some of the damage I'd done. I finally realized that I could do nothing significant to reverse the trend. The beast is out of any single person's hands. For a long time now, I've been looking for a way to make good use of all my money. Up until now, I've been unsuccessful, and it's too late for me, I'm afraid. I'm just a bitter old man."

"You are not a bitter old man," Freddy said, returning to the conversation with vitality. "I have never known anyone better."

Mr. Smith put a withered old hand on Freddy's shoulder.

"If only time could erase the past."

"Until now?" Gerald asked, his eyes narrowing. "You said, up until now."

"I don't have much political clout anymore," the old man said. "But what I do have is at Freddy's disposal. If Freddy wants to help you, I will help you too."

SEVENTY-THREE

Sadi

"Let's go get some coffee," Sadi said after they had left Mr. Smith's estate. "There's a Starbucks near my house. I can't go home just yet. I need some caffeine."

In addition to caffeine, Sadi needed to discuss how the new information affected Gerald's group and more importantly, her life. Freddy had completely changed their situation and they needed to discuss the next plan of action. Sadi needed to resolve the anxiety of an extremely uncertain future. Her body and mind craved a relaxing atmosphere.

"That's a good idea," he said.

At the coffee shop, Sadi ordered her favorite steaming hot mug of sugar, cream, and caffeine. She usually saved that kind of sugar rush for special occasions and always felt guilty for inflicting her blood with such high levels of glucose, but she needed some compensation for the trauma of the previous night. Gerald ordered an iced tea and sipped the liquid during their discussion.

"What do you plan on doing next?" she asked after they sat at a table by a south-facing window.

Gerald held his cup in both hands and Sadi looked outside, shivering at the thought of the cold glass on his skin. The sun peered through the clouds on the horizon. In less than an hour, its light would sink into the Pacific Ocean.

"I really don't know," he said. "I can hardly wrap my head around it. Eventually, I'll have to tell the others, but right now, I can't think of a way to do it."

"Can't you just tell them what happened?" Sadi asked. "Maybe they can help you work it out."

"I don't like bringing a case to someone until I have it figured out. Right now, we don't know how Freddy fits into the picture. Does the alien want only Freddy or all of us?"

"I know you and Freddy think it's an alien, but can we make that determination right now? It just doesn't feel right. I don't know."

"Maybe it just scares you, so you're trying to think of other explanations?"

She looked at him, ignoring the urge to reply with blatant irritation. She disliked others assuming they knew her thoughts, even if they were correct. But from his tone, he had meant no offense.

"Don't try to figure me out," she said and smiled. "For now, we can call it an alien, but I'm just not convinced."

"Sorry," he said in apology. "It's just the lawyer in me. I'm also looking at it from a different angle, I guess. The idea of an alien is kind of exciting. Maybe it's just the boy in me."

"If you had any kids," she said, "your approach might be a little more cautious."

"Probably," he admitted.

"I just feel bad for Freddy," Sadi said in an attempt to change the course of the conversation. "He looks scared. I'm going to help him figure out what's going on."

"And you'll keep me informed, right?"

"Of course," she said, sipping her drink and swirling the sweet liquid with her tongue. "Do you know what scares me the most about it?"

"What?"

"I didn't think about it at the time, but when we were looking into that probe, something was looking back at us. I was more worried about what it would do to me and didn't really think about that. When we first looked into the crystal, an intelligent creature took control of us and we just started driving like Freddy did, and went where it wanted us to go, without any resistance. And the funny thing is, I remember driving, but it was like a dream."

Sadi shivered and then continued.

"What if it never stopped controlling Freddy, or us? You saw how he always looks at that crystal thing. Even if he believes in his autonomy, is he making his own decisions?"

"Hmm," Gerald said. "Losing control scares most everybody, but I think we need to treat this like a court case and put the creature on trial. All we can do is consider the evidence before us and base our decisions on that. Fear can cause people to think irrationally, but I'm not saying you're acting irrationally."

"Alright, Mr. Defense Attorney," she said, and her eyes widened as though accepting a challenge. "What evidence are you talking about?"

"Instead of listening to our instincts, we should listen to our senses," he said as though starting a philosophy lesson. "Most people instinctively fall back on fear and paranoia and react from that. We can only base our decisions on evidence. What do we know about this thing?"

"It did not try to hurt us," Sadi said.

"And it could have," he replied. "We know that for sure. It could have driven us off a cliff."

"Maybe, maybe not," Sadi said, placing her cup on the table. "We just don't remember. What if we made our decisions consciously? But I agree, if it wanted to kill us, the probe could have just rammed us with that sharp tip."

"Who's to say that it didn't abduct us, and perform experiments on us," Gerald said and laughed.

"You've been watching too many movies."

"I really don't watch movies," Gerald replied with a hint of pride in his tone. "But I read enough about them to know what propaganda is being pushed. Abduction is a popular idea because it scares people. In my opinion, a creature intelligent enough to travel here is probably peaceful and might even find us boring. They would find cows and pigs a less-troublesome food supply than humans."

"More meat on them," Sadi agreed.

"That wouldn't make a very exciting movie, aliens coming down in the night and stealing cows or chickens for food."

"Well, you certainly are interested in alien movies," she said in mock triumph. But before he could respond, she continued in a more serious tone. "What if we're just thinking like humans, but normal human motivations don't apply? It might be like a little child trying to understand two adults who are sexually attracted to each other."

"Hmm," he said, pausing as though the question had stopped the conversational momentum. "That's an interesting point, and you're probably right, but its motivations may not matter. All that matters is what it does. Don't you think?"

"Not really," she said. "It could be acting falsely to manipulate us. We shouldn't take everything at face value. That's all I'm saying."

"Okay, you're probably right," he continued. "Let's finish with the evidence first and then we can try to determine its possible motives. We know it can hurt us if it wants to, and for the present, let's assume it can get us to do what it wants. For me, that gives us the leisure to act as if it means us no harm."

"For now, maybe," she said without feeling convinced. While listening to him, Sadi imagined Gerald speaking to a jury and judge.

"Can Freddy be right, that it wants us to take him into space?" he asked, his eyes narrowing. "And that's why it involved us?"

Instead of answering his question, she considered an alternative scenario.

"Can we say it doesn't have the capability? It doesn't have a ship or vessel to take Freddy on its own?"

"That might be a good assumption," he said. "I would say it's advanced enough to do it on its own, but if it knows about our group, how long has it known?"

Before she could respond, he exhaled sharply and placed his cup on the table.

"Oh damn," he said, irritated.

"What's wrong?"

When Gerald continued, he spoke more to himself than to Sadi.

"What if it's been directing our thoughts or actions for a long time? Maybe it gave Taylor the idea for her invention. She would not like that. Maybe it led me to the fusion reactor?"

"Is Taylor the name of the girl who started all this?"

While waiting for his response, she recognized the tension in his facial muscles. His irritation seemed directed at himself and not her.

"I didn't want to tell you her name yet, for your protection of course. I guess it doesn't matter, considering what we just went through."

Several questions about Taylor suddenly hijacked Sadi's thoughts like an irritating but catchy song. Did Gerald feel an attraction to the girl? Sadi imagined possible images of Taylor and attempted to fabricate a short fat girl with greasy hair.

For the next several seconds, they looked out the window in silence. While considering his new concern, the beautiful colors on the horizon attenuated her emotions. She knew how he felt. She would have felt extremely disappointed if someone else could take credit for her accomplishments. She needed to help him feel better.

"It doesn't make sense for the alien to be responsible for your group. If it wants Freddy, why bother to use you or Taylor to make the transport vessel? If it needed a human to do the work, it could have had Freddy do it easily. What about this? Take the alien, or whatever it is, out of the picture, and everything happened because of you and Taylor? Would it make a difference?"

"I hope you're right," he said and laughed. His look of concern melted. "I guess it was my turn to think irrationally, but I really do think you're right, and not just because it's what I want."

"Freddy is really smart," she continued. "He has the resources to do whatever he wants. If the alien wanted to, it could have him build it. Maybe it's been looking for someone who could take Freddy into space with them?"

"Hmm."

While his mind processed her words, Sadi recognized relief in his eyes and then made a sudden realization. She accepted the possibility of an alien controlling the probe and the crystal, and the idea no longer frightened her. All of the stupid horror movies she had watched as a kid must have warped her sense of reality. They caused an irrational and artificial fear of the unknown, an emotion that Gerald seemed to lack. She resolved to keep Helen from watching horror movies.

"When are you going to tell them?" she asked. "I mean Taylor and the others about what's happened?"

"Let's learn more from Freddy before we tell them anything," he said while rubbing his chin. "Besides, they're very busy working on the prototype ship. They don't want any distractions."

"When am I going to meet them?"

"Once they get the prototype done, we're going to have a test flight." He took a sip of his tea. "I think that would be a good time. If all goes according to plan, it'll happen in a couple of months. They are putting all their time and resources into it, and they have no red bureaucratic tape to slow them down."

SEVENTY-FOUR

Sadi

For the next few minutes, Gerald talked about how Freddy might help their group. He initially thought the extra money at their disposal would completely change the situation. But during the night, he had failed to think of any significant ways to use the money. They had already obtained most of what they needed and now they needed mainly to focus on individual tasks. Taylor and Cesar needed to complete the prototype ship, and Gerald needed to help Sadi and Freddy solve the mystery of the spider in the crystal.

As she listened to Gerald, the reality of their situation began to infect her thoughts again. She needed to seriously consider her level of involvement, and whether the situation potentially put Helen, her brother, or Jen in danger. Did she have the right to risk their future without their consent?

"There's something that's worrying me," she said when Gerald paused to yawn.

"What's that?"

"At first, it was exciting and all. You know, meeting you secretly at PF Chang's, being followed by the FBI. But after what we just went through, now it's real."

"Yes, it is."

"I've got a daughter and brother to think about," she began. "I might be putting them in danger."

"What are you saying?" he asked with concern. "You can't back out now, not after what's happened."

"I don't want to back out," she said and shook her head. "I think it's beyond that point now and I still want to help, be a part of this."

Gerald sat back against the wooden chair.

"I'll admit it, last night was pretty intense, but so far, your only crime has been to associate with me."

"But what about those agents following us?" she asked, ignoring his joke. "That was the FBI! I need to remain on the sidelines."

"I understand, really," he said more seriously. "Just focus on Freddy, and I'll remember to leave your name off any declaration of independence we sign."

"That's all I'm asking," she said. "Thank you."

"If we succeed and get Taylor's invention and the fusion reactor into the public awareness," he said, "it's going to change the world. Energy independence for the masses just might allow a new system, one based on individualism. You, your daughter, and everyone will be able to live a more complete life, a life of your own."

Sadi already understood the potential result of the group's success, but hearing the description of a brighter future for her daughter felt more motivational. She loved talking to people like Gerald about the world. Unfortunately, people who desired the collectivist ideology vastly outnumbered individualists. She needed to associate more with people who shared her view of the world.

"You're not trying to tell me what's best for my own child are you?" she asked.

"I'm taking everyone's best interest into consideration."

"I know, Gerald," she said, putting her hand on his wrist. "I was being sarcastic about that last part. I think what you're trying to do is noble, and I'm glad to be a part of it. It's just that this is big and I have to distance my family a bit. Everyone has to make their own contribution, right?"

"Sorry," he said and smiled. "Sometimes I wonder if I'm too negative. We have it pretty nice here! Compared to other places on the planet, we live in general comfort, even the poorer people do. I know the world's not perfect, and I don't expect it to be perfect, but when I think of what it could be, that's what motivates me. Sometimes, I let it make me too angry."

Sadi decided to relax and let him continue ranting.

"Powerful countries like ours have always been responsible for so many wars, so much violence and suffering. While we sit here with our drinks in this warm café, children are dying from starvation because our government or our corporations supplied their government leaders with another round of financial support. If our vampire politicians stopped taking our money through taxes and inflation, we could actually make a difference in the world. As it is now, we can donate our money to help feed the poor and build schools for them, because the system is not designed for them to feed themselves or even have a job after getting an education.

"To live in a world without taxes, without wars, no one telling you how to spend your money. Can you imagine? We wouldn't be slaves to the banks! We could pay off our houses in less than a lifetime! We could travel without having to show our papers! We could build something on our property without getting the proper authorization and without feeding the overpaid, bureaucratic system. We could drive any speed we wanted and put natural selection back to work. Idiots wouldn't have to wear seatbelts."

Gerald smiled wide during his last comment and Sadi silently suffered a painful memory, the accident that took her son's life. While he talked, Sadi rested her head in her hands and concentrated on acting extremely interested.

"That's why so many people read books and watch movies," she said. "To experience a better world, a more interesting one at least."

A young man at the table behind Gerald kept glancing away from his girlfriend to stare at the back of Gerald's head as though listening to their conversation. As a challenge, Sadi met his eyes, and he quickly looked back at his girlfriend.

"Of course, you can't say this to people," Gerald said, shaking his head. "They've been too indoctrinated by the collectivists who think they own the world. They've never seen anarchistic solutions to social problems, or if they have, some authority figure ridiculed it. By the time people are adults, they can only imagine solutions involving laws, taxes, or politicians. As you know, their laws seem to cause other social problems, and the collectivists always have more laws or more taxes ready to implement."

"Feel better," Sadi said and smiled. "I stopped trying to talk to people about this stuff. Sometimes I feel like the only honest person at a criminals' convention, trying to tell people that stealing is wrong. It's frustrating, but now we might have some hope! Are you ready to go? I need to get home."

"Sure," he said. "Like we already agreed, we need to discover more from Freddy. I think he holds the key to all of this, and I think the alien wants the same thing we do."

"Or, it wants us to think that," Sadi said silently. She stood and walked out of the café with him.

Sadi returned home at nine-thirty to find Helen in bed and Jen watching the previous week's episode of *Celebrity Apprentice* on her laptop. Sadi felt grateful to find Jen awake. She wanted to visit with another conscious human, preferably a female.

When Jen noticed Sadi enter the room, she put the video on pause and gave a status report of the day. While they spoke, the still image of the show faced them, Joan Rivers arguing with country music singer Clint Black. Jen's addiction to semi-reality television shows provided Sadi with her only source of information about the activities of the entertainment world. The next episode of the series would be aired on the major network the next night. Jen always enjoyed watching the previous episode just before the new one.

"Sadi," Jen said before turning from the screen. "You were out *pretty* late with that man. What's his name again?"

Jen stretched the word *pretty* like a rubber band ready to shoot from her finger.

"Gerald," Sadi said in confirmation.

"Yeah, Gerald. He's pretty good-looking, wouldn't you say?"

Sadi smiled and dismissed the insinuation with a laugh.

"It's not like that. We're just working on something together, but I can't talk about it."

"That's not what I see."

"Okay, Jen," Sadi said, amused and a little embarrassed. "What do you see?"

"I don't see anything," she said, holding up her hands and acting as though wrongly accused of a crime. "I just think it's strange that I haven't heard of this man until today. How long have you been keeping him a secret? Are you going to try and convince me that you're not interested in him?"

"I am not interested in him," Sadi replied and attempted to show a stern look, but Jen's suspicious expression inspired a quick change of tactics. "Jen, I think it's best if we don't talk about him right now. I've had a long two days and need to get some sleep."

Jen smiled in triumph and then returned to face her laptop. After a quiet click, the two characters on her show returned to life and continued arguing. Their voices faded as Sadi began walking away.

"I'll get it out of you," Jen said loudly, her eyes fixed on the computer screen.

"Goodnight, Jen."

Sadi checked on her sleeping daughter then entered her bedroom and shut the door. She extinguished the lights and pulled the covers over her. That night, she energized the television at the foot of her bed and then set the volume to zero. She hated to wake in the night with the television casting flickering light on the walls, but she hoped the light would help purge the darkness from her mind.

PART VI

TRIBULATION

Before the next awful bite

Relax, take a break

And see a good sight

SEVENTY-FIVE

Sadi

Just before four in the afternoon, Sadi looked at the clock on the corner of the computer screen and contemplated going home a bit early. She usually left work sometime between five thirty and six, but she had felt uncomfortable since lunch and had been glancing at the clock every few minutes. She'd worked on nothing particularly stressful in the lab or her office. Her day had passed pretty smoothly, so why would she feel so much anxiety?

From her purse, five meters away, Sadi heard the familiar vibration of her phone. In some strange way, she knew Jen was waiting for her to answer. But before answering the call, Sadi just stared at the phone as though it had fangs dripping with venom. If she touched the phone, a snake might strike. Sadi waited for three long rings until she had gained enough courage to answer.

"Hi, Jen, what's–" Sadi began, but the strange, abnormal sound of Jen crying stopped her from continuing. Her blood suddenly turned to honey.

"Ran off," Jen said through her sobs. "She ran off–"

"Calm down, Jen," Sadi said as calmly as possible. "What are you talking about?"

Sadi already knew what had happened, but she clung to the small possibility of an alternative conclusion. After making an effort to breathe deeply, Jen spoke slowly, struggling to enunciate each word.

"I was at the store register when Helen ran off," she said finally. "The fucking lady at the checkout wouldn't let me go."

"Where are you now? How long has it been?"

She asked her first two questions while fifty other questions waited impatiently behind her tongue. A panicked voice in the back of her mind screamed so loudly she could hardly think. While holding the phone to her ear, she grabbed her purse and ran from her office, leaving the door open. Without saying a word to anyone, Sadi left work and ran to her car. She talked to Jen on the phone while driving.

"I'm in the mall security office," Jen said. "They're out there looking for her. Luckily, I had her picture on my phone."

"How could you let this happen?"

Sadi made the hasty accusation before she could stop herself. Instantly, she heard Jen's sobs resume. "I'm sorry, Jen. We'll find her. I'm gonna find her."

—※—

When Sadi arrived at the mall, she saw a security guard at the entrance, watching the shoppers enter and exit. She ran to him and introduced herself as the mother of the missing girl.

"Where is she?" she asked frantically. "Have you found her yet?"

"No ma'am, but don't worry," the guard said unconvincingly. The twenty-year-old security guard spoke as though bored, as though parents lost their children all the time. A baseball cap covered his shaved head, but he had a thick beard and a goatee. "We'll find her, just go to the office. They can guide you to it at the information desk, just inside."

Without knowing how, Sadi already knew the location of the information desk. While running through the mall, she felt as though some super-drug had enhanced her senses. She noticed every person in her path, every face, and even the clothes they wore. She smelled their perfume, saw pimples on their faces, the pieces of food in their teeth. She saw everything except what she wanted to see.

After entering the security office, she first noticed Jen then the two other mall employees. Energy from her adrenaline rush crashed painfully when she failed to see her daughter in the room. Jen met Sadi's questioning gaze with bloodshot eyes and silence, apparently afraid to say anything.

"I'm sorry," she said finally, almost too low to hear.

Sadi had no remaining emotional energy for anger toward her daughter's nanny. She sat on the ugly brown leather couch next to Jen and placed her right arm protectively around the shaking girl. After a short embrace, Sadi pulled away but left her hand on Jen's shoulder.

"We'll find her," Sadi said, assuming the role of comforter. Anger would only hinder information extraction. "Tell me again what happened."

"I needed to get some things," Jen began. While speaking, she seemed to regain some of her confidence. "I brought Helen with me. I've taken her shopping with me a thousand times, but she's never run away from me before."

"Did you notice anyone suspicious following you, or watching you or Helen, or anything out of the ordinary?"

"I didn't notice anyone," she said and then explained the situation in more detail.

While Jen had stood in line at the checkout of a clothing store, Helen had run into the main mall walkway. Jen remembered thinking the transaction would take just a minute, but the store employee had complained about some issue with her cash register. When Jen had finally left the store with her purchases, Helen had disappeared. In total, Jen had searched with the mall security for an hour and twenty minutes and had called Sadi after forty minutes.

Between each word, hundreds of horrible explanations filled Sadi's mind. Waiting felt like a knife in the gut. Doing nothing felt like a hammer to her head. Instead of sitting in the office, Sadi needed to return to the central mall area and continue the search.

"Jen, take me to the store where it happened."

The mall authorities wanted Sadi to wait for them to locate Helen, but if she continued to sit without a physical outlet, she felt as though her heart would explode or at the very least she would faint. So, she ignored their request and led Jen out the door of the office. With one of the mall employees following, Sadi and Jen wound their way through narrow hallways and eventually returned to the central mall area.

As they methodically visited each store, Jen stayed close by her side and talked almost constantly, but her voice sounded like the buzzing of a fly to Sadi. She nodded in acknowledgment without understanding the meaning of her words. After the minutes turned into an hour, the voice of hope in her mind began to grow silent.

They searched all of the stores and talked with the staff of each store until Sadi had depleted all of her search options, and then a new thought revived the voice of hope in her mind. Had someone found Helen and taken her home or to the police station? But then why would they have not taken her to the mall authorities? Maybe an elderly person had found her and just failed to consider the most obvious course of action.

Maybe if Sadi went home, she would find Helen and the end of her nightmare. She told Jen her plan and started leading her to the mall exit, in the direction of her car. And then at the exit, she realized that she could call. While listening to the phone ringing, she wondered why she had neglected to consider that option until then. Sadi held her breath through six rings. No one answered.

"Maybe we should call the police first," Jen suggested. "Maybe they can find her."

"Got to get home," Sadi said to herself as though Jen's words had no meaning. "Got to get home. She might be there. You stay here for a while longer and go back to the office."

"Are you sure you can drive? I don't want you to get in an accident."

"I can drive, Jen," she said. "I'll meet you back at the house."

Sadi drove much faster than the speed limit, faster than at any time in her life. She drove as though daring the police to give her a ticket and imagined racing them to her house. That option would save a phone call to the police anyway.

When she pulled into the driveway of her home, her feeling of hope sunk even deeper inside her chest. No unrecognizable car sat in front of her house, and no light shined through any of the windows.

"Helen, Helen," she yelled after crashing through the front door. She ran up the stairs, energized every light in the house, and opened every door. She picked up the home phone and scanned through the phone numbers of the recent calls, nothing but her call from the mall.

Jen entered the open front door just a few minutes later, shutting the door loudly behind her.

"Is she here?" Jen yelled after failing to see Sadi.

Sadi did not answer but ran down the stairs to grab the phone.

"Are you calling the police?" asked Jen.

"No," Sadi replied while dialing.

SEVENTY-SIX

Sadi

After accepting that her daughter was not in the house and not at the mall, Sadi considered an alternative explanation. Did her daughter's disappearance relate to Gerald's group or that probe thing? Would she find her daughter in some barn as they had found Freddy? Maybe the probe had an interest in Helen, and Sadi had incorrectly concluded that the experience was a test for her. The dream now seemed like a foreboding of what would happen. Other alternatives were too horrible even to consider. Sadi grasped the new thought as tightly as she had held Helen in the tunnel.

She waited for three rings before anyone answered.

"Hi, Sadi," Gerald said. "It's good to hear from you."

"Hi, Gerald, I'm so sorry to call you. I, I don't know what to do."

For the first time that day, tears began falling down her cheeks. The sound of Gerald's voice had destroyed her emotional dam.

"What's wrong?" Gerald asked.

"She's gone. Helen's gone," Sadi almost shouted between sobs. Her legs began to feel so weak and had barely enough strength to support her weight, so she sat down at the kitchen table. "She disappeared at the mall. I don't know what happened to her."

Over the next forty seconds, Sadi managed to explain the story. At some points, she experienced difficulty breathing. She glanced once at Jen and cringed at the sight of her tears.

"Do you want me to talk to him?" asked Jen, her hand suddenly on Sadi's shoulder.

Sadi extended her hand, palm facing Jen, as a request for silence while she finished telling the remainder of the story. Talking helped more than it hurt.

After finishing her explanation, Sadi waited a moment for Gerald to respond. The next moment of silence passed like an eternity. Any attraction she'd previously felt for him had dissipated as the morning fog, forgotten and replaced by a need for Gerald to take control of the situation and retrieve her daughter. Only Gerald would know what to do. The situation could not be handled by the police. Sadi had no faith in them anyway.

"I'm in my car and on the way now," Gerald said. "Other than calling me, what else were you planning to do? It seems to me that you should listen to your mother's instinct. What is your head telling you to do?"

"Nothing, my brain is empty," Sadi said. All the muscles in her body felt tense, and her head pounded. "I feel helpless. What do I do? Every minute feels like she's speeding farther away from me. I can't lose her too. I've got to get her back."

"Okay, this is what I want you to do."

Gerald spoke as though giving instructions to a class of high school students. Through the phone, she heard the slam of a door and a car engine roaring to life. The sounds of Gerald driving to her aid provided her with the only comfort she'd felt after answering the phone call from Jen.

"I'm going to call Mr. Smith," Gerald began. "You need to drive over there and wait for me. Mr. Smith knows the best PI around. He has the resources you will need. Will you do that?"

"Okay," Sadi said and took a deep breath before continuing. She imagined the oxygen entering her bloodstream and flooding her brain. In a normal situation, asking a near stranger for help would have caused horror, but the action brought no anxiety. "Do you think that thing had anything to do with this?"

"I don't know, but–"

"But what?" Sadi demanded.

"But it does seem like too much of a coincidence. We can talk about it later, just let me call them. You just go over there. Can I talk to Jen for a moment?"

Sadi handed the phone to Jen.

Jen listened for a moment, said "yes" and "alright" and then cut the connection.

"He says that you know how to get to this Mr. Smith's house, but he wants me to drive."

Surprising herself, Sadi complied.

Jen staying at the house made more sense in Sadi's head, but visiting the old man with Jen seemed like the right action too. Helen knew her mother's phone number and would call if she could, whether at home or somewhere else.

—✳—

When they arrived at Mr. Smith's house, the gate opened before they could request entry. He met them alone at the door, and when she failed to see Freddy, she wondered if he was waiting inside for them.

"Oh, my dear," Mr. Smith said with as much sympathy as imaginable from an elderly man who hardly knew her.

He wrapped one arm around her and pulled her inside his home. She refrained from returning his affection too vigorously for fear of breaking his ribs. As Jen held onto her other arm, the sensation reminded Sadi of when her son had died. Jen had stayed by her side during that whole horrible affair. But the current experience felt much worse than her son dying. At least Sadi had known the fate of her son.

"Don't you worry, we'll find her," Mr. Smith said as he guided them to the same waiting room where she and Gerald had waited before beginning their search for Freddy. "I already talked to Mr. Swenson, my private investigator. He will find your daughter."

"Thank you, Mr. Smith," Sadi said, allowing herself to feel momentary relief. But then she wondered if his confidence contained only hope or a genuine belief in finding Helen. Nothing would help until they found her daughter.

"Hi, I'm Jen Andrews," said Jen. "Helen's nanny."

Mr. Smith shook her hand as though in a business meeting.

"Good to meet you. I'm sorry we have to meet under these circumstances."

Sadi turned her attention to Jen for a moment and saw tears in her beautiful brown eyes, just waiting to fall. When Jen noticed Sadi looking at her, she turned away. Like Sadi, the girl probably wanted to avoid any disturbance that might initiate another emotional flood.

"Excuse me for a moment," Mr. Smith said, leaving his cane against the piano.

He disappeared for a few minutes and returned with two mugs full of steaming liquid. "This will help calm your nerves," he said while giving them the drinks.

The herbal tea tasted of lemon and a variety of spices. The hot spicy liquid on her dry tongue sent a warm shock through her entire nervous system. The taste and smell combined into an intoxicating, almost magical substance. She declined his suggestion for her to sit and then began pacing back and forth across the room, watching the window for signs of Gerald's arrival. But after several trips across the floor, she joined Jen on the couch where she had sat with Gerald.

Mr. Smith turned to Jen.

"Miss Andrews," he said with an old voice full of concern. "I would like to speak with Sadi in private for a few minutes. Would you like to explore the house?"

"I guess," she said after seeing a nod of approval from Sadi.

"The kitchen is just down the hall to the right," he said, pointing in the direction with his cane. "If you're hungry, feel free to have whatever. Thanks, dear."

As Jen walked from the room, Sadi noticed hurt in her eyes and confusion about the dismissal, but she looked away to avoid eye contact. The current circumstances overshadowed Sadi's concern for Jen's feelings. After she left the room, Sadi waited for the old man to speak and hoped he would have some answer or explanation for her.

"I left a message on the phone for Freddy to come home as soon as possible," Mr. Smith said with no concern in his voice. "He's probably with a group from one of his classes and should be home soon."

"Has this anything to do with the probe, or what happened?"

"I don't know," he said, shaking his head. "But after you called, I went to Freddy's room and found the crystal, but it was dark and silent. I'm sorry, but I don't dare to touch or look at it too closely."

"That explanation is the only thing holding me together. I don't want to think of any other explanation. That sounds totally stupid, hoping for an alien abduction."

She wanted to laugh at the joke, but more tears suddenly threatened to fall from her eyes.

"How can it not be related?" he said and placed his hand on her shoulder. "I'm sure it's related, and your daughter is safe somewhere, just like Freddy was, but I didn't want to take any chances this time. That's why I called the PI. He really is good. With Freddy, and him, and your friend, Mr. Foster, we're sure to find her."

Sadi looked from the floor to meet his eyes and wiped the tears from her cheeks, but his cold hand on her shoulder failed to transfer any comfort.

"Do you really think so?" she asked after a deep inhale.

"I really do."

"Do you think I should have called the police?" Sadi asked.

If she neglected to call the police and failed to find her daughter, would they suspect her of foul play? That possibility would complicate the situation. Sadi suddenly felt a strange and irrational civic responsibility to make an official report. If necessary, she would make one. Sadi looked at her watch and noticed the time, ten-fifteen. Her daughter had been missing for almost seven hours.

"If you want something done," Mr. Smith said with bitterness, "don't call the police, call a private investigator. The police will tell you to wait and let them handle it. They're paid whether or not they are successful, not to get things done. If you're not famous or rich, you'll be put on a list, and it will turn into a case history, not an investigation. Even the government, if they are serious about accomplishing something, will contract with the private sector. They are only the illusion of organization."

"Are we going to tell your private investigator anything that's been happening? The probe, or the crystal?"

"That might complicate the situation," Mr. Smith said. "I was thinking the PI can do his investigation and we can look at the situation from the other angle."

Light from the window caused them to turn their heads. While Mr. Smith rose from the couch, the gate buzzer rang, and he went to answer the call. They waited only thirty seconds before the knock on the door.

"Come on in, Craig," he said.

When the giant man entered the house, his size immediately intimidated her. When he extended his hand in greeting, Sadi paused to admire the large fingers, almost twice as long as hers and three times as thick. She was relieved when his grip failed to crush her hand.

"Craig Swenson, Ma'am," he said with intense blue eyes that seemed to glow on his somewhat dull face, as the inside of an agate. She noticed a slight accent in his voice, Norwegian probably. "No need to introduce yourself, Miss Jacobsen. Mr. Smith already told me about you. We'll need to go someplace comfortable but away from the windows. Bill, what about your study?"

Craig led Sadi to the study while Mr. Smith went to the kitchen. When he met them in the study a minute later, Jen entered behind him. Her eyes widened at the site of the giant man sitting across the table from Sadi. Mr. Smith sat by the private investigator, and Jen sat by Sadi.

Craig Swenson set his laptop computer on the table then reached into his jacket and retrieved a small voice recorder. After setting the device in the middle of the table, he started the recording. His giant fingers rested on the keyboard in front of him, and Sadi wondered how he could hit only one key at a time. Everyone waited for him to speak first.

"Okay, there are two realistic possibilities," he began as soon as he got comfortable at the table. His get-down-to-business attitude made Sadi feel a little better. He would waste no time. "Helen was either deliberately chosen or a random target. Do you know of anyone who would want to take your daughter, a relative, a friend, an ex-husband, or someone with whom you've had a relationship?"

"I don't think so," she said and turned to Jen who shook her head. "The only one who might fit that description would be my ex-husband, but he has shown no interest in Helen, or me for that matter. I haven't talked to him for months."

For the next few minutes, Craig quickly and methodically reviewed all of her past acquaintances, relatives, and friends. The experience felt as though a doctor was examining a list of medical symptoms. While both speaking and listening to her answers, he typed without looking at the keyboard, and after the first few minutes, she stopped noticing his typing.

"This is a strange case," he continued, "because it happened at the mall. It is very difficult to take an unwilling child through crowds of people. I suspect an accomplice who gained Helen's confidence."

He leaned over the table and stared directly into Jen's eyes.

"Tell me what you remember. I do not want you to leave anything out, or to say you don't remember. You have to remember. Now start with why you were going shopping, how long you had the trip planned, and who knew when and where you were going."

His intensity seemed to frighten Jen, but she managed somehow to maintain her composure. No one knew of her visit to the mall, not even Sadi and she had only planned the trip that morning. She told him about all of the people she'd noticed at the mall, every face from her memory. While Jen told her version of events, Sadi felt as though she was watching Jen through a telescope, with no one else in existence. She recognized the fear in Jen's voice. If the man intended to scare the information out of her, the tactic was working.

Mr. Swenson leaned farther across the table when Jen told him of the little girl who had talked to Helen. The event had happened in a previous store, but Helen never saw the girl afterward, so she assumed it to be just a random meeting. He made Jen tell him everything about the little girl, her age, height, what she wore, and who accompanied her.

"No one seemed to be with her," Jen said. "But Helen is very outgoing. She always talks to other kids."

"In cases like this, nothing can be taken for granted."

During the interrogation, Sadi appreciated the man's professional and courteous attitude. He gave them sympathy when he could and never strayed off topic or let their emotions sway him from pursuing a line of questioning. A few times, Jen would start crying, or tears would come to Sadi's eyes. He gave them only a moment to compose themselves before bringing them back to the topic.

"Save the tears for later," he said several times, and, "I know it's hard, but you have to stay focused."

Sadi felt like a sheep being herded by an Australian Shepherd dog. After about thirty minutes of intense interrogation, Craig claimed to have acquired several leads to start following.

"You won't have to call the police," he said reassuringly to Sadi. "I'm going to talk to a friend of mine on the force. I'm not going to let them put you through more hell than what you're going through."

Like a child being scolded by a parent, Sadi nodded silently.

"Is there a–" Mr. Smith began, but the door slowly opened and Freddy appeared. He glanced at all of the people sitting at the table, and his eyes froze when they met Sadi.

SEVENTY-SEVEN

Freddy

At the barn, the alien probe had unlocked an extra sense in Freddy, a strong connection to the emotions of people in his vicinity. He had decided that until he understood the new ability and its purpose more fully, he would keep the knowledge to himself. He would tell no one, not even his employer. He hated to give people more reason to think of him as being different.

Freddy quickly discovered that each person had a unique emotional signature. He no longer required visual confirmation for identity and would not need to use *spider* as a secret code word. As soon as he entered the house, Freddy felt the presence of several familiar individuals: Sadi, her nanny, and Mr. Smith's private investigator, Craig Swenson.

Freddy thought he was prepared to see the two women, but when he saw the smeared mascara and tear-filled eyes, the blood in his veins seemed to freeze, so that he could not move. He felt pure panic from Sadi, and the nanny radiated sadness and frustration. The rush of sadness, anxiety, and panic in the room felt as though he was drinking a cup of vinegar. They quickly became his own emotions and almost choked him to death.

Mr. Smith relayed what had happened in as few words as possible, but Freddy already seemed to know, just from what he felt from Sadi. Hearing the horrible situation in words felt like the strike of a hammer on the nail already in his chest. When Sadi looked at him, he mysteriously knew what she was going to ask.

But before she could say anything, he turned to Mr. Smith.

"I am so sorry," he said. "Maybe there is something I can do? I um, I will be back in a few minutes."

Freddy tried projecting a tone of hope, but he felt totally helpless, and the emotion interfered with his ability to speak. The flood of emotions drove away all rational thought, and he had to escape their presence to think clearly. He silently shut the door and ran down the stairs to his room. After closing the bedroom door, he turned off the lights and entered his smallest closet where he could sit in the quiet of total darkness.

He needed to enter the calm abyss he had discovered as a child whenever a traumatic event happened. With his back to the wall, he sat on the ground, hugged his knees to his chest, and started counting his breaths. After counting to five, he began to feel a little better. The darkness and quiet seemed to seep into his body, helping to purge his mind of anxiety. The emotions of those in the room above him never completely disappeared, but at least he felt able to focus on his immediate surroundings.

After fifteen breaths, he saw a light burst to life under the closet door. He counted to twenty-five while watching the familiar blue and orange light flicker and dance. The light continued to grow in brightness, destroying his cherished darkness and illuminating everything in the closet.

In the two weeks since the barn incident, he had stayed away from the crystal but kept the object on top of his dresser. Occasionally, he would glance at the rainbow surface, but he would never look into the eyes of the spider. During the nights, he often dreamed about the spider moving inside the crystal as a living two-dimensional creature. But until that moment, the crystal had shown no sign of activity.

When Freddy opened the closet door again, he shielded his eyes with one hand, partly from the brightness and partly from fear of falling into another trance. With his hand blocking the light, he approached the dresser with the crystal lying on top. As soon as he touched the crystal, a singular point of light burst to life in his mind and then vanished. In the following darkness, Freddy felt different.

SEVENTY-EIGHT

Freddy

After the burst of light, Freddy felt similar to when he had run after the FBI agents from the barn. The new explosion in his mind erased all fear and anxiety. Freddy suddenly felt an enhanced ability to think with total clarity and focus. He perceived the situation in its entirety. He felt totally alive and in control of his thoughts.

But soon after feeling empowered, anger began growing deep inside his chest, the kind of anger that caused sickness as a migraine caused nausea. Thoughts of what might have happened to the poor girl became the source of his anger. The injustice of the situation stung the most, injustice to Helen, injustice to Sadi, and injustice to all the other victims of similar crimes.

Freddy knew the reasons for someone to steal a child, and he did not want to even think about them. But the situation gave him no other choice. He needed to consider everything. And then for some mysterious reason, he knew the woman from the plane had created the predicament just for him. She had appointed the task of finding Helen to Freddy. It was some kind of sick game, and he would not find Helen in a barn. This problem had a more dangerous solution. The woman from the plane no longer seemed benevolent.

Would she let him fail? Then what would happen to Helen?

He required a few moments for his eyes to adjust to the low light again, to a room illuminated only by the LED lights of his computer equipment. At the moment, he could not perceive the alien's motivation. But how could the motivation matter if the poor girl became permanently scarred or died? He attempted to direct his anger at the woman from the plane, but he only felt anger toward Helen's abductor.

"How does this relate to Gerald Foster and his other friends?" he quietly asked himself, and the sound of his voice helped him escape the darkness of his thoughts. "Why did she connect us?" That question seemed like an important clue.

Compared to other more pragmatic questions, the how and why seemed insignificant, and he should not waste his time on them. He also needed to focus on the evidence and rely on logic, and not allow fear or hope to get in the way.

The kidnapper had taken the girl from a crowded area, which meant they had gained Helen's confidence long enough to take her. Only a convincingly friendly woman or a much younger person could have accomplished that feat, not some degenerate man working alone.

Had the abductor targeted Helen specifically? He or she could have chosen a much easier place to take the child. Freddy quickly saw several good reasons to abandon that possibility. The abductor would have chosen a child from a less fortunate situation. They probably chose children of the poor and ignorant, runaways, drug addicts, or those with parents who relied on the government for help. From personal experience, he knew how many neglected children existed, children left to take care of themselves without anyone to watch over them. Abductors could easily acquire those children. Sadi also had the means and intelligence to perform a comprehensive search.

Before leaving his room and returning to the study, he made a detour to the walk-in closet of another basement room where Mr. Smith kept two pistols. Freddy had never seen Mr. Smith holding a gun, but he had found them one day on the top of a shelving unit while searching for one of Mr. Smith's canes. At first, he had resisted the almost overwhelming temptation to touch one, but then several days later, he had revisited the closet and held one in his hand.

Freddy entered the closet now, retrieved the box with the guns, and then just stared with wide eyes at the two weapons, imagining the feel of the cold metal in his hands again. The sight of them reminded him of the barn incident when he had aimed the gun at the FBI agent's head with his finger on the trigger. He expected the memory to sting, but to his surprise, he felt only excitement. Freddy suddenly wanted the experience of shooting the gun, feeling the recoil.

After removing the gun from the box, he squeezed the grip for a few seconds. The weight of the metal object felt comforting, less impotent in their horrible situation. The gun had a full clip. After sliding the clip back in place, he hid the gun in his inside jacket pocket, grabbed a handful of bullets, and then stuffed them in his other pocket. On the way to the study, he wondered why he felt compelled to get the weapon. The possible answers frightened him.

Could he trust himself with that kind of power? If the situation required him to shoot someone, could he pull the trigger?

He understood the paranoia so many people felt toward firearms, a natural fear intentionally enhanced and inflated by the news, movies, and television programs. Instead of portraying weapons as tools for self-preservation, hunting, or recreation, the media never failed to blame horrible human actions on them. Whenever a story involved someone murdering another person with a gun, they did not call it a murder, they called it a shooting. Instead of calling the criminal a murderer, they called him a shooter or a gunman. Freddy thought it would be funny to call a bear attack a clawing or a biting.

On-the-screen heroes sometimes claimed a higher moral position by refusing to use a gun. They often prevailed against those with guns by luck or the miraculous help of a god.

SEVENTY-NINE

Freddy

Freddy took a deep breath before opening the door to the study, feeling totally unprepared for the overflow of human attention. He already felt drowned in all of their emotions. While standing in the open doorway, everyone stopped talking and turned to stare at him. The pause in the conversation seemed long, but lasted only a brief moment. Sadi looked at him with moist eyes then returned her gaze to Craig who continued speaking to her.

After closing the door, Freddy considered sitting with them but decided to lean against the wall instead, next to the bookshelf. He could smell the leather-bound books, and while listening to the conversation, the familiar scent offered some comfort.

He listened as Sadi answered Craig's questions. Although he felt so many disturbing emotions from the woman, Freddy found Sadi as beautiful as ever. Occasionally, he gazed too intensely at her, and then he would shift his attention elsewhere just before anyone noticed. Then he felt guilty for appreciating her beauty and momentarily forgetting about what she needed.

While watching the scene, Freddy made a surprising realization. His new ability to sense the emotions of others had become much sharper than he had experienced at the barn. Before people spoke or performed any other action like crying or even turning their head, he detected the preceding emotional change and could correctly predict the action.

"Of course, you won't be able to work for a while," Craig said near the end of his interrogation. "I suggest you spend your energy finding Helen, rather than self-pity or worrying about her. Do you have any sleeping pills?"

Sadi could not answer, so Jen answered for her.

"I have some."

"I would suggest taking them tonight, Ms. Jacobsen. You're going to need rest to think clearly. That's what Helen needs you to do."

"Sure," she said as if coming out of a trance. "Yes. You're right, for Helen."

"What can we do?" asked Freddy.

His words brought everyone's attention to him again. Mr. Smith felt surprised at his boldness.

"Nothing for now," Craig answered, intending an end to the discussion.

"What are you going to do tonight?" Freddy asked.

Before the private investigator answered, Freddy felt a growing impatience from the large man. Craig Swenson wanted to begin his investigation, and Freddy was causing a delay.

"Tonight, I'm going to the mall," he said, staring at Freddy as though challenging him to ask another question. "I can get the security guards to let me look at the surveillance footage."

Freddy nodded and attempted to appear satisfied. After Craig stood, he led them all from the room with Freddy at the end of the line. At the front door, Craig turned and placed his giant hand on Sadi's shoulder.

"We've got some good leads to go on," he said. "Hopefully, tonight I can make some progress. Don't give up hope, because I haven't."

The giant man opened the front door and stepped outside, expecting to leave everyone inside the house. When he noticed Freddy following him, he was annoyed. The tall archway protected them from the falling rain.

"Can I talk to you for a moment?" Freddy asked.

"Yes."

"Do you think the people who took Helen are with the child sex trade?"

Craig looked at Freddy in surprise. At the beginning of the interrogation, Craig had already made that conclusion.

"Most likely," Craig said. "But if you cared at all for Miss Jacobsen, it would be best not to talk about that."

"Of course," Freddy said and nodded. "What about trying to find one of the customers, someone who would pay for a little girl like Helen? That would be the fastest way to find her, I think."

"That's a bad idea," said Craig Swenson, his eyes tightening.

"Why?" Freddy asked and he felt the man's intention to frighten him.

Before Craig responded, Freddy decided to let the man remind him of his role in the situation. Craig played the role of private investigator, and Freddy played the role of the poor woman's impotent friend. People liked to put other people in their proper place.

"It's dangerous for one," he began, sounding indignant. "I also don't want you ruining my investigation and scaring any suspects away and attracting attention."

"I just want to help find her, just as much as you do. I will not ruin anything."

"Even if you could contact someone connected to their organization, getting them to trust you would take months, and that would be too late."

Craig's frown softened a bit, and he put his giant hand on Freddy's shoulder. His grip was strong and firm, and strangely comforting. His emotions changed from annoyance to sympathy.

"These people don't just accept any potential client who comes knocking on their door. It's a business, and they will not take an unnecessary risk. Believe me. You don't want to get involved with these people anyway. They're protected by more than just the organized crime ring. They're connected to important and dangerous people, business leaders, government officials, and even federal agents. If they suspect you are a threat, they will have no problem getting rid of you, Sadi, Bill, and Helen, and no real investigation will ever take place. The media will never report it, and you'll be forgotten, end of story. I know how to handle this without scaring away all the disease-ridden flies."

"Thank you for all of your help," Freddy said. He decided against asking more questions. "If there is any way I can help, please let me know. I am willing to do anything."

"I just might," he said, removing his hand from Freddy's shoulder. "But for tonight, I need to work on this alone, without any distractions. I'll keep in touch, goodbye."

Freddy returned to the house and found Jen sitting in the waiting room on the piano stool. She had waited for him to return, so she could relay a request from Mr. Smith.

"They're back in the study, waiting for you."

The emotionally exhausted girl sighed, sad for being excluded but also wanting to ask Freddy a question. He suddenly felt sorry for the girl. Before walking away from her, he paused.

"Do not feel bad," he began. "Sadi's friend, Mr. Foster, shared confidential information with us, information he wishes to remain secret. You and the investigator cannot know of it, yet. But do not worry. If he does not find Helen, I will."

He left the girl, enjoying the small sensation of hope he had instilled in her. When he opened the door to the study, he found Mr. Smith and Sadi sitting at the table again. Without the private investigator, the room appeared larger. He already knew what Sadi wanted of him and dreaded her reaction at the likelihood of giving a disappointing answer. Sadi turned to him with desperation in her eyes, tears glistening on her beautiful cheeks.

"Does this have anything to do with the alien?" she asked. Freddy sat across from her in the chair formerly occupied by Craig Swenson.

She sounded like a woman pleading for her life. As he attempted to prepare the best response, the hope she felt in him became a stinging distraction.

"It must be related," he said. Freddy only knew one thing for certain. The alien had used the crystal to enhance his senses. But for what purpose? Did the alien care about what happened to Helen? "That is all I know."

"What about the crystal?" she asked. "If we look into the spider's eyes, will it tell me where my daughter is?"

"I already tried in my room," Freddy said, attempting to sound sympathetic. "But maybe it will answer you."

He removed the crystal from his pocket and placed the object on the table just as her cell phone began vibrating. She quickly removed her phone from her purse, looking in excitement at the caller ID. Freddy experienced a sharp pain of jealousy when he heard her say hello to Gerald Foster. The memory of how she had looked at Gerald became a bitter reminder of his childhood, how Sadi existed just beyond his reach, nothing more than a friend. He quickly removed the painful thought from his mind and waited for Sadi to finish talking with Gerald on her cell phone.

Freddy decided to act as though he had real hope for the crystal to give Sadi what she wanted. If the crystal failed to provide any answers, as he expected, her disappointment would hopefully transfer from him to the woman from the plane, to the alien.

A light had already been lit in his mind, and Freddy expected no more assistance from the alien via the crystal. While waiting for Sadi to end the phone call, Freddy wondered how the woman from the plane felt about the suffering she had caused. Was she or other invisible creatures sitting in the corner of the room with them, amused by their activity? He glanced suspiciously around the room but felt only the emotions of Sadi and Mr. Smith, and also Jen in the other room.

After Sadi ended the phone call, she slowly set her cell phone on the table. She returned her attention to the space between them, staring at the crystal with wide eyes, fear and anxiety overwhelming her other emotions. She was suddenly afraid of looking into the eyes of the spider and seeing nothing.

She silently reached across the desk and slid the crystal below her chin then focused intently on the spider's eyes. She stared at the multicolored eyes for nearly twenty seconds, blinking as she struggled to focus. Although Freddy did not expect to see any signs of altered consciousness or psychological takeover, he hoped anyway.

When he saw the disappointment in her eyes, Freddy had to look away. Her emotions were too potent. Mr. Smith looked at Freddy with a sadness in his eyes that Freddy had never seen before. His boss had also hoped for the crystal to provide the answers, almost as much as Sadi.

"Ms. Jacobsen," Mr. Smith said after another few seconds. "You should go home and get some sleep. Craig will handle the police and everything. He's really the best. We'll find her."

Sadi did not hear him but lifted the crystal with her right hand, holding the surface between her face and the ceiling. Her hand shook while holding the thin object.

"Where's my daughter? Please, where is she?"

Silence filled the room like an approaching midnight tide.

EIGHTY

John

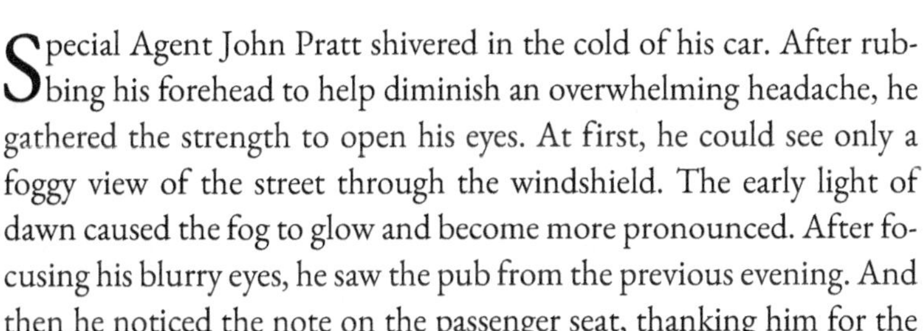

Special Agent John Pratt shivered in the cold of his car. After rubbing his forehead to help diminish an overwhelming headache, he gathered the strength to open his eyes. At first, he could see only a foggy view of the street through the windshield. The early light of dawn caused the fog to glow and become more pronounced. After focusing his blurry eyes, he saw the pub from the previous evening. And then he noticed the note on the passenger seat, thanking him for the fun evening. The author wrote in red lipstick and signed the paper with the mark of a kiss.

He tried remembering the woman's appearance or any events of the night but failed on both accounts. Should he wish to forget her appearance? Sometimes the influence of alcohol made the frightening women appear gorgeous, one reason why he never drank too much. Agent Pratt rarely drank enough to impair his judgment anyway. A good FBI agent should always be on his guard. The woman must have been beautiful to get him drinking.

As much as he wanted the memory to originate from a pleasant and random encounter, something about the memory seemed wrong. Usually, he had two drinks and then went home, but when the woman had sat next to him and started talking, he had felt compelled to buy another and then another. While recalling the memories, his thought processes became fuzzy, transforming into a psychotic fantasy where thousands of dark-eyed Muslims hid in the shadows of a giant maze. Unfortunately, none of the images in his mind even remotely resembled a naked woman.

When he attempted to identify the strange images and feelings lingering in his peripheral memory, they remained just out of reach. Maybe he needed to take a shower, have a coffee, and recover from his damned headache. But alternately, if he waited too long, his memories of the night might fade like the morning fog, like a dream and almost impossible to retrieve.

Agent Pratt started his car and waited for the heat to drive the cold from his bones. He closed his eyes, focused on breathing, and made a mental list of his unanswered questions. Had he gone to her apartment in her car or had he driven? Had he gotten a taxi back to his car? How long had he stayed at her place? Did he just have strange dreams while sleeping in his car?

If he drove somewhere, he should have remembered, but his memory of reality ended somewhere in the middle of their conversation at the bar. He looked at the control panel of his vehicle, and the odometer still showed the same distance since he had filled his gas tank, just as he remembered. Unless they had walked somewhere, or she lived nearby, he must have gone in her car.

After considering all of the benign explanations, he had to entertain the more disturbing questions. Had she put a drug in his drink? If she did give him a drug then she probably had different intentions than date rape. That ridiculous possibility suddenly made him laugh. The woman would not have needed to drug him.

"Think, John," he said while rubbing his forehead. "What's the motive?"

If he could just ignore his horrible headache, he could think more clearly. After another minute of thinking and massaging his temples, he remembered the first motive to always consider, theft. He opened his wallet and noticed the missing money and credit cards.

"Damn you, bitch!" he said in anger, holding the palm of his hand against his forehead. Although his head hurt worse after the outburst, he felt better at finally having a motive. When she'd opened his wallet, did she notice his badge? Strangely, he admired a woman who would steal from an FBI agent.

Before he could continue his investigation, his phone started vibrating in the passenger's seat. With pain in every movement, he turned his head to see the phone and noticed his girlfriend's number on the screen. The thought of talking to her made his pulse pound even harder in his temples. He retrieved the phone and noticed several missed calls, all from her. When he eventually returned home, he would hear a long lecture, so he needed to prepare a good story.

Should he use the opportunity to end the relationship, he wondered with a wry smile. If he could consider that question so indifferently, did the lack of concern indicate a weak emotional attachment to her? But if he felt no emotional attachment, then why did he care about a horrible lecture? His personal life suddenly seemed much more complicated than his job. At work, everything looked black and white. Terrorists and criminals were evil! Ignorant citizens were good! He decided to let the phone continue vibrating. Would one more unanswered call matter?

He drove home, and then after enduring the expected lecture from his girlfriend, he showered and took a nap. He lacked the energy to invent a good story, so he told her the truth, excluding the part about the woman. He had no memory of what happened, and some terrorists had drugged him. Let her chew on that story for a while! Even if he had more time and energy, he probably would have told her the truth anyway. No matter what story he told her, she would not have believed him.

During his nap, he dreamed of racing through crowded city streets, as he did in the *Grand Theft Auto* video game. But instead of shooting and running over strangers, he killed and maimed everyone he ever knew, his parents, old girlfriends, the college kids. He took great pleasure smashing into them all.

—※—

Later that afternoon, he returned to the bar, intending to get a description of the girl and eventually discover her identity. When he arrived, the only customers of the establishment were sitting around a single table. The bartender, a short, blond guy with straight hair, looked busy preparing for the rush of weekend revelers. Agent Pratt recognized him from the previous evening. He went to the bar and sat on a stool.

"Hi," he said as cheerfully as he could manage. "I was here last night. I don't know if you remember."

"Welcome back," the bartender said sarcastically. "What can I get for ya?"

Agent Pratt ordered a beer, but just as an excuse to talk.

"Do you remember me from last night?"

"Yeah, I remember you," he said with his back to Agent Pratt.

"Remember that girl I left with?" he asked with a sarcastic sneer. "What a piece of work!"

"You didn't know her?"

The guy turned and looked more interested.

"Why? Did it look like we knew each other?"

Pratt hoped the man noticed the sarcasm in his voice.

"She seemed interested in you," he said with a smile. "Didn't look like you minded."

"She might show up again tonight. That's why I'm here. I lost her damn number." Agent Pratt paused to take a sip of beer, so the man had time to consider his words. "How often does she come around here?"

The guy stopped wiping the counter for a moment.

"Never seen her before. I would have remembered her."

"Shit," Agent Pratt said and forgot to hide his anger. "I was hoping you would know her name."

"Hell, I don't even know your name," the man said, laughing. "And I've seen you a bunch of times. I see so many people here but only remember a few names, mostly the women, if you know what I mean."

"I hear ya," he replied genuinely and smiled.

"Sorry I can't help you," the barman said with a tone of finality. He gave Agent Pratt an awkward smile and then continued preparing the bar for the evening's customers.

Agent Pratt drank the rest of his beer in less than a minute. While staring at the last few drops in the bottom of the glass, he thought about his next move. Upon arriving at the establishment, he had failed to see any video surveillance equipment outside the bar. From where he sat, he noticed two video cameras inside the bar. If he identified himself as an FBI agent, the barman would probably let him see the surveillance footage without showing a warrant. But he only briefly considered that option. Agent Pratt would keep his alter ego, a financial analyst. As such, he could not ask for private information like the video footage without causing suspicion.

He thought of other options, but none of them would work in the present situation. If Pratt wanted, he could ask his fellow agents to visit the establishment and ask to see the footage. His anonymity would remain intact and the employees of the bar would not become suspicious of a pair of agents, but he could not accept that option yet. If one of his coworkers discovered what had happened, that a woman had drugged and robbed him, he would find himself with a whole shitload of other problems. He might as well quit and become a truck driver. As usual, he would need to invent a cover story.

Before sliding off the stool, he glanced casually at the seating area again and mentally reviewed what had happened to him there. After entering the previous night, he'd failed to recognize anyone, so he'd sat by himself near the same location as his present one.

He remembered the moment of noticing the woman, when she had sat and crossed her legs toward him. She had smiled, and he'd said

"Hi". The clear view of her thighs and breasts urged him to order a drink for them both. The mixture of her skin and the scent of her perfume became the closest thing to a magical potion as he thought possible. As he expected, his memory started to become fuzzy after that first drink.

"Damn!" he whispered slowly.

As he focused on the memory of her perfume, he wondered if the substance had included a human pheromone. Intelligence agencies would use a woman with such a substance but usually for another intelligence agent suspected of duplicity. That possibility seemed unlikely. Jason Smithson knew John would never betray him or the agency. Sure, Agent John Pratt often bypassed established protocol but only to accomplish agency goals.

After he returned home from the bar, Agent Pratt planned to collect a sample of his urine to submit for analysis on Monday, without a name attached. If the woman had used a drug on him, he should be able to detect the components. The identity of the drugs in his system would help shorten the list of suspects responsible. With any luck, the woman would try to use one of his credit cards. He could hope for that good fortune, but Agent Pratt knew to abandon such an expectation. Hoping for luck wasted time.

Without his girlfriend's knowledge, he put a vial of his urine in a small paper bag and hid it in the back of a rarely used drawer in the refrigerator, behind some expired shredded cheese. That night, he took his second shower of the day and while washing his legs, he felt a small stab of pain in his left thigh. "What the hell," he whispered. When he touched the tender area with his finger, it stung again.

"Fucking bugs!"

EIGHTY-ONE

John

After registering at the office on Monday, Agent Pratt quickly followed his Monday morning routine and then left for the drug testing lab. He could not consider sending the sample to the official FBI crime lab. That route involved too much paperwork. The proper procedures were a bureaucratic nightmare. They would require him to associate the sample with an official investigation and then invent a million little lies to cover his tracks. Just considering that route gave him a headache. He would not risk exposure. Using the local drug testing lab made much more sense. He knew someone at the lab who would do the test and give the results only to him without leaving any record of the transaction.

For the present, he would consider the law of parsimony and believe the simplest motive, theft. But he could not discard the most disturbing alternative explanation. Whoever drugged him could have used the robbery as a ruse and extracted information from him. Although that possibility seemed too ridiculous, he knew of many individuals and organizations who would want that kind of access. The name of Gerald Foster materialized in John's mind first, but Foster occupied the lowest position on the list of possible suspects. Foster would not want further interaction with the FBI. He also lacked the audacity.

While waiting for the drug analysis results, he focused on his main work tasks. But before beginning with the priorities of the agency, he arranged for a trace on Foster's car. Management would reject any request for more brick agents to follow Foster, so a trace became the next best option. The airlines would already notify Pratt if Gerald Foster booked a flight, but Pratt also wanted a record of where he traveled by land. Foster often drove to places such as Vancouver B.C., Portland, or Spokane.

When Agent Pratt received the urine sample analysis the next day, his jaw dropped. His worst fear had become a reality. The mass spectrometry analysis indicated the presence of Amobarbital and Midazolam. Immediately, one conclusion failed to make sense. Those drugs had to be injected to have the desired effect, but he should have evidence of an injection. Then he remembered the tender spot on the back of his leg. He felt the area again and then examined the rest of his body and found another tender spot on his other thigh.

"Stupid bitch," he swore and pounded his fist on his desk.

Agent Pratt knew enough about the use of psychoactive drugs and needed no one else to confirm his fears. The presence of the benzodiazepines in his urine would account for his memory loss. Most likely, they had used Versed, but they could have used other drugs. They obviously knew what they were doing, and probably had hired some girl from another city. Trying to locate her would be a waste of time, but he should still check the video from that bar.

The new information helped Agent Pratt eliminate several types of suspects and narrowed the scope of his investigation. In a small way, he felt an excitement for the opportunity to investigate his own case. Rage also helped.

As an FBI agent, he interfered with people's lives. They did not interfere with his life. Someone had stolen information from him, government property. Most likely, he would never remember the events, even if he went to the department psychiatrists, but he could get the information from those who had violated him.

Agent Pratt resolved to punish that serious infraction and make an example of the perpetrators.

EIGHTY-TWO

John

Agent Pratt's phone buzzed. The agent who was monitoring the location of their particular targets had called and then left a text message.

Gerald Foster, heading south. Your instructions?

Pratt lifted the phone from his desk and connected to the agent.

"How long ago did he leave?"

"He's on I-5, heading south. He left Olympia about an hour ago. If he's going to Portland, he should arrive in the next hour."

"Thank you," Pratt said, but before he could cut the connection, the voice on the line stopped him.

"Do you want me to call the Portland office to track him there?"

"No, I'll take care of it. Thank you, Agent Roberts."

Pratt needed to spend all of his time and energy investigating his own case, discovering who had abducted him, not those on his wish list like Gerald Foster. Agent Pratt decided to follow up on Foster later and for a brief moment, he considered dropping the trace on Foster and let him have an unmonitored vacation in Portland, but then he decided not to waste the opportunity.

The previous time an agent had followed Foster in Portland, Gerald had met with the woman from some pharmaceutical company, Sadi Jacobsen. Agent Pratt had investigated the woman's background himself and found her totally benign, except for an interest in the *End the Fed* movement. Unfortunately, he could find no history of legal entanglements. An intelligent and attractive woman, such as Sadi, would likely be one of Foster's romantic interests.

From whatever angle he viewed the situation, he failed to see a logical connection between his drugging and Gerald Foster. Only the most dangerous and boldest criminals would dare drug and abduct a government agent unless by mistake, which was highly unlikely. That kind of action required someone with connections and no fear of the government. Not only did Gerald lack the guts to do something so bold, he also loved to hide behind the law or behind his suspicious clients on the reservation. He worked too openly. Until other evidence presented itself, he would continue to treat Gerald Foster as a separate case.

He dialed the number for the Portland office and hesitated a moment before hitting the send button. In preparation for the conversation, he took a deep breath and practiced smiling.

"Hi, Chuck," he said. "How's the wife?"

Pratt treated Chuck like most other people, as a friend, but he had no real interest in a social connection with the man. Pratt only pretended to like the guy. He knew the usefulness of having reliable social contacts and knowing them on a first-name basis became necessary. Sometimes, when Pratt visited Portland, he spent time with the guy and acted as though they shared the same interests, such as golf, football, and global warming. He only knew the talking points on those subjects, but he personally found them tiresome. Other than rugby, lacrosse, and hockey, Agent Pratt had no other interest in sports.

"I'm doing good, as usual," Chuck responded cheerfully. "How's the girlfriend? Gonna make her a respectable woman yet?"

They both laughed.

"Getting there," said John just as cheerfully. "Hey, sorry to cut this short, but I need your help with tracking someone. We're not a hundred percent that he's going to the Portland area, but it looks like that, and if so, he might be there in an hour. I just need to know who he's meeting and where."

"Do you need a decoy team too?" Chuck asked, his tone changing from jovial to serious.

"No, I just need some pictures. Let me know if you have any problems acquiring his signal. He's not dangerous. It's Gerald Foster. He should be no problem."

The conversation finished shortly afterward. Agent Pratt wanted to spend the least amount of time working on Foster and let the Portland team get the information he wanted. When he had more time, he could follow up with what they learned. In the meantime, he planned to enter the field for his own case.

After realizing his delicate predicament, one of Agent Pratt's long-term cases kept coming to mind, a terrorist organization led by an illegal alien from Somalia, a man living in Seattle with fake identification. He was currently spending time recruiting citizens and other illegal aliens, all Muslim, with the stated intent to destroy Jewish synagogues, although strangely, they had not even attempted any yet. The FBI had been building a case against the Somali man for several years and had successfully inserted an undercover agent as the leader's confidant, and another one of the man's friends worked for the FBI as an informant. The Somali man trusted the undercover agent completely and was responding favorably to his influence.

Pratt knew the bureau could easily provide the organization with bomb materials, either real or fake, and they would have already attempted the act of terrorism, but the CIA kept telling the FBI to delay the investigation. The CIA had other plans for the group and did not want any interference. Whenever Director Smithson relayed a notification from the CIA, he would then patiently listen to Agent Pratt rant about how much he hated the CIA and how they were always meddling in his jurisdiction.

So while waiting for permission to bomb the synagogue, Agent Pratt had another plan. He wanted to use them as bait for a more significant criminal, a money laundering organization the FBI had failed to infiltrate. In a recent stroke of luck, Agent Pratt had discovered a secret back door to the organization. The Somali man had an uncle in the money laundering business, and Agent Pratt had an informant who had access to both of them.

If men from one of the organizations had arranged the abduction, why, and what had they wanted to know? They would only have attempted such a bold move if they felt threatened. Maybe they had discovered the identity of the undercover FBI agent or the informant. Their entire investigation might be ruined and all because of that woman, or his weakness for women. No one could ever discover what had happened. He had to eliminate those who knew anything, or permanently shut them up.

Agent Pratt needed to check on his informant.

Fortunately, no one had murdered the undercover FBI agent yet, but Agent Pratt found no reason to worry about the man's immediate safety. The groups would do what he would have done in the situation, use the spy to feed misinformation back to the bureau.

For that afternoon, Agent Pratt arranged a meeting with his informant to answer the pivotal question: had the man's position been compromised? If the informant was now worried about his safety, then the organization might know of his role as an informant and had acquired the information from Agent Pratt.

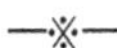

They met at one of his favorite locations, a Barnes and Noble bookstore. He liked the privacy of a specific location in the store, the end of a secluded aisle where two comfortable chairs were conveniently hidden from the public.

He dressed in sandals and old jeans with holes near the knees. A beige baseball cap and a slightly dirty shirt provided the appearance of someone who needed a shower. With just a dab of oil rubbed over his face then wiped away, he could easily pass as a vendor at a hemp festival.

He arrived at the bookstore thirty minutes before the appointment. After checking his favorite aisle, he chose a random book, sat down, and started flipping through the pages. He hardly noticed them, thinking instead about all of the possible suspects he wanted to investigate.

Without looking away from his book, Agent Pratt noticed his contact enter the aisle. The dark Somali man was of average height, five centimeters shorter than Agent Pratt. He wore a buttoned shirt with a dark plaid pattern, no hat, and appeared as a casual customer. Although his demeanor indicated refinement, his short-trimmed beard and dark eyes probably intimidated the average white American citizen.

He sat across from Pratt and opened his own hardcover book to the first few pages. The book hid his facial hair and allowed Agent Pratt to see only his nose and dark eyes. Neither man made eye contact or acknowledged the other man's existence.

"Well, I'm here," said the man after about thirty seconds of silence. "I thought we were finished meeting."

He spoke with a slight accent, diluted by several years of living in the United States.

"Did I ever say you were finished?" Pratt asked and continued without waiting for an answer. "You must have forgotten that you owe us, whatever we need, whenever."

"I do not owe you or anyone else anything," he said. "I cannot change what happened in my youth. That is not who I am anymore. It's just what I was born into. Now I am a contributing member of your society. I've paid back my debts, sevenfold."

"A worm cannot change into a butterfly," Pratt said and snorted. He loved insulting the Muslim. "It stays a worm. It will always be a worm."

"Just tell me what you want," the man answered in resignation.

If the insult had any negative effect, the man refused to give Agent Pratt the satisfaction of seeing evidence of indignation.

"I shouldn't need to remind you that we also know about your father's current involvement with Al-Shabaab."

Agent Pratt always enjoyed this part of their meeting and never failed to reference the details.

"Not to mention that we could throw him and your cousin into a Somali prison hell. That's when you'll see how your bloody Allah rewards his faithful servants. Muhammad would be so proud to see such suffering in his name."

The man visibly winced at Pratt's blasphemy. Agent Pratt kept a steady gaze on the eyes of his victim, to enjoy the reaction. Al-Shabaab, a Somali terrorist organization, claimed many sympathizers among Somali-born US citizens and residents. Several organizations, including the man's family, offered them support. The man had more connections than Pratt could even count and he was enjoying his access to the gold mine of information. Every FBI agent wanted some gold nuggets like him in their pocket.

With the Somali man's connections and those from all of the other intelligence agencies, Agent Pratt figured they could throw all the lawbreakers and terrorists in prison, or just kill them to save the paperwork, but that method was too childish. How could the FBI profit from eliminating them? Some other scum would just crawl from under the rocks to fill the holes in the market.

The FBI could act more intelligently, manipulate the current system rather than wasting time locating and fighting new players. Agent Pratt considered the situation a win-win. Keep this man on the end of a hook or throw his family in prison. Of course, Agent Pratt was not naive enough to disregard the possibility that the CIA had other plans for the organization and they were keeping the operation afloat for their own designs. Agent Pratt had to act prudently, but he despised the necessity. He often fantasized about finding a pair of CIA agents in a vulnerable situation. He considered the CIA the same as Muslims. They were un-American.

"You can insult me all you want and my religion," he said indignantly. "Your words have no power. They will only condemn you."

"Thanks for the warning," Agent Pratt answered sarcastically then changed his tone to one of concern. "Now I have a warning for you, but I don't want you to get the wrong impression. I'm only concerned because your safety is beneficial to both of us."

"What are you talking about?" The man asked, trying to hide his sudden interest.

"Do you sense lately, that they are treating you differently, like they know you've been talking to me?"

The man lowered his book and sat back in his seat. Pratt had difficulty concentrating while watching the man stroke his beard. He needed to watch for signs of deceit.

"I have noticed no such behavior," the man said, offended.

Pratt noticed other emotions in his informant's facial features, concern and insincerity. The man might have noticed irregularities in his treatment, but he was denying his true feelings. Agent Pratt was confident in his instincts. The man was not sure and planned to investigate on his own.

"That's good," Pratt answered, pretending relief. "I need you to tell me if you suspect anything. That's the only way I can help you."

"I will keep my eyes open," he said. "Why do you suspect this thing?"

"We may have an agent who is secretly trying to help your uncle," Pratt said. "I need you to discover who that is and what he told them. Hopefully, I am wrong."

"What kind of organization do you belong to? That you cannot even trust your fellow agents."

The man tried covering his anxiety with a smile.

"It's the game we all play, my Muslim friend."

EIGHTY-THREE

John

The next Monday, Pratt called Chuck, his contact at the Portland office. He had spent so much of his time during the weekend working on his own investigation that he nearly forgot about having Foster followed the previous Friday night.

"Did you get any feedback from the two agents following Gerald Foster?"

"They haven't submitted their report yet," Chuck said as though annoyed to check on another investigation rather than his own. Pratt decided against demanding an urgent response.

"When you find out, please forward it to me," he replied, "and thanks for helping me out on this one, Chuck."

"No problem," he said. "I'll try to get back to you after lunch."

"That would be great. Thanks."

While waiting for the status report, Pratt kept busy, attempting to forget the frustrating weekend with his girlfriend. Her child had ruined two nights of sleep.

When his girlfriend's daughter had awoken them after midnight, wanting to watch a Disney movie, he had expected his girlfriend to refuse and put her back to bed. But to his surprise, she'd agreed, and although he hated all Disney productions, he'd also agreed. He had assumed the girl would fall asleep after only a few minutes, but she had stayed awake in their bed for the entire movie. Agent Pratt forgave himself for relenting the first night, out of exhaustion and a lack of mental preparation, but when the same thing happened the next night, he had attempted to excuse himself to sleep on the couch, but his girlfriend had accused him of lacking spontaneity. So then to avoid a long and annoying argument in the middle of the night, he watched another movie of exaggerated Disney purity.

During lunch that day, he met with a couple of his other contacts but failed to gain any useful information about his suspected abduction. The stagnant investigation had increased his frustration almost enough to contemplate an act of desperation, take the evidence to his superiors. But he would never make such a confession, so Agent Pratt decided to let his subconscious mind work on the case for a while. He would use his conscious mental capacity for other activities.

Chuck returned his call after lunch, as expected.

"What have you got?" Pratt asked, trying to hide his impatience for having to wait.

"John," he said, and Agent Pratt cringed after noticing the tone of disappointment. "I don't know what happened."

"What do you mean?"

"Well, the two agents who followed Foster, they got nothing."

"Nothing?" Pratt asked, more confused than angry. "They don't have any pictures or any contact information, or both?"

"The two I sent are rookies," he explained hesitantly. "But very competent. I don't understand it. I'll have to talk to them more. They're both embarrassed."

A million questions materialized in his mind.

"Was their presence detected? Did Foster elude them? What?"

"No, nothing like that. They lost their cameras, and don't remember what happened."

For the next ten minutes, Pratt extracted all of the information that Chuck had acquired from the two agents. Then Chuck sent Agent

Pratt the GPS log from their vehicle, which revealed a strange story. Gerald had driven to his hotel, checked in, then went to the home of the woman, Sadi Jacobsen. Pratt already knew about her. Foster's next destination introduced another character into the story, some rich old guy. Pratt wrote down his name and would examine his identity later.

After the old man's house, they had driven about fifty kilometers away to the wilderness, to some small farm where they had stopped for a couple of hours. Then the two agents had returned to home base after the farm. Something strange had happened at that site, and Pratt doubted that two FBI agents, rookies or experienced, had just fallen asleep as they claimed.

Another option became apparent. Maybe they had lost Foster on some small forest road and were too embarrassed to confess? Despite his anger, he was compelled to admit the difficulty of remaining inconspicuous as the only other vehicle on an isolated road in the night. That explanation would have satisfied him, but they had claimed to fall asleep, an even more embarrassing confession.

The story reminded Pratt of what had happened to him. Only memory-tampering drugs would explain memory loss. For the next few seconds, Agent Pratt enjoyed an intense anger. Although the evidence failed to connect Gerald Foster directly to his abduction, the coincidence existed and Agent Pratt never let a good coincidence go to waste. If Gerald Foster had played a part in his memory loss, Pratt would find a way to eliminate him. Foster would disappear from the face of the earth, and no one would ever discover what had happened to him. Sending him to jail involved too much work.

"Chuck," Agent Pratt said after asking all of his questions. He used a tone of neutrality, as though the news had failed to affect him emotionally. "Just send me the report and please get the agents' urine and blood analyzed and have them checked for injections. I want to know if they were drugged and by what. Tell them I may want to talk to them once we get the results back. Let's give this high priority. I can take it from there."

—✳—

While waiting for the results of the drug tests, Agent Pratt experienced difficulty focusing on his work. Then the next day, his boss took Pratt to lunch. They usually ate lunch together at least once a month, but they had gone to lunch just the previous week. His boss must have noticed the change in his behavior. Pratt should have hidden the emotional impact of his abduction.

Director Smithson chose a table in an isolated corner of the bistro. After the waitress took their order, the director looked intently at Agent Pratt across the table.

"How's the girlfriend working out?" he asked casually.

"It's about to be over," John said. "That's how it's going. I used to get sleep. Now we wake up twice a night."

"You're finding it hard to throw out a woman with a little girl."

Smithson laughed hard at his friend and employee. Instead of a smile, the director received a cold stare.

"I don't think it's very funny."

"Okay," said his boss, suddenly acting seriously. "Tell me what else is going on. You're not the type to let personal matters interfere with your work. You and I are stamped from the same die."

Although Pratt had neglected to prefabricate a cover story, one came instantly to his mind.

"It's all these assholes I have to work with." He ran his fingers through his hair in a convincing simulation of someone at the point of exhaustion. While talking, he focused his thoughts on the two agents botching the simple task of watching Gerald Foster. The image of them asleep in their vehicle helped maintain a convincingly emotional outburst. "I'm approaching some critical points in some cases, but I have to deal with some real idiots."

"Do you know what makes and breaks men?" Smithson asked.

Pratt turned from his view of the front window and met his boss's eyes. "If I listen to your bullshit advice, can we talk about something else?"

Despite his tone of annoyance, Agent Pratt felt a sincere interest in the man's words. Smithson rarely gave advice or said the same thing twice to anyone. He expected them to remember.

"The people who succeed in this life," Smithson said. "They give everything they've got to get it."

"Yes, and–" Pratt began, but his boss continued as though uninterrupted.

"Those at the front of the race put all their concentration, interest, and soul, if it exists, into what they are doing. Their personal lives come second if they have any to begin with. Their devotion always keeps them one step ahead of the rest."

"Are you saying I'm letting my personal life interfere with my work?" he asked incredulously. "I don't have a personal life when I am working. I wouldn't have even mentioned it. You're the one who asked."

Director Smithson laughed and shook his head.

"That's not what I'm saying. I am telling you that devotion is a two-edged sword. If you let it, it will break you. It's my job, as your boss, to keep that from happening. What I am telling you is that I better not see you at the office for a few days."

Agent Pratt became silent for a moment and looked down at the last cut of steak on his fork. Taking time off would not deter Agent Pratt from continuing to work, as his boss knew. Smithson had given him an unspoken command. Do whatever he needed.

"Okay," he said before taking the piece of steak with his teeth.

After lunch, the director returned to the office and Pratt did not see him again. The next day, Chuck called Pratt's cell phone from the Portland office.

"Hi, Chuck," he answered while driving. "The drug tests come back yet?"

"Yeah, we got 'em," he said with obvious disappointment. "The results came back with nothing. They're clean. No trace of any drugs capable of inducing an altered psychotic state, and no injection points on their bodies."

"Damn," Pratt spat without attempting to conceal his emotions.

He had already accepted the explanation of drugs. Had he waited too long to take urine samples? Although not likely, he still assumed that someone associated with Gerald Foster had drugged the men. For the present, he would not abandon that explanation. He also planned to visit the site where they claimed to have lost their memories.

EIGHTY-FOUR

Helen

While Jen waited in the checkout line, the little girl with light brown hair, who had talked to Helen in the previous store, approached her again. Helen recognized the girl when she touched her shoulder.

"Hi, Helen," she said with a genuine smile, showing an obvious desire to become friends. "Come wait with me outside."

Helen looked back at Jen in line and then at the open area just outside the shop. "Okay," she said.

"We can wait for her out there."

Helen followed the slightly older girl outside, planning to sit on the empty couches there, but the girl did not stop and kept walking. Even after Helen yelled for her to stop, she kept moving. When Helen started running after the girl, she failed to notice her direction, toward the exit of the mall just around the corner. She looked once behind her to the shop where she had left Jen.

"Hey wait, where are you going?" she yelled again.

"My little sister just ran outside," the girl answered without looking back. "Come on. I got to go get her."

The girl ran to the mall exit and held the door open for Helen. "Hurry, so your nanny won't notice that you were gone when we get back. We'll come right back in, I promise. My sister took my favorite Bakugan, the one I wanted to show you."

Helen had an extensive collection of the popular Japanese ball toys, Bakugans, and immediately wanted to see the one the girl had planned to show her. She paused, however, in front of the open mall door and stared outside with disappointment, preparing to refuse and run back to the store where Jen waited. Fear of retribution from her nanny overpowered the urge to see a cool new toy.

But before Helen could open her mouth to speak, she felt a mysterious calm and her fear suddenly disappeared. And then the strange new sensation seemed to speak, as a quiet voice in her mind.

Go outside, the voice said softly. *You'll be all right.*

With her fear suddenly tranquilized, Helen felt no concern about following the girl who was waiting for her on the other side of the glass doors. Helen exited the mall and then followed as the girl ran to a car parked next to the curb, ugly exhaust blowing from its tailpipe. Helen's new friend opened the back door and disappeared inside the dark interior. Helen walked to the car without hesitation, but then stopped and rested her hand on the car door. She did not see any other little girl inside.

Extremely dark tinted windows blocked the bright sunlight, making the interior too dark to see clearly, so Helen leaned in for a closer look. Her new friend had scooted all the way to the other side, and she was hiding her face behind her hands as if afraid.

In her peripheral vision, Helen saw movement and began to turn and look behind her, but someone pushed her into the backseat, her legs still sticking out of the car. She struggled to reorient herself and saw a strange man pushing her feet inside the car, and then he shut the door. The older girl next to Helen had grabbed her shoulder, keeping her in place.

"It's okay," the girl said and repeated the words several times while the driver returned to his seat.

"Let go of me," Helen said in a panic, attempting to free herself from the tight grip and failing to extend her hand far enough to reach the door handle. As the car jerked into motion, an angry male voice from the front seat stopped any other attempt to move.

"What took you so long, you little shit?"

"Where are we going?" Helen asked before the girl could respond. "Please take me back."

The man in the front seat ignored her.

"Don't make me ask again, Daryn," the man growled. "What took you so long? Did anyone see you?"

"Sorry, Mr. Becerra. I did my best. I hurried! No one noticed me, I promise!"

"I've got to get back to my nanny, or else I'll get in trouble," Helen said directing her words to the girl next to her.

"Keep her quiet."

"Yes, Mr. Becerra."

In an attempt to calm Helen, the girl placed her hand on Helen's leg. Daryn opened her mouth to say something, but the man from the front seat slapped her forehead with the back of his hand. Helen jumped in fright, her eyes bursting wide open. As Daryn quietly rubbed her forehead, Helen began scooting closer to the window, farther away from the driver. When he hit Helen next, the force of the blow knocked her head back against the seat. She froze in place, eyes opened wide and tears rolling down her cheeks.

Not in her entire life had anyone ever hit Helen. She sat in shocked silence, her blood pulsating wildly through her veins. She felt like an animal in a trap, waiting to be eaten.

"Get your seatbelts on and shut up."

While they traveled, the man played loud, harsh music on the radio, the kind her mother would never let her hear. The singers used forbidden language to the rhythm of a heavy drum beat, which vibrated her chest and head. The girl whispered several things in Helen's left ear, but she could not concentrate on what the girl was saying. Helen only worried about getting hit again. Her movement had preceded the slap, so she planned on staying quiet and still. She only made movement with her eyes.

Helen required several minutes before she could ignore the horrible lyrics and think about a more pleasant topic, the feeling of peace she had experienced in the mall. *Everything's going to be alright*, she kept saying to herself. While Daryn spoke in her ear, Helen concentrated on breathing, and remembering, and by the end of the thirty-minute car trip, she had managed to get her heartbeat under control. Although the memory of getting hit never completely vanished, she could breathe calmly.

At the end of the trip, the man parked the car in a dark garage and closed the door behind them. While Helen waited for her eyes to adjust to the lower light level, the man opened her door and stood in angry silence, waiting for them to exit. Daryn pushed Helen gently in the direction of the open door, a sharp contrast to the girl's strong grip at the mall. The older girl acted as though nothing out of the ordinary was happening.

"Come on," she said with a wide smile. "It's all right."

As Helen stepped from the car, she noticed the single light bulb hanging from the ceiling and then old tools on the walls all around the garage. The light bulb provided just enough light to show their surroundings. A piece of cardboard covered the only window on the wall, bright sunlight illuminating the edges.

"It's all right, Helen," the girl said again. "I want to show you my—"

"Go tell Mrs. Becerra what's happened," the man said. "Then get to your room. I want to have a little talk with our new friend."

Before disappearing into the house, the girl glanced back at Helen with a worried but sincere smile. Helen remained standing by the car while the man shut the door quietly behind Daryn. When the door shut, Helen felt as though all of her connections to the past had also closed. Fearing to look into the man's eyes, Helen stared at his shoes.

He placed his hand on her shoulder, squatting and meeting her at eye level. He gently lifted her chin so that she looked at his face. His touch made her feel sick, but she feared to resist.

Just breathe, said the tranquil voice in her mind.

"You're going to like your new home," the man said in an almost kind tone.

The physical sound of his voice made her realize how imaginary the one in her mind seemed. That voice had told her to breathe, so she concentrated on breathing. Since the man's words failed to call for a response, Helen just waited. For several seconds, they just stared at each other. His grip tightened on her shoulder and began to cause pain, but his warm smile remained.

"Afraid to talk, huh? In the future, you will be afraid not to talk."

EIGHTY-FIVE

Helen

Helen was tempted to ask her abductor what he wanted, but her mouth failed to open. With wide eyes, he waited another few seconds for her to speak, then he stood and pushed her gently toward the door to the house. After entering the brighter interior of the home, she immediately noticed a dirty and messy kitchen, a sharp contrast to the perfectly clean environment of her home, where her toys only occasionally littered the living room floor or kitchen table.

The kitchen had dirty dishes covering every table and counter surface above the yellow linoleum floor, including some old dirty clothes in the corners. The kitchen smelled of dirty dishwater. The man led her through the kitchen and into a large, much cleaner living room.

If visitors to the home only saw the living room, they would have had a higher opinion of the caretakers, probably assuming the rest of the house to be in similar condition. Two dark leather couches sat across from a large-screen television set in an expensive entertainment center. A round coffee table with a tinted glass top sat in the center of the room.

A woman with blond hair and a cigarette between her fingers sat on one of the couches. Her skin looked old, but she seemed about the same age as Helen's mother. When the woman saw Helen and the man enter, she put her cigarette in the ashtray on the coffee table in front of her. She looked pleased but without a smile.

"Not bad," she said as Mr. Becerra pushed Helen forward for a closer inspection. The woman reached out and touched Helen's hair. When she touched her cheek, Helen flinched and then the woman pinched hard enough to cause pain. "Don't resist me when I'm checkin' you out, child. It's gonna get you hurt. What's your name?"

"Helen Jacobsen," she said quietly.

The woman turned Helen in a complete circle.

"Yep," she said with pleasure in her voice. "She's just what we were looking for. Listen to me, Helen. Next time, you are to speak so I can hear you better, understand?"

Helen nodded.

"Take her to Daryn's room," Mrs. Becerra said to the man, speaking to him as though he was her employee.

Mr. Becerra took Helen down some stairs and into a basement that smelled of mold and then to a room at the end of a hallway. After he opened the door, the man gently pushed her shoulder to step inside the room, but Helen resisted.

"Well, get in," he said, pushing Helen inside the room and then shutting the door behind her.

Surprisingly, hearing Mr. Becerra lock the door caused Helen to feel a little better, as though the locked door offered protection from her abductors. She stood motionless in front of the door, staring at the older girl who sat on the end of a dirty bed, the girl who had helped thrust Helen into her current situation. She felt sick inside, a horrible mixture of panic for herself and pity for her fellow captive.

Daryn stood, walked toward Helen, and then placed her left ear on the hollow wood door. Together, they listened to the retreating footsteps in the hallway, and then Helen heard the stairs creak as Mr. Becerra ascended to the upper level. They stopped listening after the click of the door closing at the top of the stairs.

"Okay, Helen," the girl said cheerfully and walked to her bed again. "He'll leave us alone for a while."

Helen made no response but just stood still, inspecting her surroundings. The dirty room had one bed against the wall, under a small, locked window. A small table sat against the opposite wall, and several dolls littered the floor around it. Paper and crayons lay on the table's scuffed, white surface. The only light came from a single window above the bed.

"Don't worry," Daryn said, stepping forward. "I'm not going to hurt you. I'm sorry."

After recognizing the girl's obscured but sincere sympathy, Helen began to cry, great sobs, tears pouring down her cheeks. Daryn rushed instantly to her side and embraced Helen with both arms. They stood together for over a minute. Neither of them spoke, and to Helen's astonishment, the girl began crying too.

During their embrace, several questions materialized in Helen's mind. Did the girl have no friends? How long had she been there? How to help her? Helen failed to think of any answers, but the tranquil voice from the mall returned.

Just wait, the voice said.

Helen stopped crying and wiped the tears from her cheeks with both hands.

"Mr. Becerra said I was going to get a new friend today," Daryn said when they released each other. She wiped her tears away and then spoke as though their emotional breakdown never happened.

"A new friend?" Helen asked.

"Yeah," Daryn said. "It's going to be great. We can play dolls. You like dolls don't you?" She returned to her bed and grabbed a pair of Barbie dolls from the ground. "This one is named Helen. I named her before I met you. Isn't that cool? And this one's Charlie. I know it's not a girl name, because she's a tomboy."

Daryn extended the Helen doll in her hand toward Helen who took the doll but kept her eyes on the older girl. Daryn broke eye contact and smiled at the doll in her own hand.

"Hi, Helen," the girl said in an older woman's voice, speaking for the doll. "I'm Charlie."

EIGHTY-SIX

Mr. Becerra

Mr. Becerra joined his wife in the living room then retrieved the pack of cigarettes from the coffee table and popped one between his lips. After lighting it, he sat back and took a long drag of smoke then paused three seconds before blowing. He removed the baseball cap from his head, the cap with his favorite local pub printed on the front. He placed the cap on the coffee table.

"We struck gold with that one," he said. His smile of satisfaction glistened on the oily skin of his face. "Just what Mr. Lewis has been looking for."

"How was the slip?" she asked. "Smooth?"

"Like butter," he said, taking another drag of smoke. He watched her flip the page of her magazine, the latest copy of Vogue. "That little shit pulled it off just like I taught her. She's gonna get a big thank you tonight."

"That's good," Mrs. Becerra said dismissively. "You better not lay a hand on blondie. That's the deal. He wants her fresh."

"You don't need to remind me," he said with a hint of derision in his voice.

"Good," she said, ignoring his tone.

"After we hand her over, we'll be set." He tried making eye contact, but she concentrated on the magazine. "You still excited about the plan?"

"The *gettin-the-fuck-outta-here* plan?" she asked, finally tearing her eyes from the magazine and looking to the window, to the darkening gray of dusk. "Of course, but Mexico? We'll fry our asses off."

"Yeah," he said. "But we'll be frying our asses off on the beach. That little girl just bought our tickets."

"I'm gonna give them a call," the woman said, placing the magazine on the couch beside her, face down to mark her page. "I'll bet you anything they'll want her tomorrow night. The sooner we're rid of her, the better."

"It's a shame isn't it?" he said.

"What is?"

"Daryn might only have a friend for a day," he said and laughed.

"We promised her a friend," the woman replied. "But we never said it would be forever."

Mr. Becerra stood and retrieved the phone for his wife.

"What do you think's gonna happen to the girl?" he asked, extending the phone to her.

Mr. Becerra could easily imagine a million, wonderful things he could do with their new captive, and he also knew her probable fate once she left their care, but he wanted to hear his wife give her prediction audibly. He loved hearing her talk about that sort of thing. In anticipation, saliva began pooling on the sides of his tongue. She looked at him with a wry smile on her face.

"For the money they're paying for her, it's not gonna be pretty. Those bastards are sicker than you. That girl won't last the night."

EIGHTY-SEVEN

Freddy

After the private investigator left their home, Mr. Smith attempted to provide some comfort to Sadi and Jen. He repeated his confidence in Craig's ability to find Helen. They just had to wait. He had used Craig Swenson for several years, and the man had always found success. Mr. Smith had faith in his private investigator. Craig would probably find the right clues in the security video footage at the mall security office, sufficient to lead him to Helen that night even.

Sadi's phone buzzed twenty minutes later, and Freddy cringed as she frantically answered the call. He felt her amplified emotions, a disturbing mixture of hope and foreboding, which accompanied every call. Would she hear good or bad news? Had someone found Helen? Alive or dead?

It was Gerald and he had just crossed the bridge over the Columbia River from Vancouver, Washington. He arrived several minutes later at eleven thirty. Mr. Smith told him most of what had happened, but with Jen present, he excluded the part with Sadi and the crystal.

Gerald asked many of the same questions Craig had asked. Mr. Smith answered all of his questions quickly and quietly for fear of reopening Sadi's fresh wounds. In the end, Gerald asked for the name of the investigator, so he could contact him with his other questions. When he suggested for Sadi and Jen to go home and get some sleep, Sadi agreed without protest, to Freddy's amazement. As Jen led her boss to the front door, Sadi followed, feeling dazed and exhausted.

As Sadi, Jen, and Gerald drove away, Freddy watched with a small twinge of jealousy. With his new perception of other people's emotions, he could feel the natural attraction between Gerald and Sadi. In disappointment, Freddy realized that he had no romantic future with the girl he had loved as a teenager and possibly still loved.

Freddy had to wait more than a minute before they had left his range of perception. Without the added weight of their emotions, Freddy could finally stop worrying about himself and decided to focus again on Sadi's predicament. If the worst happened and she never saw Helen again, Sadi would probably never recover and probably lose all interest in life. Freddy would never forgive himself for failing her.

"Freddy," Mr. Smith said a few minutes later. "I know you want to help, but we should let Craig handle things tonight. He needs time to think about it, by himself."

"I know," Freddy said. He felt tired and emotionally drained.

"Are you sure the alien creature won't help us find her?" Mr. Smith asked after pausing for Freddy to look at him. "The alien caused this. Didn't it?"

"I cannot explain how I know," Freddy said, feeling Mr. Smith's sudden distrust, "but this is a test for me. I do not know why."

"A test?" Mr. Smith said, rubbing his chin in thought. "I have no experience in my life to help me think about this. At the barn, I felt no malice from that probe thing, but kidnapping a child is probably the worst thing someone can do. What is your guess as to the purpose of the test?"

"The purpose depends on the outcome, I think. Helen is either rescued or not." Freddy hated to talk about the possibility of failure. "What are the consequences of her rescue? I am not sure if that will help me find her. There are too many possibilities. I need to visit my room and think."

"I need sleep," Mr. Smith said, sighing in sudden exhaustion.

The old man had no remaining energy to ask any more questions and he left Freddy alone in the waiting room. When Freddy returned to his room in the basement, he sat on the bed with the crystal in the palm of his right hand. He stared at the crystal surface for ten full minutes before recognizing an overwhelming desire to close his eyes, fall back on his bed, and succumb to the melatonin entering his bloodstream.

After lying on top of his bed and closing his eyes, scenes of Helen in different situations played in his mind, each situation worse than the last. Monsters were holding the poor girl captive, abusing her more than his foster families had abused him. Freddy could almost feel her waiting and hoping for someone to rescue her. He remembered hoping for someone to rescue him too. He fell asleep with the crystal lying on his chest, dark and visibly lifeless.

When Freddy woke up early the next morning, he still felt physically exhausted and apparently no better than the previous evening. But fortunately, the memory of his horrible dreams faded.

After a quick breakfast together, Mr. Smith and Freddy spent the rest of the morning waiting for communication from Craig, and then finally at eight-thirty, he called with a progress report. Craig had spent a good portion of the night at the mall, watching the surveillance video from the stores. He had several more hours of video to review before he could feel satisfied and he might need to review the video a second time.

Near the end of the phone call, Mr. Smith cupped his hand over the phone and turned to Freddy, his lips curved in a slight smile.

"He saw Helen speaking with another little girl," he whispered. "Craig thinks she had something to do with it."

At the end of the phone conversation, Mr. Smith gave Freddy all of the other information he had learned from the man. Craig saw a man with the little girl who had talked with Helen. He had not yet seen the man's face, but he could clearly see the unique baseball cap with the logo of a local brewery, named Breakpoint Brewing. The cap might indicate encouraging news, that the man probably lived in the area. Craig had asked Mr. Smith and Freddy to research the brewery and find all the places where one could purchase a cap with their logo.

Craig Swenson had two major leads of his own to follow that morning, acquiring more video footage from the male suspect and taking the little girl's photo to social services. Maybe he could determine her identity if she had a record of some kind. From his previous experiences, he had little hope for cooperation from social services. They had so many layers of bureaucracy that almost always impeded a private or police investigation. If he got lucky, he would acquire a good picture of the man with the little girl, and then he could take it to his contacts in the police department who would be more than happy to help him. Kidnappers were likely to have a criminal record of some sort, and Craig hoped the guy had lived in the area a long time.

Mr. Smith was sincerely hopeful during his progress report and was not just putting on an act. Hearing the optimism from his boss caused Freddy to feel better as well, and Freddy was energized at the prospect of helping with the investigation. He ran downstairs to his laptop and started searching the internet for information about that brewing company.

Freddy discovered only three stores that sold the cap with the brewery logo. He called each one to see if anyone had made a recent purchase, but no one claimed to know anything, so Freddy visited them all and asked each of the clerks personally. No one remembered selling any of the caps recently, and he located the caps in the current inventory of only one store. He quickly emailed the disappointing results of his investigation to Craig.

Efforts spent on the investigation helped diminish his anxiety a bit, but after he had completed Craig's assignment, his anxious mental state returned to full strength. He needed something else useful to do. While considering his options, he experienced an inexplicable but undeniable impression. Just wait!

Did the impression originate from him or some external source? At the moment, he could do nothing, and that made him feel like a prisoner on death row, waiting for the guards to come and take him to the electric chair.

He had a required lab at school that afternoon, but he planned to make only a brief appearance to satisfy the attendance credit. His lab partner would have to take a larger share of the work for once. To secure a good grade for himself, he usually did more than his share of the work. His lab partner, although nice, usually paid less attention to detail than he liked. His grades suddenly seemed trivial.

Craig called again a few hours later, just as Freddy was preparing to drive to his lab. As usual, Mr. Smith picked up the phone.

"Hi, Craig," he said in a tone of urgency. "Found anything?"

While Mr. Smith talked with Craig on the phone, Freddy could hear the disappointment in the investigator's voice. Mr. Smith liked to keep the phone volume high and Freddy could hear some of the conversation. The private investigator had found some better footage of the man with the little girl, but he doubted whether any could be used for identification. He planned to take what he had to the police station and hoped the police photo manipulation software could enhance the images for a positive identification.

While Mr. Smith explained what Freddy already knew about the conversation, he could feel his boss's true emotions, and fortunately, they matched his outward appearance—optimism and complete faith in Craig's abilities. The abductor had taken Helen for less than a day, Freddy reminded himself, and that felt comforting.

Before Freddy left the house for his lab, he went to his room for a book he had forgotten to put into his backpack. As he passed the dresser, the dark crystal lying on top captured his attention. At that time, the crystal had no light of its own but reflected the artificial lights in the room just as any other piece of glass would.

He felt a sudden hatred for the crystal. The object symbolized what had happened to Helen. Freddy wondered if Sadi felt the same. After slinging the backpack over his shoulder, Freddy grabbed the crystal and hid it in his pocket, out of sight.

—※—

After arriving at his lab, Freddy decided to stay for longer rather than leave immediately, which was his plan. His lab partner, a girl with light brown hair and a permanent smile, usually let Freddy take the lead, but when he failed to begin lab preparations, she awkwardly started doing them. And then after ten minutes, he turned to her.

"Erika," he said, feeling no need to fake any discomfort. "I need to go, sorry. You can take it from here, right?"

"I think so," she said without looking away from the glass burette. A solution of sodium hydroxide was slowly dripping into their acid solution. After a few more drops, she stopped the flow and looked into his eyes. She wanted to ask why he needed to leave but then changed her mind, not wanting to pry. "I'll be fine. I hope you feel better."

He forced a smile, then turned and walked out of the laboratory. Erika watched him until he disappeared from her sight then returned her attention to the titration. Her brief concern for him became the only positive emotion Freddy had felt for hours. He liked working with her. She was nice. In the parking lot, he just sat in the car, angry at himself for taking personal time when he should have been helping Sadi.

He removed the crystal from his pocket and watched the sun slowly approach the horizon, passing between the sparse clouds. He had only two and a half hours before the sun would sink out of sight. That event seemed important. He slowly opened his palm to reveal the crystal, and then without thinking, he looked into the eyes of the spider. Despite the distaste he felt for the object, he had hoped to become entranced and receive instructions. He was still unable to focus on the spider's eyes, but nothing seemed to happen.

While staring into the eyes, someone knocked on his window, and he jolted as though he was caught daydreaming in a class. He turned and saw a familiar person standing outside his window, his lab partner, Erika. For several seconds, he just stared at her blankly.

"Freddy, Freddy," she was saying, her voice muffled by the glass. "Hey, what's wrong?"

He glanced at his watch while rolling down the window and used the short time to assess the situation. In shock, he realized that while he had sat in his car, Erika had completed the lab.

"Nothing is wrong, Erika. I am okay."

"Have you been sitting there this entire time?" she asked, and her usual smile returned. "What is that thing you were staring at?"

"Just a car ornament," he said, quickly placing the crystal between his legs on the seat and out of her sight. "I, I am okay."

"Our lab is over. Can I help you with anything?"

After convincing Erika of his stable condition, he impatiently watched as she walked to her car and drove away. He had no memory of the previous forty minutes, but he somehow knew what to do.

EIGHTY-EIGHT

Freddy

Freddy felt uncomfortable in his seat and then a sensation similar to hunger urging him to get on Interstate Five and drive south. He would have followed the instinct and gone immediately, but before leaving the parking lot, he obeyed the next urge to look inside the glove compartment. Then he stared at the contents in confusion. Sitting on top of the car registration papers were the gun from Mr. Smith's closet and a silencer. After several seconds of just staring, he remembered getting up in the middle of the night, making the silencer, putting them in the glove compartment, and then returning to bed. Strange that he had forgotten.

Seeing the weapon instilled a feeling of reassurance, and for a few seconds, he imagined holding the gun in both hands and pulling the trigger. Freddy enjoyed shooting enemies in video game worlds, but he had never cared about shooting anything in the physical world, not even a lifeless target. He had never hated anyone enough to shoot them, not even in his youth. Guns would have never stopped his most dangerous enemies, the demons in his head who were always trying to make him feel worthless. After shutting the glove compartment,

Freddy took a deep breath and tried to forget about the weapon and about shooting anything. Out of sight, out of mind, he hoped.

Before following his instinct and traveling south, Freddy decided to visit Sadi. He drove on SW Broadway to the interstate and then headed north toward Hillsboro. On the drive, he gripped the wheel tightly and focused on breathing, an attempt to overcome the horrible sensation of disobeying his instinct.

His decision felt painfully wrong. Freddy needed to turn around and go south. But he also needed to get Sadi. Allowing her to participate in whatever came next would help alleviate her feeling of helplessness, the horrible consequence of stagnation.

After arriving at her house, Freddy pounded the door.

"Freddy?" Jen asked in confusion after opening the door.

"Hi. I need to see Sadi."

"Of course," she said.

Freddy had already felt Sadi's pitiful condition when he'd arrived in her driveway, and then after finally seeing her, he pretended not to notice. Her eyes had no more life in them. She wore the same clothes as the previous day. Her dark hair was now pulled into a messy ponytail. After seeing him, she smiled weakly, and the small action seemed to require all of her energy.

"Any news?" she asked, attempting to suppress the small bead of hope at seeing him. "Do you need to sit down?"

"No thanks," he replied. "I need you to come with me."

"What have you found?" she asked, leaning forward on the couch.

Freddy glanced at Jen then returned his attention to Sadi.

"It might be nothing, but you should come with me."

Freddy raised his eyebrows and nodded his head slightly toward Jen. Sadi nodded then jumped from her seat and ran to the closet by the front door to grab a jacket.

"Do I need to bring anything?"

"Get a small, sharp knife," he said, thinking only that Sadi might need something to protect herself. After leaving the house, Freddy saw Jen watching from the front window.

"Have you found her?" Sadi asked after shutting the passenger door and reaching for her seatbelt.

"I might know where she is."

His answer had the power to crush her hope, so Freddy had to choose his next words carefully. He had no idea where Helen was located, but Sadi did not need to know that. He kept his gaze on the road, Sadi's anxiety adding to his own.

"Where is she?" she asked.

"We need to drive south," he said. "That is all I can say for now."

Before going to Sadi's home, he had felt the need to get on Interstate Five, southbound, but that direction now felt wrong. Instead, he decided to take the Hillsboro Highway south. Freddy glanced out the passenger window at the setting sun and estimated just another hour before sunset.

The departure of the sun from the world seemed like a critical turning point. They needed to reach their destination before losing too much daylight but not too soon either.

"Can I call Gerald and tell him where we are?" she asked. "He went to get some food."

"No," Freddy said, silently cringing at the man's name. "We should not let anyone know our location or what we are doing. I was supposed to do this alone, I think."

"But you came to get me?"

"Yes," Freddy said and nodded.

"Thank you."

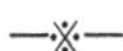

Freddy drove a long time in silence and avoided looking at Sadi. While focusing on the road, he could feel her curiosity. For some mysterious reason, Freddy knew that if he remained quiet, Sadi would refrain from asking the questions he could not answer.

The drive was taking too long, he kept thinking. Every passing minute amplified his fear of what they would find at their ultimate destination, and to make his situation even worse, the effect of so many different chemicals entering his bloodstream had produced a desperation for physical movement, forcing Freddy to constantly shift in his seat and stretch his arms and legs.

Sadi was having the opposite experience. As the terrain flew by them, Freddy could feel her growing excitement. He did not have to interpret body language. Her emotions felt like his own.

The woman from the plane had given him much more than empathy. All of the trauma from his life had already made Freddy empathetic, and seeing others experiencing emotional trauma always reminded him of his own. But after the barn experience, he could feel the emotions of those near him and not just what he imagined they were feeling. Emotions, he had discovered, also provided an accurate prediction of future actions. They motivated the individual to take action.

After the long interval of silence, Sadi suddenly felt afraid and prepared to ask him a question. But before she spoke, Freddy turned to her, anticipating a question about possible future violence.

Sadi met his eyes and flinched.

"Freddy," she said after recovering. "Why do we need a knife?"

"It is just a feeling that I have," he said apologetically, deciding to delay telling her about the gun. "Sorry if it makes you nervous."

"Do you know where we're going yet?" she asked.

"We are going to Salem," he said, suddenly knowing the answer.

Freddy unconsciously pushed a little harder on the accelerator. At their current speed, they would arrive in a little more than thirty minutes, just as the sun would set.

His answer had failed to satisfy her curiosity, so he waited patiently for her next question. He would act as though he did not already know what she was going to say.

"How do you know all these things?" she asked. "What happened to you at the barn?"

"I can feel the emotions of others," he said flatly. "I do not know how or why. The new perception hit me like a ton of bricks after I woke up at the barn."

"Can you feel my emotions?" she asked tentatively, fearing the answer.

"Yes," he said while looking at the road ahead. "I am sorry, but I cannot control it. Emotions give me clues to future actions. That does not explain everything, but it is all I know."

His answer had the opposite effect than he had predicted. Sadi felt pity for him.

"Hmm," she said. "Thanks for telling me, Freddy."

Her words needed no response, and they drove the remainder of the journey to Salem in silence. When they finally entered downtown Salem, Freddy still did not know their final destination. His instincts told him to keep driving. He turned when the feeling urged and drove straight when had no desire to drive in any specific direction. After a while, he began wondering if he had just imagined the sensations and had brought Sadi on a wild goose chase.

But his sensations changed when they passed an elegant, five-story hotel, and Freddy suddenly felt sick to his stomach. Vile humans occupied that building. Their emotions were disgusting, and he wished for the power to spit them from his mouth. The negative emotions contrasted sharply with the beautiful building, which was where the abductors were holding Helen.

"What's wrong?" Sadi asked, looking at the sweat glistening on his forehead.

"We need to find a place to park," he said, trying to ignore the feeling of disgust. "This is the place."

"Where are we going?" she asked as the traffic light thirty meters in front of them turned from yellow to red.

Freddy slowed the car obediently and stopped at the red light. Another car had stopped on their left, and the lone driver glanced at them, an older woman with long, white hair. Freddy could feel her impatience to return home and relax.

"We need to park on this block."

"There's a place," Sadi said, pointing to her side of the road.

After finding a place to park, Sadi waited on the sidewalk while Freddy opened the front passenger door. With his back to her, he removed the gun and silencer from the glove compartment. He slipped the silencer into his pocket then placed the gun deftly in his pants, touching his stomach, and then he covered it with his shirt. Sadi was inspecting her surroundings and did not notice. Before shutting the door, he removed a *Boston Red Sox* baseball cap from the back seat and pulled the visor down low to help conceal his face.

After shutting the door, he turned to Sadi and her attention immediately transferred to him. Freddy took a deep breath then glanced at the western sky. The sun now appeared as a glowing marble sitting on the horizon.

EIGHTY-NINE

Helen

Daryn took control of all the dolls after Helen lost interest in playing with them. For several hours, she just sat on the floor and watched as Daryn made the Barbie dolls talk to each other and do other normal doll activities.

After a while, Helen had gained enough motivation, partly from boredom, to participate in another tea party. Although she still felt extremely disoriented in her new surroundings, with the adults away and sharing her incarceration with another little girl, the experience seemed more bearable.

Daryn filled nearly every moment with chatter, either speaking as the dolls or as herself, so Helen could just listen if she did not feel like participating. Sometimes during their imaginary activities, Helen felt like one of the dolls.

As the older girl talked, Helen's mind raced through a million different ways to escape, but every scenario ended with one of the adults catching her. The Becerras frightened Helen more than the separation from her mother. Her only comfort came when she imagined the police or her mother breaking down the door and rescuing her. Until they did rescue her, Helen hoped they would spend all of their time in the bedroom.

After several tea parties, Daryn showed Helen all of her possessions. Introducing Helen to all of the toys required quite a while, at least a couple of hours. In the beginning, Helen winced as Daryn proudly handed the old, dirty toys to her. She was accustomed to keeping her hands clean, but Helen feared to upset the girl, so she pretended to inspect and admire all of the toys. After only a short while, Helen began to miss her own possessions.

When she noticed the room becoming noticeably darker, Helen expected Daryn to energize the overhead light, but the girl just continued to play as though unaware of the time. Helen decided not to mention it. Maybe the single light above them did not work.

The lower light levels reminded Helen of another physical sensation, the need for food. Her stomach was beginning to ache, and she tried remembering the last time she had eaten anything. Before going to the mall, she'd had a peanut butter and jelly sandwich, and Jen had promised to get her a treat from a kiosk at the mall, but they never made it that far.

Thinking about Jen made her want to cry again, but she stopped herself and focused on their games. Asking for food might result in another unpleasant encounter with one of the adults again, and Helen would rather die of starvation than see them.

—✳—

A short while later, Helen recognized another more urgent impulse. She needed to urinate. How long could she ignore the uncomfortable feeling, she wondered in dread. She did not have to wait long for the answer. A few minutes later, she heard footsteps on the stairs.

At the noise, Daryn immediately rose from the floor and stood to attention. She reminded Helen of a soldier in a movie.

"Stand up before he comes in," she said, extending her hand to help Helen to her feet.

Helen quickly stood and they waited for the door to open. Never in her life had she ever heard anything as scary as the sound of the approaching footsteps and then the turn of the doorknob. When Mr. Becerra poked his head into the room, his eyes fixed instantly on Helen then Daryn. He held a can of Coors beer in his right hand and leaned against the door frame on his left shoulder.

"Bathroom time," he said in a friendly and caring tone, but Helen recognized the man's insincerity. He spoke as though he had an embarrassing speech impediment.

To her relief, she found a bathroom just down the hall from their room and did not need to go upstairs and interact with the woman who scared her more than the man.

Before shutting the bathroom door, Helen glanced back and found Mr. Becerra looking at her through the door frame, his lips curved in a wide smile. The disturbing smile looked creepy and made her even more uncomfortable. On their way back to the bedroom, she expected Daryn to follow, but Mr. Becerra locked the door behind Helen and took Daryn with him up the stairs. The look in Daryn's eyes disturbed her almost as much as her abduction at the mall. Her face turned to stone, reminding Helen of a zombie from the movies her mother never let her watch.

Helen listened with her ear pressed against the door, and when the noise of them ascending the stairs vanished, she felt brave enough to energize the room light. As the room continued to darken, she began to imagine creepy bugs crawling out of their hiding places. To her relief, the light brought a small burst of hope. Helen climbed from the bed onto the dresser and looked through the small window. From her viewpoint, she could see the dark gray clouds in the sky, but when she tried to open the window, she could not hear even a small creak of movement.

Helen sat on the bed for what felt like hours, staring at the clutter of old toys and clothes on the dirty carpet. She would have begun crying, but her fear and feeling of disorientation were acting as an emotional dam. Her heart rate accelerated painfully whenever she heard noise from upstairs. Were they coming for her?

At the same time, every sound brought the possibility of Daryn's return, the only person in the whole world who shared in her misery, who understood her position. The girl who had lured her away from her family was now her only friend. Without Daryn in the room, demons seemed to lurk behind every shadow. Without Daryn, Helen was alone with monsters, in a room of dead dolls.

Another hour passed and Helen began to feel drowsy. Exhaustion had finally overcome her disgust at lying on the dirty bed. As she lay in the fetal position, she rested her head on her left hand, so she would not have to touch the pillow that had been white at one time but was now gray and smelled terrible.

She fought sleep as long as possible, afraid of what might happen if she closed her eyes. When Helen woke several hours later, the room was almost completely dark and she heard a noise. In panic, she opened her eyes and watched as a small shadow slowly approached the bed.

"Hi, Helen," Daryn said in a robot's voice, cold and emotionless.

Without changing her clothes, the older girl joined Helen in bed, lying on her side, motionless. Helen waited for the girl to say something else, but she remained quiet. A few minutes later, Daryn began to cry in barely audible sobs. Helen forgot her fear and the sadness of losing her Mom. She forgot the terror of being shoved into an unknown vehicle, forgot the despair of watching the familiar shopping center fall away into the distance. She wanted only to comfort Daryn, make her feel better.

Helen put her tiny arms around her new friend and held tightly. Daryn's crying stopped soon afterward, and they fell asleep together. That night, Helen dreamed of her mother having tea with Mrs. Becerra. They were laughing.

NINETY

Helen

Helen failed to hear the creaking of the stairs the next morning as Mr. Becerra descended to the basement. He opened the bedroom door and used an angry hiss to wake the girls from their deep sleep. After opening her eyes, Helen instantly noticed the man, sending her heart into a sudden sprint. Gray light leaked into the room from the window above the bed.

"Time for breakfast," he said angrily then disappeared into the hall again, leaving the door open.

Helen followed Daryn up the stairs, wearing the same clothes she had worn the previous day, and then sat at the kitchen table. Daryn shoved dirty plates out of the way so that Mrs. Becerra could place their bowls of plain oatmeal on the table. The oatmeal had no sugar or any other additives but satisfied Helen's hunger. She failed to recall a longer interval without eating or oatmeal ever tasting so good.

They ate their breakfast silently while Mr. Becerra watched the news in the living room, the back of his head to them. Helen kept her eyes on the food until Mrs. Becerra reappeared.

"Thank you for breakfast," Daryn said and put her hand on Helen's leg and squeezed.

"Yes," Helen said quickly, but she kept her eyes on the table. "Thanks for breakfast."

"You girls need a bath," she said in a stern voice.

Mrs. Becerra made them take a bath together with the bathroom door open. Mr. Becerra stood in the doorway and watched while his wife thoroughly scrubbed them. In the middle of the procedure, she turned around to face him.

"Get out of here," she barked. "Don't get any ideas."

Helen cringed at her angry tone, but the man just laughed and then walked away. When Mrs. Becerra turned back to the girls, she squinted at Helen. For a moment, Helen thought the woman had done something nice for her, but the look in her eyes felt colder than the air on her wet skin.

"You're clean," she said. "Get out and dry off while I do your hair."

After giving the girls a towel, she brushed their hair, starting with Daryn.

"Thank you, ma'am," Daryn said when Mrs. Becerra had finished with her.

"You need to look real good for a meeting with a man later this afternoon," she said after starting on Helen's hair. "You're to be polite and do whatever the man tells you. Do you understand?"

"I, I," Helen stuttered. "I don't know."

While waiting for the woman's response, Helen forgot to breathe. Mrs. Becerra shook her head and snorted as though she had just asked a dumb animal to repeat her words.

"Smile and nod your head," she commanded.

The woman smiled with wide eyes, nodding theatrically as a demonstration of what to do. Helen's heart accelerated, but she nodded her head and tried to smile.

"Good job," Mrs. Becerra said in a tone lacking any hint of sincere praise. "You're gonna be in a real nice place, so you gotta look real good. You'll meet a real nice man named Mister Lewis. Now show me what you're gonna do when you meet him!"

"I am," Helen started to say and tears began forming in her eyes, but Mrs. Becerra stopped her.

"No words, just nod, and you better wipe those tears away, real quick. You hear me?"

"Yes, Ma'am."

Mrs. Becerra gave the girls a set of new, surprisingly clean clothes and then left them alone. To Helen's relief, she closed the door and let them dress in privacy. Helen's hands shook as she pulled the pretty, satin dress over her head. Daryn dressed quickly then helped Helen with the rest. She smiled and hummed while pulling up the new stockings and then the shiny new shoes on Helen's feet. Helen felt like one of the dolls.

The girls finished dressing and then returned to their room. After Mrs. Becerra shut and locked the door, Helen recovered her morale enough to attend another tea party with Daryn. They played pretend for several minutes, and then Helen asked a question, but not through the doll in her hand.

"What's going to happen?"

The question wiped Daryn's smile from her face. When she answered, she looked at the ground.

"I don't know," she said in irritation.

After several seconds of looking angry and offended, Daryn's expression changed to excitement. She ran to her dresser and opened a drawer, and then she removed an old Japanese Bakugan toy.

"I almost forgot that I had this," she said with a renewed smile. "You like Bakugans, right?"

Helen grabbed the spherical toy from Daryn, the toy that transformed into a robotic monster. The object reminded Helen of the previous day when Daryn had presented the same toy. She spent a couple of seconds pretending to admire it again.

The next sound made both girls turn their heads toward the bedroom door. Helen stopped breathing. Someone had opened the door at the top of the stairs to the basement, and the stairs creaked as heavy footsteps descended. Daryn positioned herself protectively between

Helen and the door. Several long seconds later, Mr. Becerra opened the door. He was holding two glasses of a strawberry-red liquid.

"Brought you some Kool-Aid," he said with a smile, extending the clear plastic cups to them.

Daryn quickly drank the liquid, but Helen looked at the cup with apprehension. She had never drunk Kool-Aid in her life. Hearing the name caused a vague feeling of something sinister.

"Do you have a problem?" Mr. Becerra asked, his tone turning to anger and his eyes narrowing.

"Thank you," Helen said and then began tentatively sipping the sweet liquid.

Surprisingly, she enjoyed the cool fluid sliding down her throat. Mr. Becerra waited until she had drained all of it. After he took the empty cup, Helen felt a tingling sensation all over her body. Never before in her life had she felt so good.

Helen spent the next two hours in a mixed state of warped consciousness and sleep. As she watched a million different colors swirling around her head, she had no time to feel bad or wonder about her location. She felt like water in a small stream, slithering down a mountain slope, sunlight randomly stabbing her in the eyes. She felt no more fear, just wonder as the amazing sensations passed through her.

At one point, her mother's face floated in the sky, high above. Then a flock of birds flew through her giant cloud face, ripping the beautiful white apart.

NINETY-ONE

Freddy

As Freddy and Sadi walked toward the hotel where the kidnappers were keeping Helen, all of the emotions Freddy had felt as they drove past the building began to creep into his mind again. The emotions of both malicious and ignorant humans combined to form a net unpleasant concoction, like smelling a mixture of fresh flowers and rotting meat.

When Freddy felt Helen's emotions, his heart began beating faster in excitement, but then he had to stop and take a deep breath. He suddenly felt powerless, frightened, alone, surrounded by people who cared nothing for his welfare. Then he realized the emotions came from Helen, not him. Helen's unique emotional signature reminded him of his own painful memories.

A few seconds later, he remembered Sadi. She was looking at him with concern.

"What's wrong?" she asked.

"Nothing," he said, then decided she deserved an explanation. "It is just difficult feeling everyone's emotions."

Before starting to walk again, he took another deep breath and spent some effort focusing on himself. If he wanted to help Sadi and Helen, he had to separate his emotions from those around him. Even though he remained ignorant of the future, Freddy was in control of himself and the situation.

When they turned the corner and the hotel returned to their view, Freddy stopped to study the building. The top floor captured his attention instantly, the fifth floor. The last of the sunlight had reached the top of the windows.

"Is Helen in there?" Sadi asked, afraid of a negative answer.

"Yes," he said.

As Freddy peered at the top floor, he could feel Sadi's confusion and concern. She wanted to ask him several questions, but she chose to remain quiet for fear of ruining whatever was guiding him. Freddy had only one good solid feeling at the moment, Sadi's confidence in him. He decided to focus on that.

"We have a small obstacle," he said after thinking of a plan.

"What?" she asked.

"We need to check in and get a room, but we want to avoid getting caught on their security cameras, and not use real ID. Do you have a fake ID?"

He knew her answer before she spoke but waited for her response anyway. Of course she would not have one.

"I don't have a fake ID."

"That is okay," he said. "We can work around that."

His plan required a room on the top floor, anonymously acquired. Since they had no fake forms of identification, Freddy would have to test the validity of a widespread belief: *You can buy anything in this world with money.*

Freddy had brought a large bundle of cash, more than a person should attempt to carry at any particular time and probably more than the legal limit. With enough money, no one would ask for a credit card or identification. Rich people could get away with murder and all sorts of corruption with what money could buy. Money had its own way of doing things.

Freddy turned from the building to inspect Sadi. She needed to become less noticeable, less identifiable. With her hair pulled back as usual, everyone could clearly see her face. She needed some cover. Freddy wore a baseball cap that concealed his face well enough. But people in general noticed a pretty woman more than an average man.

"Sadi," he said tentatively. "There is one thing I think you should do. Can you let your hair down, to cover your face at all?"

He watched as Sadi untied her hair, shook her head, and arranged several strands over her face. She had no bangs, so her eyes were still visible, but she looked quite different. He found himself enjoying watching the transformation, a momentary reprieve.

"Is that good?" she asked.

"Perfect," he said without emotion.

"So what's the plan?" she asked. "How are we going to get a room without identifying ourselves?"

"I have enough money to get a room without an ID," he said confidently. "I will enter first and go to the front desk. You come in a few minutes later, but just go sit in the lobby until I can meet you at the elevator."

She looked at him in surprise but remained silent. He enjoyed sharing her sudden feelings, complete confidence in his abilities. She felt as prepared as if they had spent several months of planning. Her dependence suddenly caused him to feel even more pity for her. He hated feeling powerless and dependent on others.

Freddy walked alone into the hotel lobby, feeling like a young calf walking through a pack of jackals. He hoped none of them noticed him, so he walked while facing the ground and his hat pulled low over his face but not far down enough to raise suspicion. After sensing his emotional effect on those in the lobby, he felt better. No one felt any curiosity about him.

The front desk on his right came into view almost immediately. A short, plump woman with a pretty face stood behind the counter, looking down at a computer screen. Despite her cheerful appearance, he sensed her impatience. She planned to go home in just a short while and wanted to avoid any extra work.

He approached her slowly. When he arrived at the desk, she failed to acknowledge his presence, so he pretended to admire the painting on the wall to his right, an abstract piece of boxes with sharp corners and pastel colors. A moment later, she looked up from the computer screen and he whipped his head around to meet her eyes. She jolted at his quick action.

At the instant of eye contact, Freddy knew the woman had an awareness of illegal activities occurring on the top floor above them, but since those activities failed to affect her, she did not care. As long as she received a steady paycheck, they could do whatever they wanted. Her attitude of indifference added to his anger, but he forced his lips into a smile.

"I would like a room," Freddy said, but before she could ask a follow-up question, he placed five hundred-dollar bills in front of her. "Is something on the fourth or fifth floor available, facing west preferably? I love a good view."

She swallowed nervously before answering.

"Would you like the Emperor Suite?"

He looked curiously into her eyes and recognized the word *emperor* as a code word. She had mistakenly suggested the *Emperor Suite* instead of following the guidelines to wait for the guests to make the specific request. He needed to act confused and refuse the suggestion. If he agreed, procedure required that she notify her manager, which would delay her from leaving for the night. Her mistake suddenly caused a feeling of annoyance. Freddy glanced at the list of rooms on the wall behind her and failed to see any room listed as an *Emperor Suite*.

"No," he said, acting confused. "Nothing special, just whatever this will get me."

"Okay," she said innocently while cursing herself for her blunder. "I'll need to see a credit card."

She experienced difficulty maintaining eye contact with him when she just wanted to look at all the money on the table. Freddy reached his hand into his back pocket and acted as though he had made a disappointing discovery.

"Oh, sorry, but I forgot my credit card. Is this enough? I do not need a receipt."

He looked casually at the money on the desk between them, raising his eyebrows as if slightly annoyed.

"Yes, this will cover it," she said quickly, finally understanding what he meant. She pulled the bills toward her and they disappeared behind the desk.

Freddy recognized Sadi's proximity before she appeared in his peripheral vision. She was walking past him toward some couches in the lobby. The woman behind the desk did not notice her. She was focusing her full attention on the money and how she could maximize her share. She would give him a good room, the least expensive option with whatever discounts at her disposal, and then she could claim the remainder of the money for herself.

The woman quickly completed the transaction and extended his room access card in her left hand, an apartment on the fourth floor. As he took the card, he smiled politely but felt annoyed at the woman for profiting from him. Without saying another word, he turned and joined Sadi at the elevator.

Even though Sadi had missed taking a shower for the past few days and in general looked disheveled, standing by her made Freddy's heart skip a beat. Her dark hair hanging around her face caused her eyes to appear more mysterious and beautiful than usual. He felt a sudden temptation to put his arm around her to offer comfort. He knew the action was an appropriate gesture, but he lacked the courage.

While waiting impatiently for the elevator, Freddy realized why he probably should have visited Salem alone. Sadi's proximity was hampering his ability to concentrate. He needed to focus on Helen and her captors, not fight his sexual instincts. But despite the extra effort, he did not regret bringing her. He was standing in a pond full of alligators, but he had a friend. When the time came for them to separate, then he would feel all alone. And he would have to face all the sharp teeth by himself.

His heartbeat quickened when the elevator door opened. He let Sadi enter first then followed her inside. After the door had closed, he sighed with relief. They had completed the first step of his plan, and no one had taken any particular notice of them except for the front desk attendant, and she planned to go home in a few minutes. During the elevator ride, Freddy breathed deeply and let his body relax. He needed to prepare for the next step.

"Freddy," she said, grasping his shoulder and squeezing. She spoke in a whisper, slowly but saturated with impatience. "Where's Helen? Is she on the fourth floor?"

Freddy considered his words carefully. They had only a short time in the elevator to talk. The elevator door was going to open on the third floor for an old man and he would ruin any further verbal communication.

"Helen is not on the fourth floor," he said and pointed to the third-floor indicator light that just illuminated. "I will explain when we are safely in our room. A man will be entering soon."

As expected, the elevator door opened and a tall man in his late sixties stepped inside the carriage. After pushing the button for the first level, the old man tipped his head to Sadi and smiled.

They encountered no one else on the way to their room on the fourth floor. They walked on a light blue carpet decorated with elegant red swirls and circles. Gold-painted trim ran horizontally down the middle of each wall, separating the white surface above from the ebony below. But the beautiful hallway and quiet atmosphere failed to instill the intended tranquility.

After shutting the door to their room, Freddy ran to the window on the far wall and looked through the thick curtains. Sadi followed him hesitantly as though some predator lurked in the space behind the curtains. The only illumination came from the window. Freddy shut the curtains after Sadi reached him.

"Helen is in one of the rooms on the fifth floor," Freddy said, turning to face her. "I need you to stay here while I go get her. It may take more than an hour, so please try to be patient, although I know that will be difficult. I am sorry."

"What is she doing here?" Sadi asked, hope in her voice but fear in her eyes. She brushed hair away from her cheeks and tucked it behind her ears.

"I do not know," Freddy lied. He could not tell Sadi the horrible truth. "But I am getting her back."

Freddy returned to the apartment entrance and then paused after placing his hand on the door handle.

"Do not be concerned when the hotel loses power. That will be my distraction."

NINETY-TWO

Sadi

After Freddy left her alone in the hotel room, Sadi made several trips from the window to the door and back again. Every time she reached the door, she would put her ear to the wood and listen. But she never heard any sound from the hallway. She had expected to hear at least some noise coming from the rooms above or below her, but no sound came from them either. The silence in the apartment felt like a lead blanket of depression weighing down on her.

While waiting in the darkening room, she felt an irrational fear warning her to keep the lights off. Light had become her enemy and might attract unwanted attention. Even though no one in the hallway would know of her presence with the lights illuminated, she decided to take no chances.

As the time passed, Sadi fought a growing temptation. She wanted to run up the stairs to the fifth floor and kick in every door. If she'd had a gun, probably nothing would have stopped her from following her instinct. To help pass the time, she opened her purse, withdrew the knife, and then just sat on the bed, watching the blade reflect the low light from the window. Disturbing visions played in her imagination, wielding the knife against her daughter's captors.

"Breathe, just breathe," she whispered, and the sound of her voice seemed to help expel the invisible demons from the room. "You can't help her if you lose control. Freddy knows what he's doing."

She had to trust Freddy. He claimed to know Helen's location, the pivotal piece of information required to rescue her, and he seemed willing to risk his life for them. He had only to get her now.

Not only could Freddy feel the emotions of others, he also seemed to know what they were going to do. He had answered her unspoken questions on several occasions and he had predicted the man entering the elevator. At the time, his actions had made her feel uncomfortable, but the memories now gave her hope.

Sadi refused to entertain the idea of Freddy being wrong, traveling to the wrong hotel in the wrong city. She had no room to doubt her faith in him.

She had also made the correct decision not to call the police. The police would have ruined any chance of finding Helen. She could not call them anyway. She could not tell them the story of Freddy and the crystal, or about Gerald's group. Even if she could have convinced them to come to the hotel, what could they do, break into every room? No, the police could only knock on a door, ask a few questions, and then move on to the next door.

After fifteen minutes of standing at the window and scanning the parking lot and the traffic in the street, Sadi lay on the bed and closed her eyes. While she lacked the ability to sleep, she hoped the bed would help her focus on listening for any noise from the floor above her.

When she closed her eyes, she felt a strong desire to sleep forever, a one-way ticket to oblivion. But no matter how much she wished for an end to her suffering, she could not abandon her daughter. Without Sadi, Helen would be forgotten. That thought scared her more than anything else. Jen lacked the resources to continue the search, and her brother lacked the intelligence. Sadi could never quit.

—✳—

A few minutes later, Sadi noticed a subtle change in her surroundings. The low humming of the air conditioner had stopped, leaving the room in an eerie quiet. And then she heard the faint sounds of people moving in the rooms around her. She listened for a few seconds before sitting up on the bed and opening her eyes. The light in the room had become significantly darker, so she ran to the door to the hallway and slid her hand over the wall until she felt the light switch. When she flipped the switch, the room remained dark.

While holding the knife in her left hand, she opened the door slowly and found the hallway darker than her room. After turning to face the room again, she noticed the light from the window had also become significantly lower. Then the sound of a door opening in the hallway to the left caught her attention, and Sadi could see a low light through the newly opened door. The light was probably from a smartphone, she guessed.

"Power's out," an older woman said from the open doorway.

"I bet it comes back within five minutes," an older male voice replied. "They won't let it stay out that long."

After realizing the cause of the power outage, Sadi felt an immediate surge of hope and amazement at Freddy's success. She wanted to run from the room and start looking for her daughter, but then she remembered in disappointment that she still could not go breaking down doors. Before making any rash decisions, she shut the door and decided to follow Freddy's instructions and wait for him. While walking back to the window, she heard a series of knocks on the door.

With her heart pounding, Sadi ran back to the door and tried looking through the peephole, but she saw only darkness. She imagined Freddy and Helen standing on the other side, only centimeters away. She took a deep breath, the knife clutched tightly in her hand, and then she heard a familiar voice.

"I am back, Sadi," Freddy whispered. "You can open the door."

After recognizing Freddy's outline in the darkness, Sadi stepped out of the way to let him enter, and then a heavy disappointment swept over her after he shut the door. Helen was not with him.

"I need the knife," he said and then extended his hand.

The blade shimmered in the faint light from the window, almost becoming a light of its own. Sadi stared at the blade for a moment. Holding the knife had provided a feeling of empowerment. After forcing herself to relinquish the weapon, Freddy placed it carefully in the back of his pants.

With the weapon out of sight, several questions materialized in her mind. How had he cut the power to the hotel? What would he do next? How much time did they have?

"We are going to find Helen," he said before she could ask the first question. "She is on the fifth floor. When we get up there, I am going to find a hiding spot for you, and you need to stay there until I get you. Do you understand?"

His tone provided no option for a verbal answer, so she just nodded. She had never seen Freddy so confident, so decisive, not even at the barn. His confidence seemed to flow into her, raising her hope. For the first time since losing Helen, Sadi could actually imagine finding her daughter alive.

Freddy pulled her into the hallway and then let the door swing shut while deciding what to do. He paused for only a moment before turning to the right and then walking toward a soft green glow coming from the end of the hallway. After walking past a few doors, Sadi noticed the source of the green light, an EXIT sign hanging above the entrance to the stairwell.

When Freddy grabbed the door handle to the stairwell, Sadi suddenly felt afraid. What if hotel security was coming up the stairs looking for him? What if the kidnappers were coming down the stairs? Then she remembered his enhanced perception. Freddy would probably sense if someone was coming in their direction.

She followed him into the stairwell, which was also lit by a green EXIT sign. But despite the light, Sadi still felt afraid, so she grabbed his hand while they walked side by side up the stairs. Although each step brought her closer to her daughter, his hand felt like her only connection to reality. She remembered her vision at the barn when she had walked with Helen through the dark tunnel. If she released his hand, she might become lost.

When they reached the top step, she reluctantly let go of Freddy's hand. He quietly stepped to the door and then turned to face her.

"Wait for me at the top of those stairs," he said, nodding to the last flight of stairs on his left. "When it is safe, I will return for you."

"Why can't I go with you?" Sadi asked, looking up the stairs. They ascended into what looked like an impenetrable shadow.

Sadi shuddered at the thought of entering the darkness alone. Without waiting for her to move, Freddy returned his attention to the door. On the other side, Sadi heard muffled speech, but she failed to distinguish any words.

"There are a lot of bad people out there," he said quietly with his back to her. "These people have security, and I cannot protect us both beyond this door. Please just go to the top of the stairs and wait for me. These stairs lead to the roof, which is probably locked. No one will be going up there."

"If you don't come back, what should I do?"

"Call Craig," he said then paused. "Actually, do not make any calls. They can be used later to find you."

"I don't give a damn about that," she said. "I'm not leaving without Helen, so you might as well let me come with you."

"You cannot help Helen if you are dead," he said pleadingly. "Please, just wait for me up there. If I do not return, do whatever you feel is right."

Freddy pushed her gently in the direction of the stairs, but she resisted. All of the despair she'd felt since Helen's disappearance suddenly crashed down on her head again, and her confidence in him faltered.

"Why are you so sure that you can handle this?" she asked, his hand still on her shoulder. "This is my daughter we're talking about. Why should I put my faith in you?"

"I told you," he said, returning his attention to the door. "I know what these people are feeling. I know where they are and can anticipate what they are going to do. I will give everything to retrieve Helen."

From the tone of his voice, she knew that her emotional outburst had failed to alter his plan. He released her shoulder.

"Sorry, Freddy," she said, wiping new tears from her eyes. "I didn't mean to doubt you. Please be careful!"

"Thank you, Sadi."

Freddy waited until she had walked to the stairs and began her ascent. But after Sadi took five steps, the silence caught her attention. She turned and saw Freddy facing the door as though frozen in time. The scene reminded her of an actor in a play, listening for the cue to go on stage. Without looking back, Freddy opened the door and then disappeared.

PART VII

ANXIETY

When stuck in another head
You can't change the channel
When all turns red

NINETY-THREE

Freddy

Sadi's hand on his shoulder had shocked his whole system. Holding her hand as they ascended the stairs had sent pulsating electrical currents through his body. The energy helped pump his heart, draw in breath, and forget for a moment, the swirling rage filling his mind.

After leaving Sadi in their room, Freddy cut the power to the hotel in three different places. The hotel staff and maybe even technicians from the local power company would experience difficulty restoring the power before midnight. He knew the hotel staff would need to call the power company, but they would also call the police, an unfortunate consequence he had preferred to avoid. He hoped to finish before the police came and stopped the hotel guests from leaving.

Freddy had maneuvered stealthily through the hotel with ease. His ability to feel the emotions of others gave him a tremendous advantage. Emotions became the key to understanding people. Logic and rational thinking had less influence on humans than their feelings. He knew the location of each hotel staff member. He also knew what they would do if they encountered him and when or if they would change their location.

In the twenty minutes required to cut the power, he had also managed to destroy the computer that stored the surveillance video. Before rejoining Sadi, he had taken the disc holding the video footage. In a different situation, without the disgusting emotions of kidnappers and pedophiles, he might have even enjoyed the experience.

As Sadi began walking up the stairs, Freddy stepped to the door and waited a few seconds for his heart rate to return to normal. He needed a moment to recover from the excitement of physical contact with Sadi and prepare for the next phase of the rescue. With some reluctance, he turned his attention to the emotions of those on the fifth floor and especially to those just beyond the door in the hallway. He felt impatience and annoyance from the people in the hotel, those who waited for the restoration of electricity, and those who knew nothing of the activities at the far end of the hallway, where hideous emotions boiled—toxic gases escaping from a tar pit.

The flood of foreign emotions shocked him as Sadi's touch had shocked him. Against his will, Freddy suddenly felt a lack of concern for the welfare of others, especially defenseless children, and then he experienced the disturbing enjoyment of their suffering. He felt a lust for money stronger than a respect for life. He was beginning to feel like an empty shell, a human body without a soul.

Before entering the hallway, Freddy realized the reality of his mental situation. A potential chasm was standing just beyond the door. An emotional tsunami had already crashed over him, and if he failed to grab something substantial, the immense wall of water would sweep him away. When he put his hand on the door handle, the cool metal on his skin felt like an electrical ground to neutral Earth. He spent the next few seconds of relative calm to evaluate the situation.

Ordinary tenants filled most of the occupied rooms on the fifth floor, but the illegal sexual services took place in the last rooms at the far end of the hallway. No one would pass those rooms unless they had specific business to conduct. The hotel restricted access to the rooms and strictly enforced their scheduled maintenance and cleaning. Most of the hotel employees just thought of the rooms as reserved for VIP guests who desired anonymity, people such as wealthy foreigners, businessmen, celebrities, and the occasional well-known politician. Freddy would probably fail to recognize many of the guests, the ones never spotlighted by the media.

His new perception indicated that two wealthy men occupied the rooms that evening, men with a sense of superiority: a strange foreigner and the one who had purchased the evening with Helen.

A new thought made Freddy pause. What if he failed and they lost Helen forever? Maybe the woman from the plane had designed the situation for him to fail. Although he could not fathom a reason why, Freddy could not change course now. He had already jumped in the strong current and could not swim back to the shore.

When he focused again on Helen's unique emotional signature, her purity and terror forced him onward and erased all of his doubts. He drew a deep breath, opened the door, and noticed a small light at the end of the hallway. A tall man stood with his back to a door, holding a flashlight with the beam shining on the floor.

The door behind Freddy clicked shut and the man shined the flashlight beam down the hall. As Freddy walked toward the light, he extended his hand as a shield.

"Thanks for the light, but can you get it out of my face?"

NINETY-FOUR

Freddy

When the man guarding the door saw Freddy, his concern vanished and he felt foolish for shining the light in the face of a stranger. With the loss of the hotel's electricity, the man felt more wary than usual. But he could not remember the hotel ever losing power, and the service had never experienced any trouble either, so he felt no reason for concern by a stranger appearing in the hallway.

"Sorry," the guard said and then aimed the flashlight beam back to the ground. "Hey, do you know what's going on, when the light's coming back on?"

"As far as I know," Freddy answered, casually walking closer and counting several doors between them. He thought of a lie to help the man feel more relaxed. "The lights should return soon."

"Great, thanks," the man said. He leaned against the door again and quickly lost interest in Freddy.

While slowly walking down the hallway, Freddy turned his attention to the emotions of those occupants in the rooms before him and found most of the occupants waiting impatiently for the restoration of the power, so they could go back to watching television. Only the last few rooms were unoccupied, the ones closest to Helen. The hotel management kept those vacant as a buffer.

The fear from the children suddenly became too palpable, and a wave of dizziness forced Freddy to grasp the wall for support. Fortunately, the man did not notice. To help maintain a relaxed appearance while walking the rest of the way, he unclenched his teeth and focused on breathing deeply.

His short walk seemed like an eternity, and when he finally stopped, his heart was racing as though he had just run up a flight of stairs. Freddy stood at the last room, which would fail to raise the man's suspicion, the final room for ordinary hotel guests. Only three doors separated Freddy and the guard. He felt Helen's emotional signature two rooms over, but he had to deal with the guards first.

With the guard on his left, Freddy placed his left hand in his pocket, retrieved his door key card, and then pulled the knife with his right hand from the back of his pants, careful not to cut his skin. The gun remained strapped between his stomach and belt buckle. He liked the feel of the weapon pressed firmly against his skin.

With exaggerated impatience, Freddy pretended to slide his key card in the door lock a couple of times. An elderly couple occupied the room and did not hear him, but the man at the end of the hallway made them uncomfortable, and they preferred just to wait inside their room and avoid any possible confrontation.

"Damn it," Freddy said loud enough for the man to hear. "I forgot about the lock on the doors. The power is out."

The man shined his flashlight at Freddy again. He said nothing and just grunted in acknowledgment.

"Excuse me," Freddy said innocently, attempting to get the man's attention.

"Yeah," the man said, a feeble attempt to satisfy social propriety.

Freddy sensed the man's annoyance. The guard felt no interest in helping Freddy or anybody. He just wanted the lights restored, so he could continue with his usual routine. Freddy was relieved by the negative reaction. The man lacked the instinct to offer assistance to someone in need. His lack of common courtesy helped justify what Freddy had planned for him.

"Could you give me some light?" Freddy asked. "I might be inserting this the wrong way."

"It's not gonna work," the man said, glad for the excuse to refuse assistance.

While keeping the knife out of sight, Freddy began walking toward the guard. But after two steps, his hand began shaking, so he pressed the knife more firmly to his side.

"I thought maybe the doors were battery-operated," Freddy said. "I will just wait out here with you for a bit. The lights should be back on in a few minutes."

As Freddy slowly closed the distance between them, he attempted to keep the conversation going. For the first time in his memory, Freddy felt no concern about his proximity causing discomfort in someone. The guard pretended to act disinterested, but his anxiety levels rose slightly, not from fear, but from the need to choose a course of action.

"Are you locked out of your room too?" Freddy asked, attempting to appear interested in wasting time rather than gathering information.

The man hesitated before responding.

"No, my friend can let me in," he said.

From the man's build and stance, Freddy guessed at his defensive capabilities. From what the man felt, Freddy knew the weapons he possessed. The man had a gun in a holster under his jacket, a stun gun in one pocket, and a knife in his belt. He weighed about twenty kilograms heavier than Freddy, stood four centimeters taller, and felt no concern about Freddy posing any kind of threat.

Freddy stopped two meters from the man and leaned against the wall at his right in a manner consistent with continuing the conversation. In his life, he had experienced many people who liked to talk even when their audience showed no signs of interest, and for the first time in his memory, Freddy became one of those people. While smiling, he tightened his grasp on the knife. The darkness hid the sweat on his forehead.

"I have never heard of the power going off in a hotel before. Have you?"

The man's annoyance suddenly transformed into a higher state of tension. He flexed his muscles instinctively and shifted his stance to prepare for sudden movement. Freddy decided to delay his plan.

"I am glad to have some company in the dark," Freddy said. "Carrying a flashlight is not a normal habit for me. I should probably get one."

"Listen," the man said, exhaling in half-contained impatience. "I'm not in the mood for conversation, so just go wait by your door please, or wait in the lobby and come back later."

"Sorry," Freddy said and cleared his throat to hide the dark anger pumping through his veins. Anger suddenly calmed his shaking hands and helped prepare him for action. "It is just creepy in the stairwells. I do not want to go back in there."

The man was tempted to insult Freddy for not bringing his own flashlight, but he decided to keep his mouth shut and face the opposite wall again. He hoped the silent treatment would expedite Freddy's departure.

"Maybe that stairwell is better," Freddy said, nodding to the green EXIT sign at the end of the hallway, just past the guard.

The man made no indication of hearing Freddy and was staring at the wall like a statue in a museum. Freddy felt suddenly like the only living thing in the hallway. Not even the flashlight beam on the floor seemed alive. During the brief silence, Freddy wondered if he would lose his nerve, but then the distress he felt from Helen and the other children energized all of the muscles in his body. While squeezing the hilt of the knife, he drew a deep breath and began walking toward the exit.

After taking just a few steps, Freddy jumped at the man like a grasshopper. Although sweat from his hand made the hilt slippery and he lacked experience fighting, anger and urgency guided his aim.

Without much resistance, the knife penetrated the man's neck, slipping through his skin and stopping on his spinal column. Ignoring his instant disgust, Freddy quickly withdrew the blade while keeping pressure to the right and cutting through the internal and external jugular veins. He moved too swiftly for the man to do anything other than attempt to grab Freddy's forearm. But by the time his fingers had made contact, his muscles had lost all their strength.

Freddy kept pressure on the man's neck, holding him against the wall while his body slid slowly to the floor. The flashlight rolled from the man's hand, stopping on the floor with the beam of light shining on the opposite wall. Freddy stared into the man's eyes until the life had entirely left them. Warm blood splattered from the wound onto his hand and felt sticky between his fingers.

In the dim light, Freddy was paralyzed, staring with shock and disgust at the horrible scene in front of him. After the flow of blood from the man's neck became only a trickle, Freddy backed away from the corpse. The sweet smell of blood was making him start to gag. He wiped the blood from the knife and his hands onto the man's clothes and then slid the knife back into his pants.

Freddy needed to remove the body quickly from the hallway, so he grabbed the flashlight and found an open lobby area across from the door to the stairs. Without any other options, he decided to drag the body there.

He set the flashlight on the floor, facing the direction of the small lounge, and then dragged the hundred-kilogram corpse down the hall. The trail of blood would look menacing when the lights were restored, but in the low light, the trail appeared only as a shadow. He also needed to avoid stepping into any of the blood, so that police investigators would not easily determine his weight, height, or the pattern in the soles of his shoes.

After placing the body in the corner of the small lounge, Freddy returned to the door of the man's death. While cutting the hotel power, he had worn a pair of nitrile gloves from his lab supplies and then returned them to his pockets. The gloves would have saved Freddy from having to feel the blood, but the man would have become suspicious if Freddy had worn them in the hallway. He slipped the gloves over his hands again, put the flashlight in his jacket pocket, and prepared for the next phase of the rescue operation.

Freddy attempted to forget the shock of his violent action and focused his perception on the occupants in the first room. One of the four children remained with two adults, a young boy. With the power out, the men had decided to postpone a video with the kids.

While Freddy had killed the guard and dragged his corpse down the hallway, they had moved Helen and the two other children to the next room through a secret passage, and then they had moved Helen to the third room, to join the man who purchased her.

The remaining younger boy felt temporary relief at the loss of power, but he knew that when the power returned, the adults would probably make the video with him and the other children. The child's terror at disappointing the two adults became Freddy's terror and ultimately added to his anger. Each wave of anger transformed into energy. Freddy almost felt strong enough to break down the door with one hand.

In the adjacent room, the other boy and girl feared displeasing the client, a single adult man. The man was frustrated at having to wait for the lights, but he seemed to have no violent emotions, only a disgusting lust. The children knew that if the client gave a bad report of the experience, their handlers would punish them.

Before knocking on the door, Freddy removed the gun from under his belt and slowly twisted the silencer around the muzzle. The metal threads squeaked as they slid together, but the sound was too quiet for anyone else to hear.

With the gun aimed at the floor, he took a moment to focus on Helen. He could feel her fear of the older man in the room. The old man was acting friendly, but Helen did not trust him. She was consciously avoiding thoughts of her mother and spending all of her mental energy thinking about the time when she would rejoin the older girl, her new friend. Fortunately, nothing more horrible had happened to her yet. But Freddy needed to hurry.

With so many emotions swirling inside him, Freddy experienced difficulty keeping them sorted into the appropriate categories, his versus theirs. If he spent no effort keeping them separated, he would become all of them, criminal, abductor, terrified victim, and killer.

The anger had grown inside him his entire life, starting when his father had left them, and then had escalated when his mother had decided to focus all of her remaining attention on his sister. And then after his mother had placed him into the foster program, the psychological diseases of his foster families had found an outlet in him. While living with Mr. Smith, Freddy had kept the anger away with ease, like placing a shirt at the bottom of a clothes drawer, never to be worn again, away but not forgotten.

NINETY-FIVE

Freddy

Freddy knocked three times in quick succession and then mentally prepared for several different scenarios. If they expected a secret knock and he made the incorrect pattern, he would anticipate their suspicion and then pretend to be from the hotel. If they refused to open the door, Freddy would shoot the locking mechanism, which would make his job more difficult but might also expedite the process. Whatever happened, he felt confident he could think of a way to open the door. His enhanced perception gave him an advantage.

To his relief, the man who came to answer the door felt no concern and did not even notice that Freddy had knocked differently than the guard. He was glad for the chance to stretch his legs and was sick of waiting in the bedroom with his boss, the man who had command of the operation. His boss was waiting with a younger boy and playing on his smartphone, entirely distracted and annoyed.

The guard inside opened the door slightly and spoke while waiting for Freddy to push it the rest of the way.

"Hey, Jim," he said. "I heard you talking. Figure out when the power's coming back on?"

Freddy responded with silence and then slammed the door on the man, momentarily pinning him to the wall of the small entryway. During his sudden burst of energy, Freddy assessed the man's mass. The man behind the door weighed much heavier than the guard he had killed, so Freddy had to act quickly. Before the man had time to respond, Freddy jumped past him into the living room and let him slam the door shut.

After the door locking mechanism clicked, the man turned to find a gun pointed at his face. Freddy allowed the man enough time to recognize the gun before aiming the bright flashlight in his eyes, immediately blinding him.

"What the hell," the man said while using his hand to shield the light.

"Down the hall," Freddy said with as much confidence as he could generate. He stepped backward to increase the distance between him and the larger man, then motioned with the flashlight beam to move. "In with your boss."

"Take it easy with that thing, kid," the man said after seeing that a younger, much smaller man stood before him. He spoke with mock concern for Freddy's safety. "Neither one of us wants to get hurt."

"Just move," Freddy said and then realized the man needed more motivation. "I have no problem shooting you right here. I already killed your friend outside, but if I can help it, I do not want to kill anyone else."

The man's eyes narrowed as he tried to determine the truth of Freddy's statement. When he finally recognized Freddy's sincerity, he started moving forward. The man turned away, took a few steps in the direction indicated, and prepared to spin around and knock the gun away, but Freddy shoved him with the flashlight and knocked him off-balance. Freddy could feel the man's anger for not acting sooner.

"Nice try, now keep moving," Freddy said.

If the man felt ready to attack, Freddy would just shoot him. He was tempted to shoot him in the back of the head anyway, so he could move with ease through the apartment, but he squeezed the gun instead, keeping pressure on the trigger.

The man led Freddy to a side bedroom. A soft light seeped from beneath the door onto the plush carpet. After he opened the door, Freddy immediately noticed a movie camera atop a tall tripod that faced a large bed, its light shining on a smaller man and boy there. The smaller man had male-pattern baldness, with a mixture of dark brown and gray hair on the sides of his head. After the guard and Freddy walked into the room, he looked up casually from his smartphone. When he saw the gun, his eyes burst wide open.

He started to stand from the bed but stopped himself midway. The boy who sat on the bed behind him had his bare chest exposed, partially covered by a blanket. Even though only the blanket covered him, he was not concerned about being naked.

The bald man stared at the guard with contempt in his eyes, angry at the man for letting Freddy inside the room, but much less afraid than Freddy had expected or hoped. In the low light, his eyes looked dark, almost black.

"What is this?" the bald man asked after returning his full weight to the bed.

He set the smartphone on his lap with one hand, covering it as he would a cherished pet. The boy sat up after recognizing the angry tone of the man, supporting his weight on his elbows. His gaze shifted between the two men and Freddy. The boy felt confused and prepared for something horrible to happen.

"He says he killed Jim," the guard said.

"Shut up!" Freddy said through clenched teeth.

He held the gun firmly in his right hand, trying to think of what to do. The guard stopped at the bed and turned around to face Freddy. He looked at the gun in the bright light of the movie camera, focusing on the silencer attached to the end. He was watching for signs of weakness, an opportunity to leap at Freddy, and the bald man was wondering why the guard had failed to do it already.

"Who are you?" the bald man asked.

Freddy kept his eyes on the larger man who was still standing.

"Sit down, big guy, and stop thinking you can find a way to jump me. I am not afraid to use this."

As the man slowly lowered himself to the bed, Freddy stepped to the side of the room where a sofa lay against the wall. He took a small pillow from the sofa and placed it in front of the gun. Freddy feared that his small suppressor would fail to sufficiently muffle the sound of the exploding gas. Maybe the pillow would help contain the noise.

"I asked you a question!" the bald man said angrily and then gulped when he saw Freddy aim the pillow at his head. The man had forgotten how losing control of a situation felt. People usually treated him with fearful respect. But then his burst of fear suddenly transformed into anger again. "Who are you? We don't keep any money here, you fucking idiot!"

"I am not here for money," Freddy said, feeling an unexpected satisfaction at the man's reaction.

He felt a strong urge just to shoot them, but he stopped himself. He had no interest in striking a conversation with the men, but maybe he would feel better about executing their final judgment if they helped incriminate themselves.

"What did you do to Jim?" asked the guard finally, gaining courage from the gun aiming at someone other than himself.

"I did just what you want to do to me," Freddy said with the pleasure of being the one in control of the situation.

—✳—

The bald man wanted to use a knife on Freddy and feel the warm blood on his hands like what Freddy had experienced with the door guard. Freddy never wanted to plunge a knife into human flesh again, but he did want to pull the trigger and watch the bullet penetrate their skulls.

In the silence following his statement, Freddy made a strange realization. After killing the guard, his emotional load decreased a little.

The negative emotions he could feel from others had changed by a small but noticeable amount. Killing the two men in front of him would relieve him of even more foulness. But before delivering their final sentence, Freddy wanted to extract a confession from them. He wanted to hear them admit to their worthless state.

"Now it is my turn to ask questions," Freddy began. "What are you doing in this hotel?"

The guard looked at the smaller man next to him, waiting for him to answer. He acted as though too afraid to speak, but Freddy knew the truth. The man hoped to stall until someone came to their rescue.

The bald man had already made a phone call, informing his employers about the power loss in the hotel, and now he cursed himself for not requesting backup. Fortunately for Freddy, the hotel staff disliked contact with the men and usually avoided visiting their rooms on the fifth floor. If that situation changed, Freddy hoped to anticipate any surprise visit. Freddy had full faith that his new perception would not fail him. If the woman from the plane wanted to lead Freddy into a trap, he would know already.

"If you're hoping for me to incriminate myself, you're even stupider than you look."

The man threw insults often. They came naturally to him, and he hoped to make Freddy angry enough to make a mistake in judgment.

"Even if you get something incriminating on whatever recording device you've got, it won't hold up in any court. My associates will make sure any evidence you acquire will end up as worthless garbage, like you."

Freddy felt his lips stretch involuntarily into a sincere smile and the man recognized the look. The men were going to give him more than enough motivation to do what he so desperately wanted. But before proceeding, Freddy wanted to hear them admit to going against their conscience if they still existed.

"Then you will not object to telling me why you think it is okay to hurt children?"

The man laughed this time with relief and genuine humor. He turned to his right, directing his voice to the boy behind him.

"Hey Kristoff, are we hurting you?"

"You're not hurting me," the boy answered immediately.

Freddy could feel the boy's anxiety, his fear of making the man angry. Having another armed man in the room scared the boy much less than the bald man sitting in front of him. Adults with guns always accompanied the bald man. Freddy just happened to be a new adult to consider. Only two options came to the boy's mind. They would all be killed, or this new player would be his new handler. The boy's feeling of hopelessness amplified Freddy's desire to squeeze the trigger.

Behind the pillow, Freddy pulled the trigger several micrometers closer to firing. The only obstacle to the man's death was the insignificant resistance of the trigger or poor aim, but Freddy strangely had no fear of missing his target.

"See," he said. "We're not hurting anyone. We're paying the little shit, for Christ's sake."

"What about the other boy and the two little girls? At least, they are getting minimum wage I hope?"

"You seem to know a lot about us," the man said, squinting.

"I know more than I would like."

The bald man hoped to change the conversation from their criminal activities to a topic of his choosing and ultimately regain control of the conversation. He desperately wanted to discover Freddy's identity.

"Let me give you some advice, little man with a gun," he continued. "It's dark in here, and we won't be able to positively identify you. That's fortunate for you. Your only chance of escape is to get the hell out of here and run back to your goddamned church group or whatever hole you crawled out of. If you were smart, that's what you would be doing."

"My questions first," Freddy said, intending to inspire the man with the hope of survival. "Are the girls getting minimum wage for their services?"

"Alright," the man said with feigned disappointment. "So you want to go down that road?"

Bullies had often given Freddy the same kind of condescension at school. The man reminded Freddy of one small but popular boy who had always called Freddy a retard whenever anyone could hear him. Freddy remembered just looking at the ground in shame. Now, Freddy looked the man straight in the eyes. He recognized the fake smile.

"Yes, I want to go down that road."

NINETY-SIX

Freddy

"Let me teach you something about life," the man said, adjusting himself on the bed and preparing for a long answer.

Freddy felt a sudden impatience, an urgent need to hurry, but he wanted to hear what the man had to say.

"With enough money," the man continued, "people can get whatever they want. That's it. I'm just a businessman providing a service. If I don't provide it, someone else will. These are just business decisions. You can keep your naive and childish view on life, but it won't change reality."

"What does your older client want with the blonde girl?"

Behind the pillow, Freddy's hand began shaking with anger. Before he eliminated the men, he wanted them to understand the consequences of their actions. For some reason, Freddy wanted them to understand why they had to die.

The man shook his head, considering his words carefully, feeling more uncomfortable and planning to lie. While Freddy waited for the man's answer, he saw the truth, and it sickened him even more.

"When he's done with her, she'll be fine," he said finally.

"You lie," Freddy whispered.

Freddy changed his aim to the guard but kept his eyes on the bald man. He wanted to see the man's reaction when he pulled the trigger. When the hole exploded between the guard's eyes and he fell silently on the bed, the bald man winced. The guard's blood had splattered on the back of the bed and wall, and the bullet cracked the thick head-board.

For the first time in his life, Freddy felt a gun's recoil, but his perfect aim had failed to give Freddy as much satisfaction as seeing the fear on the bald man's face and then feeling the fear in his chest. In panic, the boy silently scrambled farther to the other side of the bed, pulling the cover up to his neck as if to separate him from the dead body. He stared at the corpse, almost expecting to see movement.

"You are so fucking dead," the man hissed in the hopes of intimidating Freddy. He scooted away from his fallen employee to avoid letting the pooling blood touch him. "You'll never make it out of here alive. We've got people all over this hotel. In fact, people are on their way up right now. If you run now, you might–"

"No one is coming to help you," Freddy said with mock sorrow and suddenly wished the first guard had been as clean of a kill as the second one.

Freddy looked into the bald man's eyes and felt the man's fresh terror and anger. It gave him a momentary pleasure, but then all of a sudden, he thought of all the kids who had passed through his business, how no one had been there to help them. Freddy no longer had any interest in the bald man. Only eliminating him mattered. Killing him would not help any of his past victims and would give Freddy no pleasure.

The man's eyes filled with shock and for a moment, his mind went blank. He knew that Freddy could see inside him.

"What are you going to do?" he asked then decided not to wait for the answer. If he could just get Freddy to keep talking, he might have a chance. "Listen, I'm just a middle-man. I can give you names. I can tell you whatever you want. Just name it."

"I do not need any more information from you," Freddy said with finality.

The bald man did not have time to say anything else. Freddy put a hole in his head, in the same spot as the guard. Contrasting with the sudden violence of his death, the man's body peacefully fell back on the bed. After a short pause, Freddy removed the pillow from the muzzle of the gun and then waited for his heartbeat to stabilize. With his two additional opponents eliminated, Freddy recognized a significant decrease in his emotional load.

While looking at the two dead men on the bed, Freddy wondered briefly if he should have killed them. Maybe he could have forced the bald man to help retrieve Helen, then kill him later. But after just a moment of reflection, he realized the truth. He would have done the same thing again. The world improved with fewer of these psychopaths. If he died or failed to rescue Helen, at least he had helped clean up some trash before his exit from the world.

Freddy turned his attention to the boy on the bed who was anticipating a similar fate. The boy almost welcomed such a clean and painless death. He had blond hair and seemed to be small for his age, maybe twelve or thirteen years old. In as non-threatening of a manner as possible, Freddy pointed the gun to the ceiling in a sign of peace. He had little time for the boy, but he could not just leave him.

"I will not hurt you," Freddy said.

He put his gun under his belt then slowly reached inside his jacket and removed a thick bundle of cash. At first, the boy winced and expected a knife or other weapon. But when he saw the money, he relaxed and became hesitantly curious. Freddy slowly extracted several fifty and hundred-dollar bills, stepping slowly toward the boy and extending his hand with the money. The boy stared at the money as if Freddy planned to trick him. He wanted to take it, but fear kept him motionless. He had just seen Freddy kill two adults and he was still shocked by the disturbing memory.

Freddy placed the money on the bed and then returned the rest of the cash to his jacket. He had several thousand dollars remaining.

"You do not want to be here when the police come, understand?"

"Yes," the boy answered then snatched the money from the bed.

"Good," Freddy said without a smile. "Take the money and when we are done here, get far away from these people. Will you do that?"

"Okay," he responded as though in a trance. He slowly gathered the blanket around his naked body. He stood from the bed and backed away from the dead men.

"This room is connected to the one next door?" Freddy asked. While waiting for the response, Freddy felt the boy's relief and his intention to lead Freddy to the back of the apartment. "Will you take me there?"

"It's in the back of a closet, to the right of the bedroom."

The boy was more relaxed with the money. He still doubted Freddy's sincerity, but his level of anxiety had become significantly lower. The boy began moving slowly toward the door, keeping himself as far away from Freddy as possible. Freddy followed with the flashlight through the dark apartment. Both of them felt better after leaving the room of corpses.

"I have a friend over there," the boy said while leading Freddy to another room. He opened the door and waited for Freddy to enter. "Please don't hurt him."

"What about the girls?" Freddy asked after stopping in the doorway and shining the flashlight into the new room.

"I only know one of them," he said. "They made me do a video with her once."

Freddy looked at the boy in the eyes, and he gulped. Freddy's gaze reminded the boy of the deaths he had just witnessed. While watching Freddy dispose of his oppressors, he had begun to think of Freddy as invincible, maybe omniscient, someone to obey. The memory of all the blood on the bed flooded his mind.

"If I enter the other apartment, will you stay here and wait? I will bring your friend back and then you can leave."

"I will wait."

"Show me how," Freddy whispered, opening the door wider.

"There's a sliding door at the back of the closet," the boy answered just as quietly.

He led Freddy to a closet in the back of the dark room. After stopping at the door, he placed his hand on the handle and prepared to open it, but Freddy stopped him. Before the boy could respond, Freddy placed his index finger over his mouth as a signal for silence.

"Wait," he whispered. "Someone is listening."

Freddy could feel the occupants in the other apartment, a man probably in his late forties, another boy, and a young girl who unfortunately did not feel like Helen. The man thought he had heard something that sounded like a gunshot from the other apartment, but he doubted his senses.

The man was standing with a knife by the adjacent closet door. He was prepared to stab at anyone who exited the closet on his side. He waited in fear of making any noise, feeling much more afraid than Freddy.

Freddy wondered what to do, thinking maybe he could go through the secret door and put a decoy into the other room, like his hat. If the man struck at the decoy, Freddy would cut his wrist and then stab him in the neck. The other option felt more reliable, wait in silence for the man to leave the closet. But unfortunately, that option required too much time. To help steady his hand, Freddy gripped the knife handle tightly. Even through the nitrile glove, he could still feel the sticky blood of the first guard on the knife and his own sweat.

"Open the door," Freddy whispered.

The boy opened the entry door to the closet, and to Freddy's relief, the door swung open without squeaking, then the boy separated some heavy coats on hooks to make room for Freddy to enter. Before stepping into the closet, Freddy handed the flashlight to the boy.

"Keep this pointed to the ground but not directly into the closet. When I am ready to open the back door, you shut this one. Nod if you understand."

The boy nodded obediently, standing motionless behind Freddy in the dark room. He looked like a statue with one hand on the closet door handle and the other hand pointing the flashlight to the ground. His feelings morphed into a mixture of relief, curiosity, and excitement. Freddy felt assured of the boy's compliance. As the boy's new potential tormentor prepared to leave him alone for a while, the boy began to enjoy the memory of seeing his former captors falling dead on the bed.

Before entering the closet, Freddy put the pillow under his arm and removed his hat. With his knife in one hand and his hat in the other, Freddy slid between the parted coats. At the back wall, he found a simple sliding door. He placed his hand on the door, turned to face the boy, and nodded. The boy quietly shut the door, leaving Freddy alone in the closet, with just enough light from under the door to see.

Freddy took a deep breath and began to slide the door open. To his surprise, the door slid open completely without a sound, allowing him to enter the other apartment's closet in complete silence. After pushing through more hanging coats, he finally reached the doorknob to the new apartment.

Without pausing, Freddy slowly turned the knob and waited for the man's reaction from the other side. The man on the other side heard the quiet click, or he thought he heard it, but in the low light, he had failed to see the knob move. He became confused and waited in vain for other sounds. Freddy also decided to wait.

After just a few seconds of silent confusion, the man chose the most desirable conclusion for himself. He had only imagined the noises and could return to the living room where his little companions waited. He felt foolish for being paranoid.

Freddy felt the man leave the room, and then he pushed the closet door open. But to his horror, the door hinges creaked loud enough for the man to hear.

NINETY-SEVEN

Freddy

While the man waited for more noise, Freddy returned the hat to his head and took a moment to familiarize himself with his new surroundings, since his eyes had already adjusted to the darkness. The room looked similar to the other room in the first apartment, and he quickly recognized the mirror-image layout and where he needed to go. The low light from the partially open door shined like a lighthouse in the night.

Judging from the flickering light spilling through the open door, the source most likely originated from a candle. Freddy stood for a brief moment just watching the animated light, and then without conscious effort, he began creeping toward the open door, drawn to the light like a mindless insect.

Freddy's appearance in the living room came as a complete shock to all of the occupants. He quickly focused on the new man and his ice-cold eyes, and he felt instant disgust. The man had a different reaction. He withered under Freddy's gaze as a strand of hair in a flame.

The man stood in front of a couch with a little girl on his right and a young boy slightly behind her. The girl wore a pretty white dress, and the boy wore a white bathrobe. They looked about the same age, maybe a year younger than the one Freddy had left in the first apartment. The sight of the captive children next to a man with such disgusting thoughts made Freddy's stomach lurch with anger again. He wished the alien would have given him the ability to fry the skin off someone with his eyes, instead of the ability to feel their horrible emotions.

"Who are you?" the man asked with a thick Colombian accent.

He held a long hunting knife, pointed like a sword at Freddy. The low light concealed his shaking hand, but Freddy felt the man's fear and the more dangerous emotion, desperation. The Colombian man slowly reached toward the girl, his hand resting on her neck and preparing to throw her into Freddy if he attacked. The girl made no protest or struggle. She just stared at Freddy with a strange mixture of fear and relief.

"Who I am does not matter," Freddy said and wondered why they all wanted to know his identity. He did not want to know theirs. "Why are you in this apartment with little children and a knife?"

Immediately after asking the question, Freddy realized his mistake. He had shown interest in the children, and the man suddenly realized his leverage in the situation.

Freddy took two small steps toward the man, forcing him to reveal his next move. In some deep part of his mind, Freddy wanted the man to threaten the girl. The cowardly act would make Freddy's job of killing him so much easier.

In response, the man stepped closer to the couch, pulling the girl in front of him as a shield. His rough handling immediately erased all of her emotions, and she moved like an inanimate doll, her lifeless eyes fixed on the floor. The absence of emotion in the girl caused Freddy to shiver. The Colombian moved the knife to her neck, as a hunter ready to skin an animal.

"You answer my question, and I'll answer yours," the man said and touched the knife to her throat. "Who are you? Come any closer, and I will hurt her!"

In the first room, the two men never even considered using the boy as leverage, so Freddy failed to consider that possibility in the second room. He should have shot the man as soon as he entered, but the thought of killing him in front of the little girl made him anxious. The children had been traumatized enough in their lives. Freddy did not want to cause more trauma.

"I just want the girl," Freddy said casually.

Freddy slowly put the knife in his belt, under his jacket then removed the gun. When the Colombian saw the gun, his eyes stretched wide, and he pulled the girl closer.

The man watched in fear as Freddy put the pillow between him and the gun. Freddy could think of no alternative to shooting the man in front of the children. He would be unable to overpower the man and also prevent him from alerting others in the hotel, including the man with Helen. His heart began pounding noticeably in his chest right before squeezing the trigger.

But before shooting, Freddy paused. If the girl heard a gunshot, she would scream. Freddy's mind became a tornado, spinning furiously. He needed to prevent the girl from screaming or at least stop her. If he acted fast enough, he could shoot the man then rush forward and put his hand over her mouth. While considering the situation, Freddy became aware of the boy.

The young boy next to the man felt more courage than the older boy who was waiting in the first apartment. While watching the situation from behind the man, in the shadows, he had waited for an opportunity to rush at Freddy and knock the gun from his hand. If he had failed to offer any resistance, his handlers might decide to punish him. While Freddy wondered how to prepare for the boy, the man interrupted his thoughts.

"If you want the girl," the man said in a tone of feigned anger. "I will give her to you in the hallway."

Freddy suddenly understood the man's plan. He wanted to close the apartment door on Freddy and the kids, so he could escape in the hallway. His escape plan helped the Colombian feel some relief, but then he began to feel another emotion. He hated to occupy the losing side of a confrontation and for someone to see him with the children. The young man in front of him, Freddy, knew his dark secret.

Freddy decided to move forward with his own plan before the boy could gather enough courage to rush at him. He hoped the boy would be too shocked to act.

Freddy fired the gun and the bullet hit the man right between the eyes, his third perfect shot of the evening. Just like the men in the other apartment, the man instantly crumpled to the floor. A splattering of blood appeared on the wall behind him with a dark hole in the center where the bullet had penetrated.

Before the corpse came to a complete rest on the floor, Freddy dropped the pillow and rushed forward, putting his hand over the girl's mouth. Fortunately, he reached the girl before she could scream. She struggled against his hand, but he managed to keep her quiet.

Unfortunately, Freddy had failed to anticipate the boy's quick response. Seeing a man shot in front of him had less effect on the boy than Freddy had hoped. Nothing could shock the boy anymore. He removed the gun from Freddy's grasp and backed several meters away, out of reach. He held the gun in shaking hands, aimed directly at Freddy's head. Freddy gulped and watched as the boy's chest rose and fell with his heavy breathing.

"Let her go," the boy said, his voice shaking as much as his hands.

NINETY-EIGHT

Freddy

"I am letting her go," Freddy said then looked down at the girl's head. "Please do not scream."

When Freddy heard the girl draw a deep breath through her nose, he knew she would remain quiet. He slowly removed his hands from the frightened child, and she ran to join the boy, positioning herself behind him. She looked back at Freddy like an animal from a cage.

"You stay away from us," the boy said, taking a step backward.

He wanted to shoot Freddy, but he feared to miss. Freddy acted just as all of the other adults he knew, manipulative and violent. The boy had intense anger inside him, and Freddy understood how he felt. Freddy slowly extended both hands above his head.

"I am not here to hurt you, just them."

"You said you came for the girl," said the boy. "Were you lying?"

"Yes, I was lying to that man, but I will not lie to you."

Freddy laughed silently at how stupid that statement sounded.

"How are we supposed to believe you?"

While holding the gun tightly in both hands, the boy began to relax and his desire to shoot Freddy diminished. He desperately wanted to believe Freddy, to believe something positive. Shooting Freddy might also hurt their chances of escape. For the first time in his life, the boy held all the leverage in a situation. He needed to devise a plan. He liked the girl with him and felt a responsibility to help her.

"Please keep your voice down," Freddy requested politely. "We cannot let the man next door hear us. He must not know what happened here."

"What are you talking about?" the boy asked in a quieter voice.

"I came here for a girl named Helen," he said slowly, hoping the children would hear the sincerity in his voice. "The girl Helen is in the next apartment. Her mother is waiting in the hallway."

The boy instantly doubted the claim, but the girl stepped out from behind him. For a brief moment, the boy made eye contact with her then returned his attention to Freddy, eyes squinted tightly.

"You came for Helen?" the girl asked. A new emotion had materialized in her mind but not the hope that Freddy had expected. He recognized sadness and panic. "And her mother?"

"I don't believe it," said the boy. In his experience, parents would not come to rescue their children. He gripped the gun with more force. He did not plan to relinquish his leverage. "It's more lies to make me give this back to him."

Freddy's precious time was slipping away. The power company might restore the power before he entered the last apartment. People would come and see all the blood in the hall. Even if he managed to convince the girl, the boy would require significantly more time. In the short pause, Freddy devised a new plan. He would let the boy keep the gun and enter the next apartment with just his knife. He lacked faith in his hand-to-hand combat skills, so he would have to depend on his new extrasensory abilities.

"Okay, keep the gun," Freddy said finally. "Go to the other apartment and find your friend and he can tell you that I am not going to hurt you. The men who held him captive are all dead. They cannot hurt you anymore, but please, I need to get the girl to her mother before the power is restored."

"You're the one to stop the electricity?" the boy asked, shocked.

"It was a diversion."

The girl stepped in front of the boy, placing herself between them. She looked at the dead body on the ground and became momentarily paralyzed. She imagined the body rising as a zombie to eat them.

"I'm going with you to see Helen," she said finally.

"It is too dangerous," said Freddy. "You cannot come."

"You won't take her away from me," said the girl, her voice rising in volume. "I won't let you."

Freddy finally understood the girl's emotions. Helen had become her new friend, her only friend. In their short time together, Helen had become like an appendage to the girl, one that could only be removed painfully. Freddy crouched down to look at her.

"I know how you feel," he said quietly, attempting to mask his impatience. "You want Helen safe? I want that too."

"Yes," she said. "I want her safe."

"Let me tell you what I will do," Freddy said. "I will find you when this is all done and you can see Helen again. That is the best I can do right now."

"You'll come and find me?"

"Yes, like I found Helen," he said, putting his hand over his heart. "I promise, but please I need you two to stay here where it is safe."

"Daryn," the boy said in panic. "Keep away from him."

The boy suddenly imagined Freddy grabbing the girl and slitting her throat.

"You can't trust him. He just killed a guy, and maybe more."

Daryn took a step backward. She wanted to go with Freddy, but she thought her companion might be right. She trusted the boy more than Freddy.

"Do you think he'll hurt Helen?" she asked.

"I don't know," the boy responded. "We've got a chance to get away, and we've got to take it. Daryn, come with me. Let's go get Kristoff and get out of here."

The boy shook the gun at Freddy and spoke in a whisper.

"Don't follow us or I'll shoot you."

The boy put one hand on the girl's shoulder and started pulling her backward. She resisted but not enough to stand still. Together, they backed away from Freddy, the boy holding the gun steadily at Freddy's head. Before they disappeared into the next room, Freddy called out to them.

"Where is the secret passage into the other apartment?"

The boy stopped and turned around.

"It's over there."

He waved the gun toward a dark corridor on the opposite side of the room. Freddy peered in the direction indicated and noticed a closet door. After turning to face the kids again, he saw only an empty doorway. They would soon join the first boy who waited anxiously by the closet joining the apartments.

When Freddy looked down at the body on the floor, he noticed the pillow lying next to it. He stared at the new bullet hole as though it meant something, and then an idea materialized. Freddy retrieved the pillow from the floor, and then grabbed the candle from the small lamp stand. Ten seconds later, he entered the next secret passageway.

In the next apartment, the man with Helen was waiting impatiently for the restoration of the hotel power, and he didn't detect any unusual activity, especially when Freddy silently entered his apartment. When Freddy stood in the empty room and watched the flickering candlelight on the walls, he felt as though he had entered a tomb.

NINETY-NINE

Freddy

Freddy paused to assess the situation. Helen was sitting in the apartment with the older man, worrying about what would happen after the electricity was restored. For the first time in her life, the dark had come to her rescue. She preferred the darkness to the stranger who kept telling her how much he liked her dress, her face, her arms, and her legs. When he called her his little darling, a cold chill entered her heart. She felt more anxiety with him than she did with Mr. Becerra and his wife combined.

She tried concentrating on seeing Daryn again, but that fleeting comfort reminded her of the pathetic little room, the dirty toys, and how her mother would not be there. Still, she preferred to be anywhere other than her present location. To keep herself from crying, she breathed deeply as her mother had taught her to do when she became upset. The man might dislike the sound of her crying.

The sadness and anxiety Freddy felt from Helen caused tears to well in his eyes, but his anger vaporized them before they could fall. He extinguished the candle flame with a silent exhale and carefully opened the door to the short hallway. As he approached the room containing Helen and the old man, they did not notice his quiet footsteps. When

Freddy got close enough, he could hear the old man whispering, so he stopped at the edge of the open door into the room and just listened.

When he heard Helen's voice for the first time, his heart almost exploded with energy and excitement. The mental image of Sadi embracing her daughter again made Freddy want to run into the room. But the memory of losing his gun quickly deflated his euphoria. Without the gun, he had a much more difficult task.

"Come on, my little darling," the older man said. He had a deep voice, one that would have been respectable had Freddy met him in another circumstance. His age probably exceeded fifty years, maybe even sixty. "There's no need to be afraid of the dark. The power will be restored in a few minutes, I'm sure."

"Okay," Helen answered.

"Just sit here with me, my darling. I'll keep you safe."

Freddy instantly recognized the manipulation tactic. The man was giving Helen an alternative cause for her fear, the dark, not him. He would be the one to comfort her.

"Am I going back with my friend?" Helen asked tentatively.

"Of course, of course," said the man with amusement in his voice at her silly question. "Like I said, we're just going to play some fun games then you can go back to your little friend. Just relax with me. Yes, like that."

A steady light shined from the room into the hallway. The light looked different than the candlelight from the other apartment, probably from the street lights outside. From the dark hallway, Freddy stared at the partially open bedroom door and considered his limited options.

A beautiful plan materialized in his mind. At least, the plan seemed beautiful. He could creep to the front door and knock. Then the man would leave Helen in the room and come to answer the door, assuming the service wanted to talk to him. Freddy would attack from the dark and plunge the knife into his heart. The plan's execution flowed beautifully in his imagination, but it seemed too easy. Easy seemed extremely wrong. Maybe the service had a secret knock. If Freddy knocked incorrectly, the man would probably not leave Helen.

While considering his options, Freddy felt his precious time quickly diminishing. He needed to decide on a plan quickly. If he delayed action too long, his anxiety level would push his body forward with or without his conscious permission. So Freddy made a decision, take advantage of his second asset, surprise, and then depend on his new ability the alien creature had given him. He would rush into the room and attempt to stab the man.

But before moving forward, he recognized something different about his next opponent. The man was different from the other men he had killed that night. Not only did he fill Freddy with more disgust, but the man also scared him, the first time that evening he experienced true fear. And he suddenly understood one reason why. His enhanced senses and the gun had helped conceal his fear and insecurity. Without the gun, he felt more susceptible to failure. Freddy desperately wanted to hold the gun again, feel the kick of the escaping bullet.

The man in the next room also seemed composed of pure malice. Greed had motivated the other men. A disregard for the welfare of their victims had enabled those men. The next man got pleasure from inflicting pain on others, a true sadist. Sexual pleasure satisfied only half of his needs. Violence satisfied the rest.

Freddy decided to change tactics again. A surprise attack might put Helen in danger. Since Freddy could not see their position, he doubted the success of rushing into the room and stabbing the man. As soon as the new plan materialized, he executed it.

"Hey, mister," Freddy whispered as quietly as he could.

The man in the next room felt immediate confusion, not sure if he could trust his senses. He stopped breathing, so he could focus on listening. For a long moment, the silence became a tangible object between them, and it felt as though the air had solidified. Without thought, Freddy's lips quietly formed the next words.

"Let go of the little girl and be a man for once in your life."

The following silence continued for almost ten seconds, the longest ten seconds of his life. Freddy hoped the man would stand and investigate, but he never did or would. As quietly and slowly as possible, Freddy withdrew the knife from his belt, but unfortunately, the blade slid across his belt buckle and made a scraping sound that pierced the silence like a sword.

Freddy quickly placed the knife behind the pillow and stepped into the doorway, holding the pillow in a way that showed the holes from the bullets. Hopefully, the room had enough light for the man to see the obliterated fabric.

When Freddy made his appearance, the man sat more erect on the bed, and his blue eyes narrowed to slits. He had gray hair and a large waist covered by a white shirt that hung over black slacks. He looked as though he had just returned home from a long day at the office.

In a flash, the man produced a large knife from beside him. He held the blade in his right hand while his left hand rested on Helen's leg. The blade length surpassed the one in Freddy's hand by several centimeters, and the white hilt appeared to be composed of ivory.

When Freddy saw how fast the man had moved, he took an inconspicuous gulp. Freddy's adversary had a lot of experience using a knife and would enjoy using one on Freddy.

Helen was sitting in the man's lap and wore a pink dress with lace. He moved the knife to the side of her head, and she failed to notice the blade stopping so close to her delicate skin. The light pouring into the room from the open window reflected off the sharp metal.

Helen held her hand to the top of her dress just under her neck as though she feared her clothes would fall off. The man had probably unzipped her dress in the back. When Freddy saw her predicament, his anger increased and helped displace his fear just a little. Freddy imagined inserting the knife into the man's neck and slicing it like a peach.

"Who the hell are you?" the man asked with the tone of someone accustomed to being obeyed.

The man turned slightly to face Helen, and Freddy's anger suddenly evaporated. With the hand holding the knife, he brushed her blond hair away from her ear, but she still failed to see the knife. He pulled her head closer to his lips.

"Do you know this man, my darling?"

Helen looked at Freddy closely for a moment. After feeling her sudden recognition, he waited with dread for her verbal admission. If he could communicate telepathically, he would have instructed Helen to deny knowing him. She hesitated before answering, but her fear of the man prevailed.

"He's my mom's friend," Helen said finally with some confusion. Her fear was mixed with the relief of seeing a familiar face.

"Your mom's friend?" the man asked and then turned to Freddy. "Come all this way just for me?"

"Just for you," Freddy said with sarcasm.

The man paused and considered the situation. He possessed confidence and the kind of courage difficult to intimidate. He glanced at the pillow in Freddy's hand then suppressed a smile at how silly he thought Freddy looked with the object. Pillows with bullet holes failed to inspire fear in the man. He considered throwing Helen from his lap and attacking Freddy, but the bullet holes in the pillow did cause him to pause. His desired action carried too much risk. He would use the girl to shield himself until he assessed Freddy's true offensive capabilities.

The man lifted Helen higher on his lap and crouched a bit, so her head shielded the lower half of his face then he moved the knife to her throat. His charade of pretending to care for the girl had come to an end. When she looked down and finally saw the knife, she stopped breathing.

"After I kill the girl," he said through gritted teeth, his feeling of anger suddenly exploding. "After I kill this girl, I'm going to find her mother and kill her."

ONE HUNDRED

Freddy

The man pulled Helen's hair so that her head pressed against his lips. She squealed with terror, and muffled sobs exited her mouth in short bursts. While keeping his eyes on Freddy, he spoke in her ear.

"You wouldn't want me to do something to your mother my dear, would you? If this man leaves us alone and goes away, I will let you and your mother live."

"Mom?" Helen said through her tears, not comprehending.

"Do not listen to him, Helen," Freddy said. "If he tries to hurt you, I will kill him, and he knows it."

"There's something not right about that pillow you're holding," the man said, releasing her hair and looking directly into Freddy's eyes. His curiosity had returned, but he would only believe in the gun's existence if he saw it. "I see what looks like bullet holes in the pillow. You probably used it on the others. Otherwise you wouldn't have made it into this apartment, but something happened didn't it? Your hand looks a little too close to the back of the pillow."

"You want me to show my gun?" Freddy asked with a shaking voice and an attempted smirk. "I am not here to give you what you want. If you move the girl's head just a little farther down, I can show you what I have."

"Are we at an impasse?" the man asked sarcastically, with a mocking imitation of the same smirk Freddy had given him. "Let us just wait until the police come. I already dialed nine-one-one. The power will be restored soon. You do not have much time."

Freddy recognized the facade with some satisfaction. The man was only pretending to appear unconcerned, but he was beginning to believe in the existence of a gun. Somehow, Freddy forced himself to keep smiling. He had to play the man's game at least until he could find a resolution to the stalemate.

"So when they come, your knife will be at the child's throat? How will you explain that?"

The man looked at Freddy with respect, anger, and annoyance.

"You really are a stupid asshole, aren't you? The police will see you and me, and notice the blood all over you. I can see it splattered on your clothes. I was protecting the child."

Freddy looked down briefly at his jacket and pants. He had forgotten about the blood on his own clothes. Freddy laughed quietly and enjoyed the effect on the man, a twinge of fear.

"You did not call the police," Freddy said blandly while shaking his head.

The old man answered with a cold stare.

"This is your last chance," Freddy said, taking a step closer. "Give me the girl, or I shoot you. Although, the first shot might just graze the top of your head."

Since he could see no other option, the man decided to accept the challenge. He loved to gamble, loved the rush of taking on high risk. He enjoyed betting his life on pure instinct.

"Go ahead. Shoot me," he said fiercely and leaned forward. Helen jumped in shock. "If you miss, you're dead!"

"Willing to take that chance?" Freddy asked in a desperate last attempt. His smile melted and the man noticed. "Is your life that worthless, to bet it on a hunch?"

The man slowly stood on his feet, setting Helen on the ground in between them. He pushed the knife to her throat so hard the blade penetrated her delicate skin. A dark trickle of blood became a red trail down her neck. She squealed and closed her eyes.

"I knew it," the man said in triumph and some disappointment. "I just have to press a little bit harder, and this girl starts dying. How do you like that?"

Never in Freddy's life had he felt so many conflicting and overpowering emotions. Most came from within himself, but also from the man and Helen. They wrapped around his chest like a boa constrictor. Frustration at his helpless situation kept him from lunging at the man and attempting to stab him directly in the heart. Helen's eyes pleaded for him to help her. When she looked at him, Freddy almost exploded with frustration.

Freddy dropped the pillow and extended the knife in front of him. The man had a larger knife, but the dried blood on Freddy's knife made his weapon more menacing. Somehow, he found the strength to remain under control.

"Let the girl go, and we can settle this like men. I would rather use the knife anyway."

"Is this what you want?" the man spat, his voice rising like a madman. "Do you want this girl dead? Do you? Do you? You shithead. She will be, once I get done with you."

Freddy felt the man's excitement at the new development. He threw Helen violently to the ground and faked a lunge at Freddy, smiling wide. But before he moved, Freddy anticipated the action and took two steps backward.

After the fake lunge, the man stopped and took two slow steps toward him. Freddy backed away at the same pace and cringed at the feeling of dark euphoria emanating from the man. As he advanced, Freddy remembered school and his foster brothers and the joy they seemed to receive from hurting him. This man was the same, just older and wearing an expensive suit.

"Let me tell you what's going to happen," the man said while licking his lips in anticipation. "First, I'm going to take that fucking kitchen knife out of your hands and–"

The man stopped in mid-sentence, groaning in sudden pain and taking a quick step backward to prevent himself from falling. In his panic, Freddy had failed to notice the creature waiting in the shadows. She'd jumped from the darkness of the hallway, darted into the room, and hit the man behind the leg with a heavy object. Daryn had come to the aid of her only friend.

ONE HUNDRED ONE

Freddy

After hitting the man in the legs, Daryn jumped away from him and ran to Helen who had scooted across the floor to the wall. Daryn positioned herself protectively in front of Helen, holding a tall crystal vase in front of her, the weapon she had used to hit the man. Without consciously planning his next move, Freddy's body acted spontaneously. He jumped forward and attempted to grab the knife from the man's hand. But instead of taking hold of the knife, Freddy had grasped his wrist.

"You little shit," the old man said to the little girl while Freddy's grip tightened on his wrist. His expensive cologne tasted sickeningly sweet on Freddy's tongue.

Both girls watched while Freddy struggled with the older, more massive human. Each opponent held a knife in his right hand, attempting to plunge the blade into the flesh of the other.

After a few seconds of grappling, the old man managed to pin Freddy to the ground. And then to his horror, Freddy quickly realized his inferior strength and fighting skills. The old man also outweighed Freddy by at least thirty kilograms of fat and muscle.

While struggling to keep the longer knife away from his chest, Freddy realized the only fortunate aspect of his present position. Helen could escape to her mother. Freddy followed the only plan his mind could produce.

"Get out of here," he yelled to Helen. "Your mother is in the stairwell. Tell her she has to take you away from here."

The old man pinned Freddy's right hand to the ground then began slamming it against the soft carpet until the knife flew from his grasp and landed somewhere near the bed. With his more massive weight, the older man had effectively pinned his opponent's whole body to the ground. Freddy pulled his hand free and grabbed the man's other hand that held the knife.

"You're gonna pay for this," the man said with an angry smile. He stopped putting downward pressure on the knife and seemed to prepare for a final push. "Do you know how much money that little girl cost me? But don't worry, I can still get my money's worth out of her, and now I get to kill you too."

Freddy turned his head toward the two girls. They reminded him suddenly of stone statues in a garden.

"Get out of here, Helen," he yelled. "Run, please!"

Daryn was the first to emerge from her trance. She began pulling Helen toward the hallway and after just a few seconds, they were out of sight, heading toward the front of the apartment. With relief, Freddy heard the door to the hallway open and then the quiet click of it closing. Not even his imminent death could destroy the satisfaction of hearing Helen's escape.

Freddy hoped to experience the reunion of mother and daughter, feel their overwhelming joy and relief. He hoped to delay his death long enough to feel that. The request seemed reasonable.

With Freddy's attention distracted, the old man released his right hand from Freddy's grasp and hit him on the left side of his head. The sudden blow to his temple brought his fixation on the emotions of the girls to an abrupt end. He required several seconds for his eyes to focus again.

"They're gone," Freddy said, his vision still a blur. "Out of your reach."

The older man growled like an animal, slammed his hand against the side of Freddy's head again, and then spit in his eyes, effectively ending Freddy's ability to see clearly. He quickly returned both hands to his knife and resumed the downward pressure. Then his growl transformed into maniacal laughter when he noticed Freddy's resistance beginning to crumble. The man's horrible laughter was more frightening than his feeling of satisfaction.

As the man closed the distance between the tip of the knife and Freddy's chest, a strange relief washed over him. Freddy experienced the beautiful reunion of mother and daughter in the dark stairwell. He imagined Sadi's tears of joy sliding down his own cheeks. But when the knife began penetrating his flesh, just over his heart, the reunion had ended.

The old man suddenly stopped pushing so hard. He twisted the knife for a few seconds until he found a space between two of Freddy's ribs. Strangely, the pain meant nothing to him. After the man began applying pressure again, Freddy knew the knife would soon enter his heart. He did not want to die at the hands of such a monster.

But if Freddy died, his final act would have been worthwhile. He had saved children from a band of monsters and eliminated at least four sadistic psychopaths from the world.

When Freddy felt warm blood begin to soak into his clothes, he knew the end had come. The knife was going to pierce his heart, his muscles would lose all of their energy, and then his arms would go limp. Instead of blood flowing to his brain, his life would soak the carpet beneath him. Although his vision was blurry, Freddy stared into the eyes of his murderer, a pathetic final view of the world.

Freddy closed his eyes and imagined Sadi and Helen reunited. "She is safe from you now," he said with the last of his breath.

His strength vanished and then his arms dropped, but instead of feeling the knife enter his heart, the blade tip slid violently across his chest, leaving a trail of pain and blood like the wake behind a boat.

"Get the fuck off him," an angry female voice growled.

—✳—

Freddy heard a loud thud as the heavy body fell to the floor. The man began groaning and rocking back and forth next to Freddy, holding the bloody side of his head where the woman had kicked him. Breathing hard, Freddy wiped the sweat and spit from his eyes and turned to see a blurry vision of Sadi standing over the body of the old man. She was looking at the man, her eyes wide with rage.

For the next few seconds, Freddy forgot about how close he had come to death. With his left hand, he wiped his eyes again, and then while sitting up, he felt the man's knife begin sliding down his chest. Instinctively, he caught the weapon before it slid any farther. He did not want any of his blood on the floor. After sitting up, he was relieved when he saw that none of his blood had touched the floor around him. He knew that police investigators could use his blood to identify him.

"I thought I was dead," he said, gasping for breath and then laughing with relief. Real tears fell from his eyes, which helped remove the remaining saliva. "I really thought it was the end. Thank you, Sadi, for coming back for me."

"Don't mention it," she said, keeping her gaze on the old man. When she continued speaking, she seemed to be addressing herself. "When I saw Helen again, I just wanted to run away and never look back, but I couldn't leave without you."

Sadi watched the old man writhing on the floor for five long seconds, checking for signs of his former vitality returning and fighting the temptation to crack his skull with another kick. She wanted to stop him from moving altogether. She felt a strange mixture of anger and panic. Freddy spent a moment enjoying her emotions, an immense satisfaction at incapacitating the man who had wanted to hurt her daughter. The intense emotional rush felt like a deep breath of fresh air. It helped chase the dark thoughts and memories from his mind.

When Sadi was convinced of their safety, she knelt at his side, parted his clothes, and then spent a few seconds feeling the wounds on his chest. She brushed the hair from his wet forehead. Her touch felt like fire on his skin.

"I think you'll be all right," she said. "The cut's not too deep. Can you stand? We need to get out of here."

"Yes," he answered and felt dizzy while attempting to stand. "Just give me a second. He hit me pretty hard on my head. Do you think he can hear us?"

Freddy felt nothing but pain and confusion from the man on the floor.

"I kicked him hard," she said and smiled. "Probably gave him brain damage, but he definitely has a pretty bad concussion."

Helen, Daryn, and the boy with his gun were standing behind Sadi, all staring at the old man. Freddy had not noticed them until then. Helen was suddenly afraid of being taken from her mother again and began pulling on her jacket.

"Mom, can we go home?" she asked. "I don't like it here."

"Of course," Sadi answered, grasping Freddy's shoulder to help steady him. "Freddy's been hurt, so we have to help him."

"You really did come to save her, didn't you?" the boy asked from behind Sadi, the one who had taken the gun from Freddy. His gaze was fixed on the man on the ground.

Everyone turned to stare at him. The boy was afraid the man might stand and attack them all. He stepped around Sadi and extended his hand with the gun, pointing it at the man's head. He bent down until the gun reached just a couple of centimeters from his skull. The boy held the gun as though it was a natural extension of his arm.

"Yes, I did come to help them," Freddy answered softly. He spoke as though attempting to prevent a man from committing suicide. "Will you please return my gun now?"

The boy looked at Freddy with confusion and then turned back to the old man, squinting as though in deep thought. He wanted to shoot the man, transform his head into a pool of blood, torn flesh, and broken bones. He began murmuring to himself. Freddy failed to distinguish any words, but he felt the conflicting emotions. The man represented everything the boy hated in the world. Only his conditioning of obedience and fear kept him from pulling the trigger.

"Come on, Freddy, we need to leave," Sadi pleaded.

She cared only about escaping safely with her daughter and did not care if the boy shot the man. Helen clung to her mother's jacket and Daryn stood behind them.

"We cannot leave without the gun," Freddy said, speaking to the boy. "It will point the police to us. Do you understand? I cannot let you keep it."

"This is a bad one," the boy said in a whisper, tears falling down his cheeks. "Can't let him live. He doesn't deserve to live."

"I will take care of him," Freddy said, extending his hand. "After you leave the room. I do not want the girls to see."

"Can't let him live," the boy said to himself. "The police will believe whatever he says, no matter what."

He turned slowly, facing Freddy but not recognizing his presence. He thought only about the gun in his hand and the complete control he had over the destiny of his enemy, a position he had never before experienced.

After looking at the man again, the boy pulled the trigger and a chunk of the man's head exploded under him, leaving a bloody mess of bone, brain, and hair on the carpet. The silence was shattered by the scream of a woman in the apartment below them when the bullet had passed through the floor.

Everyone stood in shock for several seconds. Helen buried her face in Sadi's hip, but Daryn and the boy just stared at the body, emotionless. The gun fell from the boy's hand, hitting the carpet with a soft thud. Freddy stepped forward, careful to avoid stepping into the bloody mess on the floor, and retrieved the gun. He put the weapon under his belt.

With every movement, the cut on his chest felt like multiple wasp stings. Ignoring the pain, he slowly withdrew half of the remaining cash from his pocket and extended the money to the boy who turned from the corpse and stared at the money in Freddy's hand as though it was inside a glass case.

"I gave your friend some money too," Freddy said and suddenly felt the impatience of the other boy who was waiting for them in the hallway. "This is enough for you to go anywhere you want. Do you have anywhere you can go, safe from here?"

The boy nodded his head. Freddy placed his hand on the boy's shoulder and gently pushed him away from the horrible scene, and then his attention shifted from the body to the money in his hand.

"Kristoff has a brother we haven't seen in a long time," the boy said softly. "I think he remembers where he lives."

"Does his brother know about this?" Freddy asked, motioning with his hand to indicate the apartment and the activities that happened there.

"I think so," said the boy.

The thought of letting the other children go somewhere on their own felt like a foolish idea, but he had not considered how to fit them into his escape plan. Too bad he could not have thought about this complication beforehand. He would need to get them into an area where no one would find them, where they could hopefully start a new life. That thought helped produce an idea. He knew where they might take the three other children.

"No," Freddy said. "That will not work. You can come with us, but we have to hurry."

The emotions of the people in the apartment below them were raising Freddy's anxiety levels. A man had just called the police and would explain to the operator what he had heard. Another person was worried and prepared to call the hotel staff. For the moment, everyone feared to leave their rooms, but some people would soon gain the courage to investigate.

"Freddy, we need to go," Sadi said, desperation in her voice.

Freddy sensed members of the hotel staff heading to the stairs from the ground floor, the stairwell leading to the apartments of death. In just a few minutes, they would pass the dead guard or see his blood on the floor. Freddy quickly led them from the apartment and into the hallway, the beam of his flashlight lighting the way. They traveled through the hallway to the stairwell on the other side where he had left Sadi.

ONE HUNDRED TWO

Freddy

Freddy led the traumatized band of humans down the stairs to a back exit of the hotel. The door opened to the parking lot where a few of the other tenants could be seen heading to their cars. Freddy made eye contact with no one and soon stepped onto the sidewalk by the street.

The two boys had already found their clothing and looked like normal kids while the two girls looked out of place in their pretty dresses. The people driving on the road who happened to notice the group just thought of them as a young couple walking with their four children. Freddy knew the police were on their way and somehow knew the direction they would travel, so he took the group in the opposite direction.

No one spoke as they walked, but the boys began to doubt Freddy's good intentions. The older one considered running off into the night a few times and taking his friend with him. His instincts told him to escape the new adults who were suddenly in control of them. He would have run away already, but he hesitated to tell his friend or Daryn for fear of alerting Freddy. He was tempted to let them go, but Freddy put faith in his plan as the best course of action.

Daryn felt completely different and thought of their journey as an exciting new adventure with a new set of friends. During her life, she had become accustomed to thinking only of the present, not the future. She cared only about escaping the bad men who wanted to abuse her and how much she liked her new friends.

"You are free to go," Freddy said after they reached the car. "But I will be taking you somewhere safe, where I hope no one will find you. But if you choose to leave now, please get far away."

He held the door open and waited for them to make their decisions. Both boys required only a few seconds to arrive at the same conclusion. They believed him. Freddy had only spoken kindly, and they had failed to hear any threat of violence in his tone, unlike any other adult they ever knew. And no one had ever given them the option of leaving before.

Daryn sat behind Freddy near the window, with Helen in the middle and Sadi next to the other window. The boys sat in the front seats next to Freddy. Instead of taking the same route, he drove back to Portland on Interstate Five.

When they left the lights of Salem behind them and entered the country darkness, Sadi began breathing more calmly and stopped looking behind them, fearful of seeing the police. Her relief quickly helped calm Freddy's nerves. Maybe he would forget about the whole affair as she was desperately trying to do. Just another hour and they might be able to relax in her home.

Freddy drove directly to their next destination, the home of his old caseworker from Hungary, Malika. He believed she would keep the boys safe, at least temporarily. By some miracle, he remembered where she used to live, and by another miracle, she still lived there. He knocked on her door a few minutes past midnight.

Before Malika answered the door, he knew her state of mind. She was slightly annoyed at being awakened just after falling asleep, but she was more worried that someone needed her help. She opened the door as much as the chain lock would allow, looked at him, and then the car idling in the driveway. When she returned her attention to Freddy, he did not see any sign of recognition. He knew she would remember him after introducing himself.

"Hello, Malika," he said. "I am so sorry to bother you this late, but I need your help."

"Do I know you?" she asked.

She had the distinct features of an Eastern European woman, dark blond hair, sharp eyes, and a full figure. Old age had begun to encroach on her once-beautiful face. She looked tired, physically and emotionally.

"I used to be one of your foster case kids," he said, the words tasting bitter on his tongue. "I am Freddy Carlson."

Before continuing, he waited and wondered what he should tell her. He had everyone's safety to consider. Knowledge could also put her in danger. She squinted in an attempt to recognize his face then opened the door and stepped into the cool night air.

"How can I help you?" she asked, her face turned to the car.

"I know this is an inconvenience and will sound unbelievable," he began, "but we have two boys and a girl who need protection. We rescued them from a child pornography ring, and they need to be taken someplace safe."

The woman put her hand to her mouth when he mentioned the rescue, and then she looked at his chest and noticed the blood on his clothes. His zipped jacket failed to hide all the blood stains. But instead of fearing the sight of the blood, she recognized the evidence of a violent effort to rescue the kids.

"Oh my god," she said in shock and concern. "Are they hurt? Bring them inside and tell me what happened."

On his short walk to the car, he felt her eyes on his back and her sincere desire to help. She suspected no deceit and only cared for the children. Freddy opened the driver's door then crouched down to the boys' eye level.

"You are going to stay with this nice lady," he said while wincing at the sting in his chest. "She will keep you away from the bad men. She is my friend who helped me when I was your age."

While waiting for their response, Freddy focused on the feelings of any prying eyes from the neighborhood homes and failed to detect anyone's notice. The two boys looked at him for a moment then shifted their attention to the lady standing in the doorway. The woman looked less threatening than Freddy, and they instantly liked her.

Both boys shrugged their shoulders.

"Okay," said Kristoff.

"She will not let anyone abuse you again," Freddy said.

As the boys began to exit the vehicle, Freddy turned to Daryn in the back seat. She had pressed her head back against the seat, holding onto Helen's arm.

He would have to spend extra effort convincing the young girl to leave her new friend. Her sudden sorrow and panic caused Freddy to pause and remind himself that Malika would take good care of her. He opened her door and put his hand on her small shoulder.

"This woman will take care of you now," he said slowly. "Helen can come visit you. Will that be okay?"

"Come on, Daryn, let's go," the older boy said while standing next to Freddy.

The boy extended his hand to Daryn, but she looked away from him and turned to Helen. She grabbed her new friend with both hands, a look of terror in her eyes. Tears began falling from Helen's eyes too.

"We can't leave Daryn," Helen said, turning to her mother.

Freddy looked at Sadi who turned to him with a blank look on her face. He waited for her to speak, but she remained silent. During their drive home, Sadi had let the horrible events of the evening consume her thoughts, the killings, and how close her daughter had come to an awful death. She could only think about getting home and locking the doors.

"Helen," Freddy said, turning to point at the lady standing in the doorway. "This lady and the boys will take good care of Daryn."

"She can't go back," Helen said, not understanding. "They'll keep hurting her. They'll keep her in her room and never let her out again. We can't leave her."

Sadi opened her mouth to protest, but the pleading in her daughter's voice silenced her. Then her tears started falling. In the next instant, she smiled for the first time since entering the car.

"She can come with us."

ONE HUNDRED THREE

Freddy

After leaving the boys at the social worker's house, Sadi and the girls remained in the backseat, and Freddy drove the rest of the way home as the chauffeur. Images and emotions from the evening played in a continuous loop inside his head, the killings, his near demise, and finally the moment when Sadi had saved his life. The silence of so many horrible people became his greatest respite, amplified by the silence in the car.

Freddy noticed the occasional glance of his passengers at the other people who shared the highway with them. Occupants in the other vehicles seemed like aliens from another planet, living their comfortable and secure lives, disconnected from the trauma of their fellow travelers. Freddy envied them.

As they took the westbound exit to Highway Twenty-Six toward Hillsboro, a new sensation ripped Freddy from his musings, a feeling of excitement from Helen. She recognized her surroundings, and her heartbeat instantly accelerated.

"Daryn," she said, sitting forward. "We're almost to your new home. You're going to love it."

"Really?"

"Just a few more minutes," Sadi said and put her hand on Daryn's knee, the first time she touched the little girl.

Sadi's touch caused the girl's tension to elevate, but she showed no outward sign. Only Freddy noticed her reaction, and it produced additional anger at how life had emotionally damaged the poor girl. The show of compassion from Sadi should have helped calm her unease instead of increasing it.

Freddy stopped in Sadi's driveway at one-fifteen in the morning then paused before opening the car door. His passengers seemed to feel his elevated alertness and waited for his signal to move. He felt exposed, as a deer about to enter a clearing.

Would one of Sadi's neighbors notice their arrival? A witness might remember the event and tell a future investigator. If the events of the evening ever became known, he doubted anyone would make the truth public. The story involved high-profile people and an organization protected by corrupt government officials. If the police revealed anything to the press, it would be false information, justified by a need to keep the investigation a secret. The press usually only regurgitated the story presented by government or intelligence officials, Freddy assumed. Most likely, a higher-level government agency would commandeer the investigation.

Sadi waited for him to give some signal to exit the car.

"No one is taking notice of us," he said, looking directly at Daryn. "We can go inside. Helen and Sadi will go first, then you and I will follow them."

Sadi opened the door and led Helen by the hand into the night. As mother and daughter walked to the front door, Freddy smiled in anticipation of experiencing their emotional reunion. Before Sadi could touch the doorknob, the front door burst open and Jen appeared, tears streaming down her cheeks. Helen exploded into tears also then melted into Jen's outstretched arms. While watching them hug, Freddy wiped tears from his own eyes.

"It is our turn, Daryn."

Freddy held her hand while they walked to the front door. She grasped his hand tightly, afraid of being released. On their short walk together, he felt a new emotional connection begin to form with the girl, like two pieces of metal welded together.

Sadi held the door open for them, glancing at the houses on the street, and then guided Freddy gently into the house with her hand on his back. Once inside, she crouched down to Daryn's eye level and placed both hands on her shoulders.

"It's alright," Sadi said gently, and everyone turned their attention to Daryn. "This is your new home now. No one will hurt you here."

The girl stood in the entryway, staring with surprise at the clean interior of the home. She was suddenly frightened of all the adults and the new environment. After a long moment of silence, Helen came forward and extended her hand. The frightened girl looked up at Freddy, and he released her hand with some reluctance.

"Welcome to your new home," Helen said with a smile.

After Sadi closed the door, Freddy felt all of the attention switch from Daryn and Helen to him. More people were waiting for their return than he had anticipated. Before entering the house, he had felt the presence of several other people inside but had neglected to concentrate sufficiently on identifying them.

Mr. Smith sat on the couch in the living room with a concerned look in his eyes, one hand on his cane as though preparing to stand. He was waiting impatiently for his turn to intrude on the happy reunion, an overwhelming sense of relief briefly energizing him. Brian Jacobsen stood with one hand on his sister's shoulder, smiling wide.

Gerald Foster silently watched the scene from a couple of meters away. He was concerned about the unfamiliar little girl who had just walked into the house and was waiting for an opportunity to ask about her. The adults noticed the blood all over Freddy's clothes.

While Jen, Sadi, and Brian spoke with the two girls, Freddy approached Mr. Smith on the couch. The old man slowly rose to his feet with the help of his cane then peered into Freddy's eyes as though looking for something lost. Instead of answering his employer's unspoken question, Freddy followed human protocol and waited for the question first.

"Are you okay?" he asked finally and then placed his old hand on Freddy's shoulder. Mr. Smith feared to learn the answer to his next question, but he asked anyway. "Is that your blood?"

"It is mostly mine," Freddy answered, looking briefly at his chest. "I can tell you all about it on the ride home. I would rather not talk about it here."

"That's probably a good idea."

During the brief exchange, Gerald had left his silent observation point between the two groups and approached the two men. He had dark shadows under his eyes, and his hair looked as though he had run his hands through it a hundred times. He spoke quietly, so the others would not notice.

"I know you probably just want to go home, but before you leave, could I talk to you both outside."

Freddy suddenly felt tired, more exhausted than he ever remembered feeling. He needed his boss to take control of the situation. Mr. Smith recognized the look in Freddy's eyes and then nodded and turned to the woman.

"Sadi," he said politely, and she immediately turned her attention to him. "I need to get Freddy home. I'm sure you understand. I know you'll want to get these two girls situated."

Before allowing them to leave, Sadi embraced Freddy and held him close. She squeezed tightly as though afraid he would attempt to escape. Her breasts put pressure against his stinging chest, but the exhilaration of contact with the woman completely buried the pain. Freddy had fantasized for much of his life about holding Sadi, and the real experience felt far superior to his imagination. He wished the contact could continue forever, despite the pain.

"We will never forget what you did for us."

When she finally released him, he had to wait a moment for the euphoria to end.

"I owe you too," he said quietly. "You saved my life, so we are even. We did it together, remember?"

Sadi smiled, nodding silently. Disturbing memories of the evening began to replace her relief. She needed to sleep, then maybe her subconscious mind could begin the healing process.

Before getting in their cars and leaving, Gerald spoke to Freddy and Mr. Smith on the porch. Freddy quickly glanced around the neighborhood and felt no awareness of the three men from any of Sadi's neighbors. The only other people in his sensory range were unconscious.

"Sadi said that the people who had the kids are all dead?" Gerald asked quietly but did not wait for the answer. "Will anyone be looking for them? Does anyone know where they live? Are they going to be safe tonight?"

Mr. Smith and Gerald turned to Freddy. He looked at the ground, avoiding eye contact and afraid of giving too many details. Mr. Smith might form a negative impression of him.

"I did my best not to leave any fingerprints or blood," Freddy said as confidently as possible, attempting to convince them and himself. He would not mention the two boys they left at his case worker's house. He just wanted to go home. "All the witnesses are dead. No one followed us or knows anything about us, for now."

"Craig should know what to do," Mr. Smith said confidently. "He can learn what they are up to. Tomorrow, we'll need to discuss the situation with him, but tonight, you need sleep, and I'll need to check your injuries. You're holding your chest like it hurts."

"It does hurt," Freddy admitted. "But, I should not need stitches."

"What do your friends think about all of this?" Mr. Smith asked, turning to Gerald.

Freddy felt a mixture of confusion from Gerald and a small amount of guilt. The man considered lying but then changed his mind. He hesitated only briefly.

"I'm still trying to figure out how and what to tell them. I need to figure it out first."

"Well," Mr. Smith said almost accusingly and barely containing a sudden burst of anger. Freddy cringed. "You need to discuss these things with this group of yours. Everything started happening when you came into our lives."

"I will tell them," Gerald said, failing to notice the anger. He considered asking Freddy about the alien and his new abilities but changed his mind. His desire to return to the house and see Sadi overpowered his curiosity. "When I do discuss this with my friends, I'll let you know our conclusions, but we can all talk about that later. I know you need to get home and rest. I'd better go back inside."

After Gerald left them alone on the porch, a new emotion suddenly overshadowed all others, jealousy. Freddy had already accepted the eventuality of never having an intimate relationship with Sadi, but seeing a possible relationship with Gerald caused a sting more painful than his chest wounds.

When Sadi entered his life again, all of the buried feelings for her had resurfaced. Freddy wished that he could stop thinking about her. Her image kept playing in his mind like an infectious melody, repeating over and over and over. Only after entering his car and driving away from her home could he push the feeling of jealousy from his mind, leaving him with only the physical pain in his chest.

PART VIII

CLASH

Do you really want to be
The architect and builder
Of your destiny?

ONE HUNDRED FOUR

Freddy

On the way home, Freddy's emotional dam broke when he explained the events of the evening to his boss. With so many lives depending on him, he had maintained a high level of control, exerting more emotional energy than his strength would allow for long. The story flowed without any filter. He decided to keep nothing from his boss or pause to think about the consequences.

When they finally arrived in the darkness of their garage, Freddy turned off the car and they just sat there for a moment. Mr. Smith sat in silence and let the overload of information sink into his consciousness. For several seconds, Freddy waited for his boss to become angry at how he had handled the situation, but the old man was only shocked and amazed. While waiting for a response, Freddy unzipped his jacket and then winced every time he touched his chest. Although he knew how much more pain it would produce, he anticipated a hot shower with pleasure. He disliked the idea of soaking in a bath of soap and blood.

"I feel somehow that I should not have killed those men," Freddy said to break the silence. "Although, I know they deserved it."

"You did what you had to do," Mr. Smith said. "Try to keep your emotions from influencing your reasoning. Children were in danger, and you brought them out of the situation. I would have done the same thing if I could have."

"Thank you, sir," Freddy said, feeling Mr. Smith's sincerity.

Would he ever regret killing those men, he wondered. Were they just a product of their environment and did that justify their termination? Did he, in essence, value their lives less than the lives of his friends? Yes, he did, and he accepted that. After a few seconds, he came to a conclusion that put his mind temporarily at ease. The men had accepted the risk of death when they had chosen that line of work.

"So the alien," Mr. Smith said, "or whatever it is, gave you the ability to know what others are feeling? Is that going to be part of you from now on?"

"I feel what those around me are feeling. It has gradually become stronger since the barn incident. I think it is permanent."

"I feel old," Mr. Smith said with a sigh and then laughed. "So I guess you feel old too, huh?"

"I do not feel physical sensations from others, only emotions."

Freddy put his hand on the car door handle and then paused when he understood the old man's joke. He had failed to recognize the sarcastic tone of his voice. Would his new ability help him be more normal?

"Oh, I get it."

Although he did not feel like laughing, he made a feeble attempt. Mr. Smith smiled, patted him on the shoulder, and then they went inside the main house.

During his shower, Freddy fell into a short trance while watching the bloody water disappear down the drain. The shower process stung more than when the old man had slashed his chest, but at least he felt clean, as though the shower also helped remove the painful memories.

After his shower, Mr. Smith tried convincing Freddy to let his personal doctor come and stitch his wounds, but Freddy said he had some medical tape that might work. In the morning, they could reevaluate his condition, and if he still needed it, he would not object to calling the doctor. For that night, he just wanted sleep. When Mr. Smith suggested sleeping pills, Freddy declined, fearing that unnatural chemicals would interfere with the healing process.

Before getting into bed, he held the crystal spider and then placed it on top of a table under a lamp. He wanted to look into the eyes of the spider but then lost his nerve. Did he really want to see the woman from the plane again? The creature or entity had brought only stress into his life. He almost wished everything would just go back to normal.

He went to bed that night lying on his side, the crystal six centimeters from his face, and the irrational thought that if he kept the crystal in his view, nothing would happen. For a long while, he lay on his bed with his eyes open and concentrated on breathing to help himself relax. He preferred the darkness of his room more than the images of death in his mind. After a while, keeping his eyes open began to require a lot of effort.

ONE HUNDRED FIVE

Freddy

When Freddy opened his eyes, he expected to see a dimly lit bed-room, but instead, he found himself standing in complete darkness in the middle of an infinite flat plane. Although he saw and heard nothing, he could feel the flat stone under his bare feet stretching to infinity in every direction. He felt insignificant.

He stood motionless for what seemed an infinite length of time with nothing to disturb his tranquility. He felt no surprise at being there. All of his care and pain had vanished, his fear for Helen, for Sadi, for himself. His mind became as empty as the plane where he stood. If dying led to his current state of existence, he would never fear death again.

When he first noticed the faint noise, the familiar sensation tore him from his state of nirvana. The sound instantly consumed his entire attention, and then the physical sensation of wind hit him in the face, and the cool fluctuation of pressure reminded him of the world he once knew.

Light was the next change to his world, brilliant oranges and blues, intensifying slowly all around him. The light shined down from the sky as though from a glowing fog. After a while, the lights slowly faded to nothing and then began to slowly grow again. The transitions reminded him of day and night, the concept of time. The cycle repeated more times than he could count, the light in the sky growing, dying, and then growing again.

After several cycles of light and then dark, the light dimmed and did not return, immersing him in total darkness again. He remembered being a small boy and fearing the dark, fearing what his eyes could not see, but what his imagination had created. That life seemed so far away, the distant memory of another time and another world, another Freddy.

When a yellow light began illuminating the space just above the horizon, Freddy expected to see the sun. But instead of a brighter light, three black stars in a row ascended a few degrees into the sky, three dark dots against a bright yellow background. After they stopped, the center star began stretching vertically, eventually touching the horizon and then transforming into the silhouette of a woman walking toward him. The woman had slender legs, long hair.

Although walking casually, the woman was soon close enough for him to distinguish her features. Dark brown hair fell loosely down her back, and she was wearing a tight, dark gray dress with black sandals, her legs exposed just above the knees. A single line of black pearls was embedded in the silky material of her dress, winding around her body in a spiral and ending just below her right shoulder. The oily blackness of the pearls shined with a black light of their own, brighter than the two black stars that had remained in the sky behind her.

When he could see the dark blue of her eyes, he thought the woman was looking through him, as though unaware of his presence. And when she came within reach, he expected her to crash into him, but she changed direction at the last moment and walked slowly around him. The woman walked one complete revolution around him and then stopped a few centimeters from his face.

"Hello again, Freddy," she said after finally looking into his eyes. While waiting for his response, the left corner of her mouth curved into a slight smile.

Her proximity suddenly made him nervous, and the intensity of her gaze seemed to burn his eyes, a sensation broken only by looking away from her face and down at her feet. They were encased in sandals with straps as black as the pearls on her dress. The smooth white skin of her legs drew his attention next, but he looked quickly back to her face and focused on her pink lips.

"I know you," he said, thinking she looked familiar. Speaking helped him feel human again, but the action failed to restore his memory. "I am sorry. I forgot your name."

"You'll remember soon enough," she said, smiling wider. "Why don't you tell me how you feel? Talking about your emotions might be therapeutic."

He looked away from her pink lips to the whiteness of her feet wrapped in the shiny black straps. While attempting to assess his emotional state, he closed his eyes.

"I feel like I *should* be tired, but I feel nothing."

"You won't be tired here."

"Why?" he asked and then felt brave enough to look into her dark blue eyes again. "Is this a dream? It feels real."

"I am supplying the background information," she said and her smile transformed into a look of concern. "What do you think of it?"

"I feel relaxed," he said after a short pause.

"I want you to be relaxed," she said while laying her left hand on his right shoulder. The warmth and pressure of her hand reminded him of a similar experience, another woman in a dark stairwell.

"I can show you whatever you want to see," she said, and her smile returned. "I can give you any sensation you want. I will *do* whatever you want."

He looked at her neck and then her breasts and suddenly lacked the strength to turn away. His sexual attraction felt magnetic, as a living thing, and he was standing too close. If he extended his hand, she would let him touch her. If he asked to remove her clothes, she would let him. She offered herself to him as a waitress would offer to refill a glass of water.

After returning his attention to her face, he considered the offer. She was waiting patiently, staring at him with those two, beautiful blue eyes. He tried to consider all of his options, but he was having trouble remembering other interests.

"Why don't I choose something for you?" she asked with a hint of disappointment. "At first, your imagination will be limited."

"Okay," he said, and then cold liquid began rising above his feet.

ONE HUNDRED SIX

Freddy

Freddy looked down at his feet and saw rising black water, and then he noticed the entire plane was filling with water and he was standing in a shallow ocean. The light on the horizon reflected off the water, rippling on the fluid surface. The dark ocean quickly reached his chin, but he had no time to panic. The water soon passed over his mouth and nose and finally his head. Before he could gasp for breath, something was at his lips, trying to enter his mouth. It was a tube providing air. He opened his mouth and allowed the cool air to enter his lungs.

The surrounding water was ice-cold, but it felt comfortable. He looked to his side and noticed the woman standing next to him still. She had no such tube in her mouth and did not appear bothered by the surrounding water. When she opened her mouth to speak, her words entered his consciousness through a different route than through his ears. He expected to see bubbles escaping her mouth, but he saw none.

"You don't need to breathe here," she explained. "If you remove the tube, you'll be fine. I just didn't want you to panic."

Without answering, Freddy looked upward and saw the sky getting darker and farther away. He enjoyed watching the yellow light rippling through the water interface. When he looked back at the woman, she was gone. Then a new sensation stole his attention. He could feel a muddy sea floor under his feet and between his toes.

Pressure from all of the seawater began to intensify, squeezing him from every side, but the sensation caused no pain. The pressure was comforting, like being wrapped in heavy cold blankets on a hot day. His environment was also beginning to darken, and when the sky turned completely black, other lights began to surround him.

All kinds of sea creatures approached him and many had lights of their own. He saw anglerfish with large fangs, strange sharks, eels with sharp noses, all kinds of starfish, crabs. Beautiful glowing jellyfish swam around and above him, shining like electric lamps.

Most of the creatures swam close and seemed curious about him. When he extended his hand, they allowed him the pleasure of feeling their cold, slimy skin. He enjoyed the experience so much, the woman and the plane quickly fled from his memory.

He watched the creatures for a long time and soon forgot about his identity as a human, a stranger in the ocean. He watched the creatures eat each other, defend their young, fight for food and territory. They mated and produced offspring. He watched countless cycles of life and death. For what felt like an eternity, he experienced the diversity of ocean life. It eventually felt like home.

—✳—

When the woman spoke again, her voice was a sharp reminder of his life outside the water, when he had breathed air. The tube was no longer in his mouth. It was long forgotten.

"Your world is full of beauty," she said. "Endless experience in the deep."

The woman was standing beside him again, just out of sight. When he turned and saw her, he did not know what to say. He remembered her effect on him. The sea creatures were beautiful, but he did not desire to hold them in his arms.

While looking into her eyes, the ocean life began swimming and crawling away and soon left his view. The ocean was suddenly dark again, but only for a short time. He looked up and saw the shimmering sky high above him, getting closer and brighter. The surface of the water quickly reached the top of his head and then he was no longer submerged but standing in the dry air again.

All of the water quickly disappeared, and he was standing on the flat plane, dry and comfortable. The two black stars remained just above the horizon, but now the whole sky was brighter. Although he was not alone, he suddenly felt an immense loss. He was standing in a barren world. He missed the comfort of the water pressure, the company of other living creatures, the feeling of being in an inaccessible place.

He remembered the woman saying she would show him anything, so he began thinking of several other things he wanted to see, other experiences. A thousand ideas entered his mind and he had difficulty deciding on what to choose first.

"What's next?" she asked.

"I would like my memories," he said quickly, surprising himself.

His lack of memories suddenly felt like a painful void, a loss of identity. But did he really want to remember his identity?

"Remember what exactly?" she asked.

"Before being here," he said slowly, "I was somewhere else. Can you help me remember?"

"Let's not do that just yet," she said as though she had already seriously considered the request. "I've got something better first."

Before he could respond, the ground suddenly drew his attention. He looked down and noticed his shadow on the plane, black and stretching from his feet to the horizon in front of him. When his shadow had stretched to an infinite distance, time seemed to stop, and then the top of his shadow began racing to meet him again. When his shadow came directly under him, he turned to look at the sky behind him and had to shield his eyes from the intense lights.

His eyes soon grew accustomed to all of the lights, a beautiful galaxy with two arms spiraling around each other. While looking at the billions of stars, he discovered an exciting new ability. He could focus on any one of the stars and see the smaller celestial bodies near them. Although the galactic light became more intense toward the center, he could still see each star system distinctly.

In his peripheral vision, he saw the woman turn from watching the sky and focus on him. She reminded him of a parent appreciating the curiosity of a child. He remembered having a mother, but he could not remember her face.

"Why are you keeping my memory from me?" he asked after turning away from the galaxy and looking into her eyes again.

"You require a respite," she said while returning her gaze to the sky. "Another occupation for your consciousness. Experiencing this with you also gives me pleasure."

He fought the urge to return his attention to the sky. Only her feminine form provided the necessary counter-temptation.

"Has something happened to me?" he asked.

"I can show you anything," she said, keeping her gaze skyward. "We can explore molecules, the atom, or even smaller energies. Those have immense beauty."

The offer tempted him, but fragments of his memory floated just out of reach, as a fading dream. He suddenly wanted to remember his past more than anything she could show him.

"I appreciate what you are showing me," he said, fearing to disappoint her. "But I want to remember."

Instead of receiving a look of disappointment, the woman turned to him, her smile growing wider. She walked slowly around him and stopped just behind his back. After placing her warm hand on his shoulder, she pointed to the horizon with her other hand.

"Watch," she whispered and then the light from the sky vanished, leaving them in darkness.

ONE HUNDRED SEVEN

Freddy

Her cool breath on his cheek felt like the soft breeze and smelled of cinnamon. As he waited for something to happen, the touch of her warm hand on his shoulder replaced his memory of the beautiful galaxy.

When the small white light materialized just above the horizon, its reflection on the black marble extended in a straight line from the edge of the world to his feet. The new light initially looked like another star, but when he looked closer, he saw that the light was pulsating, swirling as though composed of several other lights. The woman stepped beside him, entering his peripheral vision. The faint white light illuminated the outline of her face.

"What is that?" he asked.

"Go and see."

After taking his first step, the woman's outline disappeared from view and he suddenly felt all alone again. He turned around to see her, but she was gone and he saw nothing behind him, not even the plane. After facing the star again and following the reflection on the ground, he began to feel like a robot executing a simple program, an insect attracted by light. As he walked, the star ascended higher in the sky, expanding and growing brighter but only illuminating the ground in front of him, a trail of reflection.

When he finally recognized the composition of the light, he stopped and stared. Hundreds of creatures were flying around each other in the sky, forming a swirling cloud of light. They were human in form but swarming like insects, glowing and translucent. Several words to describe them came to his mind, phantoms, specters, ghosts. No word seemed quite appropriate, maybe ghosts. He could not look away, and he no longer felt alone.

He attempted to focus on individual ghosts, but they moved too quickly and always disappeared into the swarm before he could distinguish their faces. Did he want to identify them? If he recognized one, then it might also recognize him. While deciding what to do, one of the creatures flew high above the swarm and faced him, the ghost of a familiar woman.

She was slightly overweight with greasy brown hair and tight-fitting clothes. He knew her, but he had no time for the memory to form. The woman's eyes suddenly opened wide and she dove toward him. Freddy did not move and just stood in place, more curious than afraid.

When the woman, his mother, crashed into him finally, the impact restored several disturbing memories. He remembered when she had blamed him for his father leaving. He remembered when she had sent him to live with his first foster family. He remembered her embarrassment and anger when the court had sent him to juvenile detention for shoplifting. Then another woman flew out of the swarm, the ghost of his sister. When she crashed into him, he remembered her spite and manipulation. Then each member of his first foster family escaped the swarm. Freddy cringed at every impact.

Ghosts continued diving from the sky, restoring other painful memories. Then the teenage ghosts of Sadi and her brother restored some of his first pleasant experiences, fun and a sense of belonging. After the Jacobsens, he had a short reprieve of ghostly encounters, and he felt the presence of the woman. She was standing next to him again. She resembled Sadi in every way imaginable.

Next, the ghosts of teachers and lab partners restored even more pleasant memories, his love of learning, the wonder of contemplating life and the universe. And then Mr. Smith restored memories of feeling needed, appreciated, and self-sufficient. Several other acquaintances also joined. Freddy remembered valuable and unique experiences from each.

After the ghosts of his classmates, professors, and friends from the internet, a demon rushed toward him like a rocket, the first human he had killed. The man had a large gash on his neck and eyes nearly exploding with pain. Then his other victims from that nightmare followed. One by one they crashed into him and Freddy extended his hands in a failed attempt to shield the impacts.

After the entire swarm had crashed into him, a new light appeared in the sky, a giant rectangular crystal encasing a two-dimensional spider. Brilliant blue and orange lights were shining from the eyes and Freddy remembered how the light could erase his memory, so he kept his right hand extended in the air as a shield from the view.

While the beautiful orange and blue lights shined around his hand, Freddy remembered the hotel room with Sadi, watching the street lights through the curtains. He remembered leaving her in the stairwell, slicing through the guard's neck, and then shooting the other men in the head. He remembered experiencing their terror mixed with his own.

"If you want to forget again, just look into the spider's eyes," the woman said. She was standing beside him again.

Freddy turned to her and quickly considered the option of forgetting. The suggestion tempted him, but he did not want to endure another restoration of his memories. He also wanted to keep his pleasant ones.

He opened his mouth to tell her his decision, but the eyes of the spider stopped shining and another light returned to the sky. When he looked up, he saw the galaxy again and the sight quickly swallowed all of his attention, relieving Freddy from the burden of his restored memories. He spent a long time watching the swirling mass of stars and other celestial objects. The rings of Saturn, the great eye storm on Jupiter, the colossal magnetic storms in the atmosphere of the Sun, unimaginable displays of energy.

—✳︎—

"Helen was not kidnapped by chance," he said eventually, not turning away from the sky. Freddy no longer felt the presence of the woman, but he knew she would hear him.

"Nothing is by chance," the woman answered solemnly from behind him.

Freddy tore his gaze away from the amazing objects in the sky. He turned and stared at her. Although she resembled Sadi in every imaginable way, the figure beside him seemed like an alien. Her human form looked like a costume.

"You set this up," he accused, a familiar anger providing his courage. "What was the purpose? To turn me into some sort of hero?"

"There's no reason to speak rudely," she said with a frown. "You are my guest here, and you're not returning the hospitality. Have I not been hospitable?"

"Yes," he answered without attempting to conceal his hostile tone. "But this is my imagination. How can I possibly be a guest in my own imagination?"

She raised her eyebrows in shock but remained silent.

"It is an impossible coincidence," he said. "You come in contact with me, then Helen is abducted? Do not deny it. It was wrong of you to put her in that position and permanently scar her."

She took a step closer to him.

"You saved her, did you not?" she said, her eyes opening wide. "Damage averted and justice served."

"How did damaging that poor little girl serve justice?" he asked, feeling justified in his anger. "To serve justice, you would be punished for what you did. Those who put people in dangerous situations are just as liable and sometimes more than those who do the actual damage. Not only will Helen be scarred for life, but who knows what will happen to Sadi because of it. When those men connect her to what happened, her life could be over."

Freddy did not wait for her response.

"I killed people," he yelled at her with clenched fists, the disturbing memory feeding his anger. Freddy wanted to crush her beautiful neck, but he restrained himself. "I killed them! I did not want to kill anyone!"

While maintaining eye contact, she tilted her head to the left. The action reminded him of a lizard preparing to eat a cricket.

"What child would you prefer they stole?" she asked as though sincerely interested in his response.

"No other child," Freddy said. "Of course, no other child."

"The human who took Helen would have chosen another child," the woman said regretfully.

Freddy felt as though the woman had poured a large bucket of ice water over his head, extinguishing his anger with a sizzle and transforming it into hot steam. He suddenly felt drained, but then a new emotion, sadness for what could have been.

"What are you?" Freddy asked finally.

"What do you think I am?"

"Will every answer be another question?"

"What do you think?" she asked, laughing. "I'm definitely not a creation of your imagination."

"Why did you do it?" Freddy asked, deciding to change the subject. "Why me? Why Helen?"

Before answering, the woman who resembled Sadi shrugged and raised her eyebrows as though she had acted on a whim.

"So you could practice."

"Practice?"

His next thought never fully formed.

The ground under his feet began shaking and a tornado suddenly appeared in the plane before him. The massive swirling cloud sucked the sky into itself, and all of its celestial objects combined into a singularity of blinding brilliance. When he turned away from the bright light and faced the woman, her blue eyes opened wide and consumed the world.

Continues in Book 2

About the Author

Hyrum is the product of a large family and the Utah desert. He's an Eagle Scout, has degrees in chemistry and chemical engineering, and spent a few years as the Libertarian Chairman of his county. After he and his wife raised their family in the Pacific Northwest, they all moved to Kentucky, where they now reside. Other than the people in his life, he loves exploring the world and creating things.